GOLDEN AGE SUSPENSE STORIES

OTTO PENZLER,
EDITOR

AMERICAN MYSTERY CLASSICS

Penzler Publishers
New York

Published in 2026 by Penzler Publishers
58 Warren Street, New York, NY 10007

penzlerpublishers.com

Distributed by Simon & Schuster

OTTO PENZLER PRESENTS
AMERICAN MYSTERY CLASSICS

GOLDEN AGE SUSPENSE STORIES

Otto Penzler, the creator of American Mystery Classics, is also the founder of the Mysterious Press (1975); MysteriousPress.com (2011), an electronic-book publishing company; and New York City's Mysterious Bookshop (1979). He has won a Raven, the Ellery Queen Award, two Edgars (for the *Encyclopedia of Mystery and Detection*, 1977, and *The Lineup*, 2010), and lifetime achievement awards from NoirCon and *The Strand Magazine*. He has edited more than 80 anthologies and written extensively about mystery fiction.

Cover image: Andy Ross
Cover design: Mauricio Diaz

Paperback ISBN 978-1-61316-789-2
Hardcover ISBN 978-1-61316-788-5
eBook ISBN 978-1-61316-790-8

Library of Congress Control Number: 2025948244

Printed in the United States of America

9 8 7 6 5 4 3 2 1

GOLDEN AGE SUSPENSE STORIES

CONTENTS

INTRODUCTION

WHAT, EXACTLY, makes a story "the best"? In all candor, it is no more than the favorites of the series editor and the guest editor for any given year. Granted, as someone who has been professionally involved in the world of mystery literature for more than a half-century, and read countless short stories (well, no, not countless, but a lot, probably 20,000 at minimum), I like to think my taste is a bit more seasoned than someone who is new to the genre.

The designation of "Suspense", also has more nuance than most of the anthologies for which I am responsible. The subjects of such books as *The Big Book of Female Detectives*, *The Big Book of Sherlock Holmes Stories*, *Golden Age Christmas Mysteries*, *Murder for Love*, *Golden Age Locked Room Mysteries*, *Bibliomysteries*, and many others are self-evident.

Suspense? Since this book is identified as a member of the mystery genre, it is reasonable to expect that the possibility of a crime exists and the suspense may be generated by the expectation of mayhem, or the hope that it can be avoided, or how severe it will be, or who is the potential victim of a despicable act, or who will be the perpetrator, or *when* will be the seemingly unavoidable tragedy occur.

In virtually all of narrative fiction, suspense is an element of the work. *Waiting for Godot* offers very little other than suspense. When will Godot arrive, or will he arrive at all?

Will Romeo and Juliet find the happiness together that we want for them? Will Indiana Jones escape the snake pit unharmed? Will the young narrator of *All Quiet on the Western Front* survive the war? Will Winston Smith and Julia be able to continue their love affair and find peace and liberty in *1984*?

In the mystery category, suspense can be created in many ways, often with an innocent or unsuspecting victim caught in a web from which escape appears to be hopeless. Sometimes, it is.

On other occasions, as is common in noir fiction and films, people make plans that go horribly wrong. One such satisfying event occurred when Ludovico Sforza invented the unutterably cruel Iron Shroud and became the first individual to be agonizingly killed at its hands in William Mudford's 1830 short story. It is reasonable to say he brought it upon himself without regarding the potential consequence of his vile contraption.

Similarly, the Regent Morton in Scotland invented the Maiden, a variant of the guillotine deliberately designed to inflict more pain than that infamous French device (charitably created to make executions fast, certain, and painless, at all of which it was successful). He was himself beheaded on it. Speaking of the guillotine, it is inexorably linked to the Bastille, which was built by Hugues Aubriot, Provost of Paris. When the doors of that dark, unforgiving structure opened, Aubriot was the first person to be led through the door and introduced to one of its cells, having been found guilty of heresy.

If one can have a favorite moment of schadenfreude when contemplating horrors, my uncharitable memory conjures an event in ancient Greece when Perillos of Athens attempted to curry favor with the dictator Phalaris by creating a device designed to execute criminals in an especially barbaric manner. He constructed a hollow bronze bull into which a criminal could be locked in its belly, after which a large fire could be set beneath it to roast (or would it be bake?) the miscreant. Phalaris was immediately taken by this monstrous contraption but claimed that he wanted to be certain it would work as described, so he asked Perillos to step inside, whereupon it was locked and the makings of a fire ignited. The macabre device proved to work exactly as described.

Novels and stories of suspense have been a staple of storytelling since the first caveman told of his adventures with a saber tooth tiger and it retains its popularity to the present day. The suspense involved with the presumably exciting encounter with a saber tooth (which is not, in fact, related to the animal we know as a tiger today) was probably minimal as we know that the hunter lived to tell about it. Suspense (and its related cousin, terror) may vary in degree and can emanate from any source but readers have enjoyed being terrified—in the comfort of their easy chair or pillow-stacked bed since the invention of storytelling.

It has been said that reading mystery and suspense carries great value, allowing the catharsis of homicidal tendencies to be satisfied in fictional form. I know this is true for many of the authors who have created scenarios in which they place characters who inspired by real-life figures that they despise and who consequently emerge less well than they had been. This notion of punishing or polishing off undesirable acquaintances between the covers of a book can be effective in any sub-genre of mystery fiction, ranging from suspense to detective stories to noir tales and beyond.

The suspense story is rarely a whodunnit. It should more accurately be described as when-will-it-be-done. There are innumerable ways to approach the creation of a suspense story, resulting in an enormously varied type of suspense story. As the cliché goes, there is more than one way to skin a cat. I do not know if this is true, having neither seen nor performed the skinning of a cat, but the adage has been around so long I am forced to give it credence.

I do know it is true for the invention of suspense stories and the results in the following pages will provide ample evidence of the fact.

Otto Penzler
New York
October 2025

THE TWENTY-FOURTH HOUR

Jerome Beatty

Cornell Woolrich, writing as William Irish, wrote the heart-stopping suspense novel *Phantom Lady* with its race against the clock to prevent an execution of an innocent man. Jerome Beatty (1886-1967), beat him to it by a decade in this story.

Born in Lawrence, Kansas, Beatty was educated at the University of Kansas and began his writing career as a newspaper reporter, dramatist, and sports editor for a number of publications and organizations, including the *Kansas City Star, New York Globe,* American Press Association, and *New York Tribune.* He contributed articles to various film magazines and wrote numerous stories for *Collier's, Munsey's, McClure's. Reader's Digest,* and other magazines.

He moved to the film business as the publicity director with Essanay, handling the popular serial *The Strange Case of Mary Page.* For the Thanhouser Studio, he prepared news releases and articles for *Picture-Play, Photoplay,* and other magazines. In 1916 he moved to McClure Pictures and then Famous Players-Lasky, later known as Paramount. In the mid-1920s he served as assistant to Will Hays, who was named to monitor and regulate the motion picture industry in the wake of several scandals. In 1927-1928 he was publicity director for First National Pictures.

Beatty died in Newtown, Connecticut; his sole survivor was Jerome Beatty, Jr., a successful author of children's books who also wrote for *The Saturday Review* and other publications.

"The Twenty-Fourth Hour" was originally published in the January 4, 1930, issue of *Collier's*; it was first published in book form in *Best American Mystery Stories of the Year, Volume 1*, edited by Carolyn Wells (New York, Dutton, 1931).

The Twenty-Fourth Hour

Jerome Beatty

THEY HAD been there for three hours, the girl and the man. It was now noon and a white-haired old Negro set the catch on the high carved doors that led from the Governor's regal anteroom, where they sat, out into the wide foyer. No more callers were admitted after noon on Saturdays.

As the morning passed many visitors had presented their names to the Governor's secretary, were admitted to the sanctum and had gone. There were state senators, representatives, a judge or two, fifteen members of the baseball team that had won the state championship, a delegation of club women who lodged a protest about something or other, the mayor of a near-by city who wanted the Governor to deliver a Memorial Day address.

But the Governor's secretary had ignored the two, now the huge room's only occupants, who sat in the high-backed throne-like chairs by the broad window.

The man shook his head in doubt. His name was Montgomery H. Latham and he was known as one of the greatest criminal lawyers in the state. He was a sturdy man of sixty, with bushy black hair. He was immaculate in a blue suit and gray gaiters. On a table beside him lay his camel's-hair topcoat and his brown velours hat.

"Looks bad," he said to the girl. "I'm afraid—"

"I'm not," she said sharply.

"We've got only a little more than twelve hours," he reminded her.

"*Fourteen* hours," she declared firmly. "Fourteen hours and," she looked at her wrist watch, "and twenty-six minutes!"

She rose and walked to the window. There was firmness in her carriage. In her soft brown eyes was a competent gleam and the pitch of her chin showed a fighting heart. She was young, she was beautiful, she was lithe—like a thoroughbred.

Hundreds of girls could sing and dance and deliver lines better than Alice Rankin but her's was the name that shone in electric lights, while the others still were in the chorus. She had charm. Not sex appeal, charm. When men and women looked at Alice Rankin they knew at once that she was all right.

Her fox fur was loose at her throat. She pushed back her coat and set her knuckles on her lips. Her tiny feet were apart and she looked out of the window at the world and defied it.

"After all," the lawyer said, "you must admit that we haven't a very strong argument for the Governor."

She did not turn her head. "Jack didn't do it," she retorted. "That's the strongest argument in the world. They don't hang innocent men."

Latham shrugged his shoulders and picked up a morning newspaper that he already had read four times.

The Governor ran a hand through his long, tawny hair and

looked over the gold-rimmed glasses that perched perilously on the end of his nose.

"Did you want me, Governor?" The Attorney General had entered through a private door that led from a secret hallway into the Governor's office. The Attorney General was tall and gray and lean, and his mouth was small and hard.

"Yes, General," said the Governor.

"Sit down." He waved a hand toward a massive leather chair on the other side of the elaborately carved mahogany desk. "I was just talking to G. W.," indicating with a nod the Lieutenant Governor, who was sprawled out in another chair, chewing a long cigar.

The Attorney General lighted a cigarette, kicked a suitcase out of his way and dropped into the chair and crossed his knees.

"G. W. and I are going to drive to Pine Lake to spend Sunday," the Governor observed. "Want to go along?"

The Attorney General shook his head. "I bought a new set of matched clubs. My golf is getting good."

"We need a quart or two of rye," said the Lieutenant Governor. "Can you——"

"Sure. Stop at my house. I'll phone the missus." He looked inquiringly from the Governor to the Lieutenant Governor. "Is that why you got me in here?"

"Oh, no. I forgot for a moment." The Governor picked up a pencil and began to make crosses and squares on his blotter. "The Rankin girl is outside. Latham, Van Dyke's attorney, is with her. I'm rather inclined——"

The Attorney General threw his legs apart and lunged forward. He pounded a fist on the desk. "For crimeny's sake, Governor, don't be a fool!"

"That's what I told him," the Lieutenant Governor agreed promptly.

"I thought," the Governor offered, "I thought I might grant a stay of, maybe, a week."

The Attorney General was emphatic. "Jack Van Dyke is guilty. You've granted two stays already. The execution is set for tonight. Let him hang!"

"The girl phoned my secretary this morning. She says she has absolute evidence that Jessie Duke is in town and that she'll have a statement from her before Monday."

"Jessie Duke!" the Lieutenant Governor laughed. "Ha!"

"That's the song and dance they gave you twice before," the Attorney General protested. "Don't be a sucker! The papers are riding you hard enough now, and if you mention Jessie Duke once more you'll be the biggest joke in the state. The cartoonists and funny writers haven't entirely forgotten yet and if you give them another opening—good night!"

"But just a week—" the Governor suggested.

"Don't you remember all those cartoons last Christmas when you gave Van Dyke a stay on this same cock and bull yarn?" the Attorney General declaimed. "How Jessie Duke must be Santa Claus and all that? We got an election in November, and if you don't sit tight the papers will Jessie-Duke us right out of these jobs. He shot Bernstein. Let him hang!"

"Sure," the Lieutenant Governor put in. "The jury said he was guilty, the Court of Appeals said he was guilty, everybody in this state agrees. There's been too much talk already about how Van Dyke will never hang because he's a rich man's son. You've given him almost a year——"

"Ten months," said the Governor. "This is the last of April."

"If they can't find their witness in ten months," the Attorney General sneered, "there isn't any witness."

"But there's Latham," the Governor began. "I don't want to offend him."

"Rats!" The Attorney General dismissed Latham with a wave of a hand. "Latham himself thinks Van Dyke is guilty. He's just going through the motion. He put up the best defense he could and now he's paid off and ready to wash up. Old Man Van Dyke and all the relatives believe the boy did it and are ready to let him ride. It's the Rankin girl that's keeping things hot. I'll bet a thousand dollars that Latham knows this Jessie Duke story is all a lot of hooey."

"I sort of feel sorry for the boy," said the Governor. "He's a nice kid."

"Humph!" the Attorney General snorted. "He's a Van Dyke. His father stole every cent he's got. The sisters are tramps. Society folks!" He snorted his disgust. "He murdered a man. Let him hang!"

"That's what I say," the Lieutenant Governor declared.

The Governor shrugged his shoulders. "All right, then," he agreed. "The sentence stands." He looked at the clock. "We better be going, G. W. Won't you change your mind, General?"

"Not me. I'm just about set to shoot me a ninety with my new clubs."

"Steel shafts?" the Governor asked.

"No, wood. You can't get——"

"I changed to steel shafts," the Governor began, "and . . ."

While the man and the girl waited outside, alone in the big room, the question of steel shafts vs. wooden shafts was debated for fifteen minutes. When the argument reached an impasse the Governor picked up his bag and told his secretary to go out and say that under no circumstances would he interfere with the due process of law in the case of the State vs. John Van Dyke, legally convicted of the murder of Lucky Joe Bernstein, and sentenced by the court to hang at 2:30 A.M. on Sunday, April 28th. That moment now was less than fourteen hours away.

As the Governor's secretary opened the door, Alice whirled from the window and stepped toward him, her eyes seeking an answer. The Governor's secretary looked past her at Latham, who had risen slowly to his feet.

"Well?" the girl demanded.

"What news, Dockery?" Latham asked.

The secretary shook his head. "Nothing doing."

"He'll see us, though?" Alice asked quickly.

"I'm sorry. He's gone for the day."

"Gone! Where?" she protested.

"On a personal matter."

She seized his coat. "Where's he gone?" she snapped.

"Er—Pine Lake—to the hotel. Over Sunday."

"There's a telephone there, if we need him?" Latham asked.

"Oh, yes. But, Mr. Latham, really—there's no hope. Really."

"No hope!" Alice disputed. "Don't talk nonsense. Jack didn't shoot Bernstein. They don't hang innocent men!"

"I trust not, Miss Rankin," the secretary offered.

She looked at her watch.

"Now, Dockery," Latham began, "don't you suppose we could catch the Governor? If I could just have a little talk with him, perhaps——"

"Never mind that talking thing," the girl interrupted sharply. "We have work to do. Come on!"

"I'm afraid we're sunk, Miss Rankin," said Latham. They were in his limousine, riding from the state capitol to his office.

She turned on him fiercely. "Are you going to be like all the rest?"

"What do you mean?" he asked, uneasily.

"You believe Van, don't you? You know there is such a person as Jessie Duke?"

"Of course." There was a strut in his voice as he added: "Didn't I establish that at the trial?"

She ignored his boast. "You know, don't you, that she saw the murder committed—that she knows who was standing behind Van and who did the shooting?"

"If we find her, Miss Rankin," he evaded, "she won't tell."

"She will tell," she muttered through clenched teeth. She gripped Latham's arm so tight that it hurt him.

"Well," he agreed, "if we find her, at least that may be sufficient to make the Governor give us another stay. But, Miss Rankin, the real murderer—" he paused, "if, er, if it——"

"If what?" she demanded. "Do you mean, if it wasn't Van?"

"No, no," he said hastily. "The real murderer knows that Jessie Duke saw him. Even if she wanted to tell, he and his gang would stop her. Look at this sensibly. We——"

"Sensibly!" she raged. "That's what has left Van without a friend but me—looking at it 'sensibly'! That stuffed shirt of a father of his and his sisters—they're being 'sensible.' Look at it sensibly! That's the alibi of quitters. They all believe he's guilty—everybody but me. Me—" she added, "and Jessie Duke and the man who really fired the shot. Van's people know that if he's freed he'll marry me—me, a musical comedy actress. They'd rather see him dead! And that isn't all! His sisters and the other relatives know that if Van dies they'll get more of the old man's money. What a fine lot of swine. *They're* murderers! Killing Van for his money!"

"You might as well be calm," Latham tried to soothe her. "Perhaps, as you say, we'll save him. But if we can't find Jessie Duke in time—I would advise you to prepare. The shock, I'm afraid——"

"I'm no quitter, Mr. Latham. I love Jack and he loves me and I'm a one-man dog. I'm going to get him out of there. I told him I would and he believes me. I'm going to make good!"

"Jessie Duke may be dead. They may have killed her."

"Why should that priest telephone me then?"

"He may not have been a priest," he suggested. "I'm afraid that it was some cruel practical joker."

"He said she was dying of tuberculosis and wanted to see me."

"But he was evasive. He would not tell his name, nor when you could see her, nor where. It doesn't hold water, that story."

"There's nothing the matter with that story. It was true talk. Those gunmen, he said, were going away over Sunday and probably I could sneak in and see her."

"Well," Latham resignedly gestured with his hands, "it will do no harm to hope." He looked at his watch. "At three o'clock, he was to call?"

"Yes, and he'll call, too."

"Umm," said Latham, as the limousine stopped at their destination.

They pushed through the group of reporters who were waiting in Latham's outer office.

"No news yet, boys," he said. "I may turn up something though. I'm working with might and main."

"Humph!" said Alice, who had gone on ahead.

They sat down in Latham's office and he glanced at the evening paper that lay on his desk. A headline all the way across the page read: VAN DYKE TO HANG BEFORE DAYBREAK.

Alice leaned forward.

"Liars!" she said.

She looked at the bronze clock on the desk.

"We'll get a call in five minutes," she predicted. "He'll phone at three."

Latham was looking through some papers on his desk.

"Isn't it queer," he mused, "how little things affect lives? Here is a case that I am trying next month. If a man had not stopped to tie his shoe, he would be alive today."

"That's nothing. If Van hadn't forgotten about daylight-saving time he would have been on a train for New York when the murder was committed."

"This is a most interesting case. Down at Thirty-second and Main——"

"I'm interested in only one case, Mr. Latham." She rose and went to the window. "Go ahead with your work. Don't mind me."

The telephone bell rang sharply. She strode toward the desk as Latham took off the French phone.

"Hello," he said.

Alice stood tense beside him.

"Oh, hello, Bill," he said, and looked up at her and shook his head.

Her tired shoulders sagged as she walked back to the window and she clenched her fists as Latham and a man named Bill decided whom they would get to make the fourth in their Sunday golf game.

Finally Latham replaced the phone.

"Wasn't him," he said.

"So I gathered."

Five minutes passed. Ten minutes. Half an hour. The execution was only eleven hours away.

Latham looked up from his papers. The girl still was standing by the window, looking at the sky as if searching for inspiration from the sunshine.

"Won't you sit down?" he said.

She shook her head and smiled wanly. "I'm praying," she said, simply.

Suddenly the telephone bell rang. Latham reached out, but Alice was ahead of him.

"Hello!" she said. . . .

"Yes, this is Miss Rankin. . . ."

She turned to Latham. "It's Jessie Duke!" she exclaimed.

Latham leaped to his feet.

"Yes, yes, I hear you," Alice was saying. "Apartment 4D, Number 2236 North Dollinger Place."

Latham hastily wrote down the address. His fingers were trembling.

"Yes," Alice said. "I'll start immediately. Thank you, thank you. . . . What's that? Hello! Hello!"

She quickly hung up the telephone.

"She's ready to talk!" she cried. "Let's go!"

A group of men and women were talking excitedly with a policeman on the sidewalk in front of the dingy apartment on Dollinger Place as Alice and Latham jumped out of Latham's limousine.

"Hey, where you goin'?" the policeman yelled.

"A business call," said Latham, with dignity.

"Where?" the policeman insisted.

"I fail to see that it is any concern of yours," Latham declared.

"Apartment 4D," Alice said quickly. "Come on," she said to Latham.

"Wait a minute, wait a minute, whoa there!" the policeman blocked their way. "Maybe you know somepin."

A dozen people crowded around them.

"Here is my card," said Latham.

"Oh." There was awe in the policeman's manner now. He stepped aside. "I'll go up with you, Mr. Latham."

"What's happened?" Alice demanded.

"You come too," said the policeman. "Get back, all of yuh!" he growled at the bystanders.

They climbed three flights of stairs to Apartment 4D. It consisted of two tiny rooms and a bath, cheaply furnished, but clean.

"She's gone!" Alice exclaimed.

"Yeah," the policeman agreed. "Just a little while ago two men carried her out, screamin', and put her in a car and drove away. The neighbors called me, but it was all over when I got here. Know anything about it?"

"They overheard her talking to me!" Alice declared. "I thought I heard a funny noise, sort of like a scream, just before the phone was hung up." She turned to the policeman. "You've got to find her, you've got to! Right away!"

Under the lash of frantic demands from Montgomery H. Latham, the police were searching the city. Now the great criminal lawyer was alert, eager. If he found Jessie Duke it would be one more triumph. He would save a man's life—but more important than that, Montgomery H. Latham's picture would be in the papers.

Alice was waiting with him in his office. She sat beside his desk. It was now after midnight. The late editions of the afternoon papers lay on the desk. Alice glanced at the headlines, which promised an execution at 2:30 A.M.

At the first click of the bell he seized the telephone.

"Yes?" he said. There was a long silence as he listened. Alice leaned forward, taut, her clenched fists on the newspapers.

"Great!" Latham said. "I'll be right down." He jumped up.

"They've found her!" he shouted and reached for his hat and coat. "Shot in the back, beside a road out in Engledale. She's still alive—at the city hospital. They're operating. She'll live!"

Alice pointed to the telephone. "Call the Governor."

"Right!"

He got the little hotel in Pine Lake and asked to speak to the Governor.

"Lots of noise," he said to Alice. "They must be having a wild party." He turned quickly to the phone. "Hello! Hello, Governor? . . . Oh, it's you, G. W. The Governor there? . . . When will he be back? . . . Well, listen, G. W. . . ."

He told the Lieutenant Governor about Jessie Duke.

Evidently the Lieutenant Governor answered, "Well, what of it?"

"What of it?" Latham yelled. "I want the Governor to telephone the Warden and order a stay! That's what of it! . . . How do I know it's Jessie Duke? Well, I know! I'm certain of it. . . . Yes, that's true, but, G. W., this time I've got her. . . . Hey, wait a minute!" He turned to Alice, crestfallen. "He hung up. He said to get the Chief of Police to telephone the Governor that the Chief has positive evidence that it's Jessie Duke and that she is ready to talk."

"All right," said Alice, promptly. "Let's go find the Chief."

"But," Latham was in despair, "they don't know. There's nothing on her to identify her, and nothing in her apartment."

"Ask her who she is! Get a statement from her! My God!" she raged, "are you going to stand there and——"

"Don't you understand!" he interrupted. "She's on the operating table, under ether, and she won't be able to talk until morning! We're lost!"

"Lost!" she denied fiercely. "They don't hang innocent men, I tell you!" Her eyes fell on the headlines in the newspaper. "Liar! Liar!" she shouted. "He'll never—" she stopped suddenly.

Latham was putting on his coat. She looked at the newspaper. She read something there. Tense, like a mechanical man, holding her breath, she raised a hand to her temple and let her hand, pressing hard, slide down her face, her eyes fixed on the words she read. "I'll go to the prison," she said softly, as if she hardly dared to speak aloud. She grasped the newspaper tight.

"You can see the boy at two o'clock," the gray-haired old Warden said, kindly. "Just before he goes—er, into the yard. That won't be long."

"He's not going into the yard," she declared.

The Warden shook his head doubtfully. "I wish you were right, Miss Rankin. I—I've talked a lot to that boy and, Miss Rankin, I don't believe he did it."

"Of course he didn't do it! And you're not going to hang him! Will you please let me see the court order?"

He took it out of his desk. She held the newspaper in one hand pressed against her breast and reached for the document with the other. The order commanded the Warden to hang John Van Dyke at 2:30 A.M. on Sunday, April 28th.

She nodded and returned the legal form to him.

"Thanks," she said, and relaxed in her chair. "You can't hang Jack on that order."

He looked at it quickly, then his eyes met hers. He was irritated. This was no time for joking and he was about to tell her so, but in her eyes he saw something that stopped him.

"Why not?" he asked, scanning the document with its legal seal and three signatures.

"You are ordered to execute him at 2:30 A.M."

"Yes."

"You can't execute him at two o'clock—nor at three o'clock?"

"No, of course not. Half-past two is the time."

She unfolded the newspaper. She pointed to a box on the front page. She read the headline to him, "Set Your Watches Forward Before You Go to Bed."

She glanced quickly at the Warden's puzzled face and resumed reading aloud: "By act of Legislature, Daylight Saving Time officially goes into effect at two o'clock tomorrow morning. One hour is dropped out of the twenty-four, so tomorrow legally is only twenty-three hours long. The lost hour will be picked up when Standard Time is restored in September."

The Warden seized the paper and read the item.

"I don't get you," he said.

"There is no 2:30 A.M. this morning. The state orders you to set your clock ahead one hour at 2 A.M. Two o'clock legally becomes three o'clock. An hour is lost—utterly lost."

"But—why—it can't be possible that——"

"The same authority that commands you to hang Jack at 2:30 has legally wiped out that hour. There is no such time in this state. Understand?"

"I think I see what you mean," he guessed vaguely. "But—" He picked up the court order and read it carefully. Then he reached for the newspaper. He read the item again and he scratched his head. He muttered to himself, confused.

"By George!" he exclaimed. "I hope you're right! But—but it doesn't seem reasonable, someway. I guess I better phone the Attorney General."

"You can get his opinion tomorrow. It's up to you to use your own judgment. You think Jack is innocent, don't you? Well, you can't legally hang him tonight."

"I don't want to do anything I oughtn't to," he said cautiously. "I'll call the Attorney General."

The Attorney General, roused from a sound sleep, listened to the Warden's problem, then gave his opinion.

"All right, sir," said the Warden, despairingly, and hung up the receiver. He turned to Alice. "He says it's nonsense and for me to go ahead with the execution at 2:30 A.M., Standard Time."

"It's not nonsense! You've got to wait for a new court order!"

She looked up. Latham had just opened the door and, before he entered the office, was assuring the newspaper men, waiting outside, that he was moving heaven and earth. He came in and closed the door.

"Not a chance," he lamented. "She can't talk for hours."

"Listen to me!" Alice ordered.

She told him of her discovery.

"Great!" he exclaimed. "Wonderful!" he rubbed the palms of his hands together and looked questioningly at the Warden. "That ought to settle it, don't you think?"

"The Attorney General says to go ahead," the Warden said.

Latham's face fell. "You don't mean that you will go ahead—illegally?"

"What else can I do?"

"Well," Latham pondered. "The Attorney General knows his law. If he says so——"

"To hell with the Attorney General!" Alice raged, and pointed to the telephone. "Get the Governor!"

The Governor was called to the telephone at Pine Lake. Latham began to explain the situation. The Governor interrupted.

"You can too, be bothered," Latham yelled. . . . "I say the execution cannot legally take place until the court issues another order. You have got to grant a stay. Hear me?"

Latham turned to Alice. "There's a lot of noise there," he said. "I can't make him understand." He turned back to the telephone. "I'll tell you again, Governor. It's this way. . . ." He sighed. "He doesn't get it," he said. "He says to let the Attorney General decide."

"Let me talk to him!" Alice seized the telephone. Her voice was crisp and sharp: "Governor, you signed a Daylight Saving Bill that abolishes one hour to-day. In that hour Jack Van Dyke is sentenced to hang. If you do not stop the execution you will have allowed an innocent man to be murdered! To-morrow morning Jessie Duke will make a statement that will clear Jack. And you will be run out of the state because I am going to tell the newspapers— What's that?" She turned to the Warden. "The Governor wants to speak to you," she said.

The Warden flung open the door of his office. Close behind him was Alice, followed by Latham.

"The Governor has granted a stay, boys!" the Warden announced.

The reporters rushed toward him, asking questions furiously.

Alice dragged him by the hand. "Come quick!" she ordered. She spoke to the reporters: "Mr. Latham will tell you all about it." She dragged the Warden toward the doors that led to the cell block.

"Well, boys," Latham began, "I happened to get an idea. . . ."

The iron doors behind her, Alice ran down the corridor toward the cells of the condemned.

"It's all right, honey," she cried. "It's all right. Didn't I tell you?"

RED WINE

Lawrence G. Blochman

"Red Wine" was one of the most successful stories written by Lawrence G(oldtree) Blochman's (1900-1975), whose more than fifty books and hundreds of short stories were adventure and popular fiction, often set in the Far East. He created two series characters, Inspector Leonidas Prike in India and Dr. Daniel Webster Coffee in the fictional midwestern town of Northbank, but most of his novels and stories were standalones, as is "Red Wine."

Set in a jungle outpost, the solution to a wonderfully constructed dilemma is solved in a surprise ending. The story served as the basis for several episodes of the popular radio anthology series *Escape* and other programs.

A Californian born in San Diego and a graduate of the University of California at Berkeley (1921), Blochman's career in journalism began in California but he soon was assigned to posts in Japan, Hong Kong, Calcutta, and France, after which he resigned to become a full-time free-lance writer.

A television series titled *Diagnosis: Unknown*, based on his

Dr. Coffee stories, aired in the early 1960s, starring Patrick O'Neal as the pathologist and Chester Morris as the policeman. Films made from his work include *Bombay Mail* (1934), based on his novel of the same name, starring Edmund Lowe; *Chinatown Squad* (1935), based on an original Blochman story, starring Lyle Talbot and Valerie Hopkins; and *Quiet Please, Murder* (1942), based on "Death Walks in Marble Halls," starring George Sanders, Gail Patrick, and Richard Denning.

"Red Wine" was originally published in the June 1, 1930, issue of *Adventure* magazine; its first book appearance was in *Best American Mystery Stories*, edited by Carolyn Wells (New York, Albert & Charles Boni, 1931).

Red Wine

Lawrence G. Blochman

A RAUCOUS toot from the whistle of the yellow funneled K.P.M. steamer echoed from the jungle covered headlands to arouse Heer Controleur Koert from his afternoon nap. Heer Koert did not swear; the day was too hot for any such exertion as swearing. He opened one eye and peered through the haze of his mosquito netting. Below his veranda lay a collection of glaring tin roofed sheds, whitewashed Chinese shops, and *attap* huts clinging to the green edge of the low river bank.

Some distance offshore, beyond the muddy swirl made by the river as it pushed brown fingers into the unruffled blue of the sea, the mail steamer was smoking impatiently, the only connection between Tanjong Samar and civilization. And since Heer Koert was the official representative of civilization in Tanjong Samar, he opened the other eye.

He watched the swarm of *praus* and *sampans* streaking for

the ship, and estimated that he would have half an hour before being forced to make any further movement. In half an hour he would arise, dash tepid water on himself from a Java bath jar, drink a cup of coffee and button his white duck jacket high about his neck. Thus he would be fit to sit at his desk and properly receive the official communications and two weeks' accumulations of the *Bataviasch Nieuwsblad* which his dusky skinned *aspirant-controleur* would bring ashore.

The *controleur's* leisurely routine was somewhat rushed, however, when he saw that the first boat ashore did not debark his slow moving assistant, but a brisk walking white man he had never seen before. The stranger made such a rapid climb to the *controleur's* bungalow that Heer Koert had barely time to make himself dignified before there was a knock on the screen door of the veranda. He waddled ponderously to answer.

A man in a pongee suit and white topee stood there, wiping his perspiring face with a silk handkerchief. He was a well fed appearing man whose movements were good natured and deliberate. His frank smile caused deep dimples to dot either side of a face that gave an impression of virile intelligence—an impression somehow strengthened by the droop of his right eyelid over a vaguely pale eye. The alert vitality of the good eye was penetrating enough for two.

"Are you Mr. Koert?" asked the man in the pongee suit. "My name is Paul Vernier. The governor-general promised me your coöperation. Has he written you?"

"You are here before the mail," said the *controleur*. "But you have my coöperation anyhow. Won't you sit down please?"

"I'll come right to the point," said Vernier, sinking into a high, fan backed Bilibid chair. "I'm looking for a killer."

"Dayaks, maybe?" said the rotund *controleur*. "You must go

far up the river to find them. And they are not killing so much any more. Instead of letting them hunt new heads for marriage ceremonies, we are persuading them to use old heads——"

"Dayaks don't interest me," said Vernier. "I'm looking for an American—an American murderer named Jerome Steeks. I've traced him to Tanjong Samar."

Koert clapped his hands and shouted something in Malay, which was answered by a grunt in another room.

"I am offering you coffee," he explained. "This is coffee time. Later is gin time. Where is your baggage?"

"I have all the baggage I need in my inside pocket—extradition papers for Jerome Steeks, approved by the governor-general in Batavia. I'll pick up Steeks as soon as you tell me where he is, and I'll take him aboard the steamer before she sails."

"You can't do that," said the *controleur* simply.

"Why not? I'm positive Jerome Steeks is in Tanjong Samar."

"There is nobody with that name in my district."

"Naturally, he wouldn't be using his own name. But it shouldn't be so hard to locate my man in this bustling metropolis. Isn't there an American here?"

"There are three Americans." Vernier's eyebrows raised slightly as Koert continued, "All three are on the Kota Bharu rubber estate up the river. The round trip to the plantation will take two hours, not counting time for looking for the Americans. The steamer leaves in one hour. Shall I send out for your baggages?"

Vernier's gaze fixed Koert for a moment. Then his pursed lips spread into a smile.

"All right," he said. "If it won't be too much trouble."

Koert clapped his hands again and muttered more Malay. A servant appeared with a tray.

"They will get it for you," said the *controleur.* "And now we can drink our coffee."

There was no coffee pot on the tray—only cups, sugar bowl, a pitcher of hot milk and a small jug. Vernier watched Koert pour a spoonful of black essence from the jug into each cup, then add the steaming milk. The resultant liquid looked and smelled a little like coffee.

"And now," said Koert, passing a cup, "tell me about this man you want to arrest. Does he know you?"

"No."

"Good. In that case he will not suspect. You can arrest him a few hours before the next ship calls. That will save unpleasant makeshifts. We have no good jail here. You will recognize this American? You have his photograph?"

"Jerome Steeks is a very clever man," said Vernier. "He planned a perfect escape from a nearly perfect crime. There isn't a single picture or set of fingerprints of him in existence. I know him only by description; medium height, slight build, pale complexion, dark hair and small black mustache."

The *controleur* suddenly grasped his ample girth with both hands, threw back his head, opened his mouth wide and emitted loud cackling sounds. After a moment Vernier decided Heer Koert was laughing.

"You must have come to the wrong *dessa,*" laughed the *controleur.* "All three men are medium height, but all are quite strong looking, clean shaven, brown as coffee by the sun, and none has dark hair."

"I told you Steeks was clever." Vernier smiled, a little wistfully. "But I'm positive he is here. He came here from Batavia six months ago."

"All three men came from Batavia six months ago, by the

same boat. The estate changed hands and the new owner wanted Americans to run it, because American planters know how to bud the trees and double the rubber yield . . . What sort of man is the murderer?"

Vernier gulped the bitterish coffee.

"Utterly ruthless," he said, "yet a polished gentleman. Strange combination. He has lived a great deal in Europe, where he was known as a connoisseur of music, women, good cooking and fine wines. I heard of him first when I was in France."

"Ah, France," said Heer Koert, looking steadfastly at Vernier's drooping eyelid. "Then it was in France that you——"

He made a vague gesture, as though afraid to touch on a delicate subject. Vernier saw the gesture and smiled.

"Yes," he said. "A piece of shrapnel. It started me on my present career, I guess. One eye isn't enough for the infantry, so they took me off the line and put me into the Intelligence. I made so many French contacts that after the Armistice I followed them up. Stayed on in Paris to study Bertillon methods with the French Sûreté. Just before I came home I remember reading of Jerome Steeks attending the annual banquet of Paris vintners, entering the usual wine tasting contest and identifying by taste as many unlabeled vintages as the oldest professional taster."

Heer Koert made clucking sounds with his tongue.

"A gourmet," he commented.

"He was rich. Nobody questioned the source of his money, which was undoubtedly—well, extralegal. Three years ago he married a San Francisco heiress, took her to Europe, brought her back to California. Shortly after their return, Mrs. Steeks's body was found lying on the end of a little used pier, a bullet in the brain. Tire marks on the pier led to a search for the Steeks's car, which was found in the bay. Steeks was supposed to have been drowned in the plunge. A note told of a suicide pact. They had run through the heiress's fortune, lost staggering sums at Monte Carlo and decided on death rather than poverty. Although Steeks's body was never found, in view of the tides, the discovery of two empty shells in a revolver, and the fact that Mrs. Steeks's fortune was indeed dissipated, the police accepted the double suicide theory."

"And of course it was false?"

"Of course. It was a case of cold-blooded murder for profit. A year later a prominent shyster lawyer got into a jam, was arrested, and in his safe cops found a letter from Steeks, written from Batavia. The lawyer had apparently been salting away the wife's missing fortune and was to notify Steeks when he could come back safely. Well, the Secretary of State asked for extradition right away, and I slid out to Batavia to pick up the trail. Clews can get pretty cold in a year, and evidence can be camouflaged. But I've got Mr. Steeks here now. With no steamer for two weeks, he can't very well get away from me."

Controleur Koert shook his head in a puzzled manner.

"I am not so sure," he said. "There is no gourmet and no polished gentleman at Kota Bharu estate. There is just Americans."

"One of them is a murderer. When can we go and pick him out, Mr. Koert?"

The *controleur* scratched himself behind the ear.

"First I must attend to the steamer," he said. "Then I will talk with you about best methods."

"In the meantime I'll walk about the town a bit," said Vernier, arising. "It's cooler now. Maybe I can learn something."

"Mr. Vernier, please don't open that screen door yet," cried Koert, rushing after the detective in a panic. "Wait."

He rolled a newspaper into a small torch, lighted it and

waved the flame against the screen to cremate whatever mosquitoes had gathered on the outside waiting a chance to enter.

"Now," he said. "Go. And shut the door quickly. In an hour and a half come back. We will have gin *pahits* and discuss methods."

The *controleur* persuaded Paul Vernier to wait until next morning before starting his man hunt. The sun glinted with hard brilliance on the coffee colored river when the two men—Koert in whites, Vernier in khaki—walked down to the shore. They threaded their way among carved, high stemmed *praus*, drawn up on the beach, with red and blue demons grinning from their leaning masts. The two white men crawled under the palm thatched canopy shading the middle of a long narrow *sampan*. Paddles dug into the brown water, churning the current. The craft swung upstream.

The *sampan* slid between low banks of mangrove and nipa palms, behind which arose mountains of verdure, cliffs of tangled palms and creepers, slashed by the broad fresh green blades of plantains, flecked by the white puffs of ripe tree cotton, the yellow of cannas and the flame of *lantana*.

Four naked mahogany torsos glistened as four paddles swung in unison. The steersman aft of the canopy chanted.

After a few minutes on the river Vernier drew Koert's attention to another *sampan* following them, stroke for stroke.

"Yes," said Koert. "That is your baggages. I had them sent by another *sampan* because we are already crowded in this one."

"But I don't need baggage," said Vernier. "I won't have to stay at the plantation. I'll pick my man and come back to stay with you—if you don't mind."

"I would be more than pleased. But I am afraid you will have to stay longer. I know the three Americans. None of them fits your description. You will have to study them closer. The governor-general said I should help you, so I sent word ahead that we would come for *makan* at noon today and that you might want to stay on for a few days to see how rubber is made."

The round faced detective's dimples appeared.

"I wouldn't like to do that—accept a man's hospitality and then clamp the bracelets on him. If I find I have to stay there to complete my identification, I'll tell them so right out. Not likely that my man will escape from this place. That way it will make it an open battle of wits, and I'll feel better about staying with the men."

"Oh, no, no!" exclaimed the *controleur.* "You can't do that. I have already said you were a stockholder and for that reason wished to stay on the plantation. You can not contradict the *controleur.*" Vernier's dimples disappeared.

"Can't you say you misunderstood me?" he inquired.

"Should the governor-general hear I was misunderstanding people, I might not get my promotion to be sub-resident in Java. Besides, it will be easier for you to work quietly like I plan."

"Well, all right. We'll try it for awhile," said Vernier soberly. A pucker grew between his eyebrows.

A rickety little pier, two tin roofed sheds and a clearing of the jungle to make way for the symmetrical rows of *hevea* trees marked the place where the Kota Bharu rubber plantation reached the river. From the river it was a five-minute walk to the large bungalow, raised on piles, which served as quarters for the white plantation managers.

The three managers puzzled Vernier as they were introduced—Prale, Wilmerding and Doran. The *controleur* had been right. There was nothing of a cultured *bon vivant* among these rough and ready Americans, and all were light. Prale was a bland looking, sandy haired fellow with a smart Aleck twist to the corners of his mouth and a turned up nose. Wilmerding was blond, almost tow headed, with a vigorous handshake. Doran, keen eyed and restless, had light reddish hair. Which one of the trio was the black haired Jerome Steeks? None of them, Vernier would have said, had he not definite information that the murderer was here. One of them *must* be Steeks.

"Hope you don't object to *rystaffel*," said Doran as they filed into a darkened room for lunch. "That's all our cook ever gives us for noon."

"From what I had of it in Java," said Vernier, "I rather like it."

"I don't," said Wilmerding. "*Rystaffel*'s enough to give dyspepsia to a herd of buffaloes."

Whatever the reaction of buffaloes to the national dish of the Dutch colonial in the Indies, Wilmerding was apparently not afraid of dyspepsia for himself. He heaped his plate high with rice and proceeded to decorate it with all the accessories which two servants brought to the table: curried eggs, fried bananas, onions, chutneys, shredded cocoanut, tiny red dried fish, peppers and various unidentified spiced meats and vegetables. Vernier watched Wilmerding mix the conglomeration in approved Dutch East Indies style. Wilmerding caught Vernier's eye, guessed his judgment on the score of inconsistency, and said——

"Well, we have to eat something."

"*Rystaffel's* not bad with a glass of beer," said Vernier.

"We never have any real cold beer out here," Wilmerding complained. "No ice. And warm beer is nasty."

Vernier studied Wilmerding a moment. He was attacking his *rystaffel* with as much gusto as his two companions, but for a flash, Vernier thought he had detected a styled movement on the lifting of a fork. Perhaps not, inasmuch as Wilmerding wiped his mouth with the back of his hand after taking a draft of beer. Still——

"I ran across some pretty good wine down in Batavia and Sourabaya. Why don't you fellows get some of it sent up?" Vernier suggested.

"Never learned to drink wine," said Wilmerding. "We got plebeian tastes. Just beer—and a little gin or Scotch at night. Prale over there talks a lot about the wine he drank, but if you ask me, he'd a lot rather have an ice cream soda. A lot of us would, I guess."

He ran his fingers through his blond hair, thoughtfully sipped some beer, then went after his rice with renewed vigor.

Talk ranged from baseball back in the States to the classic argument as to which is worse, mosquitoes or citronella oil; the amours of the contract Javanese laborers and reports of a head hunting expedition by Dayaks in a neighboring district occupied some of the conversation. It wasn't until an amazing amount of rice had been consumed, however, that Vernier saw his first indication as to which of the three might be the cultured murderer. The detective pricked up his ears when Wilmerding suggested that Doran give him some music.

"Music?" echoed Vernier.

"Yeh. Doran plays," said Prale. "He plays a mean phonograph."

Yes, the phonograph was his, Doran admitted. What would Mr. Vernier like to hear? Probably nothing, because it was damned hard to keep up a decent repertoire out there in Borneo, where the new records had to be shipped in and half the time arrived broken.

"May I look?" said Vernier.

He slid back the disks, one after the other, expecting to find recordings of operas, symphonies and other more serious compositions—probably French composers dominating. He found only jazz numbers, out-of-date sentimental ballads, Irving Berlin, pre-Gershwin dance music. No trained, cosmopolitan taste here.

"Play anything," he said.

The phonograph squealed, sang and strummed away. Wilmerding sat smoking a pipe with Heer Koert. Prale walked to the edge of the veranda and looked through the screen toward the river. Doran was sorting over his precious records. Vernier walked slowly about the room, taking in details with his one alert eye. He stopped in front of a bookcase and began reading the titles.

"Hello," he said. "Who owns the French books?"

"They were here when we came," said Wilmerding. "There was a French planter on the estate before us. He left the books."

"Anybody here read them?" Vernier inquired, taking down a volume bound in yellow paper covers.

"Prale practically invented the French language," said Doran. "Just ask him."

Vernier was holding the French book close to his face, slowly turning pages. "I studied French," he said, as if to himself. Then, watching the room over the top of his book, he said, as though reading, "*Il y a un meurtrier dans cette maison.*"

He paused, watching for a reaction to his announcement in French that there was a murderer in the house. He was disappointed. Prale looked stupidly sheepish as the others overwhelmed him with banter.

"What's it all about, Prale?" demanded Wilmerding.

"Translate for us," ordered Doran.

"Why, it's all about houses," said Prale. "*Maison*—that's French for house."

When the laughter had subsided, Heer Controleur Koert arose and mopped his ruddy face.

"You will excuse me, I have to return to the *dessa* for important official business," he said, with as much equanimity as if every one present did not know that the important business was his daily *siesta*. "And you, Mr. Vernier? Are you going to pay a visit of some days to this estate?"

"If I'm not in the way," said Vernier.

The drooping lid of his sightless eye quivered just a trifle.

"Plenty of room," said Wilmerding.

"Even if there wasn't, we'd make room by putting Doran out to sleep with the mosquitoes," said Prale.

"Which would spare me from listening to Prale's wisecracks," countered Doran.

"I would like very much to have a chance to see how you fellows get a dozen golf balls and a set of balloon tires out of a tree," said Vernier. "But I warn you—" he paused and looked at Koert—"I warn you that you'll have me prowling all over the place, asking questions like a woman at a ball game. I'm curious—about all sorts of things."

He worked his curiosity overtime during the next few days. He prowled and asked questions at all hours. He would follow Prale down the estate in the misty dawn at tapping time, listening as he offered profane suggestions, half English, half broken Malay, to the Javanese who were shaving the diagonal scars on the trunks of the *hevea* trees so that the milky latex would ooze out into grooves, through a spigot into tiny porcelain cups. After the sun had become hot enough to stop the flow of sap he would make the rounds with Wilmerding, watching Javanese women in gay *sarongs* collecting latex in buffalo drawn tank carts. Then he would stand, where Doran, at the chemical shack, received the latex, pouring it into vats to be coagulated into rubber.

But in three days he got nowhere. He still believed that one of the planters was Jerome Steeks. And he still did not know whether it was Prale, Doran, or Wilmerding. One thing he did know for certain: Steeks's hair had changed color in the last eighteen months. The dark murderer of San Francisco had become a blond. Hydrogen peroxide or some other bleaching agent must have been in use here. In use constantly, too, because for three days Vernier had looked closely to find one head of hair that was darker at the roots. Vain search. The new growth was apparently being bleached as fast as it came out. This might be a clew.

The following day, when the three planters had gone out into the steamy morning, Vernier remained at the bungalow, pleading a headache. He lay on his springless tropical bed until he no longer heard the servants stirring about. Then he arose, went directly to Prale's room and started systematically to examine every corner of it. He ran hurriedly through a chest of drawers, and a steamer trunk green with the quick mold of the tropics. He had little expectation that a man as clever as Jerome Steeks would leave telltale papers around, but he hoped to find that bleaching agent. As a matter of fact, he found nothing but clothes, a photograph of an old woman in a moldy leather case, a catalog from a Chicago mail order house——

He repeated the procedure in Wilmerding's room. As he was opening a trunk he thought he heard steps outside the door. He arose quickly, listened, looked out. He saw no one. He returned to his task; again fruitless. Doran's room was equally devoid of evidence.

But Doran was in the chemical shack most of the day! Just the place to hide a bleach and a little henna dye. A bottle more or less among the other chemicals would not be noticed. So Vernier went out to do a little noticing. He asked questions of Doran, who was busy with the latex. He picked up bottles and tapped metal drums. Doran gave a satisfactory explanation for everything. Another blind clew.

Prale? Wilmerding? Doran? He shut himself up alone that afternoon to reflect, to work out some plan of attack. He was so wrapped in thought that he was late for dinner. An animated conversation was in progress before he reached the table, but it stopped suddenly as he appeared in the doorway. As he sat down, conversation was resumed on trivial matters, obviously forced in an effort by the planters to cover up a change of subject. Vernier knew they had been talking about him.

After dinner there was a poker game. The four men sat about a table on the veranda. Perspiration glistened on faces and naked arms, golden in the lamplight.

A cloud of insects buzzed and flickered about the lamp, one occasionally diving into the flame with an odorous sizzle, sometimes falling among the cards in a wing beating frenzy. Vernier was unusually quiet. He was studying his three opponents.

Jerome Steeks had been somewhat of a gambler. He might betray himself at the game. One of the three planters did, in fact, display considerable more card sense than the others—Prale. Luck was against him, however, and the chips piled up in front of Vernier. The trio were not good sports about losing, either. At least, Vernier attributed a certain tensity in the hot atmosphere to his consistent winnings. Conversation seemed strained, tonight, and what little talk there was was rarely directed at him.

Finally, when he had raked in a jack pot with four sixes over Prale's ace full, Doran tossed his cards to the center of the table and cleared his throat.

"Say, Vernier," he began, looking the detective full in the face. "Just exactly what are you doing in Borneo, anyhow?"

"I thought Koert explained," said Vernier. "I'm——"

"We mean the real reason," said Wilmerding. "Of course, the stockholder story is out, because there aren't any stockholders in Kota Bharu rubber. The whole estate belongs to one man. I know that for certain."

Vernier laughed. It was a genuine laugh, for although he felt the situation rapidly growing more uneasy, he could appreciate the joke he had played on himself by accepting the *controleur's* suggestion to act the rôle of stockholder.

"Do you boys think I'm out here to sell you gold bricks or something?" he said genially.

His joviality was not reflected by the three planters. There was an embarrassed silence for several seconds. Then Prale said with a drawl——

"What kind of gold bricks were you looking for in my room this morning?"

Again a leaden moment of silence. All eyes were fixed on Vernier. The detective held the deck of cards between his hands and was ruffling the edge of the pack with his thumb. It made a sharp crackling noise, repeated several times as he scanned the three faces around the lamp. He was thinking about the footsteps he had heard while he was in Wilmerding's room that morning. A spying servant, seeking to ingratiate himself by bearing tales to his employer?

"In your room?"

"Yes," said Wilmerding. "We understand you did a little prospecting to-day—to cure your headache."

"I don't like this business—your coming here lying to us, Vernier," put in Doran. "How do we know what crooked game you're up to? You're probably a spy of some kind."

"Don't be ridiculous."

"He's not ridiculous." It was Wilmerding speaking. "We're living on the frayed edge of civilization here. We've got to look out for our-selves. We've got a perfect right to be suspicious of strangers. There's nothing ridiculous in a man protecting himself against potential enemies."

"How did you just happen to come to Tanjong Samar, which most people never heard of?" demanded Prale. "Why did you pick Kota Bharu estate out of the hundreds of rubber plantations in the East Indies?"

Vernier was still ruffling the pack of cards with his thumb. The three men about the table looked at him in ominous silence. They were serious, these faces that perspired in the lamplight; suspicious, challenging and perhaps just a bit contemptuous. Vernier dropped the cards to the table carelessly. A *gecko* in some dark corner of the veranda uttered a series of explosive cries that sounded uncannily like human words. Insects continued their monotonous buzzing about the lamp. Vernier leaned forward easily on his elbows.

"I'll tell you why I came to Tanjong Samar," he said at last. "I came here to arrest a murderer."

There was a little movement by each of the three planters. Surprise, perhaps. Resentment——

"I'll be quite frank with you boys," Vernier continued. "I told the *controleur* he'd better pass me off as a stockholder until I found out which one of you three was the man I wanted. I had definite information that the murderer was on the Kota Bharu rubber estate."

Vernier's smile again flashed, and his one eye shone so with frankness that the planters leaned back in their chairs. The tension was eased for a moment.

"I'll bet Doran is the guy you're after," said Prale.

"If you stick around long enough, you can pick me up for killing Prale. I feel it coming on," said Doran.

"What's the murderer's name?" asked Wilmerding.

"Jerome Steeks."

Vernier's keen glance shifted from one face to another, but he detected not so much as the flicker of an eyelash.

"Never heard of him."

"Sounds like a vegetable to me."

"Which one of us is he?"

Vernier leisurely lighted a cigarette over the lamp chimney before he replied.

"None of you," he said. "I hadn't been here long before I decided that the tip I had was wrong. Jerome Steeks had dark hair. You men are all naturally light—nothing phony about your wigs. So I'm going to go back to Java on the next K.P.M. steamer. Then home. I kick myself, though, for having had you all under false suspicion, even if it wasn't my fault. To put myself right, to show there's no ill will on my part, I want to throw a party for you boys. We'll make it on steamer day, and you can declare a holiday, because I know the captain of the *Van Laar* is a real epicure. He has a fine cellar aboard—specializes in Chambertin—and has a great cook. I'll have him lend me the cook and a few rare old bottles for the occasion. You're invited to take a rest from *rystaffel* and have a real feed. How about it?"

There was no immediate response to the invitation. The planters seemed a little bit wary. Wilmerding spoke first.

"Sure, we'll eat your chow," he said.

"Fine," said Vernier. "I'll promise you a banquet you won't forget. How would boar with Madeira and mushroom sauce do for the roast? I'll furnish the wine sauce if there's boar to be had around here. I'll shoot one myself if some one will lend me a gun."

"I'll shoot you a pig," said Doran. "I don't like strangers using my gun."

Next morning Vernier went down the river to Tanjong Samar and called on the *controleur.*

"Mr. Koert," he said, "when does the East Borneo steamer leave Batavia?"

The *controleur* studied red lines on a wall map and consulted books.

"Is there any way for me to get through a communication to the ship before she leaves Java?" said Vernier, while Koert turned pages.

The *controleur* stroked his two chins a moment before replying.

"There is wireless at Balik Papan," he said. "For twenty-five guilders I can get an *Orung Laut* to paddle up the coast to Balik Papan to the wireless station. He would get there in time. Why?"

"I want the U. S. consul in Batavia to get some things on that boat for me. The consul knows a good cellar in Batavia. I want him to get me some Chambertin of the same vintage he produced when I was there. And I'll want other wines, and a cook. He can get me a cook from the Hôtel des Indes and put him on the boat, too, with ingredients for a menu I'm going to indicate. And ice. We must have ice——"

He sat down and began drafting his message.

"Very good," said the *controleur.* "If you will give me the twenty-five guilders, and the price of the message, I will see it goes at once. And in the meantime I am glad you are here. If you had not come, I should have gone after you this afternoon. You must stay with me until your steamer comes."

"Why so?"

"Because your life is no longer safe on the plantation."

"What makes you think so?"

"I know. I hear from natives. Servants talk. Talk travels. In the end, it always reaches me. You told the planters at Kota Bharu of your mission——"

"I protected you. The governor-general will never know anything derogatory."

"But your man will certainly kill you before steamer day."

"Oh, no," said Vernier, smiling. "We're all good friends now. I'm giving this dinner to show there's no hard feelings. Besides, I must go back to the estate. Everything depends upon my being there."

"Well, suit yourself; but remember I warned you."

"I consider myself warned. And in the meantime hurry that SOS for food, wine, and ice. You're invited, of course."

Cordial relations were apparently reëstablished when Vernier returned to the rubber estate. The three planters gave no outward evidence that they had not accepted Vernier's profession of good faith, yet the detective sensed an undercurrent of suspicion. He had an idea one of the trio was fomenting ill feelings, or at least keeping it alive, for his own private ends. And for that reason Vernier slept lightly and kept his loaded automatic under his "Dutch Wife"—the cylindrical bolster found beneath every mosquito netting in the East Indies, used as an aid to ventilation of the body and to reduce perspiration during sleep.

During the entire week that preceded the arrival of the K.P.M. steamer, Vernier acted as enthusiastic press agent for his farewell dinner. He outlined his menu and told of the wines he would serve with each course—particularly the Chambertin, king of red Burgundies, robust, fragrant, heady, Napoleon's favorite wine——

"Any Chambertin is fine," Vernier would tell the planters, "but 1911 Chambertin is beyond comparison. It is the superlative in wine. Burgundy produced real nectar that year. You'll see."

Three days before the arrival of the steamer the matter of boar again came up. All three planters decided to go shooting.

"Come with us," said Prale to Vernier.

"I haven't a gun," said Vernier, looking at Doran.

Doran looked away and did not reply.

"I have two rifles," said Wilmerding. "You can take one."

At the last minute, however, Wilmerding found that the packing of smoked crêpe for shipment on the next boat was not going rapidly enough. He decided to stay on the estate to push the coolies a bit.

Prale and Doran accompanied Vernier into the jungle beyond the limits of the plantation. Vernier noticed casually that he was the only one wearing a white topee. The other two wore khaki sun helmets.

"We won't have to go far," said Prale. "Sometimes they come right down in the trees. Just keep plugging straight ahead."

That was the plan. Vernier was to keep on straight ahead,

while Prale and Doran were to oblique to the right and left. Several Malays were out in front.

As a matter of fact, as soon as the two men were out of sight in the chest high thicket, Vernier stopped walking. He wanted those two men ahead of him, not behind. Jerome Steeks was a ruthless person——

The detective took off his white topee and perched it atop a *lantana* bush. Then he walked several paces away and squatted down in the damp growth, his rifle between his knees. They could not possibly see him there, but they could see his sun helmet—a flash of white in the dense greenery.

For twenty minutes he waited, whisking away flies and insects. Then he heard a shot, followed by two more, a fourth shot, and his sun helmet leaped spinning into the air, struck a tree, bounded to the ground at his feet. Jerome Steeks could shoot, too. Which was he? Vernier picked up the helmet. Did the shot come from the left—Prale? or the right—Doran? He turned the helmet in the direction it had been facing atop the bush. He looked at the holes. Then he looked again. The shot had come from neither left nor right. It had come from behind. One of the pair had succeeded in circling around behind him, despite his precautions. But which one?

Putting on his helmet he started back toward the estate. He hoped to cross the trail of the man who had fired from behind. But he was disappointed. He reached the bungalow without meeting any one. It was half an hour later that Prale and Doran came back, with their Malays carrying the dead pig.

There was no more stray shooting before steamer day, and when the yellow funneled steamer again hove-to off the river mouth, Vernier was still in the dark as to who fired the shot.

The ship arrived one gray, sweltering afternoon, and the *controleur* got the skipper to lay over until nearly midnight, instead of making the usual hurried call. He could be in Balik Papan by dawn, anyhow.

The cook imported from Batavia came ashore in a *sampan* loaded with crates, boxes and a huge cake of ice wrapped in burlap. He repaired immediately to the bungalow of Heer Koert where he shooed his Chinese predecessor into a corner and began to exercise his art. In view of the *controleur's* superior kitchen, and the time that would have been lost by transporting the supplies up the river, the three planters had agreed to come down to the *dessa*.

In deference to Dutch colonial custom, the dinner was preceded by a few rounds of gin *pahits* on the veranda. Vernier proudly produced a menu written in French, which he passed around, watching the expression on the faces of the three Americans as they read:

FOIE GRAS AU PORTO

HOMARD À L'ARMORICAINE

TRUFFES SOUS LA CENDRE

SANGLIER À LA MADÈRE

POMMES SOUFFLÉES

ZABAGLIONE

PETITS FOURS ROQUEFORT

DEMI-TASSE

MONTRACHET 1904 CHAMBERTIN-CRÉSIGNY 1911 CHAMPAGNE IRROY 1919

The eyes of the Dutch *controleur* and the steamship captain, who also was a guest, grew large and bright as they scanned the menu. Those of the three Americans did not show a flicker of comprehension.

The planters smacked their lips over the goose liver in port wine jelly, however, and breathed noisily in unison—Ah-h-h—when the lobster appeared, steaming in its savory fumes of white wine, brandy, essence of tomatoes.

Paul Vernier, as he presided over the table, glittering with the crystal ware and cutlery from Batavia, seemed to be thoroughly enjoying himself. At times he could be as boisterous as the three Americans. Yet when he mentioned his wines, he spoke reverently in low tones.

"This Montrachet," he said, as he poured the fragrant golden wine that accompanied the lobster, "beats any other white wine in the world. Can't compete with Chambertin, of course, but in 1904 it was as good as white Burgundy ever was or will be."

The planters approved profanely. There was plenty of white wine, so they drank plenty. And Montrachet is a heady wine. . . . They probably did not fully appreciate the truffles. Each truffle had been imbedded in a potato and baked in live coals. One had only to peel off the charred potato to find the truffle in all its succulence. . . .

Then came the boar, bathed in its mauve wine sauce, studded with mushrooms, exhaling a glorious aroma.

"And now," announced Vernier, "the king of wines. There never was a better wine than Chambertin, and there never was a better Chambertin than 1911. Look!"

Carefully cradled in a special basket with a handle at one end, the bottle was passed around. Vernier called attention to the cobwebs on the bottle. Then he poured a little in his own glass, holding it up to be admired.

"Look at that color!" he said. "Rubies. Clear, leaping flame. The fire of a thousand sunsets. And the bouquet! Just have a whiff of it. Sheer poetry! That's wine for you—Chambertin!"

He held out the glass to the nostrils of each of the guests, watching them as they breathed the spirituous fragrance.

"And now, pass me your large wine glasses, please. Thanks."

Scarcely moving the bottle, he poured each glass three-fourths full. His one keen eye darted quick glances about the table. Then he suddenly plunged a spoon into a dish of cracked ice and began to tinkle the crystal chunks into each glass of red wine.

Wilmerding instantly half rose from his chair directly opposite, his mouth open as though he had witnessed something horrible.

"My God, man! Don't put ice in that Chambertin!" he said in low, shocked tones.

Vernier dropped the spoon, made a swipe for his pocket and lunged across the table before Wilmerding could sit down again. There was a metallic click, a grunt—and a pair of handcuffs glistened around Wilmerding's wrists.

Straightening up, Vernier said quietly——

"Jerome Steeks!"

The room was immediately in an uproar. The diners were on their feet shouting, gesticulating. The *controleur* was yelling in Dutch at the steamship captain who was nodding his head furiously. Prale was pounding the table and hurling pyrotechnic language at Vernier. Doran had an arm around Wilmerding and was assuring him that everything was all right. Wilmerding continued to stare at Vernier, his mouth open.

"Jerome Steeks!" repeated Vernier.

"Liar!" yelled Doran.

"You can't get away with that stuff!" Prale was advancing toward Vernier with a chair swung above his head.

"Wait!" Vernier made a pacific gesture with both hands. Prale paused. "I'll tell you how I know this man is Jerome Steeks." Prale put down the chair. "Only an epicure, a gourmet such as Jerome Steeks, would have been shocked by my putting ice in Chambertin. Only a man who knows thoroughly how to eat and drink appreciates wines enough to understand that the bouquet of Chambertin would be destroyed, frozen up, by cold. Steeks knows that red wine should always be drunk at the temperature of the room. This, gentlemen, is Jerome Steeks, epicure—wanted in San Francisco for murder."

"How about it, Willy? What's the inside?" demanded Prale.

Steeks, lately Wilmerding, did not turn his head. He was looking forlornly at a growing purple stain on the table cloth. In his excitement of snapping on the handcuffs, Vernier had upset three glasses of wine.

"Say, Vernier," said the manacled man at last. "Will you do me one last and quite reasonable favor?"

"Sure," said Vernier, "if you'll do me one. Tell me how you kept your hair blond without bleaching agents."

Wilmerding-Steeks smiled faintly.

"It was always blond," he said. "When I started living by my wits I figured I'd probably have to hide out some day. So I dyed it black and kept it that way, knowing I could let it grow out blond when I wanted to. And now, will you do me that favor?"

"What is it?" asked Vernier.

"Pour me a glass of your Chambertin," came the reply, "without ice."

RANSOM

Pearl S. Buck

A seemingly unusual author to find in a volume devoted to mystery and suspense, Pearl S(ydenstricker) Buck (1892-1973) was a distinguished storyteller in whichever category of literature she chose to work, including more than forty novels, twenty nonfiction books, twenty short story collections, twenty children's books, and several television and screenwriting credits.

Born in West Virginia, her parents took her to China as an infant to continue their missionary work. After graduating from Virginia's Randolph-Macon Women's College, she returned to China and married John Lossing Buck, also a missionary. She taught English to Chinese university students until 1931, when her novel, *The Good Earth*, was published, immediately becoming an international bestseller and making her a world-famous literary figure. She soon returned to the United States with her daughters, divorced her husband, and married Richard J. Walsh, the president of John Day Company, her publisher.

Along with *The House of Earth* and *A House Divided*, the third volume of the trilogy, *The Good Earth* provided the history of a Chinese family through several generations and gave much of the Western world an open, honest look at an unknown, alien culture in a secretive country.

In addition to its extraordinary success, remaining at the top of the bestseller lists for more than two years, *The Good Earth* received countless critical accolades, including the Pulitzer Prize, the Howells Medal of the American Academy of the Arts, and was a major element in Buck's Nobel Prize for Literature.

Three of her novels inspired motion pictures: *The Good Earth* (1937), *Dragon Seed* (1944), and *China Sky* (1945).

"Ransom" was originally published in the October 1938 issue of *Cosmopolitan*.

Ransom

Pearl S. Buck

The Beethoven symphony stopped abruptly. A clear metallic voice broke across the melody of the third movement.

"Press radio news. The body of Jimmie Lane, kidnaped son of Mr. Headley Lane, has been found on the bank of the Hudson River near his home this afternoon. This ends the search of—"

"Kent, turn it off, please!" Allin exclaimed.

Kent Crothers hesitated a second. Then he turned off the radio.

In the silence Allin sat biting her lower lip. "That poor mother!" she exclaimed. "All these days—not giving up hope."

"I suppose it is better to know something definite," he said quietly, "even though it is the worst."

Perhaps this would be a good time to talk with her, to warn her that she was letting this kidnaping business grow into an obsession. After all, children did grow up in the United States, even in well-to-do families like theirs. The trouble was that they were not quite rich enough and still too rich—not rich enough to hire guards for their children, but rich enough, because his father owned the paper mill, to make them known in the neighborhood, at least.

The thing was to take it for granted that they did not belong to the millionaire class and therefore were not prize for kidnappers. They should do this for Bruce's sake. He would be starting to school next autumn. Bruce would have to walk back and forth on the streets like millions of other American children. Kent wouldn't have his son driven three blocks, even by Peter the outdoor man; it would do him more harm than . . . after all, it was a democracy they lived in, and Bruce had to grow up with the crowd.

"I'll go and see that the children are covered," Allin said. "Betsy throws off the covers whenever she can."

Kent knew that she simply wanted to make sure they were there. But he rose with her, lighting his pipe, thinking how to begin. They walked up the stairs together, their fingers interlaced. Softly she opened the nursery door. It was ridiculous how even he was being affected by her fears. Whenever the door opened his heart stood cold for a second, until he saw the two beds, each with a little head on the pillow.

They were there now, of course. He stood beside Bruce's bed and looked down at his son. Handsome little devil. He was sleeping so soundly that when his mother leaned over him he did not move. His black hair was a tousle; his red lips pouted. He was dark, but he had Allin's blue eyes.

They did not speak. Allin drew the cover gently over his outflung arm, and they stood a moment longer, hand in hand, gazing at the child. Then Allin looked up at Kent and smiled, and he kissed her. He put his arm about her shoulder, and they went to Betsy's bed.

Here was his secret obsession. He could say firmly that Bruce must take his chances with the other children, because a boy had to learn to be brave. But this baby—such a tiny feminine creature, his little daughter. She had Allin's auburn coloring, but by some miracle she had his dark eyes, so that when he looked into them he seemed to be looking into himself.

She was breathing now, a little unevenly, through her tiny nose.

"How's her cold?" he whispered.

"It doesn't seem worse," Allin whispered back. "I put stuff on her chest."

He was always angry when anything happened to this baby. He didn't trust her nurse, Mollie, too much. She was good-hearted, maybe, but easygoing.

The baby stirred and opened her eyes. She blinked, smiled and put up her arms to him.

"Don't pick her up, darling," Allin counseled. "She'll only want it every time."

So he did not take her. Instead, he put her arms down, one and then the other, playfully, under the cover.

"Go to sleep-bye, honey," he said. And she lay, sleepily smiling. She was a good little thing.

"Come—let's put out the light," Allin whispered. They tiptoed out and went back to the living room.

Kent sat down, puffed on his pipe, his mind full of what he wanted to say to Allin. It was essential to their life to believe that nothing could happen to their children.

"Kidnaping's like lightning," he began abruptly. "It happens, of course—once in a million. What you have to remember is all the rest of the children who are perfectly safe."

She had sat down on the ottoman before the fire, but she turned to him when he said this. "What would you do, honestly, Kent, if some night when we went upstairs—"

"Nonsense!" he broke in. "That's what I've been trying to tell you. It's so unlikely as to be—it's these damned newspapers! When a thing happens in one part of the country, every little hamlet hears of it."

"Jane Eliot told me there are three times as many kidnapings as ever get into the newspapers," Allin said.

"Jane's a newspaperwoman," Kent said. "You mustn't let her sense of drama—"

"Still, she's been on a lot of kidnaping cases," Allin replied. "She was telling me about the Wyeth case—"

This was the time to speak, now when all Allin's secret anxiety was quivering in her voice. Kent took her hand and fondled it as he spoke. He must remember how deeply she felt everything, and this thing had haunted her before Bruce was born. He had not even thought of it until one night in the darkness she had asked him the same question, "What would we do, Kent, if " Only then he had not known what she meant.

"If what?" he had asked.

"If our baby were ever kidnaped."

He had answered what he had felt then and believed now to be true. "Why worry about what will never happen?" he had said. Nevertheless, he had followed all the cases since Bruce was born.

He kissed her palm now. "I can't bear having you afraid," he said. "It isn't necessary, you know, darling. We can't live under the shadow of this thing," he went on. "We have to come to some rational position on it."

"That's what I want, Kent. I'd be glad not to be afraid—if I knew how."

"After all," he went on again, "most people bring up their families without thinking about it."

"Most mothers think of it," she said. "Most of the women I know have said something about it to me—some time or other—enough to make me know they think about it all the time."

"You'd be better off not talking about it," he said.

But she said, "We keep wondering what we would do, Kent."

"That's just it!" he exclaimed. "That's why I think if we decided now what we would do—always bearing in mind that it's only the remotest possibility—"

"What *would* we do, Kent?" she asked.

He answered half playfully, "Promise to remember it's as remote as—an airplane attack on our home?"

She nodded.

"I've always thought that if one of the children were kidnaped I'd simply turn the whole thing over to the police at once."

"What police?" she asked instantly. "Gossipy old Mike O'Brien, who'd tell the newspapers the first thing? It's fatal to let it get into the papers, Jane says."

"Well, the Federal police, then—the G-men."

"How does one get in touch with them?"

He had to confess he did not know. "I'll find out," he promised. "Anyway, it's the principle, darling, that we want to determine. Once we know what we'll do, we can put it out of our minds. No ransom, Allin—that I feel sure about. As long as we keep on paying ransoms, we're going to have kidnapings. Somebody has to be strong enough to take the stand. Then maybe other people will see what they ought to do."

But she did not look convinced. When she spoke, her voice was low and full of dread. "The thing is, Kent, if we decided not to pay ransom, we just couldn't stick to it—not really, I mean. Suppose it were Bruce—suppose he had a cold and it was winter—and he was taken out of his warm bed in his pajamas, we'd do anything. You know we would!" She rushed on. "We wouldn't care about other children, Kent. We would only be thinking of our own little Bruce—and no one else. How to get him back again, at whatever cost."

"Hush, darling," he said. "If you're going to be like this we can't talk about it, after all."

"No, Kent, please. I do want to talk. I want to know what we ought to do. If only I could be not afraid!" she whispered.

"Come here by me," he said. He drew her to the couch beside him. "First of all, you know I love the children as well as you do, don't you?" She nodded, and he went on, "Then, darling, I'd do anything I thought would be best for our children, wouldn't I?"

"You'd do the best you knew, Kent. The question is, do any of us know what to do?"

"I do know," he said gravely, "that until we make the giving and taking of ransoms unlawful we shall have kidnapers. And until somebody begins it, it will never be done. That's the law of democratic government. The people have to begin action before government takes a stand."

"What if they said not to tell the police?" she asked.

Her concreteness confounded him. It was not as if the thing could happen!

"It all depends," he retorted, "on whether you want to give in to rascals or stand on your principle."

"But if it were our own child?" she persisted. "Be honest, Kent. Please don't retire into principles."

"I am trying to be honest," he said slowly. "I think I would stick by principle and trust somehow to think of some way—" He looked waveringly into her unbelieving eyes.

"Try to remember exactly what happened!" he was shouting at the silly nurse. "Where did you leave her?"

Allin was quieter than he, but Allin's voice on the telephone half an hour ago had been like a scream: "Kent, we can't find Betsy!"

He had been in the mill directors' meeting, but he'd risen instantly. "Sorry," he'd said sharply. "I have to leave at once."

"Nothing serious, Kent?" His father's white eyebrows had lifted.

"I think not," he'd answered. He had sense enough not to say what Allin had screamed. "I'll let you know if it is."

He had leaped into his car and driven home like a crazy man. He'd drawn up in a spray of gravel at his own gate. Allin was there, and Mollie, the silly nurse. Mollie was sobbing.

"We was at the gate, sir, watchin' for Brucie to come home from school, like we do every day, and I put 'er down—she's heavy to carry—while I went in to get a clean hankie to wipe her little hands. She'd stepped into a puddle from the rain this morning. When I came back, she wasn't there. I ran around the shrubs, sir, lookin'—and then I screamed for the madam."

"Kent, I've combed the place," Allin whispered.

"The gate!" he gasped.

"It was shut, and the bar across," Mollie wailed. "I'd sense enough to see to that before I went in."

"How long were you gone?" he shouted at her.

"I don't know, sir," Mollie sobbed. "It didn't seem a minute!"

He rushed into the yard. "Betsy, Betsy!" he cried. "Come to Daddy! Here's Daddy!" He stooped under the big lilac bushes. "Have you looked in the garage?" he demanded of Allin.

"Peter's been through it twice," she answered.

"I'll see for myself," he said. "Go into the house, Allin. She may have got inside, somehow."

He tore into the garage. Peter crawled out from under the small car.

"She ain't hyah, suh," he whispered. "Ah done looked ev'ywheah."

But Kent looked again, Peter following him like a dog. In the back of his mind was a telephone number, National 7117. He had found out about that number the year before, after he and Allin had talked that evening. Only he wouldn't call yet. Betsy was sure to be somewhere.

The gate clicked, and he rushed out. But it was only Bruce.

"Why, what's the matter with you, Daddy?" Bruce asked.

Kent swallowed—no use scaring Bruce. "Bruce, did you—you didn't see Betsy on the way home, did you?"

"No, Daddy. I didn't see anybody except Mike to help me across the square 'cause there was a notomobile."

"Wha' dat?" Peter was pointing at something. It was a bit of white paper, held down by a stone.

As well as he knew anything, Kent knew what it was. He had read that note a dozen times in the newspaper accounts. He stooped and picked it up. There it was—the scrawled handwriting.

"We been waiting this chanse." The handwriting was there,

illiterate, disguised. "Fifty grand is the price. Your dads got it if you aint. Youll hear where to put it. If you tell the police we kill the kid."

"Daddy, what's—" Bruce began.

"Bring him indoors," he ordered Peter.

Where was Allin? He had to—he had promised her it would not happen! The telephone number was—but—

"Allin!" he shouted.

He heard her running down from the attic.

"Allin!" he gasped. She was there, white and piteous with terror—and so helpless. God, they were both so helpless! He had to have help; he had to know what to do. But had not he—he had decided long ago what he must do, because what did he know about crooks and kidnapers? People gave the ransom and lost their children, too. He had to have advice he could trust.

"I'm going to call National 7117!" he blurted at her.

"No, Kent—wait!" she cried.

"I've got to," he insisted. Before she could move, he ran to the telephone and took up the receiver. "I want National 7117!" he shouted.

Her face went white. He held out his hand with the crumpled note. She read it and snatched at the receiver.

"No, Kent—wait. We don't know. Wait and see what they say!"

But a calm voice was already speaking at the other end of the wire: "This is National 7117." And Kent was shouting hoarsely, "I want to report a kidnaping. It's our baby girl. Kent Crothers, 134 Eastwood Avenue, Greenvale, New York."

He listened while the voice was telling him to do nothing, to wait until tomorrow, and then at a certain village inn, fifty miles away, to meet a certain man who would wear a plain gray suit.

And all the time Allin was whispering, "They'll kill her—they'll kill her, Kent."

"They won't know," he whispered back. "Nobody will know." When he put the receiver down he cried at her angrily, "They won't tell anybody—those fellows in Washington! Besides, I've got to have help, I tell you!"

She stood staring at him with horrified eyes. "They'll kill her," she repeated.

He wanted to get somewhere to weep, only men could not weep. But Allin was not weeping, either. Then suddenly they flung their arms about each other, and together broke into silent terrible tears.

He was not used to waiting, but he had to wait. And he had to help Allin wait. Men were supposed to be stronger.

At first it had been a comfort to have the directions to follow. First, everybody in the house—that was easy: simply the cook Sarah, the maid Rose, and Mollie and Peter. They of course were beyond blame, except Mollie. Perhaps Mollie was more than just a fool. They all had to be told they were to say absolutely nothing.

"Get everybody together in the dining room," Kent had told Allin. He had gone into the dining room.

"Daddy!" He saw Bruce's terrified figure in the doorway. "What's the matter? Where's Betsy?"

"We can't find her, son," Kent said, trying to make his voice calm. "Of course we will, but just now nobody must know she isn't here."

"Shall I go out in the yard?" Bruce asked. "Maybe I could find her."

"No," Kent said sharply. "I'd rather you went upstairs to your own room. I'll be up—in a minute."

The servants were coming in, Allin behind them.

"I'll go with Bruce," she said.

She was so still and so controlled, but he could tell by the quiver about her lips that she was only waiting for him.

"I'll be up in a very few minutes," he promised her. He stood until she had gone, Bruce's hand in hers. Then he turned to the four waiting figures. Mollie was still crying. He could tell by their faces that they all knew about the note.

"I see you know what has happened," he said. Strange how all these familiar faces looked sinister to him! Peter and Sarah had been in his mother's household. They had known him for years. And Rose was Sarah's niece. But they all looked hostile, or he imagined they did. "And I want not one word said of this to anyone in the town," he said harshly. "Remember, Betsy's life depends on no one outside knowing."

He paused, setting his jaws. He would not have believed he could cry as easily as a woman, but he could.

He cleared his throat. "Her life depends on how we behave now—in the next few hours." Mollie's sobbing burst out into wails. He rose. "That's all," he said. "We must simply wait."

The telephone rang, and he hurried to it. There was no way of knowing how the next message would come. But it was his father's peremptory voice: "Anything wrong over there, Kent?"

He knew now it would never do for his father to know what had happened. His father could keep nothing to himself.

"Everything is all right, Dad," he answered. "Allin's not feeling very well, that's all."

"Have you had the doctor?" his father shouted.

"We will if it is necessary, Dad," he answered and put up the receiver abruptly. He could not go on with that.

He thought of Bruce and went to find him. He was eating his supper in the nursery, and Allin was with him. She had told Mollie to stay downstairs. She could not bear to see the girl any more than he could.

But the nursery was unbearable, too. This was the time when Betsy, fresh from her bath . . .

"I'm—I'll be downstairs in the library," he told Allin hurriedly, and she nodded.

In the library the silence was torture. There was nothing to do but wait.

And all the time who knew what was happening to the child? Tomorrow, the man had said an hour ago. Wait, he had said. But what about tonight? In what sort of place would the child be sleeping?

Kent leaped to his feet. Something had to be done. He would have a look around the yard. There might be another letter.

He went out into the early autumn twilight. He had to hold himself together to keep from breaking into foolish shouts and curses. It was the agony of not being able to do anything. Then he controlled himself. The thing was to go on following a rational plan. He had come out to see if he could find anything.

He searched every inch of the yard. There was no message of any sort.

Then in the gathering darkness he saw a man at the gate. "Mist' Crothers!" It was Peter's voice. "Fo' God, Mist' Crothers, Ah don' know why they should pick on mah ole 'ooman. When Ah come home fo' suppah, she give it to me—she cain't read, so she don' know what wuz in it. Ah run all de way."

Kent snatched a paper from Peter's shaking hand and ran to the house. In the lighted hall he read:

> Get the dough ready all banknotes dont mark any or well get the other kid too. Dont try double-crossing us. You cant get away with nothing. Put it in a box by the dead oak at the mill creek. You know where. At twelve o'clock tomorrow night.

He knew where, indeed. He had fished there from the time he was a little boy. The lightning had struck that oak tree one summer when he had been only a hundred yards away, standing in the doorway of the mill during a thunderstorm. How did they know he knew?

He turned on Peter. "Who brought this?" he demanded.

"Ah don' know, suh," Peter stammered. "She couldn't tell me nothin' 'cep'n'it wuz a white man. He chuck it at 'er and say, 'Give it to yo' ole man.' So she give it to me, and Ah come a-runnin'."

Kent stared at Peter, trying to ferret into that dark brain. Was Peter being used by someone; bribed, perhaps, to take a part? Did he know anything?

"If I thought you knew anything about Betsy, I'd kill you myself," he said.

"Fo' God, Ah don', Mist' Crothers—you know me, suh! Ah done gyardened for yo' since yo' and Miss Allin got mah'ied. 'Sides, whut Ah want in such devilment? Ah got all Ah want—mah house and a sal'ry. Ah don' want nuthin'."

It was all true, of course. The thing was, you suspected everybody.

"You tell Flossie to tell no one," he commanded Peter.

"Ah done tole 'er," Peter replied fervently. "Ah tole 'er Ah'd split 'er open if she tole anybody 'bout dat white man."

"Get along, then," said Kent. "And remember what I told you."

"Yassuh," Peter replied.

"Of course we'll pay the ransom!" Allin was insisting.

They were in their own room, the door open into the narrow passage, and beyond that the door into the nursery was open, too. They sat where, in the shadowy light of a night lamp, they could see Bruce's dark head on the pillow. Impossible, of course, to sleep. Sarah had sent up some cold chicken and they had eaten it here, and later Kent had made Allin take a hot bath and get into a warm robe and lie down on the chaise longue. He did not undress. Someone might call.

"I'll have to see what the man says tomorrow," he answered.

Terrifying to think how he was pinning everything on that fellow tomorrow—a man whose name, even, he did not know. All he knew was he'd wear a plain gray suit and he'd have a blue handkerchief in his pocket. That was all he had to save Betsy's life. No, that wasn't true. Behind that one man were hundreds of others, alert, strong, and ready to help him.

"We've got to pay it," Allin was saying hysterically. "What's money now?"

"Allin!" he cried. "You don't think I'm trying to save the money, in God's name!"

"We have about twenty thousand, haven't we, in the bank?" she said hurriedly. "Your father would have the rest, though, and we could give him the securities. It isn't as if we didn't have it."

"Allin, you're being absurd! The thing is to know how to—"

But she flew at him fiercely. "The thing is to save Betsy—that's all; there's nothing else—absolutely nothing. I don't care if it takes everything your father has."

"Allin, be quiet!" he shouted at her. "Do you mean my father would begrudge anything—?"

"You're afraid of him, Kent," she retorted. "Well, I'm not! If you don't go to him, I will."

They were quarreling now, like two insane people. They were both stretched beyond normal reason.

Suddenly Allin was sobbing. "I can't forget what you said that night," she cried. "All that standing on principle! Oh, Kent, she's with strangers, horrible people, crying her little heart out; perhaps they're even—hurting her, trying to make her keep quiet. Oh, Kent, Kent!"

He took her in his arms. They must not draw apart now. He must think of her.

"I'll do anything, darling," he said. "The first thing in the morning I'll get hold of Dad and have the money ready."

"If they could only *know* it," she said.

"I could put something in the paper, perhaps," he said. "I believe I could word something that no one else would understand."

"Let's try, Kent!"

He took a pencil and envelope from his pocket and wrote. "How's this?" he asked. "Fifty agreed by dead oak at twelve."

"I can't see how it could do any harm," she said eagerly. "And if they see it, they'll understand we're willing to do anything."

"I'll go around to the newspaper office and pay for this in cash," he said. "Then I won't have to give names."

"Yes, yes!" she urged him. "It's something more than just sitting here!"

He drove through the darkness the two miles to the small town and parked in front of the ramshackle newspaper office. A red-eyed night clerk took his advertisement and read it off.

"This is a funny one," he said. "We get some, now and then. That'll be a dollar, Mr.—"

Kent did not answer. He put a dollar bill on the desk.

"I don't know what I've done, even so," he groaned to himself.

He drove back quietly through the intense darkness. The storm had not yet come, and the air was strangely silent. He kept his motor at its most noiseless, expecting somehow to hear through the sleeping stillness Betsy's voice, crying.

They scarcely slept, and yet when they looked at each other the next morning the miracle was that they had slept at all. But he had made Allin go to bed at last, and then, still dressed, he had lain down on his own bed near her. It was Bruce who waked them. He stood hesitatingly between their beds. They heard his voice.

"Betsy hasn't come back yet, Mommie."

The name waked them. And they looked at each other.

"How could we!" Allin whispered.

"It may be a long pull, dearest," he said, trying to be steady. He got up, feeling exhausted.

"Will she come back today?" Bruce asked.

"I think so, son."

At least it was Saturday, and Bruce need not go to school today.

"I'm going to get her tonight," Kent said after a moment.

Instantly he felt better. They must not give up hope—not by a great deal. There was too much to do: his father to see and the money to get. Secretly, he still reserved his own judgment about the ransom. If the man in gray was against it, he would tell Allin nothing—he simply would not give it. The responsibility would be his.

"You and Mommie will have to get Betsy's things ready for her tonight," he said cheerfully. He would take a bath and get into a fresh suit. He had to have all his wits about him today, every moment—listen to everybody, and use his own judgment finally. In an emergency, one person had to act.

He paused at the sight of himself in the mirror. Would he be able to keep it from Allin if he made a mistake? Suppose they never got Betsy back. Suppose she just—disappeared. Or suppose they found her little body somewhere.

This was the way all those other parents had felt—this sickness and faintness. If he did not pay the ransom and *that* happened, would he be able *not* to tell Allin—or to tell her it was his fault? Both were impossible.

"I'll just have to go on from one thing to the next," he decided.

The chief thing was to try to be hopeful. He dressed and went back into the bedroom. Bruce had come in to dress in their room. But Allin was still in bed, lying against the pillows, white and exhausted.

He bent over her and kissed her. "I'll send your breakfast up," he said. "I'm going to see Father first. If any message comes through, I'll be there—then at the bank."

She nodded, glanced up at him and closed her eyes. He stood looking down into her tortured face. Every nerve in it was quivering under the set stillness.

"Can't break yet," he said sharply. "The crisis is ahead."

"I know," she whispered. Then she sat up. "I can't lie here!" she exclaimed. "It's like lying on a bed of swords, being tortured. I'll be down, Kent—Bruce and I."

She flew into the bathroom. He heard the shower turned on instantly and strongly. But he could wait for no one.

"Come down with Mother, son," he said. And he went on alone.

"If you could let me have thirty thousand today," he said to his father, "I can give it back as soon as I sell some stock."

"I don't care when I get it back," his father said irritably. "Good God, Kent, it's not that. It's just that I—it's none of my business, of course, but thirty thousand in cold cash! I'd like to ask what on earth you've been doing, but I won't."

Kent had made up his mind at the breakfast table when he picked up the paper that if he could keep the thing out of the papers, he would keep it from his father and mother. He'd turned to the personals. There it was, his answer to those scoundrels. Well, he wouldn't stick to it unless it were best for Betsy. Meanwhile, silence!

To Rose, bringing in the toast, he'd said sharply, "Tell everybody to come in now before your mistress comes down."

They had filed in, subdued and drooping, looking at him with frightened eyes.

"Oh, sir!" Mollie had cried hysterically.

"Please!" he'd exclaimed, glancing at her. Maybe the man in gray ought to see her. But last night he had distrusted Peter. This morning Peter looked like a faithful old dog, and as incapable of evil.

"I only want to thank you for obeying me so far," he'd said wearily. "If we can keep our trouble out of the papers, perhaps we can get Betsy back. At least, it's the only hope. If you succeed in letting no one know until we know—the end, I shall give each of you a hundred dollars as a token of my gratitude."

"Thank you, sir," Sarah and Rose had said. Mollie only

sobbed. Peter was murmuring, "Ah don' wan' no hundred dollahs, Mist' Crothers. All Ah wan' is dat little chile back."

How could Peter be distrusted? Kent had wrung his hand. "That's all I want, too, Peter," he'd said fervently.

Strange how shaky and emotional he had felt!

Now, under his father's penetrating eyes, he held himself calm. "I know it sounds outrageous, Father," he admitted, "but I simply ask you to trust me for a few days."

"You're not speculating, I hope. It's no time for that. The market's crazy."

It was, Kent thought grimly, the wildest kind of speculation—with his own child's life.

"It's not ordinary speculation, certainly," he said. "I can manage through the bank, Dad," he said. "Never mind. I'll mortgage the house."

"Oh, nonsense!" his father retorted. He had his checkbook out and was writing. "I'm not going to have it get around that my son had to go mortgaging his place."

"Thanks," Kent said briefly.

Now for the bank!

Step by step the day went. It was amazing how quickly the hours passed. It was noon before he knew it, and in an hour he must start for the inn. He went home and found Allin on the front porch in the sunshine. She had a book in her hand, and Bruce was playing with his red truck out in the yard. Anyone passing would never dream there was tragedy here.

"Do you have it?" she asked him.

He touched his breast pocket. "All ready," he answered.

They sat through a silent meal, listening to Bruce's chatter. Allin ate nothing and he very little, but he was grateful to her for being there, for keeping the outward shape of the day usual.

"Good sport!" he said to her across the table in the midst of Bruce's conversation. She smiled faintly. "Thank you, no more coffee," he said to Rose. "I must be going, Allin."

"Yes," she said, and added, "I wish it were I—instead of waiting."

"I know," he replied, and kissed her.

Yesterday, waiting had seemed intolerable to him, too. But now that he was going toward the hour for which he had been waiting, he clung to the hopefulness of uncertainty.

He drove alone to the inn. The well-paved roads, the tended fields and comfortable farmhouses were not different from the landscape any day. He would have said, only yesterday, that it was impossible that underneath all this peace and plenty there could be men so evil as to take a child out of its home, away from its parents, for money.

There was, he pondered, driving steadily west, no other possible reason. He had no enemies; none, that is, whom he knew. There were always discontented people, of course, who hated anyone who seemed successful. There was, of course, too, the chance that his father had enemies he was ruthless with idle workers.

"I can't blame a man if he is born a fool," Kent had heard his father maintain stoutly, "but I can blame even a fool for being lazy." It might be one of these. If only it were not some perverted mind!

He drove into the yard of the inn and parked his car. His heart was thudding in his breast, but he said casually to the woman at the door, "Have you a bar?"

"To the right," she answered quickly. It was Saturday afternoon, and business was good. She did not even look at him as he sauntered away.

The moment he entered the door of the bar he saw the man. He stood at the end of the bar, small, inconspicuous, in a gray suit and a blue-striped shirt. He wore a solid blue tie, and in his pocket was the blue handkerchief. Kent walked slowly to his side.

"Whisky and soda, please," he ordered the bartender. The room was full of people at tables, drinking and talking noisily. He turned to the man in gray and smiled. "Rather unusual to find a bar like this in a village inn," he said.

"Yes, it is," the little man agreed. He had a kind, brisk voice, and he was drinking a tall glass of something clear, which he finished. "Give me another of the same," he remarked to the bartender. "London Washerwoman's Treat, it's called," he explained to Kent.

It was hard to imagine that this small hatchet-faced man had any importance.

"Going my way?" Kent asked suddenly.

"If you'll give me a lift," the little man replied.

Kent's heart subsided. The man knew him, then. He nodded. They paid for their drinks and went out to the car.

"Drive due north into a country road," the little man said with sudden sharpness. All his dreaminess was gone. He sat beside Kent, his arms folded. "Please tell me exactly what's happened, Mr. Crothers."

And Kent, driving along, told him.

He was grateful for the man's coldness; for the distrust of everything and everybody. He was like a lean hound in a life-and-death chase. Because of his coldness, Kent could talk without fear of breaking.

"I don't know your name," Kent said.

"Don't matter," said the man. "I'm detailed for the job."

"As I was saying," Kent went on, "we have no enemies—at least, none I know."

"Fellow always has enemies," the little man murmured.

"It hardly seems likely a gangster would—" Kent began again.

"No, gangsters don't kidnap children," the little man told him. "Adults, yes. But they don't monkey with kids. It's too dangerous, for one thing. Kidnaping children's the most dangerous job there is in crime, and the smart ones know it. It's always some little fellow does it—him and a couple of friends, maybe."

"Why dangerous?" Kent demanded.

"Always get caught," the little man said, shrugging. "Always!"

There was something so reassuring about this strange sharp creature that Kent said abruptly, "My wife wants to pay the ransom. I suppose you think that's wrong, don't you?"

"Perfectly *right*," the man said. "Absolutely! We aren't magicians, Mr. Crothers. We got to get in touch somehow. The only two cases I ever knew where nothing was solved was where the parents wouldn't pay. So we couldn't get a clue."

Kent set his lips. "Children killed?"

"Who knows?" the little man said, shrugging again. "Anyway, one of them was. And the other never came back."

There might be comfort, then, in death, Kent thought. He had infinitely rather hold Betsy's dead body in his arms than never know . . .

"Tell me what to do, and I'll do it," he said.

The little man lighted a cigarette. "Go on just as though you'd never told us. Go on and pay your ransom. Make a note of the numbers of the notes, of course—no matter what that letter says. How's he going to know? But pay it over—and do what he says next. You can call me up here." He took a paper out of his coat pocket and put it in Kent's pocket. "I maybe ought to tell you, though, we'll tap your telephone wire."

"Do anything you like," Kent said.

"That's all I need!" the man exclaimed. "That's our orders—to do what the parents want. You're a sensible one. Fellow I knew once walked around with a shotgun to keep off the police. Said he'd handle things himself."

"Did he get his child back?"

"Nope—paid the ransom, too. Paying the ransom's all right—that's the way we get 'em. But he went roarin' around the neighborhood trying to be his own law. We didn't get a chance."

Kent thought of one more thing. "I don't want anything spared—money or trouble. I'll pay anything, of course."

"Oh, sure," the man said. "Well, I guess that'll be all. You might let me off near the inn. I'll go in and get another drink."

He lapsed into dreaminess again, and in silence Kent drove back to the village.

"All right," the little man said. "So long. Good luck to you." He leaped out and disappeared into the bar.

And Kent, driving home through the early sunset, thought how little there was to tell Allin—really nothing at all, except that he liked and trusted the man in gray. No, it was much more than that: the fellow stood for something far greater than himself—he stood for all the power of the government organized against crimes like this. That was the comfort of the thing. Behind that man was the nation's police, all for him, Kent Crothers, helping him find his child.

When he reached home, Allin was in the hall waiting.

"He really said nothing, darling," Kent said, kissing her, "except you were right about the ransom. We have to pay that. Still, he was extraordinary. Somehow I feel—if she's still alive, we'll get her back. He's that sort of fellow." He did not let her break, though he felt her trembling against him. He said very practically, "We must check these banknotes, Allin."

And then, when they were checking them upstairs in their bedroom with doors locked, he kept insisting that what they were doing was right.

At a quarter to twelve he was bumping down the rutted road to the forks. He knew every turn the road made, having traveled it on foot from the time he was a little boy. But that boy out on holiday had nothing to do with himself as he was tonight, an anxious, harried man.

He drew up beneath the dead oak and took the cardboard box in which he and Allin had packed the money and stepped out of the car. There was not a sound in the dark night, yet he knew that somewhere not far away were the men who had his child.

He listened, suddenly swept again with the conviction he had had the night before, that she would cry out. She might even be this moment in the old mill. But there was not a sound. He stooped and put the box at the root of the tree.

And as he did this, he stumbled over a string raised from the ground above a foot. What was this? He followed it with his hands. It encircled the tree—a common piece of twine. Then it went under a stone, and under the stone was a piece of paper. He seized it, snapped on his cigarette lighter, read the clumsy printing.

> If everything turns out like we told you to do, go to your hired mans house at twelve tomorrow night for the kid. If you double-cross us you get it back dead.

He snapped off the light. He'd get her back dead! It all depended on what he did. And what he did, he would have to do alone. He would not go home to Allin until he had decided every step.

He drove steadily away. If he did not call the man in gray, Betsy might be at Peter's alive. If he called, and they did not find out, she might be alive anyway. But if the man fumbled and they did find out, she would be dead.

He knew what Allin would say: "Just so we get her home, Kent, nothing else! People have to think for themselves, first." Yes, she was right. He would keep quiet; anyway, he would give the kidnapers a chance. If she were safe and alive, that would be justification for anything. If she were dead . . .

Then he remembered that there was something courageous and reassuring about that little man. Only he had seemed to know what to do. And anyway, what about those parents who had tried to manage it all themselves? Their children had never come back, either. No, he had better do what he knew he ought to do.

He tramped into the house. Allin was lying upstairs on her bed, her eyes closed.

"Darling," he said gently. Instantly she opened her eyes and sat up. He handed her the paper and sat down on her bed. She lifted miserable eyes to him.

"Twenty-four more hours!" she whispered. "I can't do it, Kent."

"Yes, you can," he said harshly. "You'll do it because you damned well have to." He thought, She can't break now, if I have to whip her! "We've got to wait," he went on. "Is there anything else we can do? Tell Mike O'Brien? Let the newspapers get it and ruin everything?"

She shook her head. "No," she said.

He got up. He longed to take her in his arms, but he did not dare. If this was ever over, he would tell her what he thought of her—how wonderful she was; how brave and game—but he could not now. It was better for them both to stay away from that edge of breaking.

"Get up," he said. "Let's have something to eat. I haven't really eaten all day."

It would be good for her to get up and busy herself. She had not eaten either.

"All right, Kent," she said. "I'll wash my face in cold water and be down."

"I'll be waiting," he replied.

This gave him the moment he had made up his mind he would use—damned if he wouldn't use it! The scoundrels had his money now, and he would take the chance on that queer fellow. He called the number the man had put into his pocket. And almost instantly he heard the fellow's drawl.

"Hello?" the man said.

"This is Kent Crothers," he answered. "I've had that invitation!"

"Yes?" The voice was suddenly alert.

"Twelve tomorrow!"

"Yes? Where? Midnight, of course. They always make it midnight."

"My gardener's house."

"Okay, Mr. Crothers. Go right ahead as if you hadn't told us." The phone clicked.

Kent listened, but there was nothing more. Everything seemed exactly the same, but nothing was the same. This very telephone wire was cut somewhere, by someone. Someone was listening to every word anyone spoke to and from his house. It was sinister and yet reassuring—sinister if you were the criminal.

He heard Allin's step on the stair and went out to meet her. "I have a hunch," he told her, smiling.

"What?" She tried to smile back.

He drew her toward the dining room. "We're going to win," he said.

Within himself he added, If she were still alive, that little heart of his life. Then he put the memory of Betsy's face away from him resolutely.

"I'm going to eat," he declared. "And so must you. We'll beat them tomorrow."

But tomorrow very nearly beat them. Time stood still—there was no making it pass. They filled it full of a score of odd jobs about the house. Lucky for them it was Sunday; luckier that Kent's mother had a cold and telephoned that she and Kent's father would not be over for their usual visit.

They stayed together, a little band of three. By midafternoon Kent had cleaned up everything—a year's odd jobs—and there were hours to go.

They played games with Bruce, and at last it was his suppertime and they put him to bed. Then they sat upstairs in their bedroom again, near the nursery, each with a book.

Sometime, after these hours were over, he would have to think about a lot of things again. But everything had to wait now, until this life ended at midnight. Beyond that no thought could reach.

At eleven he rose. "I'm going now," he said, and stooped to kiss her. She clung to him, and then in an instant they drew apart. In strong accord they knew it was not yet time to give way.

He ran the car as noiselessly as he could and left it at the end of the street, six blocks away. Then he walked past the few tumble-down bungalows, past two empty lots, to Peter's rickety gate. There was no light in the house. He went to the door and knocked softly. He heard Peter's mumble: "Who dat?"

"Let me in, Peter," he called in a low voice. The door opened. "It's I, Peter—Kent Crothers. Let me in. Peter, they're bringing the baby here."

"To mah house? Lemme git de light on."

"No, Peter, no light. I'll just sit down here in the darkness, like this. Only don't lock the door, see? I'll sit by the door. Where's a chair? That's it." He was trembling so that he stumbled into the chair Peter pushed forward.

"Mist' Crothers, suh, will yo' have a drink? Ah got some corn likker."

"Thanks, Peter."

He heard Peter's footsteps shuffling away, and in a moment a tin cup was thrust into his hand. He drank the reeking stuff down. It burned him like indrawn flame, but he felt steadier for it.

"Ain't a thing Ah can do, Mist' Crothers?" Peter's whisper came ghostly out of the darkness.

"Not a thing. Just wait."

"Ah'll wait here, then. Mah ole 'ooman's asleep. Ah'll jest git thrashin' round if Ah go back to bed."

"Yes, only we mustn't talk," Kent whispered back.

"Nosuh."

This was the supremest agony of waiting in all the long agony that this day had been. To sit perfectly still, straining to hear, knowing nothing, wondering . . .

Suppose something went wrong with the man in gray, and they fumbled, and frightened the man who brought Betsy back. Suppose he just sat here waiting and waiting until dawn came. And at home Allin was waiting.

The long day had been nothing to this. He sat reviewing all his life, pondering on the horror of this monstrous situation in which he and Allin now were. A free country, was it? No one was free when his lips were locked against crime, because he dared not speak lest his child be murdered. If Betsy were dead, if they didn't bring her back, he'd never tell Allin he had telephoned the man in gray. He was still glad he had done it. After all, were respectable men and women to be at the mercy of—but if Betsy were dead, he'd wish he had killed himself before he had anything to do with the fellow!

He sat, his hands interlocked so tightly he felt them grow cold and bloodless and stinging, but he could not move. Someone came down the street roaring out a song.

"Thass a drunk man," Peter whispered.

Kent did not answer. The street grew still again.

And then in the darkness—hours after midnight, it seemed to him—he heard a car come up to the gate and stop. The gate creaked open and then shut, and the car drove away.

"Guide me down the steps," he told Peter.

It was the blackest night he had ever seen. But the stars were shining when he stepped out. Peter pulled him along the path. Then, by the gate, Peter stooped.

"She's here," he said.

And Kent, wavering and dizzy, felt her in his arms again, limp and heavy. "She's warm," he muttered. "That's something."

He carried her into the house, and Peter lighted a candle and held it up. It was she—his little Betsy, her white dress filthy and a man's sweater drawn over her. She was breathing heavily.

"Look lak she done got a dose of sumpin," Peter muttered.

"I must get her home," Kent whispered frantically. "Help me to the car, Peter."

"Yassuh," Peter said, and blew out the candle.

They walked silently down the street, Peter's hand on Kent's arm. When he got Betsy home, he—he—

"Want I should drive you?" Peter was asking him.

"I—maybe you'd better," he replied.

He climbed into the seat with her. She was so fearfully limp. Thank God he could hear her breathing! In a few minutes he would put Betsy into her mother's arms.

"Don't stay, Peter," he said.

"Nosuh," Peter answered.

Allin was at the door, waiting. She opened it and without a word reached for the child. He closed the door behind them.

Then he felt himself grow sick. "I was going to tell you," he gasped, "I didn't know whether to tell you—" He swayed and felt himself fall upon the floor.

Allin was a miracle; Allin was wonderful, a rock of a woman. This tender thing who had endured the torture of these days was at his bedside when he woke next day, smiling, and only a little pale.

"The doctor says you're not to go to work, darling," she told him.

"The doctor?" he repeated.

"I had him last night for both of you—you and Betsy. He won't tell anyone."

"I've been crazy," he said, dazed. "Where is she? How—"

"She's going to be all right," Allin said.

"No, but—you're not telling me!"

"Come in here and see," she replied.

He got up, staggering a little. Funny how his legs had collapsed under him last night! His withers still felt all unstrung.

They went into the nursery. There in her bed she lay, his beloved child. She was more naturally asleep now, and her face bore no other mark than pallor.

"She won't even remember it," Allin said. "I'm glad it wasn't Bruce."

He did not answer. He couldn't think—nothing had to be thought about now.

"Come back to bed, Kent," Allin was saying. "I'm going to bring your breakfast up. Bruce is having his downstairs."

He climbed back into bed, shamefaced at his weakness. "I'll be all right after a little coffee. I'll get up then, maybe."

But his bed felt wonderfully good. He lay back, profoundly grateful to it—to everything. But as long as he lived he would wake up to sweat in the night with memory.

The telephone by his bed rang, and he picked it up. "Hello?" he called.

"Hello, Mr. Crothers," a voice answered. It was the voice of the man in gray. "Say, was the little girl hurt?"

"No!" Kent cried. "She's all right!"

"Fine. Well, I just wanted to tell you we caught the fellow last night."

"You *did!*" Kent leaped up. "No! Why, that's—that's extraordinary."

"We had a cordon around the place for blocks and got him. You'll get your money back, too."

"That—it doesn't seem to matter. Who was he?"

"Fellow named Harry Brown—a young chap in a drugstore."

"I never heard of him!"

"No, he says you don't know him—but his dad went to school with yours, and he's heard a lot of talk about you. His dad's a poor stick, I guess, and got jealous of yours. That's about it, probably. Fellow says he figured you sort of owed him something. Crazy, of course.

"Well, it was an easy case—he wasn't smart, and scared to death, besides. You were sensible about it. Most people ruin their chances with their own fuss. So long, Mr. Crothers. Mighty glad."

The telephone clicked. That was all. Everything was incredible, impossible. Kent gazed around the familiar room. Had this all happened? It had happened, and it was over. This was one of those cases of kidnaping that went on in this mad country, unheard of until they were all over and the criminals arrested.

When he went downstairs he would give the servants their hundred dollars apiece. Mollie had had nothing to do with it, after all. The mystery had dissolved like a mist at morning.

Allin was at the door with his tray. Behind her came Bruce, ready for school. She said, so casually Kent could hardly catch the tremor underneath her voice, "What would you say, darling, if we let Peter walk to school with Bruce today?"

Her eyes pleaded with him: "No? Oughtn't we to? What shall we do?"

Then he thought of something else that indomitable man in gray had said, that man whose name he would never know, one among all those other men trying to keep the law for the nation. "We're a lawless people," the little man had said that day in the car. "If we made a law against paying ransoms, nobody would obey it any more than they did Prohibition. No, when the Americans don't like a law, they break it. And so we still have kidnapers. It's the price you pay for a democracy."

Yes, it was the price. Everybody paid—he and Allin; the child they had so nearly lost; that boy locked up in prison.

"Bruce has to live in his own country," he said. "I guess you can go alone, can't you son?"

"Course I can," Bruce said sturdily.

THE BABY IN THE ICEBOX

James M. Cain

Born in Annapolis, MD, James M(allahan) Cain (1892-1977) grew up in Maryland and returned permanently (after seventeen years as a screenwriter in California) in 1947. He received his B.A. from Washington College at the age of 18, then taught mathematics and English for four years before receiving his M.A. He became a journalist, also submitting articles and stories to magazines while still in his twenties.

"The Baby in the Icebox" was filmed by Paramount in 1934 as *She Made Her Bed*, starring Richard Arlen, Sally Eilers, and Robert Armstrong. A bizarre review appeared in *Photoplay Magazine*, which called it "(a) gay merry-go-'round that makes for good entertainment."

Cain's first full-length novel, *The Postman Always Rings Twice* (1934) became a huge best-seller and was filmed by MGM (with a script by Raymond Chandler) in 1946 starring Lana Turner and John Garfield, and again in 1981 with Jessica Lange and Jack Nicholson. Cain did not write detective stories but is lumped with other hard-boiled writers for his tough, gritty crime novels of sex and violence, most of which follow a familiar plot of a man falling for a woman, engaging in a criminal plot for her, only to have her betray him. In addition to *Postman*, the formula also worked in *Double Indemnity* (1943), filmed by Billy Wilder in 1944 with Barbara Stanwyck, Fred MacMurray and Edward G. Robinson. The other classic film noir made from his work, *Mildred Pierce* (1941) was as bleak as his other books and films, but this time it is the titular character who is betrayed by a woman–her daughter.

"The Baby in the Icebox" was first published in the January 1933 issue of *American Mercury* and was first collected in book form in *The Baby in the Icebox* (New York, Holt, 1981).

The Baby in the Icebox

James M. Cain

Of course there was plenty pieces in the paper about what happened out at the place last Summer, but they got it all mixed up, so I will now put down how it really was, and specially the beginning of it, so you will see it is not no lies in it.

Because when a guy and his wife begin to play leapfrog with a tiger, like you might say, and the papers put in about that part and not none of the stuff that started it off, and then one day say X marks the spot and next day say it wasn't really no murder but don't tell you what it was, why I don't blame people if they figure there was something funny about it or maybe that somebody ought to be locked up in the booby-hatch. But there wasn't no booby-hatch to this, nothing but plain oneriness and a dirty rat getting it in the neck where he had it coming to him, as you will see when I get the first part explained right.

Things first began to go sour between Duke and Lura when

they put the cats in. They didn't need no cats. They had a combination auto camp, filling-station, and lunchroom out in the country a ways, and they got along all right. Duke run the filling-station, and got me in to help him, and Lura took care of the lunchroom and shacks. But Duke wasn't satisfied. Before he got this place he had raised rabbits, and one time he had bees, and another time canary birds, and nothing would suit him now but to put in some cats to draw trade. Maybe you think that's funny, but out here in California they got every kind of a farm there is, from kangaroos to alligators, and it was just about the idea that a guy like Duke would think up. So he begun building a cage, and one day he showed up with a truckload of wildcats.

I wasn't there when they unloaded them. It was two or three cars waiting and I had to gas them up. But soon as I got a chance I went back there to look things over. And believe me, they wasn't pretty. The guy that sold Duke the cats had went away about five minutes before, and Duke was standing outside the cage and he had a stick of wood in his hand with blood on it. Inside was a dead cat. The rest of them was on a shelf, that had been built for them to jump on, and every one of them was snarling at Duke.

I don't know if you ever saw a wildcat, but they are about twice as big as a house cat, brindle gray, with tufted ears and a bobbed tail. When they set and look at you they look like a owl, but they wasn't setting and looking now. They was marching around, coughing and spitting, their eyes shooting red and green fire, and it was an ugly sight, specially with that bloody dead one down on the ground. Duke was pale, and the breath was whistling through his nose, and it didn't take no doctor to see he was scared to death.

"You better bury that cat," he says to me. "I'll take care of the cars."

I looked through the wire and he grabbed me. "Look out!" he says. "They'd kill you in a minute."

"In that case," I says, "how do I get the cat out?"

"You have to get a stick," he says, and shoves off.

I was pretty sore, but I begun looking around for a stick. I found one, but when I got back to the cage Lura was there. "How did that happen?" she says.

"I don't know," I says, "but I can tell you this much: If there's any more of them to be buried around here, you can get somebody else to do it. My job is to fix flats, and I'm not going to be no cat undertaker."

She didn't have nothing to say to that. She just stood there while I was trying the stick, and I could hear her toe snapping up and down in the sand, and from that I knowed she was choking it back, what she really thought, and didn't think no more of this here cat idea than I did.

The stick was too short. "My," she says, pretty disagreeable, "that looks terrible. You can't bring people out here with a thing like that in there."

"All right," I snapped back. "Find me a stick."

She didn't make no move to find no stick. She put her hand on the gate. "Hold on," I says. "Them things are nothing to monkey with."

"Huh," she says. "All they look like to me is a bunch of cats."

There was a kennel back of the cage, with a drop door on it, where they was supposed to go at night. How you got them back there was bait them with food, but I didn't know that then. I yelled at them, to drive them back in there, but nothing happened. All they done was yell back. Lura listened to me a while, and then she give a kind of gasp like she couldn't stand it no longer, opened the gate, and went in.

Now believe me, that next was a bad five minutes, because she wasn't hard to look at, and I hated to think of her getting mauled up by them babies. But a guy would of had to of been blind if it didn't show him that she had a way with cats. First thing she done, when she got in, she stood still, didn't make no sudden motions or nothing, and begun to talk to them. Not no special talk. Just "Pretty pussy, what's the matter, what they been doing to you?"—like that. Then she went over to them.

They slid off, on their bellies, to another part of the shelf. But she kept after them, and got her hand on one, and stroked him on the back. Then she got a-hold of another one, and pretty soon she had give them all a pat. Then she turned around, picked up the dead cat by one leg, and come out with him. I put him on the wheelbarrow and buried him.

Now, why was it that Lura kept it from Duke how easy she had got the cat out and even about being in the cage at all? I think it was just because she didn't have the heart to show him up to hisself how silly he looked. Anyway, at supper that night, she never said a word. Duke, he was nervous and excited and told all about how the cats had jumped at him and how he had to bean one to save his life, and then he give a long spiel about cats and how fear is the only thing they understand, so you would of thought he was Martin Johnson just back from the jungle or something.

But it seemed to me the dishes was making quite a noise that night, clattering around on the table, and that was funny, because one thing you could say for Lura was: she was quiet and easy to be around. So when Duke, just like it was nothing at all, asks me by the way how did I get the cat out, I heared my mouth saying, "With a stick," and not nothing more. A little bird flies around and tells you, at a time like that. Lura let it pass. Never said a word. And if you ask me, Duke never did find out how easy she could handle the cats, and that ain't only guesswork, but on account of something that happened a little while afterward, when we got the mountain-lion.

A mountain-lion is a cougar, only out here they call them a mountain-lion. Well, one afternoon about five o'clock this one of ours squat down on her hunkers and set up the worst squalling you ever listen to. She kept it up all night, so you wanted to go out and shoot her, and next morning at breakfast Duke come running in and says come on out and look what happened. So we went out there, and there in the cage with her was the prettiest he mountain-lion you ever seen in your life. He was big, probably weighed a hundred and fifty pounds, and his coat was a pearl gray so glossy it looked like a pair of new gloves, and he had a spot of white on his throat. Sometimes they have white.

"He come down from the hills when he heard her call last night," says Duke, "and he got in there somehow. Ain't it funny? When they hear that note nothing can stop them."

"Yeah," I says. "It's love."

"That's it," says Duke. "Well, we'll be having some little ones soon. Cheaper'n buying them."

After he had went off to town to buy the stuff for the day, Lura sat down to the table with me. "Nice of you," I says, "to let Romeo in last night."

"Romeo?" she says.

"Yes, Romeo. That's going to be papa of twins soon, out in the lion cage."

"Oh," she says, "didn't he get in there himself?"

"He did not. If she couldn't get out, how could he get in?"

All she give me at that time was a dead pan. Didn't know nothing about it at all. Fact of the matter, she made me a little sore. But after she brung me my second cup of coffee she kind of smiled. "Well?" she says. "You wouldn't keep two loving hearts apart, would you?"

So things was, like you might say, a little gritty, but they got a whole lot worse when Duke come home with Rajah, the tiger. Because by that time, he had told so many lies that he begun to believe them hisself, and put on all the airs of a big animal-trainer. When people come out on Sundays, he would take a black-snake whip and go in with the mountain-lions and wildcats, and snap it at them, and they would snarl and yowl, and Duke acted like he was doing something. Before he went in, he would let the people see him strapping on a big six-shooter, and Lura got sorer by the week.

For one thing, he looked so silly. She couldn't see nothing to going in with the cats, and specially couldn't see no sense in going in with a whip, a six-shooter, and a ten-gallon hat like them cow people wears. And for another thing, it was bad for business. In the beginning, when Lura would take the customers' kids out and make out the cat had their finger, they loved it, and they loved it still more when the little mountain-lions come and they had spots and would push up their ears to be scratched. But when Duke started that stuff with the whip it scared them to death, and even the fathers and mothers was nervous, because there was the gun and they didn't know what would happen next. So business begun to fall off.

And then one afternoon he put down a couple of drinks and figured it was time for him to go in there with Rajah. Now it had took Lura one minute to tame Rajah. She was in there sweeping out his cage one morning when Duke was away, and when he started sliding around on his belly he got a bucket of water in the face, and that was that. From then on he was her cat. But what happened when Duke tried to tame him was awful. The first I knew what he was up to was when he made a speech to the people from the mountain-lion cage telling them not to go away yet, there was more to come. And when he come out he headed over to the tiger.

"What's the big idea?" I says. "What you up to now?"

"I'm going in with that tiger," he says. "It's got to be done, and I might as well do it now."

"Why has it got to be done?" I says.

He looked at me like as though he pitied me.

"I guess there's a few things about cats you don't know yet," he says. "You got a tiger on your hands, you got to let him know who's boss, that's all."

"Yeah?" I says. "And who *is* boss?"

"You see that?" he says, and cocks his finger at his face.

"See what?" I says.

"The human eye," he says. "The human eye, that's all. A cat's afraid of it. And if you know your business, you'll keep him afraid of it. That's all I'll use, the human eye. But of course, just for protection, I've got these too."

"Listen, sweetheart," I says to him. "If you give me a choice between the human eye and a Bengal tiger, which one *I* got the most fear of, you're going to see a guy getting a shiner every time. If I was you, I'd lay off that cat."

He didn't say nothing: hitched up his holster, and went in. He didn't even get a chance to unlimber his whip. That tiger, soon as he saw him, begun to move around in a way that made your blood run cold. He didn't make for Duke first, you understand. He slid over, and in a second he was between Duke and the gate. That's one thing about a tiger you better not forget if you ever meet one. He can't work examples in arithmetic, but when it comes to the kind of brains that mean meat, he's the brightest boy in the class and then some. He's born knowing more about cutting off a retreat than you'll ever know, and his legs do it for him, just automatic, so his jaws will be free for the main business of the meeting.

Duke backed away, and his face was awful to see. He was straining every muscle to keep his mouth from sliding down in his collar. His left hand fingered the whip a little, and his right pawed around, like he had some idea of drawing the gun. But the tiger didn't give him time to make up his mind what his idea was, if any.

He would slide a few feet on his belly, then get up and trot a step or two, then slide on his belly again. He didn't make no noise, you understand. He wasn't telling Duke, Please go away: he meant to kill him, and a killer don't generally make no more fuss than he has to. So for a few seconds you could even hear Duke's feet sliding over the floor. But all of a sudden a kid begun to whimper, and I come to my senses. I run around to the back of the cage, because that was where the tiger was crowding him, and I yelled at him.

"Duke!" I says. "In his kennel! Quick!"

He didn't seem to hear me. He was still backing, and the tiger was still coming. A woman screamed. The tiger's head went down, he crouched on the ground, and tightened every muscle. I knew what that meant. Everybody knew what it meant, and specially Duke knew what it meant. He made a funny sound in his throat, turned, and ran.

That was when the tiger sprung. Duke had no idea where he was going, but when he turned he fell through the trap door and

I snapped it down. The tiger hit it so hard I thought it would split. One of Duke's legs was out, and the tiger was on it in a flash, but all he got on that grab was the sole of Duke's shoe. Duke got his leg in somehow and I jammed the door down tight.

It was a sweet time at supper that night. Lura didn't see this here, because she was busy in the lunchroom when it happened, but them people had talked on their way out, and she knowed all about it. What she was plenty. And Duke, what do you think he done? He passed it off like it wasn't nothing at all. "Just one of them things you got to expect," he says. And then he let on he knowed what he was doing all the time, and the only lucky part of it was that he didn't have to shoot a valuable animal like Rajah was. "Keep cool, that's the main thing," he says. "A thing like that can happen now and then, but never let a animal see you excited."

I heard him, and I couldn't believe my ears, but when I looked at Lura I jumped. I think I told you she wasn't hard to look at. She was a kind of medium size, with a shape that would make a guy leave his happy home, sunburned all over, and high cheekbones that give her eyes a funny slant. But her eyes was narrowed down to slits, looking at Duke, and they shot green where the light hit them, and it come over me all of a sudden that she looked so much like Rajah, when he was closing in on Duke in the afternoon, that she could have been his twin sister.

Next off, Duke got it in his head he was such a big cat man now that he had to go up in the hills and do some trapping. Bring in his own stuff, he called it.

I didn't pay much attention to it at the time. Of course, he never brought in no stuff, except a couple of raccoons that he probably bought down the road for $2, but Duke was the kind of a guy that every once in a while has to sit on a rock and fish, so when he loaded up the flivver and blew, it wasn't nothing you would get excited about. Maybe I didn't really care what he was up to, because it was pretty nice, running the place with Lura with him out of the way, and I didn't ask no questions. But it was more to it than cats or 'coons or fish, and Lura knowed it, even if I didn't.

Anyhow, it was while he was away on one of them trips of his that Wild Bill Smith the Texas Tornado showed up. Bill was a snake-doctor. He had a truck, with his picture painted on it, and two or three boxes of old rattlesnakes with their teeth pulled out, and he sold snake-oil that would cure what ailed you, and a Indian herb medicine that would do the same. He was a fake, but he was big and brown and had white teeth, and I guess he really wasn't no bad guy. The first I seen of him was when he drove up in his truck, and told me to gas him up and look at his tires. He had a bum differential that made a funny rattle, but he said never mind and went over to the lunchroom.

He was there a long time, and I thought I better let him know his car was ready. When I went over there, he was setting on a stool with a sheepish look on his face, rubbing his hand. He had a snake ring on one finger, with two red eyes, and on the back of his hand was red streaks. I knew what that meant. He had started something and Lura had fixed him. She had a pretty arm, but a grip like iron, that she said come from milking cows when she was a kid. What she done when a guy got fresh was take hold of his hand and squeeze it so the bones cracked, and he generally changed his mind.

She handed him his check without a word, and I told him what he owed on the car, and he paid up and left.

"So you settled his hash, hey?" I says to her.

"If there's one thing gets on my nerves," she says, "it's a man that starts something the minute he gets in the door."

"Why didn't you yell for me?"

"Oh, I didn't need no help."

But the next day he was back, and after I filled up his car I went over to see how he was behaving. He was setting at one of the tables this time, and Lura was standing beside him. I saw her jerk her hand away quick, and he give me the bright grin a man has when he's got something he wants to cover up. He was all teeth.

"Nice day," he says. "Great weather you have in this country."

"So I hear," I says. "Your car's ready."

"What I owe you?" he says.

"Dollar twenty."

He counted it out and left.

"Listen," says Lura: "we weren't doing anything when you come in. He was just reading my hand. He's a snake doctor, and knows about the zodiac."

"Oh, wasn't we?" I says. "Well, wasn't we nice!"

"What's it to you?" she says.

"Nothing," I snapped at her. I was pretty sore.

"He says I was born under the sign of Yin," she says. You would of thought it was a piece of news fit to put in the paper.

"And who is Yin?" I says.

"It's Chinese for tiger," she says.

"Then bite yourself off a piece of raw meat," I says, and slammed out of there. We didn't have no nice time running the joint *that day.*

Next morning he was back. I kept away from the lunchroom, but I took a stroll, and seen them back there with the tiger. We had hauled a tree in there by that time, for Rajah to sharpen his claws on, and she was setting on that. The tiger had his head in her lap, and Wild Bill was looking through the wire. He couldn't even draw his breath. I didn't go near enough to hear what they was saying. I went back to the car and begin blowing the horn.

He was back quite a few times after that, in between while Duke was away. Then one night I heard a truck drive up. I knowed that truck by its rattle. And it was daylight before I heard it go away.

Couple weeks after that, Duke comes running over to me at the filling-station. "Shake hands with me," he says. "I'm going to be a father."

"Gee," I says, "that's great!"

But I took good care he wasn't around when I mentioned it to Lura.

"Congratulations," I says. "Letting Romeos into the place seems to be about the best thing you do."

"What do you mean?" she says.

"Nothing," I says. "Only I heard him drive up that night. Look like to me the moon was under the sign of Cupid. Well, it's nice if you can get away with it."

"Oh," she says.

"Yeah," I says. "A fine double cross you thought up. I didn't know they tried that any more."

She set and looked at me, and then her mouth begin to twitch and her eyes filled with tears. She tried to snuffle them up but it didn't work. "It's not any double cross," she says. "That night, I never went out there. And I never let anybody in. I was supposed to go away with him that night, but—"

She broke off and begin to cry. I took her in my arms. "But then you found this out?" I says. "Is that it?" She nodded her head. It's awful to have a pretty woman in your arms that's crying over somebody else.

From then on, it was terrible. Lura would go along two or three days pretty nice, trying to like Duke again on account of the baby coming, but then would come a day when she looked like some kind of a hex, with her eyes all sunk in so you could hardly see them at all, and not a word out of her.

Them bad days, anyhow when Duke wasn't around, she would spend with the tiger. She would set and watch him sleep, or maybe play with him, and he seemed to like it as much as she did. He was young when we got him, and mangy and thin, so you could see his slats. But now he was about six year old, and had been fed good, so he had got his growth and his coat was nice, and I think he was the biggest tiger I ever seen. A tiger, when he is really big, is a lot bigger than a lion, and sometimes when Rajah would be rubbing around Lura, he looked more like a mule than a cat.

His shoulders come up above her waist, and his head was so big it would cover both her legs when he put it in her lap. When his tail would go sliding past her it looked like some kind of a constrictor snake. His teeth were something to make you lie awake nights. A tiger has the biggest teeth of any cat, and Rajah's must have been four inches long, curved like a cavalry sword, and ivory white. They were the most murderous-looking fangs I ever set eyes on.

When Lura went to the hospital it was a hurry call, and she didn't even have time to get her clothes together. Next day Duke had to pack her bag, and he was strutting around, because it was a boy, and Lura had named him Ron. But when he come out with the bag, he didn't have much of a strut.

"Look what I found," he says to me, and fishes something out of his pocket. It was the snake ring.

"Well?" I says. "They sell them in any dime store."

"H'm," he says, and kind of weighed the ring in his hand. That afternoon, when he come back, he says, "Ten-cent store, hey? I took it to a jeweler today, and he offered me two hundred dollars for it."

"You ought to sold it," I says. "Maybe save you bad luck."

Duke went away again right after Lura come back, and for a little while things was all right. She was crazy about the little boy, and I thought he was pretty cute myself, and we got along fine. But then Duke come back and at lunch one day he made a crack about the ring. Lura didn't say nothing, but he kept at it, and pretty soon she wheeled on him.

"All right," she says. "There was another man around here, and I loved him. He give me that ring, and it meant that he and I belonged to each other. But I didn't go with him, and you know why I didn't. For Ron's sake. I'ved tried to love you again, and maybe I can yet. God knows. A woman can do some funny things if she tries. But that's where we're at now. That's right where we're at. And if you don't like it, you better say what you're going to do."

"When was this?" says Duke.

"It was quite a while ago. I told you I give him up, and I give him up for keeps."

"It was just before you knowed about Ron, wasn't it?" he says.

"Hey," I cut in. "That's no way to talk."

"Just what I thought," he says, not paying no attention to me. "Ron. That's a funny name for a kid. I thought it was funny, right off when I heard it. Ron. Ron. That's a laugh, ain't it?"

"That's a lie," she says. "That's a lie, every bit of it. And it's not the only lie you've been getting away with around here. Or think you have. Trapping up in the hills, hey? And what do you trap?"

But she looked at me, and choked it back. I begun to see that the cats wasn't the only things that had been gumming it up.

"All right," she wound up. "Say what you're gong to do. Go on. Say it!"

But he didn't.

"Ron," he cackles, "that's a hot one," and walks out.

Next day was Saturday, and he acted funny all day. He wouldn't speak to me or Lura, and once or twice I heard him mumbling to himself. Right after supper he says to me, "How are we on oil?"

"All right," I says. "The truck was around yesterday."

"You better drive in and get some," he says. "I don't think we got enough."

"Enough?" I says. "We got enough for two weeks."

"Tomorrow is Sunday," he says, "and there'll be a big call for it. Bring out a hundred gallon and tell them to put it on the account."

By that time, I would give in to one of his nutty ideas rather than have an argument with him, and besides, I never tumbled that he was up to anything. So I wasn't there for what happened next, but I got it out of Lura later, so here is how it was:

Lura didn't pay much attention to the argument about the oil, but washed up the supper dishes, and then went in the bedroom to make sure everything was all right with the baby. When she come out she left the door open, so she could hear if he cried. The bedroom was off the sitting-room, because these here California houses don't have but one floor, and all the rooms connect. Then she lit the fire, because it was cool, and sat there watching it burn. Duke come in, walked around, and then went out back. "Close the door," she says to him. "I'll be right back," he says.

So she sat looking at the fire, she didn't know how long, maybe five minutes, maybe ten minutes. But pretty soon she felt the house shake. She thought maybe it was a earthquake, and looked at the pictures, but they was all hanging straight. Then she felt the house shake again. She listened, but it wasn't no truck outside that would cause it, and it wouldn't be no State road blasting or nothing like that at that time of night. Then she felt it shake again, and this time it shook in a regular movement, one, two, three, four, like that. And then all of a sudden she knew what it was, why Duke had acted so funny all day, why he had sent me off for the gas, why he had left the door open, and all the rest of it. There was five hundred pounds of cat walking through the house, and Duke had turned him loose to kill her.

She turned around, and Rajah was looking at her, not five foot away. She didn't do nothing for a minute, just set there thinking what a boob Duke was to figure on the tiger doing his dirty work for him, when all the time she could handle him easy as a kitten, only Duke didn't know it. Then she spoke. She expected Rajah to come and put his head in her lap, but he didn't. He stood there and growled, and his ears flattened back. That scared her, and she thought of the baby. I told you a tiger has that kind of brains. It no sooner went through her head about the baby than Rajah knowed she wanted to get to that door, and he was over there before she could get out of the chair.

He was snarling in a regular roar now, but he hadn't got a whiff of the baby yet, and he was still facing Lura. She could see he meant business. She reached in the fireplace, grabbed a stick that was burning bright, and walked him down with it. A tiger is afraid of fire, and she shoved it right in his eyes. He backed past the door, and she slid in the bedroom. But he was right after her, and she had to hold the stick at him with one hand and grab the baby with the other.

But she couldn't get out. He had her cornered, and he was kicking up such a awful fuss she knowed the stick wouldn't stop him long. So she dropped it, grabbed up the baby's covers, and threw them at his head. They went wild, but they saved her just the same. A tiger, if you throw something at him with a human smell, will generally jump on it and bite at it before he does anything else, and that's what he done now. He jumped so hard the rug went out from under him, and while he was scrambling to his feet she shot past him with the baby and pulled the door shut after her.

She run in my room, got a blanket, wrapped the baby in it, and run out to the electric icebox. It was the only thing around the place that was steel. Soon as she opened the door she knowed why she couldn't do nothing with Rajah. His meat was in there, Duke hadn't fed him. She pulled the meat out, shoved the baby in, cut off the current, and closed the door. Then she picked up the meat and went around outside of the house to the window of the bedroom. She could see Rajah in there, biting at the top of the door, where a crack of light showed through. He reached to the ceiling. She took a grip on the meat and drove at the screen with it. It gave way, and the meat went through. He was on it before it hit the floor.

Next thing was to give him time to eat. She figured she could handle him once he got something in his belly. She went back to the sitting-room. And in there, kind of peering around, was Duke. He had his gun strapped on, and one look at his face was all she needed to know she hadn't made no mistake about why the tiger was loose.

"Oh," he says, kind of foolish, and then walked back and closed the door. "I meant to come back sooner, but I couldn't help looking at the night. You got no idea how beautiful it is. Stars is bright as anything."

"Yeah," she says. "I noticed."

"Beautiful," he says. "Beautiful."

"Was you expecting burglars or something?" she says, looking at the gun.

"Oh, that," he says. "No. Cats been kicking up a fuss. I put it on, case I have to go back there. Always like to have it handy."

"The tiger," she says. "I thought I heard him, myself."

"Loud," says Duke. "Awful loud."

He waited. She waited. She wasn't going to give him the satisfaction of opening up first. But just then there come a growl from the bedroom, and the sound of bones cracking. A tiger acts awful sore when he eats. "What's that?" says Duke.

"I wonder," says Lura. She was hell-bent on making him spill it first.

They both looked at each other, and then there was more growls, and more sound of cracking bones. "You better go in there," says Duke, soft and easy, with the sweat standing out on his forehead and his eyes shining bright as marbles. "Something might be happening to Ron."

"Do you know what I think it is?" says Lura.

"What's that?" says Duke. His breath was whistling through his nose like it always done when he got excited.

"I think it's that tiger you sent in here to kill me," says Lura.

"So you could bring in that woman you been running around with for over a year. That redhead that raises rabbit fryers on the Ventura road. That cat you been trapping!"

"And stead of getting you he got Ron," says Duke. "Little Ron! Oh my, ain't that tough? Go in there, why don't you? Ain't you got no mother love? Why don't you call up his pappy, get him in there? What's the matter? Is he afraid of a cat?"

Lura laughed at him. "All right," she says. "Now you go." With that she took hold of him. He tried to draw the gun, but she crumpled up his hand like a piece of wet paper and the gun fell on the floor. She bent him back on the table and beat his face in for him. Then she picked him up, dragged him to the front door, and threw him out. He run off a little ways. She come back and saw the gun. She picked it up, went to the door again, and threw it after him. "And take that peashooter with you," she says.

That was where she made her big mistake. When she turned to go back in the house, he shot, and that was the last she knew for a while.

Now, for what happened next, it wasn't nobody there, only Duke and the tiger, but after them State cops got done fitting it all together, combing the ruins and all, it wasn't no trouble to tell how it was, anyway most of it, and here's how they figured it out:

Soon as Duke seen Lura fall, right there in front of the house, he knowed he was up against it. So the first thing he done was to run to where she was and put the gun in her hand, to make it look like she had shot herself. That was where he made *his* big mistake, because if he had kept the gun he might of had a chance. Then he went inside to telephone, and what he said was, soon as he got hold of the State police:

"For God's sake come out here quick. My wife has went crazy and throwed the baby to the tiger and shot herself and I'm all alone in the house with him and—*Oh, my God, here he comes*!"

Now, that last was something he didn't figure on saying. So far as he knowed, the tiger was in the room, having a nice meal off his son, so everything was hotsy-totsy. But what he didn't know was that that piece of burning firewood that Lura had dropped had set the room on fire and on account of that the tiger had got out. How did he get out? We never did quite figure that out. But this is how I figure it, and one man's guess is good as another's:

The fire started near the window, we knew that much. That was where Lura dropped the stick, right next to the cradle, and that was where a guy coming down the road in a car first seen the flames. And what I think is that soon as the tiger got his eye off the meat and seen the fire, he begun to scramble away from it, just wild. And when a wild tiger hits a beaverboard wall, he goes through, that's all. While Duke was telephoning, Rajah come through the wall like a clown through a hoop, and the first thing he seen was Duke, at the telephone, and Duke wasn't no friend, not to Rajah he wasn't.

Anyway, that's how things was when I got there, with the oil. The State cops was a little ahead of me, and I met the ambulance with Lura in it, coming down the road seventy mile an hour, but just figured there had been a crash up the road, and didn't know nothing about it having Lura in it. And when I drove up, there was plenty to look at all right. The house was in flames, and the police was trying to get in, but couldn't get nowheres near it on account of the heat, and about a hundred cars parked all around, with people looking, and a gasoline pumper cruising up and down the road, trying to find a water connection somewheres they could screw their hose to.

But inside the house was the terrible part. You could hear Duke screaming, and in between Duke was the tiger. And both of them was screams of fear, but I think the tiger was worse. It is a awful thing to hear a animal letting out a sound like that. It kept up about five minutes after I got there, and then all of a sudden you couldn't hear nothing but the tiger. And then in a minute that stopped.

There was nothing to do about the fire. In a half hour the whole place was gone, and they was combing the ruins for Duke. Well, they found him. And in his head was four holes, two on each side, deep. We measured them fangs of the tiger. They just fit.

Soon as I could I run to the hospital. They had got the bullet out by that time, and Lura was laying in bed all bandaged around the head, but there was a guard over her, on account of what Duke said over the telephone. He was a State cop. I sat down with him, and he didn't like it none. Neither did I. I knowed there was something funny about it, but what broke your heart was Lura, coming out of the ether. She would groan and mutter and try to say something so hard it would make your head ache. After a while I got up and went in the hall. But then I see the State cop shoot out of the room and line down the hall as fast as he could go. At last she had said it. The baby was in the electric icebox. They found him there, still asleep and just about ready for his milk. The fire had blacked up the outside, but inside it was as cool and nice as a new bathtub.

Well, that was about all. They cleared Lura, soon as she told her story, and the baby in the icebox proved it. Soon as she got out of the hospital she got a offer from the movies, but stead of taking it she come out to the place and her and I run it for a while, anyway the filling-station end, sleeping in the shacks and getting along nice. But one night I heard a rattle from a bum differential, and I never even bothered to show up for breakfast the next morning.

I often wish I had. Maybe she left me a note.

SPIDER
Mignon G. Eberhart

Known as "America's Agatha Christie" during the 1930s and 1940s (although, to be fair, the same analogy was made of Mary Roberts Rinehart), Mignon G(ood) Eberhart (1899-1996) was one of America most popular and beloved writers for decades, enjoying a career that produced sixty books, beginning with *The Patient in Room 18* (1929) and concluding with *Three Days for Emeralds* (1988).

While most of her books were stand-alones, she did create several series characters. Her first five books featured Sarah Keate, a middle-aged spinster, nurse, and amateur detective who works closely with Lance O'Leary, a promising young police detective in an unnamed Midwestern city. This unlikely duo functions effectively, despite Keate's penchant for stumbling into dangerous situations from which she must be rescued. She is inquisitive and supplies O'Leary with valuable information.

Equally unlikely is the fact that five films featuring Nurse Keate and O'Leary were filmed over a three-year period in the 1930s. *While the Patient Slept* (1935) featured Aline MacMahon as Nurse Keate and Guy Kibbee as O'Leary. *The Murder of Dr. Harrigan* (1936) starred Kay Linaker in the lead role, renamed Nurse Sally Keating and now much younger. *Murder by an Aristocrat* (1936) has Marguerite Churchill as Keating, and *The Great Hospital Mystery* 1937) features a much older Jane Darwell, before Warner Brothers-First National decided to go younger again with a lovely Ann Sheridan starring in both *The Patient in Room 18* (1938) and *Mystery House* (1938).

Eberhart's other series detective is Susan Dare who, like her creator, is a mystery writer. Young, attractive charming, romantic, and gushily emotional, she has a habit of stumbling into or being pushed into situations that result into real-life murders.

"Spider" was originally published in the May 1934 issue of *The Delineator*; it was first collected in *The Cases of Susan Dare* (New York, Doubleday, Doran, 1934).

Spider

Mignon G. Eberhart

"But it is fantastic," said Susan Dare, clutching the telephone. "You can't just be afraid. You've got to be afraid of something." She waited, but there was no reply.

"You mean," she said presently, in a hushed voice, "that I'm to go to this perfectly strange house, to be the guest of a perfectly strange woman—"

"To you," said Jim Byrne. "Not, I tell you, to me."

"But you said you had never seen her—"

"Don't maunder," said Jim Byrne sharply. "Of course I've

never seen her. Now, Susan, do try to get this straight. This woman is Caroline Wray. One of the Wrays."

"Perfectly clear," said Susan. "Therefore I'm to go to her house and see why she's got an attack of nerves. Take a bag and prepare to spend the next few days as her guest. I'm sorry, Jim, but I'm busy. I've got to do a murder story this week and—"

"Sue," said Jim, "I'm serious."

Susan paused abruptly. He *was* serious.

"It's—I don't know how to explain it, Susan," he said. "It's just—well, I'm Irish, you know. And I'm—fey. Don't laugh."

"I'm not laughing," said Susan. "Tell me exactly what you want me to do."

"Just—watch things. There ought not to be any danger—don't see how there could be. To you."

Susan realized that she was going. "How many Wrays are there, and what do you think is going to happen?"

"There are four Wrays. But I don't know what is going on that has got Caroline so terrified. It was that—the terror in her voice—that made me call you."

"What's the number of the house?" said Susan.

He told her. "It's away north," he said. "One of those old houses—narrow, tall, hasn't changed, I suppose, since old Ephineas Wray died. He was a close friend, you know, of my father's. Don't know why Caroline called me: I suppose some vague notion that a man on a newspaper would know what to do. Now let me see—there's Caroline. She's the daughter of Ephineas Wray. David is his grandson and Caroline's nephew and the only man—except the houseman—in the place. He's young—in his twenties, I believe. His father and mother died when he was a child."

"You mean there are three women?"

"Naturally. There's Marie—she is old Wray's adopted daughter—not born a Wray, but more like him than the rest of them. And Jessica—she's Caroline's cousin; but she's always lived with the Wrays because her father died young. People always assume that the three women are sisters. Actually, of course, they are not. But old Ephineas Wray left his fortune divided equally among them."

"And they all live there together?"

"Yes. David's not married."

"Is that," said Susan, at the note of finality in his voice, "all you know about them?"

"Absolutely everything. Not much for you to go on, is it? It was just," said Jim Byrne soberly, with the effect of a complete explanation, "that she was so—so horribly scared. Old Caroline, I mean."

Susan retraced the address slowly before she said again: "What was she afraid of?"

"I don't know," said Jim Byrne. "And—it's queer—but I don't think she knew either."

It was approaching five o'clock, with a dark fog rolling up from the lake and blending itself with the early winter twilight, when Susan Dare pressed the bell beside the wide old door—pressed it and waited. Lights were on in the street, but the house before her was dark, its windows curtained. The door was heavy and secretive.

But they were expecting her—or at least Caroline Wray was; it had all been arranged by telephone. Susan wondered what Caroline had told them; what Jim Byrne had told Caroline to say to explain her presence; and, suddenly, what Caroline was like.

Little Johnny hung his sister.
She was dead before they missed her.
Johnny's always up to tricks,
Ain't he cute, and only six—

The jingle had been haunting her with the persistency of a popular dance tune, and it gave accent to the impatient little beat of her brown Oxford upon the stone step. Then a light flashed on above the door. Susan took a deep breath of the moist cold air and felt a sudden tightening of her nerves. The door was going to open.

It swung wider, and a warm current of air struck Susan's cheeks. Beyond was a dimly lit hall and a woman's figure—a tall, corseted figure with full sweeping skirts.

"Yes?" said a voice harshly out of the dimness.

"I am Susan Dare," said Susan.

"Oh—oh, yes." The figure moved aside and the door opened wider. "Come in, Miss Dare. We were expecting you."

Afterward Susan remembered her own hesitation on the dark threshold as the door closed with finality behind her, and the woman turned.

"I am Miss Jessica Wray," she said.

Jessica. This was the cousin, then.

She was a tall woman, large-boned, with a heavy, dark face, thick, iron-gray hair done high and full on her head, and long, strong hands. She was dressed after a much earlier fashion; one which, indeed, Susan was unable to date.

"We were expecting you," she said. "Caroline, however, was obliged to go out." She paused just under the light and beside a long mirror.

Susan had a confused impression of the house in that moment; an impression of old, crowded elegance. The mirror was wavery and framed in wide gilt; there were ferns in great marble urns; there were marble figures.

"We'll go up to your room," said Jessica. "Caroline said you would be in Chicago for several days. This way. You can leave your bag here. James will take it up later; he is out just now."

Susan put down her small suitcase, and followed Jessica. The newel post and stair rail were heavy and carved. The steps were carpeted and thickly padded. And the house was utterly, completely still. As they ascended the quiet stairs it grew increasingly hot and airless.

At the top of the stairs Jessica turned with a rigid motion of her strong body.

"Will you wait here a moment?" she said. "I'm not sure which room—"

Susan made some assenting gesture, and Jessica turned along the passage which ran toward the rear of the house.

So terrifically hot the house was. So crowded with old and almost sentient furniture. So very silent.

Susan moved a bit restively. It was not a pleasant house. But Caroline had to be afraid of something—not just silence and heat and brooding, secretive old walls. She glanced down the length of hall, moved again to put her hand upon the tall newel post of the stair rail beside her. The carved top of it seemed to shift and move slightly under the pressure of her hand and confirmed in the strangest way her feeling that the house itself had a singular kind of life.

Then she was staring straight ahead of her through an open, lighted doorway. Beyond it was a large room, half bedroom and half sitting room. A lamp on a table cast a circle of light, and beside the table, silhouetted against the light, sat a woman with a book in her lap.

It must be Marie Wray—the older sister; the adopted Wray who was more like old Ephineas Wray than any of them.

Her face was in shadow with the light beyond it, so Susan could see only a blunt, fleshy white profile and a tight knot of shining black hair above a massive black-silk bosom. She did not, apparently, know of Susan's presence, for she did not turn. There was a kind of patience about that massive, relaxed figure; a waiting. An enormous black female spider waiting in a web of shadows. But waiting for what?

The suggestion was not one calculated to relieve the growing tension of Susan's nerves. The heat was making her dizzy; fanciful. Calling a harmless old woman a black spider merely because she was wearing a shiny black-silk dress! Marie Wray still, so far as Susan could see, did not look at her, but there was suddenly the flicker of a motion on the table.

Susan looked and caught her breath in an incredulous little gasp.

There was actually a small gray creature on that table, directly under the lamplight. A small gray creature with a long tail. It sat down nonchalantly, pulled the lid off a box and dug its tiny hands into the box.

"It's a monkey," thought Susan with something like a clutch of hysteria. "It's a monkey—a spider monkey, is it?—with that tiny face."

It was turning its face jerkily about the room, peering with bright, anxious eyes here and there, and busily, furiously eating candy. It failed somehow to see Susan; or perhaps she was too far away to interest it. There was suddenly something curiously unreal about the scene. That, thought Susan, or the heat in this fantastic house, and turned at the approaching rustle of skirts down the passage. It was Jessica, and she looked at Susan and then through the open doorway and smiled coldly.

"Marie is deaf," she said. "I suppose she didn't realize you were here."

"No," said Susan.

"I'll tell her—" She made a stiff gesture with her long hand and turned to enter the room beyond the open door. As her gray silk rustled through the door the little monkey jerked around, gave her one piercing black glance and was gone from the table in a swift gray streak. He fled across the room, darted under an old sofa.

But Jessica did not reprove him. "Marie," she said loudly and distinctly.

There was a pause. Jessica's flowing gray-silk skirts were now silhouetted against the table lamp, and the monkey absently began to lick its paw.

"Yes, Jessica." The voice was that of a person long deaf—entirely without tone.

"Susan Dare is here—you know—the daughter of Caroline's friend. Do you want to see her?"

"See her? No. No, not now. Later."

"Very well. Do you want anything?"

"No."

"Your cushions?"

Jessica's rigid back bent over Marie as she arranged a cushion. Then she turned and walked again toward Susan. Susan felt queerly fascinated and somehow oddly shocked to note that, as Jessica turned her rigid back to the room, the monkey darted out from under the sofa and was suddenly skittering across the room again in the direction of the table and the candy.

He would be, thought Susan, one very sick monkey. The

house was too hot, and yet Susan shivered a bit. Why did people keep monkeys?

"This way," said Jessica firmly, and Susan preceded her down the hall and into exactly the kind of bedroom she might have expected it to be.

But Jessica did not intend to leave her alone to explore its Victorian fastnesses. Under her somewhat unnerving dark gaze, Susan removed her cockeyed little hat, smoothed back her light hair and put her coat across a chair, only to have it placed immediately by Jessica in the enormous gloomy wardrobe. The servants, said Jessica, were out; the second girl and James because it was their half day out, the cook to do an errand.

"You are younger than I should have expected," she said abruptly to Susan. "Shall we go down now?"

As they passed down the stairs to the drawing room, a clock somewhere struck slowly, with long trembling variations.

"Five," said Jessica. "Caroline ought to return very soon. And David. He usually reaches home shortly after five. That is, if it isn't rainy. Traffic sometimes delays him. But it isn't rainy tonight!"

"Foggy," said Susan and obeyed the motion of Jessica's long gray hand toward a chair. It was not, however, a comfortable chair. And neither were the moments that followed comfortable, for Jessica sat sternly erect in a chair opposite Susan, folded her hands firmly in her silk lap and said exactly nothing. Susan started to speak a time or two, thought better of it, and herself sat in rather rigid silence. And was suddenly aware that she was acutely receptive to sight and sound and feeling.

It was not a pleasant sensation.

For she felt queerly as if the lives that were living themselves out in that narrow old house were pressing in upon her—as if long-spoken words and long-stifled whispers were living yet in the heated air.

She stirred restively and tried not to think of Marie Wray. Queer how difficult it was, once having seen Marie and heard her speak, not to think of that brooding figure—sitting in its web of shadows, waiting.

Three old women living in an old house. What were their relations to one another? Two of them she had seen and had heard speak, and knew no more of them than she had known. What about Caroline—the one who was afraid? She stirred again and knew Jessica was watching her.

They heard the bell, although it rang in some back part of the house. Jessica looked satisfied and rose.

"It's David," she said. At the door into the hall she added in a different tone: "And I suppose Caroline, too."

Susan knew she was tense. Yet there was nothing in that house for her—Susan Dare—to fear. It was Caroline who was afraid.

Then another woman stood in the doorway. Caroline, no doubt. A tall slender woman, a blonde who had faded into tremulous, wispy uncertainty. She did not speak. Her eyes were large and blue and feverish, and two bright pink spots fluttered in her thin cheeks, and her bare thin hands moved. Susan rose and went to her and took the two hands.

"But you're so young," said Caroline. Disappointment throbbed in her voice.

"I'm not really," said Susan.

"And so little—" breathed Caroline.

"But that doesn't matter at all," said Susan, speaking slowly, as one does to a nervous child. There were voices in the hall, but she was mainly aware of Caroline.

"No, I suppose not," said Caroline, finally looking into Susan's eyes. Terrified, Jim had said. Curious how right Jim managed to be.

Caroline's eyes sought into Susan's, and she was about to speak when there was a rustle in the doorway. Caroline's uncertain lips closed in a kind of gasp, and Jessica swept into the room.

"But I must know what she's afraid of," thought Susan. "I must get her alone—away from Jessica."

"Take off your coat, Caroline," said Jessica. "Don't stand there. I see you've spoken to Susan Dare. Put away your hat and coat and then come down again."

"Yes, Jessica," said Caroline. Her hands were moving again, and she looked away.

"Go on," said Jessica. Her voice was not sharp, it was merely undefeatable.

"Yes, Jessica," said Caroline.

"Marie is reading," said Jessica. "You needn't speak to her now unless you wish to do so. You may take Susan Dare in to see her later."

"Yes, Jessica."

Caroline disappeared and in her place stood a man, and Susan was murmuring words of acknowledgment to Jessica's economical introduction.

David, too, was blond, and his eyes were darkly blue. He was slender and fairly tall; his mouth was fine and sensitive, and there was a look about his temples and around his eyes that was—Susan sought for the word and found it—wistful. He was young and strong and vibrant—the only young thing in the house—but he was not happy. Susan knew that at once. He said:

"How do you do, Miss Dare?"

"Don't go upstairs yet, David," said Jessica. Her voice was less harsh, she watched him avidly. "You ought to rest."

"Not now, Aunt Jessica. I'll see you again, Miss Dare."

He walked away. "Aunt Marie all right?" he called from the stairway.

"Perfectly," said Jessica. Her voice was harsh again. "She's reading . . ."

Afterward Susan tried to remember whether she could actually hear David's steps upon the padded stairs or whether she was only half consciously calculating the time it took to climb the stairs—the time it took, or might have taken to walk along the hall, to enter a room. She was sure that Jessica did not speak. She merely sat there.

Why did Jessica become rigid and harsh again when David spoke of Marie? Why did—

A loud, dreadful crash of sound forever shattered the silence in the house. It fell upon Susan and immersed her and shook the whole house and then receded in waves. Waves that left destruction and intolerable confusion.

Susan realized dimly that she was on her feet and trying to move toward the stairway, and that Jessica's mouth was gray, and that Jessica's hands were clutching her.

"Oh, my God—David—" said Jessica intelligibly, and Susan pushed the woman away from her.

She reached the stairway, Jessica beside her, and at the top of the stairs two figures were locked together and struggling in the upper hall.

"Caroline," screamed Jessica. "What are you doing? Where's Marie—where—"

"Let me go, Caroline!" David was pulling Caroline's thin

clutching arms from around him. "Let me go, I tell you. Something terrible has happened. You must—"

Jessica brushed past them and then was at the door of Marie's room.

"*It's Marie!*" she cried harshly. "*Who shot her?*"

Susan was vaguely conscious of Caroline's sobbing breaths and of David's shoulder pressing against her own. Somehow they had all got to that open doorway and were crowding there together.

It *was* Marie.

She sat in the same chair in which she'd been sitting when Susan saw her so short a time ago. But her head had fallen forward, her whole body crumpled grotesquely into black-silk folds.

Jessica was the first to enter the room. Then David. Susan, feeling sick and shaken, followed. Only Caroline remained in the doorway, clinging to the casing with thin hands, her face like chalk and her lips blue.

"She's been shot," said Jessica. "Straight through the heart." Then she looked at David. "Did Caroline kill her, David?"

"*Caroline* kill Marie! Why, Caroline couldn't kill anything!" he cried.

"Then who killed her?" said Jessica. "You realize, don't you, that she's dead?"

Her dark gaze probed deeper and she said in a grating whisper: "Did you kill her, David?"

"No!" cried David. "*No!*"

"She's dead," said Jessica.

Susan said as crisply as she could: "Why don't you call a doctor?"

Jessica's silk rustled, and she turned to give Susan a long cold look. "There's no need to call a doctor. Obviously she's dead."

"The police, then," said Susan softly. "Obviously, too—she's been murdered."

"The police," cried Jessica scornfully. "Turn over my own cousin—my own nephew—to the police. Never."

"I'll call them," Susan said crisply, and whirled and left them with their dead.

On the silent stairway her knees began to shake again. So this was what the house had been waiting for. Murder! And this was why Caroline had been afraid. What, then, had she known? Where was the revolver that had shot Marie? There was nothing of the kind to be seen in the room.

The air was hot—the house terribly still—and she, Susan Dare, was hunting for a telephone—calling a number—talking quite sensibly on the whole—and all the time it was entirely automatic action on her part. It was automatic, even, when she called and found Jim Byrne.

"I'm here," she said. "At the Wrays'. Marie has been murdered—"

"My God!" said Jim and slammed up the receiver.

The house was so hot. Susan sat down weakly on the bottom step and huddled against the newel post and felt extremely ill. If she were really a detective, of course, she would go straight upstairs and wring admissions out of them while they were shaken and confused and before they'd had time to arrange their several defenses. But she wasn't a detective, and she had no wish to be, and all she wanted just then was to escape. Something moved in the shadows under the stairs—moved. Susan flung her hands to her throat to choke back a scream, and the little monkey whirled out, peered at her worriedly, then darted up the window curtain and sat nonchalantly on the heavy wooden rod.

Her coat and hat were upstairs. She couldn't go out into the cold and fog without them—and Jim Byrne was on the way. If she could hold out till he got there—

David was coming down the stairs.

"She says it's all right to call the police," he said in a tight voice.

"I've called them."

He looked down at her and suddenly sat on the bottom step beside her.

"It's been hell," he said quite simply. "But I didn't think of—murder." He stared at nothing, and Susan could not bear the look of horror on his young face.

"I understand," she said, wishing she did understand.

"I didn't," he said. "Until—just lately. I knew—oh, since I was a child I've known I must—"

"Must what?" said Susan gravely.

He flushed quickly and was white again.

"Oh, it's a beastly thing to say. I was the only—child, you know. And I grew up knowing that I dared have no—no favorite—you see? If there'd been more of us—or if the aunts had married and had their own children—but I didn't understand how—how violent—" the word stopped in his throat, and he coughed and went on—"how strongly they felt—"

"Who?"

"Why, Aunt Jessica, of course. And Aunt Marie. And Aunt Caroline."

"Too many aunts," said Susan dryly. "What was it they were violent about?"

"The house. And each other. And—and other things. Oh, I've always known, but it was all—hidden, you know. The surface was—all right."

Susan groped through the fog. The surface was all right, he'd said. But the fog parted for a rather sickening instant and gave her an ugly glimpse of an abyss below.

"Why was Caroline afraid?" said Susan.

"*Caroline?*" he said, staring at her. "*Afraid!*" His blue eyes were brilliant with anxiety and excitement. "See here," he said, "if you think it was Caroline who killed Marie, it wasn't. She couldn't. She'd never have dared. I m-mean—" he was stammering in his excitement—"I mean, Caroline wouldn't hurt a fly. And Caroline wouldn't have opposed Marie about anything. Marie—you don't know what Marie was like."

"Exactly what happened in the upstairs hall?"

"You mean—when the shot—"

"Yes."

"Why, I—I was in my room—no, not quite—I was nearly at the door. And I heard the shot. And it's queer, but I believe—I believe I knew right away that it was a revolver shot. It was as if I had expected—" He checked himself. "But I *hadn't* expected—I—" He stopped; dug his fists desperately into his pockets and was suddenly firm and controlled—"But I hadn't actually expected it, you understand."

"Then when you heard the shot you turned, I suppose, and looked."

"Yes. Yes, I think so. Anyway, there was Caroline in the hall, too. I think she was screaming. We were both running. I thought of Marie—I don't know why. But Caroline clutched at me and held me. She didn't want me to go into Marie's room. She was terrified. And then I think you were there and Jessica. Were you?"

"Yes. And there was no one else in the hall? No one came from Marie's room?"

His face was perplexed, terribly puzzled.

"Nobody."

"Except—Caroline?"

"But I tell you it couldn't have been Caroline."

The doorbell began to ring—shrill sharp peals that stabbed the shadows and the thickness of the house.

"It's the police," thought Susan, catching her breath sharply. The boy beside her had straightened and was staring at the wide old door that must be opened.

Behind them on the padded stairway something rustled. "It's the police," said Jessica harshly. "Let them in."

Susan had not realized that there would be so many of them. Or that they would do so much. Or that an inquiry could last so long. She had not realized either how amazingly thorough they were with their photographs and their fingerprinting and their practised and rapid and incredibly searching investigation. She was a little shocked and more than a little awed, sheerly from witnessing at first hand and with her own eyes what police actually did when there was murder.

Yet her own interview with Lieutenant Mohrn was not difficult. He was brisk, youthful, kind, and Jim Byrne was there to explain her presence. She had been very thankful to see Jim Byrne, who arrived on the heels of the police.

"Tell the police everything you know," he had said.

"But I don't know anything."

And it was Lieutenant Mohrn who, oddly enough, brought Susan into the very center and hub of the whole affair.

But that was later—much later. After endless inquiry, endless search, endless repetitions, endless conferences. Endless waiting in the gloomy dining room with portraits of dead and vanished Wrays staring fixedly down upon policemen. Upon Susan. Upon servants whose alibis had, Jim had informed her, been immediately and completely established.

It was close to one o'clock when Jim came to her again.

"See here," he said. "You look like a ghost. Have you had anything to eat?"

"No," said Susan.

A moment later she was in the kitchen, accepting provender that Jim Byrne brought from the icebox.

"You do manage to get things done," she said. "I thought newspapermen wouldn't even be permitted in the house."

"Oh, the police are all right—they'll give a statement to all of us—treat us right, you know. More cake? And don't forget I'm in on this case. Have you found out yet what Caroline was afraid of?"

"No. I've not had a chance to talk to her. Jim, who did it?"

He smiled mirthlessly.

"You're asking me! They've established, mainly, three things: the servants are clear; there was no one in the house besides Jessica and David and Caroline."

"And me," said Susan with a small shudder. "And—Marie."

"And you," agreed Jim imperturbably. "And Marie. Third, they can't find the gun. Jessica and you alibi each other. That leaves David and Caroline. Well—which of them did it? And why?"

"I don't know," she said. "But, Jim, I'm frightened."

"*Frightened!* With the house full of police? Why?"

"I don't know," said Susan again. "It's nothing I can explain. It's just—a queer kind of menace. Somewhere—somehow—in this house. It's like Marie—only Marie is dead and this is alive.

Horribly alive." Susan knew she was incoherent and that Jim was staring at her worriedly, and suddenly the swinging door behind her opened, and Susan's heart leaped to her throat before the policeman spoke.

"The lieutenant wants you both, please," he said.

As they passed through the hall, the clock struck a single note that vibrated long afterward. It had been, then, eight hours and more since she had entered that wide door and been met by Jessica.

Lights were on everywhere now, and there were policemen, and the old-fashioned sliding doors between the hall and the drawing room had been closed, and they shut in the sound of voices.

"In there," said the policeman and drew back one of the doors.

It was entirely silent in the heavily furnished room. Lights were on in the chandelier above and it was eerily, dreadfully bright. The streaks showed in the faded brown-velvet curtains at the windows, and the wavery lines in the mantelpiece mirror, and the worn spots in the old Turkish rug. And every gray shadow on Jessica's face was darker, and the fine, sharp lines around Caroline's mouth and her haunted eyes showed terribly clear, and there were two bright-scarlet spots in David's cheeks. Lieutenant Mohrn had lost his look of youth and freshness and looked the weary, graying forty that he was. A detective in plain clothes was sitting on the small of his back in one of the slippery plush chairs.

The door slid together again behind them, and still no one spoke, although Jessica turned to look at them. And, oddly, Susan had a feeling that everything in that household had changed. Yet Jessica had not actually changed; her eyes met Susan's with exactly the same cold, remote command. Then what was it that was different?

Caroline—Susan's eyes went to the thin bent figure, hunched tragically on the edge of her chair. Her fine hair was in wisps about her face; her mouth tremulous.

Why, of course! It was not a change. It was merely that both Jessica and Caroline had become somehow intensified. They were both etched more sharply. The shadows were deeper, the lines blacker.

Lieutenant Mohrn turned to Caroline. "This is the young woman you refer to, isn't it, Miss Caroline?"

Caroline's eyes fluttered to Susan, avoided Jessica, and returned fascinated to Lieutenant Mohrn. "Yes—yes."

David whirled from the window and crossed to stand directly above Caroline.

"Look here, Aunt Caroline, you realize that whatever you tell Miss Dare she'll be bound to tell the police? It's just the same thing—you know that, don't you?"

"Oh, yes, David. That's what—*he*—said."

Lieutenant Mohrn cleared his throat abruptly and a bit uncomfortably.

"She understands that, Wray. I don't know why she won't tell me. But she won't. And she says she will talk to Miss Dare."

"Caroline," said Jessica, "is a fool." She moved rigidly to look at Caroline, who refused to meet her eyes, and said: "You'll find Caroline's got nothing to tell."

Caroline's eyes went wildly to the floor, to the curtains, to David, and both her hands fluttered to her trembling mouth.

"I'd rather talk to her," she said.

"Caroline," said Jessica, "you are behaving irrationally. You have been like this for days. You brought this—this Susan Dare into the house. You lied to me about her—told me it was a daughter of a school friend. I might have known you had no such intimate friend!" She shot a dark look at Susan and swept back to Caroline. "Now you've told the police that you were afraid and that you telephoned to a perfect stranger—"

"Jim Byrne," fluttered Caroline. "His father and my father—"

"That means nothing," said Jessica harshly. "Don't interrupt me. And then this young woman comes into our house. Why? Answer me, Caroline. Why?"

"I—was afraid—"

"Of what?"

"I—I—" Caroline stood, motioning frantically with her hands—"I'll tell. I'll tell Miss Dare. She'll know what to do."

"This is the situation, Miss Dare," said Lieutenant Mohrn patiently.

"Miss Caroline has admitted that she was alarmed about something and why you are here. She has also admitted that there was an urgent and pressing problem that was causing dissension in the household. But she's—very tired, as you see—a little nervous, perhaps. And she says she is willing to tell, but that she prefers talking to you." He smiled wearily. "At any rate—it's asking a great deal of you, but will you hear what she has to tell? It's—a whim, of course." There was something friendly and kind in the look he gave Caroline. "But we'll humor her. And she understands—"

"I understand," said Caroline with a flash of decision. "But I don't want—anyone but Susan Dare."

"Nonsense, Caroline," said Jessica, "I have a right to hear. So has David."

Caroline's eyes, glancing this way and that to avoid Jessica, actually met Jessica's gaze, and she succumbed at once.

"Yes, Jessica," she said obediently.

"All right, then. Now, we are going outside, Miss Caroline. You can say anything you want to say. And remember we are here only to help." Lieutenant Mohrn paused at the sliding door, and Susan saw a look flash between him and Jim Byrne. She also saw Jim Byrne's hand go to his pocket and the brief little nod he gave the lieutenant.

"Do you mind if I stay in the room but out of earshot, Miss Jessica?" Jim asked.

"No," Jessica agreed grudgingly.

"We'll be just outside," said Lieutenant Mohrn, speaking to Jim. Something in his voice added: "Ready for any kind of trouble." She saw, too, the look in Jim's eyes as he glanced at her and then back to the lieutenant, and all at once she understood the meaning of that look and the meaning of his gesture toward his pocket. He had a revolver there, then. And the lieutenant was promising protection. But that meant that they were going to leave her alone with the Wrays. Alone with three people one of whom was a murderer.

But she was not entirely alone. Jim Byrne was there, in the far corner, his eyes wary and alert and his smile unperturbed.

"Very well now, Caroline," said Jessica. "Let's hear your precious story."

"It's about the house," began Caroline, looking at Susan as if she dared not permit her glance to swerve. "The police dragged it out of me—"

Jessica laughed harshly and interrupted.

"So that's your important evidence. I can tell it with less foolishness. It is simply that we have had an offer of a considerable sum of money for the purchase of this house. We happen to hold this house—all four of us—with equal interest. Thus it is necessary for us to agree before we can sell or otherwise dispose of the property. That's really all there is to it. Caroline and David wanted to sell. I didn't care."

"But Marie didn't want to sell," cried Caroline. "And Marie was stronger than any of us."

"Miss Caroline," said Susan softly. "Why were you afraid?"

For a dreadful second or two there was utter silence.

Then, as dreadfully, Caroline collapsed into her chair again and put her hands over her mouth and moaned.

But Jessica was ready to speak.

"She had nothing to be afraid of. She's merely nervous—very nervous. I know, Caroline, what you have been doing with every cent of money you could get your silly hands upon. But I intended to do nothing about it."

Caroline had given up her effort to avoid Jessica. She was staring at her like a terrified, panting bird.

"You—know—" she gasped in a thin, high voice.

"Of course, I know. You are completely transparent, Caroline. I know that you were gambling away your inheritance—or at least what you could touch—"

"Gambling!" cried David. "What do you mean?"

"Stocks," said Jessica harshly. "Speculative stocks. It got her like a fever. Caroline has always been susceptible. So you have no money at all left, Caroline? Is that why you were so anxious to sell the house? You surely haven't been fool enough to buy on margin."

Caroline's distraught hands confessed what her trembling lip could not speak.

David was suddenly standing beside her, his hand on her thin shoulder.

"Don't worry, Aunt Carrie," he said. "It'll be all right. You've got enough in trust to take care of you."

Over Caroline's head he looked at Jessica. The look or the tenderness in his voice when he spoke to Caroline seemed to infuriate Jessica, and she arose amid a rustling of silk and stood there tall and rigid, facing him.

"Why don't you offer to take care of her yourself, David?" she said gratingly.

David was white, and his eyes brilliant with pain, but he replied steadily: "You know why, Aunt Jessica. And you know why she gambled, too. We were both trying to make enough money to get away. To get away from this house. To get away from—" He stopped.

"From what, David?" said Jessica.

"From Marie," said David desperately. "And from you."

Jessica did not move. Her face did not change. There was only a queer luminous flash in her eyes. After a horribly long moment she said:

"I loved you far better than Marie loved you, David. You feared her. I intended to give you money when you came to me. You *had* to come to me. You would have begged me for help—me, Jessica! Why did you or Caroline kill Marie? Was it because she refused to sell the house? I know why she refused. She pretended that it was sentiment; that she, the adopted daughter, was more a Wray than any of us. But it wasn't that, really. She hated us. And we wanted to sell. That is, you and Caroline wanted to sell for your own selfish interests. I—it made no difference to me."

Caroline sobbed and cried jerkily:

"But you did care, Jessica. You wanted the money. You—you love money." There was a strangely incredulous wail in her thin voice. "*Money—money!* Not the things it will buy. Not the freedom it might give you. But money—bonds, mortgages, gold. You love money first, Jessica, and you—"

"*Caroline,*" said Jessica in a terrible voice. Caroline babbled and sobbed into silence. "Caroline, you are not responsible. You forget that there are strangers here. That Marie has been murdered. Try to collect yourself. At once. You are making a disgusting exhibition."

All three looked at Susan.

And as suddenly as they had been diverted from each other they were, for a moment, united in their feeling against Susan. She was the intruder, the instrument of the police, placed there by the law for the purpose of discovering evidence.

Their eyes were not pleasant.

Susan smoothed back her hair, and she was acutely aware of the small telegram of warning that ran along her nerves. One of them had murdered. She turned to Caroline.

"Then were you afraid that Marie would discover what you had been doing with your money?" she asked gently.

Caroline blinked and was immediately ready to reply, her momentary feeling against Susan disseminated by the small touch of kindness in Susan's manner.

"No," she said in a confidential way. "That wasn't what I was afraid of."

"Then was there something unusual about the house? Something that troubled you?"

"Oh, yes, yes," said Caroline.

"What was it?" asked Susan, scarcely daring to breathe. If only Jessica would remain silent for another moment.

But Caroline was fluttering again.

"I don't know. I don't know. You see, it was all so queer, Marie holding out against us all, and we all—except Jessica sometimes—obeyed Marie. We've always obeyed Marie. Everything in the house has done that. Even Spider—the—the monkey, you know."

Susan permitted her eyes to flicker toward Jessica. She stood immovable, watching David. Susan could not interpret that dark look, and she did not try. Instead she leaned over to Caroline, took her fluttering, ineffectual hands, and said, still gently: "Tell me exactly why you telephoned to Jim Byrne. What was it that happened in the morning—or maybe the night before—that made you afraid?"

"How did you know?" said Caroline. "It happened that night."

"What was it?" said Susan so softly that it was scarcely more than a whisper.

But Caroline quite suddenly swerved.

"I wasn't afraid of Marie," she said. "But everyone obeyed Marie. Even the house always seemed more Marie's house than—than Jessica's. But I didn't kill Marie."

"Tell me," repeated Susan. "What happened last night that was—queer?"

"Caroline," said Jessica harshly, dragging herself back from some deep brooding gulf, "you've said enough."

Susan ignored her and held Caroline's feverishly bright eyes with her own. "*Tell me*—"

"It was—Marie—" gasped Caroline.

"Marie—what did she do?" said Susan.

"She didn't do anything," said Caroline. "It was what she said. No, it wasn't that exactly. It was—"

"If you insist upon talking, Caroline, you might at least try to be intelligible," said Jessica coldly.

Could she get Jessica out of the room? thought Susan; probably not. And it was all too obvious that she was standing by, permitting Caroline to talk only so long as Caroline said nothing that she, Jessica, did not want her to say. Susan said quietly: "Did you hear Marie speak?"

"Yes, that was just it," cried Caroline eagerly. "And it was so very queer. That is, of course we—that is, I—have often thought that Marie must be about the house much more than she pretended to be, in order to know all the things she knew. That is, she always knew everything that happened in the house. It—sometimes it was queer, you know, because it was like—like magic or something. It was quite," said Caroline with an unexpected burst of imagery, "as if she had one of those astral-body things, and it walked all around the house while Marie just sat there in her room."

"Astral—body—things," said Jessica deliberately. Caroline crimsoned and Jessica's hands gestured outward as much as to say: "You see for yourself what a state she's in."

The old room was silent again. Susan's heart was pounding, and again those small tocsins of warning were sounding in some subconscious realm. All those forces were silently, invisibly combating—struggling against each other. And somewhere amid them was the truth—quite tangible—altogether real.

"But the astral body," said Caroline suddenly into the silence, "couldn't have talked. And I heard Marie speak. She was in Jessica's room, and the door was closed, and I heard her talking to Jessica. And then—that's what's queer—I went straight on past the door and into Marie's room, and there was Marie sitting there. Isn't it queer?"

"Why were you frightened?"

"Because—because—" Caroline's hands twisted together. "I don't know why. Except that I had a—a feeling."

"Nonsense." Jessica laughed. There was again the luminous flash in her shadowed eyes, and she spoke more rapidly than usual. "You see, Susan Dare, how nonsensical all this is. How utterly fantastic!"

"There was Marie," said Caroline. "She was talking to you."

Jessica's silks rustled, and she walked rigidly and quickly to Caroline and leaned over so that she could grip Caroline's shoulder and force Caroline to meet her eyes. David tried to intervene, and she brushed him away and said hoarsely:

"Caroline, you poor little fool. You thought you'd get this young woman here and try to establish your innocence of the crime. All this talk is sheer nonsense. You are cunning after the way of fools such as you. Tell me this, Caroline—" She paused long enough to take a great gasp of breath. She was more powerful, more invincible than Susan had seen her. "Tell me. Where was David when the revolver was fired?"

Caroline was shrinking backward. David said quickly: "She'll say anything to protect me. She'll say anything, and you—"

"Be quiet, David. Caroline, answer me."

"He was at the door of his room," said Caroline.

For a long moment Jessica waited. Then with terrible deliberation she relaxed her grip and straightened and looked slowly from one to the other.

"You've as good as confessed, Carrie," she said. "There was no one else. You admit that it was not David. Why did you kill her, Carrie?"

"She didn't kill her!" David was between the two women, his face white and his eyes blazing. "It was you, Jessica. You—"

"*David! Stop!*" The two sharp exclamations were like lashes. "I was here in this room when the shot was fired. I didn't kill

Marie. I couldn't have killed her. You know that. Come, Caroline."

She put her gray hand upon Caroline's shoulder. Caroline, as if mesmerized by that touch, arose, and Jessica turned to the doorway. No one moved as the two women crossed the room. Jim Byrne glanced at Susan unrevealingly and then, at Jessica's imperious gesture, opened the door. Susan was vaguely aware that there were men in the hall outside, but she was held as if enchanted by the extraordinary scene she was witnessing.

No one moved, and there was no sound save the rustle of Jessica's silks while she led Caroline to the stairway. At the bottom step Jessica turned, and there was suddenly something less harsh in her face; it was for an instant almost kind, and there was a queer sort of tenderness in the pressure of her hand upon Caroline's shrinking shoulder.

But that hand was nevertheless compelling.

"Go upstairs," she said to Caroline, in a voice loud enough so that they all heard. "Go upstairs and do what is necessary. There's enough veronal on my dresser. We'll give you time."

She turned as if to barricade the stairway with her own rigid body and looked slowly and defiantly around her. "I'll *make them* give you time, Carrie. *Go on.*"

There was the complete and utter silence of sheer horror. And in that silence something small and gray and quick flashed down from the curtain and up the stairs.

"Holy Mother," cried someone. "What was that?"

And David sprang forward.

"You can't do that—you can't do that! Caroline, don't move—" Susan knew that he was thrusting himself between Jessica and Caroline, that there was sudden confusion. But she was mainly aware of something that had clicked in her own mind.

Somehow she got through the confusion in the hall to Lieutenant Mohrn, and Jim Byrne was at her side. Both of them listened to the brief words she said; Lieutenant Mohrn ran rapidly upstairs, and Jim disappeared toward the dining room.

Jim was back first. He pulled Susan to one side.

"You are right," he said. "The cook and the houseman both say that Marie was very strict about the monkey and that the monkey always obeyed her. But what do you mean?"

"I'm not sure, Jim. But I've just told Lieutenant Mohrn that I think there should be a bullet hole somewhere upstairs. It was made by the second bullet. It is in the ceiling, perhaps—or wall. I think it's in Jessica's room."

Lieutenant Mohrn was coming down the stairway. He reached the bottom of the stairs and looked wearily and a bit sadly at the group there. At Caroline crumpled against the wall. At David white and taut. At Jessica, a rigid figure of hatred. Then he sighed and looked at the policeman nearest him and nodded.

"Will you go into the drawing room, please?" he asked Susan. "And you, Jim."

The doors slid together and, still wearily, Lieutenant Mohrn pulled out from his pocket a revolver, a long cord, a piece of cotton, and a small alarm clock.

"They were all there hidden in the newel post at the top of the stairway. The carved top was loose as you remembered it, Miss Dare. And there's two shots gone from the revolver, and there's a bullet hole in the wall of Jessica's bedroom. How did you know it was Jessica, Miss Dare?"

"It was the monkey," said Susan. Her voice sounded unnatural in her own ears, terribly tired, terribly sad. "It was the monkey all the time. You see, he was sitting there, stealing candy *right beside Marie's chair.* He would have been afraid to do that if he had not known she was dead. And when Jessica entered the room he fled. When I thought of that, the whole thing fell together: the hot house, obviously to keep Marie's body warm and confuse the time of death; everyone out of the house to permit Jessica to do murder; then this thing you've found—"

"It's simple, of course," said Lieutenant Mohrn. "The cord fastened tight between the alarm lever and the trigger—the bit of cotton to pad the alarm. The clock is set for ten minutes after five. When did she hide it in the newel post?"

"When I went down to telephone the police, I suppose, and David and Caroline were in Marie's room—I want to go home," said Susan wearily.

"Look here," said Jim Byrne. "This sounds all right, Susan, but, remember, Marie couldn't have been dead then. You heard her talk."

"I had never heard her speak before. And I heard the flat, dead tone of a person who has been deaf a long time. It was Caroline who actually solved the thing. And Jessica knew it. She knew it and at once tried to fasten the blame upon Caroline—to compel her to commit suicide."

"What did Caroline say?" Lieutenant Mohrn was very patient.

"She said that she'd heard Marie speaking with Jessica in Jessica's room behind a closed door. And that she'd gone straight on past that door to Marie's room and found Marie sitting there. Caroline was confused, frightened, talked of astral bodies. Naturally, we knew that Jessica was—rehearsing—her imitation of Marie's way of speaking."

"Premeditated," said Jim. "Planned to the last detail. And your coming merely gave her the opportunity. You were to provide the alibi, Susan."

Susan shivered.

"That was the trouble. She was sitting directly opposite me when the shot was fired upstairs. Yet she was the only person who hated Marie sufficiently to—murder her. It wasn't money. It was hatred. Growing for years in this horrible house, nourished by jealousy over David, brought to a climax that was inevitable." Susan smoothed her hair. "Please may I go?"

"Then Marie was dead when you entered the house?"

"Yes. Propped up by pillows. I—I saw the whole thing, you know. Saw Jessica approach her and talk, heard the reply—and how was I to know it was Jessica speaking and not Marie? Then Jessica bent and did something to her cushions, pulled them away, I suppose, so the body was no longer erect. And she turned at once and was between me and Marie all the way to the door so I could not see Marie, then, at all. (I couldn't see Marie very well at any time, because she was in the shadow.) And when David and Caroline came upstairs, Jessica warned both of them that Marie was reading. I suppose she knew that they were only too glad to be relieved of the necessity to speak to Marie." Susan shivered again and smoothed back her hair and felt dreadfully that she might cry. "It's a t-terrible house," she said indecisively, and Jim Byrne said hurriedly:

"She can go now, can't she? I've got a car out here. She doesn't have to see them again."

The air was cold and fresh and the sky very black before dawn, and the pavements glistened.

They swerved onto the Drive and stopped for a red light, and

Jim turned to her as they waited. Through the dusk in the car she could feel his scrutiny.

"I didn't expect anything like this," he said gravely. "Will you forgive me?"

"Next time," said Susan in a small clear voice, "I'll not get scared."

"Next time!" said Jim derisively. "There won't be a next time! I was the one that was scared. I had my finger on the trigger of a revolver all the time you were talking to them. No, indeedy, there won't be a next time—not if I can help it!"

THE MOMENT OF DECISION
Stanley Ellin

"The Moment of Decision" was adapted for a sixty-minute episode of *The United States Steel Hour* in 1961. The lead actor was a song-and-dance man who took the opportunity to show what he could do as a purely dramatic actor. It seemed to work out well as Fred Astair went on to star in many other motion pictures and television shows.

The three-time Edgar Allan Poe Award winner and the Mystery Writers of America's Grand Master honoree in 1981, Stanley Ellin was one of America's greatest short story writers of the twentieth century. His first story, "The Specialty of the House" (1948), went on to become a relentlessly anthologized classic of crime fiction and was adapted for an episode of the television series, *Alfred Hitchcock Presents*. Six of his stories were nominated for Edgars, two of which won: "The House Party" (1954) and "The Blessington Method" (1956); his superb novel, *The Eighth Circle* (1958), also won an Edgar.

Other Ellin works have been produced as feature films. *Dreadful Summit* (1948), his first novel, was filmed by Joseph

Losey as *The Big Night* (1951), starring John Drew Barrymore, Preston Foster, and Joan Lorring. A short story, "The Best of Everything" (1952) became *Nothing but the Best* (1964), directed by Clive Donner and starring Alan Bates, Denholm Elliott, and Harry Andrews. *House of Cards* (1967) was filmed with the same title in 1968, directed by John Guillerman and starring George Peppard, Inger Stevens, and Orson Welles.

"The Moment of Decision" was originally published in the March 1955 issue of *Ellery Queen's Mystery Magazine*; it was first collected in *Mystery Stories* (New York, Simon & Schuster, 1956).

The Moment of Decision

Stanley Ellin

HUGH LOZIER was the exception to the rule that people who are completely sure of themselves cannot be likable. We have all met the sure ones, of course—those controlled but penetrating voices which cut through all others in a discussion, those hard forefingers jabbing home opinions on your chest, those living Final Words on all issues—and I imagine we all share the same amalgam of dislike and envy for them. Dislike, because no one likes to be shouted down or prodded in the chest, and envy, because everyone wishes he himself were so rich in self-assurance that he could do the shouting down and prodding.

For myself, since my work took me regularly to certain places in this atomic world where the only state was confusion and the only steady employment that of splitting political hairs, I found absolute judgments harder and harder to come by. Hugh once observed of this that it was a good thing my superiors in the department were not cut of the same cloth, because God knows what would happen to the country then. I didn't relish that, but—and there was my curse again—I had to grant him his right to say it.

Despite this, and despite the fact that Hugh was my brother-in-law—a curious relationship when you come to think of it—I liked him immensely, just as everyone else did who knew him. He was a big, good-looking man, with clear blue eyes in a ruddy face, and with a quick, outgoing nature eager to appreciate whatever you had to offer. He was overwhelmingly generous, and his generosity was of that rare and excellent kind which makes you feel as if you are doing the donor a favor by accepting it.

I wouldn't say he had any great sense of humor, but plain good humor can sometimes be an adequate substitute for that, and in Hugh's case it was. His stormy side was largely reserved for those times when he thought you might have needed his help in something and failed to call on him for it. Which meant that ten minutes after Hugh had met you and liked you, you were expected to ask him for anything he might be able to offer. A month or so after he married my sister Elizabeth she mentioned to him my avid interest in a fine Copley he had hanging in his gallery at Hilltop, and I can still vividly recall my horror when it suddenly arrived, heavily crated and with his gift card attached, at my barren room-and-a-half. It took considerable effort, but I finally managed to return it to him by forgoing the argument that the picture was undoubtedly worth more than the entire building in which I lived and by complaining that it simply didn't show to advantage on my wall. I think he suspected I was lying, but being Hugh he would never dream of charging me with that in so many words.

Of course, Hilltop and the two hundred years of Lozier tradition that went into it did much to shape Hugh this way. The first Loziers had carved the estate from the heights overlooking the river, had worked hard and flourished exceedingly; its successive generations had invested their income so wisely that money and position eventually erected a towering wall between Hilltop and the world outside. Truth to tell, Hugh was very much a man of the eighteenth century who somehow found himself in the twentieth, and simply made the best of it.

Hilltop itself was almost a replica of the celebrated, but long untenanted, Dane house nearby, and was striking enough to open anybody's eyes at a glance. The house was weathered stone, graceful despite its bulk, and the vast lawns reaching to the river's edge were tended with such fanatic devotion over the years that they had become carpets of purest green which magically changed luster under any breeze. Gardens ranged from the other side of the house down to the groves which half hid the stables and outbuildings, and past the far side of the groves ran the narrow road which led to town. The road was a courtesy road, each estate holder along it maintaining his share, and I think it safe to say that for all the crushed rock he laid in it Hugh made less use of it by far than any of his neighbors.

Hugh's life was bound up in Hilltop; he could be made to leave it only by dire necessity; and if you did meet him away from it you were made acutely aware that he was counting off the minutes until he could return. And if you weren't wary you would more than likely find yourself going along with him when he did return, and totally unable to tear yourself away from the place while the precious weeks rolled by. I know. I believe I spent more time at Hilltop than at my own apartment after my sister brought Hugh into the family.

At one time I wondered how Elizabeth took to this marriage, considering that before she met Hugh she had been as restless and flighty as she was pretty. When I put the question to her directly, she said, "It's wonderful, darling. Just as wonderful as I knew it would be when I first met him."

It turned out that their first meeting had taken place at an art exhibition, a showing of some ultramodern stuff, and she had been intently studying one of the more bewildering concoctions on display when she became aware of this tall, good-looking man staring at her. And, as she put it, she had been about to set him properly in his place when he said abruptly, "Are you admiring that?"

This was so unlike what she had expected that she was taken completely aback. "I don't know," she said weakly. "Am I supposed to?"

"No," said the stranger, "it's damned nonsense. Come along now, and I'll show you something which isn't a waste of time."

"And," Elizabeth said to me, "I came along like a pup at his heels, while he marched up and down and told me what was good and what was bad, and in a good loud voice, too, so that we collected quite a crowd along the way. Can you picture it, darling?"

"Yes," I said, "I can." By now I had shared similar occasions with Hugh, and learned at firsthand that nothing could dent his cast-iron assurance.

"Well," Elizabeth went on, "I must admit that at first I was a little put off, but then I began to see that he knew exactly what he was talking about, and that he was terribly sincere. Not a bit self-conscious about anything, but just eager for me to understand things the way he did. It's the same way with everything. Everybody else in the world is always fumbling and bumbling over deciding anything—what to order for dinner, or how to manage his job, or whom to vote for—but Hugh always *knows*. It's *not* knowing that makes for all those nerves and complexes and things you hear about, isn't that so? Well, I'll take Hugh, thank you, and leave everyone else to the psychiatrists."

So there it was. An Eden with flawless lawns and no awful nerves and complexes, and not even the glimmer of a serpent in the offing. That is, not a glimmer until the day Raymond made his entrance on the scene.

We were out on the terrace that day, Hugh and Elizabeth and I, slowly being melted into a sort of liquid torpor by the August sunshine, and all of us too far gone to make even a pretence at talk. I lay there with a linen cap over my face, listening to the summer noises around me and being perfectly happy.

There was the low, steady hiss of the breeze through the aspens nearby, the plash and drip of oars on the river below, and now and then the melancholy *tink-tunk* of a sheep bell from one of the flock on the lawn. The flock was a fancy of Hugh's. He swore that nothing was better for a lawn than a few sheep grazing on it, and every summer five or six fat and sleepy ewes were turned out on the grass to serve this purpose and to add a pleasantly pastoral note to the view.

My first warning of something amiss came from the sheep—from the sudden sound of their bells clanging wildly and then baa-ing which suggested an assault by a whole pack of wolves. I heard Hugh say "Damn!" loudly and angrily, and I opened my eyes to see something more incongruous than wolves. It was a large black poodle in the full glory of a clownish haircut, a bright-red collar, and an ecstasy of high spirits as he chased the frightened sheep around the lawn. It was clear the poodle had no intention of hurting them—he probably found them the most wonderful playmates imaginable—but it was just as clear that the panicky ewes didn't understand this, and would very likely end up in the river before the fun was over.

In the bare second it took me to see all this, Hugh had already leaped the low terrace wall and was among the sheep, herding them away from the water's edge, and shouting commands at the dog who had different ideas.

"Down, boy!" he yelled. "Down!" And then as he would to one of his own hounds, he sternly commanded, "Heel!"

He would have done better, I thought, to have picked up a stick or stone and made a threatening gesture, since the poodle paid no attention whatever to Hugh's words. Instead, continuing to bark happily, the poodle made for the sheep again, this time with Hugh in futile pursuit. An instant later the dog was frozen into immobility by a voice from among the aspens near the edge of the lawn.

"*Assieds!*" the voice called breathlessly. "*Assieds-toi!*"

Then the man appeared, a small, dapper figure trotting across the grass. Hugh stood waiting, his face darkening as we watched.

Elizabeth squeezed my arm. "Let's get down there," she whispered. "Hugh doesn't like being made a fool of."

We got there in time to hear Hugh open his big guns. "Any man," he was saying, "who doesn't know how to train an animal to its place shouldn't own one."

The man's face was all polite attention. It was a good face, thin and intelligent, and webbed with tiny lines at the corners of the eyes. There was also something behind those eyes that couldn't quite be masked. A gentle mockery. A glint of wry perception turned on the world like a camera lens. It was nothing anyone like Hugh would have noticed, but it was there all the same, and I found myself warming to it on the spot. There was also something tantalizingly familiar about the newcomer's face, his high forehead, and his thinning gray hair, but as much as I dug into my memory during Hugh's long and solemn lecture I couldn't come up with an answer. The lecture ended with a few remarks on the best methods of dog training, and by then it was clear that Hugh was working himself into a mood of forgiveness.

"As long as there's no harm done—" he said.

The man nodded soberly. "Still, to get off on the wrong foot with one's new neighbors—"

Hugh looked startled. "Neighbors?" he said almost rudely. "You mean that you live around here?"

The man waved toward the aspens. "On the other side of those woods."

"The *Dane* house?" The Dane house was almost as sacred to Hugh as Hilltop, and he had once explained to me that if he were ever offered a chance to buy the place he would snap it up. His tone now was not so much wounded as incredulous. "I don't believe it!" he exclaimed.

"Oh, yes," the man assured him, "the Dane house. I performed there at a party many years ago, and always hoped that someday I might own it."

It was the word *performed* that gave me my clue—that and the accent barely perceptible under the precise English. He had been born and raised in Marseilles—that would explain the accent—and long before my time he had already become a legend.

"You're Raymond, aren't you?" I said. "Charles Raymond."

"I prefer Raymond alone." He smiled in deprecation of his own small vanity. "And I am flattered that you recognize me."

I don't believe he really was. Raymond the Magician, Raymond the Great would, if anything, expect to be recognized wherever he went. As the master of sleight of hand who had paled Thurston's star, as the escape artist who had almost outshone Houdini, Raymond would not be inclined to underestimate himself.

He had started with the standard box of tricks which makes up the repertoire of most professional magicians; he had gone far beyond that to those feats of escape which, I suppose, are known to us all by now. The lead casket sealed under a foot of lake ice, the welded-steel strait jackets, the vaults of the Bank of England, the exquisite suicide knot which nooses throat and doubles legs together so that the motion of a leg draws the noose tighter around the throat—all these Raymond had known and escaped from. And then at the pinnacle of fame he had dropped from sight and his name had become relegated to the past.

When I asked him why, he shrugged.

"A man works for money or for the love of his work. If he has all the wealth he needs and has no more love for his work, why go on?"

"But to give up a great career—" I protested.

"It was enough to know that the house was waiting here."

"You mean," Elizabeth said, "that you never intended to live any place but here?"

"Never—not once in all these years." He laid a finger along his nose and winked broadly at us. "Of course, I made no secret of this to the Dane estate, and when the time came to sell I was the first and only one approached."

"You don't give up an idea easily," Hugh said in an edged voice.

Raymond laughed. "Idea? It became an obsession really. Over the years I traveled to many parts of the world, but no matter how fine the place, I knew it could not be as fine as that house on the edge of the woods there, with the river at its feet and the hills beyond. Someday, I would tell myself, when my travels are done I will come here, and, like Candide, cultivate my garden."

He ran his hand abstractedly over the poodle's head and looked around with an air of great satisfaction. "And now," he said, "here I am."

Here he was, indeed, and it quickly became clear that his arrival was working a change on Hilltop. Or, since Hilltop was so completely a reflection of Hugh, it was clear that a change was being worked on Hugh. He became irritable and restless, and more aggressively sure of himself than ever. The warmth and good nature were still there—they were as much part of him as his arrogance, but he now had to work a little harder at them. He reminded me of a man who is bothered by a speck in the eye, but can't find it, and must get along with it as best he can.

Raymond, of course, was the speck, and I got the impression at times that he rather enjoyed the role. It would have been easy enough for him to stay close to his own house and cultivate his garden, or paste up his album, or whatever retired performers do, but he evidently found that impossible. He had a way of drifting over to Hilltop at odd times, just as Hugh was led to find his way to the Dane house and spend long and troublesome sessions there.

Both of them must have known that they were so badly suited to each other that the easy and logical solution would have been to stay apart. But they had the affinity of negative and positive forces, and when they were in a room together the crackling of the antagonistic current between them was so strong you could almost see it in the air.

Any subject became a point of contention for them, and they would duel over it bitterly: Hugh armored and weaponed by his massive assurance, Raymond flicking away with a rapier, trying to find a chink in the armor. I think that what annoyed Raymond most was the discovery that there was no chink in the armor. As someone with an obvious passion for searching out all sides to all questions and for going deep into motives and causes, he was continually being outraged by Hugh's single-minded way of laying down the law.

He didn't hesitate to let Hugh know that. "You are positively medieval," he said. "And of all things men should have learned since that time, the biggest is that there are no easy answers, no solutions one can give with a snap of the fingers. I can only hope for you that someday you may be faced with the perfect dilemma, the unanswerable question. You would find that a revelation. You would learn more in that minute than you dreamed possible."

And Hugh did not make matters any better when he coldly answered, "And *I* say, that for any man with a brain and the courage to use it there is no such thing as a perfect dilemma."

It may be that this was the sort of episode that led to the trouble that followed, or it may be that Raymond acted out of the most innocent and aesthetic motives possible. But, whatever the motives, the results were inevitable and dangerous.

They grew from the project Raymond outlined for us in great detail one afternoon. Now that he was living in the Dane house he had discovered that it was too big, too overwhelming. "Like a museum," he explained. "I find myself wandering through it like a lost soul through endless galleries."

The grounds also needed landscaping. The ancient trees were handsome, but, as Raymond put it, there were just too many of them. "Literally," he said, "I cannot see the river for the trees, and I am one devoted to the sight of running water."

Altogether there would be drastic changes. Two wings of the house would come down, the trees would be cleared away to make a broad aisle to the water, the whole place would be enlivened. It would no longer be a museum, but the perfect home he had envisioned over the years.

At the start of this recitative Hugh was slouched comfortably in his chair. Then as Raymond drew the vivid picture of what was to be, Hugh sat up straighter and straighter until he was as rigid as a trooper in the saddle. His lips compressed. His face became blood-red. His hands clenched and unclenched in a slow deadly rhythm. Only a miracle was restraining him from an open outburst, and it was not the kind of miracle to last. I saw from Elizabeth's expression that she understood this, too, but was as helpless as I to do anything about it. And when Raymond, after painting the last glowing strokes of his description, said complacently, "Well, now, what do you think?" there was no holding Hugh.

He leaned forward with deliberation and said, "Do you really want to know what I think?"

"Now, Hugh," Elizabeth said in alarm. "Please, Hugh—"

He brushed that aside.

"Do you really want to know?" he demanded of Raymond.

Raymond frowned. "Of course."

"Then I'll tell you," Hugh said. He took a deep breath. "I think that nobody but a damned iconoclast could even conceive the atrocity you're proposing. I think you're one of those people who take pleasure in smashing apart anything that's stamped with tradition or stability. You'd kick the props from under the whole world if you could!"

"I beg your pardon," Raymond said. He was very pale and angry. "But I think you are confusing change with destruction. Surely, you must comprehend that I do not intend to destroy anything, but only wish to make some necessary changes."

"Necessary?" Hugh gibed. "Rooting up a fine stand of trees that's been there for centuries? Ripping apart a house that's as solid as a rock? *I* call it wanton destruction."

"I'm afraid I do not understand. To refresh a scene, to reshape it—"

"I have no intention of arguing," Hugh cut in. "I'm telling you straight out that you don't have the right to tamper with that property!"

They were on their feet now, facing each other truculently, and the only thing that kept me from being really frightened was the conviction that Hugh would not become violent, and that Raymond was far too level-headed to lose his temper. Then the threatening moment was magically past. Raymond's lips suddenly quirked in amusement, and he studied Hugh with courteous interest.

"I see," he said. "I was quite stupid not to have understood at once. This property, which, I remarked, was a little too much like a museum, is to remain that way, and I am to be its custodian. A caretaker of the past, one might say, a curator of its relics."

He shook his head smilingly. "But I am afraid I am not quite suited to that role. I lift my hat to the past, it is true, but I prefer to court the present. For that reason I will go ahead with my plans, and hope they do not make an obstacle to our friendship."

I remember thinking, when I left next day for the city and a long, hot week at my desk, that Raymond had carried off the affair very nicely, and that, thank God, it had gone no further than it did. So I was completely unprepared for Elizabeth's call at the end of the week.

It was awful, she said. It was the business of Hugh and Raymond and the Dane house, but worse than ever. She was counting on my coming down to Hilltop the next day; there couldn't be any question about that. She had planned a way of clearing up the whole thing, but I simply had to be there to back her up. After all, I was one of the few people Hugh would listen to, and she was depending on me.

"Depending on me for what?" I said. I didn't like the sound of it. "And as for Hugh listening to me, Elizabeth, isn't that stretching it a good deal? I can't see him wanting my advice on his personal affairs."

"If you're going to be touchy about it—"

"I'm *not* touchy about it," I retorted. "I just don't like getting mixed up in this thing. Hugh's quite capable of taking care of himself."

"Maybe too capable."

"And what does that mean?"

"Oh, I can't explain now," she wailed. "I'll tell you everything tomorrow. And, darling, if you have any brotherly feelings you'll be here on the morning train. Believe me, it's serious."

I arrived on the morning train in a bad state. My imagination is one of the overactive kind that can build a cosmic disaster out of very little material, and by the time I arrived at the house I was prepared for almost anything.

But, on the surface, at least, all was serene. Hugh greeted me warmly, Elizabeth was her cheerful self, and we had an amiable lunch and a long talk which never came near the subject of Raymond or the Dane house. I said nothing about Elizabeth's phone call, but thought of it with a steadily growing sense of outrage until I was alone with her.

"Now," I said, "I'd like an explanation of all this mystery. The Lord knows what I expected to find out here, but it certainly wasn't anything I've seen so far. And I'd like some accounting for the bad time you've given me since that call."

"All right," she said grimly, "and that's what you'll get. Come along."

She led the way on a long walk through the gardens and past the stables and outbuildings. Near the private road which lay beyond the last grove of trees she suddenly said, "When the car drove you up to the house didn't you notice anything strange about this road?"

"No, I didn't."

"I suppose not. The driveway to the house turns off too far away from here. But now you'll have a chance to see for yourself."

I did see for myself. A chair was set squarely in the middle of the road and on the chair sat a stout man placidly reading a magazine. I recognized the man at once: he was one of Hugh's stable hands, and he had the patient look of someone who has been sitting for a long time and expects to sit a good deal longer. It took me only a second to realize what he was there for, but Elizabeth wasn't leaving anything to my deductive powers. When we walked over to him, the man stood up and grinned at us.

"William," Elizabeth said, "would you mind telling my brother what instructions Mr. Lozier gave you?"

"Sure," the man said cheerfully. "Mr. Lozier told us there was always supposed to be one of us sitting right here, and any truck we saw that might be carrying construction stuff or such-like for the Dane house was to be stopped and turned back. All we had to do was tell them it's private property and they were trespassing. If they laid a finger on us we just call in the police. That's the whole thing."

"Have you turned back any trucks?" Elizabeth asked for my benefit.

The man looked surprised. "Why, you know that, Mrs. Lozier," he said. "There was a couple of them the first day we were out here, and that was all. There wasn't any fuss either," he explained to me. "None of those drivers wants to monkey with trespass."

When we were away from the road again I clapped my hand to my forehead. "It's incredible!" I said. "Hugh must know he can't get away with this. That road is the only one to the Dane place, and it's been in public use so long that it isn't even a private thoroughfare anymore!"

Elizabeth nodded. "And that's exactly what Raymond told Hugh a few days back. He came over here in a fury, and they had quite an argument about it. And when Raymond said something about hauling Hugh off to court, Hugh answered that he'd be glad to spend the rest of his life in litigation over this business. But that wasn't the worst of it. The last thing Raymond said was that Hugh ought to know that force only invites force, and ever since then I've been expecting a war to break out here any minute. Don't you see? That man blocking the road is a constant provocation, and it scares me."

I could understand that. And the more I considered the matter, the more dangerous it looked.

"But I have a plan," Elizabeth said eagerly, "and that's why I wanted you here. I'm having a dinner party tonight, a very small, informal dinner party. It's to be a sort of peace conference. You'll be there, and Dr. Wynant—Hugh likes you both a great deal—and," she hesitated, "Raymond."

"No!" I said. "You mean he's actually coming?"

"I went over to see him yesterday and we had a long talk. I explained everything to him—about neighbors being able to sit down and come to an understanding, and about brotherly love and—oh, it must have sounded dreadfully inspirational and sticky, but it worked. He said he would be there."

I had a foreboding. "Does Hugh know about this?"

"About the dinner? Yes."

"I mean, about Raymond's being here."

"No, he doesn't." And then when she saw me looking hard at her, she burst out defiantly with, "Well, *something* had to be done, and I did it, that's all! Isn't it better than just sitting and waiting for God knows what?"

Until we were all seated around the dining room table that evening I might have conceded the point. Hugh had been visibly shocked by Raymond's arrival, but then, apart from a sidelong glance at Elizabeth which had volumes written in it, he managed to conceal his feelings well enough. He had made the introductions gracefully, kept up his end of the conversation and, all in all, did a creditable job of playing host.

Ironically, it was the presence of Dr. Wynant which made even this much of a triumph possible for Elizabeth, and which then turned it into disaster. The doctor was an eminent surgeon, stocky and gray-haired, with an abrupt, positive way about him. Despite his own position in the world he seemed pleased as a schoolboy to meet Raymond, and in no time at all they were as thick as thieves.

It was when Hugh discovered during dinner that nearly all attention was fixed on Raymond and very little on himself that the mantle of good host started to slip, and the fatal flaws in Elizabeth's plan showed through. There are people who enjoy entertaining lions and who take pleasure in reflected glory, but Hugh was not one of them. Besides, he regarded the doctor as one of his closest friends, and I have noticed that it is the most assured of men who can be the most jealous of their friendships. And when a prized friendship is being impinged on by the man one loathes more than anything else in the world—! All in all, by simply imagining myself in Hugh's place and looking across the table at Raymond who was gaily and unconcernedly holding forth, I was prepared for the worst.

The opportunity for it came to Hugh when Raymond was deep in a discussion of the devices used in effecting escapes. They were innumerable, he said. Almost anything one could seize on would serve as such a device. A wire, a scrap of metal, even a bit of paper—at one time or another he had used them all.

"But of them all," he said with a sudden solemnity, "there is only one I would stake my life on. Strange, it is one you cannot see, cannot hold in your hand—in fact, for many people it does not even exist. Yet it is the one I have used most often and which has never failed me."

The doctor leaned forward, his eyes bright with interest. "And it is—?"

"It is a knowledge of people, my friend. Or, as it may be put, a knowledge of human nature. To me it is as vital an instrument as the scalpel is to you."

"Oh?" said Hugh, and his voice was so sharp that all eyes were instantly turned on him. "You make sleight of hand sound like a department of psychology."

"Perhaps," Raymond said, and I saw he was watching Hugh

now, gauging him. "You see there is no great mystery in the matter. My profession—my art, as I like to think of it—is no more than the art of misdirection, and I am but one of its many practitioners."

"I wouldn't say there were many escape artists around nowadays," the doctor remarked.

"True," Raymond said, "but you will observe I referred to the art of misdirection. The escape artist, the master of legerdemain, these are a handful who practice the most exotic form of that art. But what of those who engage in the work of politics, of advertising, of salesman-ship?" He laid his finger along his nose in the familiar gesture, and winked. "I am afraid they have all made my art their business."

The doctor smiled. "Since you haven't dragged medicine into it I'm willing to go along with you," he said. "But what I want to know is, exactly how does this knowledge of human nature work in your profession?"

"In this way," Raymond said. "One must judge a person carefully. Then, if he finds in that person certain weaknesses he can state a false premise and it will be accepted without question. Once the false premise is swallowed, the rest is easy. The victim will then see only what the magician wants him to see, or will give his vote to that politician, or will buy merchandise because of that advertising." He shrugged. "And that is all there is to it."

"Is it?" Hugh said. "But what happens when you're with people who have some intelligence and won't swallow your false premise? How do you do your tricks then? Or do you keep them on the same level as selling beads to the savages?"

"Now that's uncalled for, Hugh," the doctor said. "The man's expressing his ideas. No reason to make an issue of them."

"Maybe there is," Hugh said, his eyes fixed on Raymond. "I

have found he's full of interesting ideas. I was wondering how far he'd want to go in backing them up."

Raymond touched the napkin to his lips with a precise little flick, and then laid it carefully on the table before him. "In short," he said, addressing himself to Hugh, "you want a small demonstration of my art."

"It depends," Hugh said. "I don't want any trick cigarette cases or rabbits out of hats or any damn nonsense like that. I'd like to see something good."

"Something good," echoed Raymond reflectively. He looked around the room, studied it, and then turned to Hugh, pointing toward the huge oak door which was closed between the dining room and the living room, where we had gathered before dinner.

"That door is not locked, is it?"

"No," Hugh said, "it isn't. It hasn't been locked for years."

"But there is a key to it?"

Hugh pulled out his key chain, and with an effort detached a heavy, old-fashioned key. "Yes, it's the same one we use for the butler's pantry." He was becoming interested despite himself.

"Good. No, do not give it to me. Give it to the doctor. You have faith in the doctor's honor, I am sure?"

"Yes," said Hugh dryly, "I have."

"Very well. Now, doctor, will you please go to that door and lock it."

The doctor marched to the door, with his firm, decisive tread, thrust the key into the lock, and turned it. The click of the bolt snapping into place was loud in the silence of the room. The doctor returned to the table holding the key, but Raymond motioned it away. "It must not leave your hand or everything is lost," he warned.

"Now," Raymond said, "for the finale I approach the door, I flick my handkerchief at it"—the handkerchief barely brushed the keyhole—"and presto, the door is unlocked!"

The doctor went to it. He seized the doorknob, twisted it dubiously, and then watched with genuine astonishment as the door swung silently open.

"Well, I'll be damned," he said.

"Somehow," Elizabeth laughed, "a false premise went down easy as an oyster."

Only Hugh reflected a sense of personal outrage. "All right," he demanded, "how was it done? How did you work it?"

"I?" Raymond said reproachfully, and smiled at all of us with obvious enjoyment. "It was you who did it all. I used only my little knowledge of human nature to help you along the way."

I said, "I can guess part of it. That door was set in advance, and when the doctor thought he was locking it, he wasn't. He was really unlocking it. Isn't that the answer?"

Raymond nodded. "Very much the answer. The door *was* locked in advance. I made sure of that, because with a little forethought I suspected there would be such a challenge during the evening, and this was the simplest way of preparing for it. I merely made certain that I was the last one to enter this room, and when I did I used this." He held up his hand so that we could see the sliver of metal in it. "An ordinary skeleton key, of course, but sufficient for an old and primitive lock."

For a moment Raymond looked grave, then he continued brightly, "It was our host himself who stated the false premise when he said the door was unlocked. He was a man so sure of himself that he would not think to test anything so obvious. The doctor is also a man who is sure, and he fell into the same trap. It is, as you now see, a little dangerous always to be so sure."

"I'll go along with that," the doctor said ruefully, "even though it's heresy to admit it in my line of work." He playfully tossed the key he had been holding across the table to Hugh, who let it fall in front of him and made no gesture toward it. "Well, Hugh, like it or not, you must admit the man has proved his point."

"Do I?" said Hugh softly. He sat there smiling a little now, and it was easy to see he was turning some thought over and over in his head.

"Oh, come on, man," the doctor said with some impatience. "You were taken in as much as we were. You know that."

"Of course you were, darling," Elizabeth agreed.

I think that she suddenly saw her opportunity to turn the proceedings into the peace conference she had aimed at, but I could have told her she was choosing her time badly. There was a look in Hugh's eye I didn't like—a veiled look which wasn't natural to him. Ordinarily, when he was really angered, he would blow up a violent storm, and once the thunder and lightning had passed he would be honestly apologetic. But this present mood of his was different. There was a slumbrous quality in it which alarmed me.

He hooked one arm over the back of his chair and rested the other on the table, sitting halfway around to fix his eyes on Raymond. "I seem to be a minority of one," he remarked, "but I'm sorry to say I found your little trick disappointing. Not that it wasn't cleverly done—I'll grant that, all right—but because it wasn't any more than you'd expect from a competent locksmith."

"Now there's a large helping of sour grapes," the doctor jeered.

Hugh shook his head. "No, I'm simply saying that where

there's a lock on a door and the key to it in your hand, it's no great trick to open it. Considering our friend's reputation, I thought we'd see more from him than that."

Raymond grimaced. "Since I had hoped to entertain," he said, "I must apologize for disappointing."

"Oh, as far as entertainment goes I have no complaints. But for a real test—"

"A real test?"

"Yes, something a little different. Let's say, a door without any locks or keys to tamper with. A closed door which can be opened with a fingertip, but which is nevertheless impossible to open. How does that sound to you?"

Raymond narrowed his eyes thoughtfully, as if he were considering the picture being presented to him. "It sounds most interesting," he said at last. "Tell me more about it."

"No," Hugh said, and from the sudden eagerness in his voice I felt that this was the exact moment he had been looking for. "I'll do better than that. I'll *show* it to you."

He stood up brusquely and the rest of us followed suit—except Elizabeth, who remained in her seat. When I asked her if she wanted to come along, she only shook her head and sat there watching us hopelessly as we left the room.

We were bound for the cellars, I realized, when Hugh picked up a flashlight along the way, but for a part of the cellars I had never seen before. On a few occasions I had gone downstairs to help select a bottle of wine from the racks there, but now we walked past the wine vault and into a long, dimly lit chamber behind it. Our feet scraped loudly on the rough stone, the walls around us showed the stains of seepage, and warm as the night was outside, I could feel the chill of dampness turning my chest to gooseflesh. When the doctor shuddered and said hollowly,

"These are the very tombs of Atlantis," I knew I wasn't alone in my feeling, and felt some relief at that.

We stopped at the very end of the chamber, before what I can best describe as a stone closet built from floor to ceiling in the farthest angle of the walls. It was about four feet wide and not quite twice that in length, and its open doorway showed impenetrable blackness inside. Hugh reached into the blackness and pulled a heavy door into place.

"That's it," he said abruptly. "Plain solid wood, four inches thick, fitted flush into the frame so that it's almost airtight. It's a beautiful piece of carpentry, too, the kind they practiced two hundred years ago. And no locks or bolts. Just a ring set into each side to use as a handle." He pushed the door gently and it swung open noiselessly at his touch. "See that? The whole thing is balanced so perfectly on the hinges that it moves like a feather."

"But what is it for?" I asked. "It must have been made for a reason."

Hugh laughed shortly. "It was. Back in the bad old days, when a servant committed a crime—and I don't suppose it had to be more of a crime than talking back to one of the ancient Loziers—he was put in here to repent. And since the air inside was good for only a few hours at the most, he either repented damn soon or not at all."

"And that door?" the doctor said cautiously. "That impressive door of yours which opens at a touch to provide all the air needed—what prevented the servant from opening it?"

"Look," Hugh said. He flashed his light inside the cell and we crowded behind him to peer in. The circle of light reached across the cell to its far wall and picked out a short, heavy chain hanging a little above head level with a U-shaped collar dangling from its bottom link.

"I see," Raymond said, and they were the first words I had heard him speak since we had left the dining room. "It is truly ingenious. The man stands with his back against the wall, facing the door. The collar is placed around his neck, and then—since it is clearly not made for a lock—it is clamped there, hammered around his neck. The door is closed, and the man spends the next few hours like someone on an invisible rack, reaching out with his feet to catch the ring on the door which is just out of reach. If he is lucky he may not strangle himself in his iron collar, but may live until someone chooses to open the door for him."

"My God," the doctor said. "You make me feel as if I were living through it."

Raymond smiled faintly. "I have lived through many such experiences and, believe me, the reality is always a little worse than the worst imaginings. There is always the ultimate moment of terror, of panic, when the heart pounds so madly you think it will burst through your ribs, and the cold sweat soaks clear through you in the space of one breath. That is when you must take yourself in hand, must dispel all weakness, and remember all the lessons you have ever learned. If not—!" He whisked the edge of his hand across his lean throat. "Unfortunately for the usual victim of such a device," he concluded sadly, "since he lacks the essential courage and knowledge to help himself, he succumbs."

"But you wouldn't," Hugh said.

"I have no reason to think so."

"You mean," and the eagerness was creeping back into Hugh's voice, stronger than ever, "that under the very same conditions as someone chained in there two hundred years ago you could get this door open?" The challenging note was too strong to be brushed aside lightly. Raymond stood silent for a long minute, face strained with concentration, before he answered.

"Yes," he said. "It would not be easy—the problem is made formidable by its very simplicity—but it could be solved."

"How long do you think it would take you?"

"An hour at the most."

Hugh had come a long way around to get to this point. He asked the question slowly, savoring it. "Would you want to bet on that?"

"Now, wait a minute," the doctor said. "I don't like any part of this."

"And I vote we adjourn for a drink," I put in. "Fun's fun, but we'll all wind up with pneumonia, playing games down here."

Neither Hugh nor Raymond appeared to hear a word of this. They stood staring at each other—Hugh waiting on pins and needles, Raymond deliberating—until Raymond said, "What is this bet you offer?"

"This. If you lose, you get out of the Dane house inside of a month, and sell it to me."

"And if I win?"

It was not easy for Hugh to say it, but he finally got it out. "Then I'll be the one to get out. And if you don't want to buy Hilltop I'll arrange to sell it to the first comer."

For anyone who knew Hugh it was so fantastic, so staggering a statement to hear from him, that none of us could find words at first. It was the doctor who recovered most quickly.

"You're not speaking for yourself, Hugh," he warned. "You're a married man. Elizabeth's feelings have to be considered."

"Is it a bet?" Hugh demanded of Raymond. "Do you want to go through with it?"

"I think before I answer that, there is something to be explained." Raymond paused, then went on slowly, "I am afraid I gave the impression—out of pride, perhaps—that when I retired from my work it was because of a boredom, a lack of interest in it. That was not altogether the truth. In reality, I was required to go to a doctor some years ago, the doctor listened to the heart, and suddenly my heart became the most important thing in the world. I tell you this because, while your challenge strikes me as being a most unusual and interesting way of settling differences between neighbors, I must reject it for reasons of health."

"You were healthy enough a minute ago," Hugh said in a hard voice.

"Perhaps not as much as you would want to think, my friend."

"In other words," Hugh said bitterly, "there's no accomplice handy, no keys in your pocket to help out, and no way of tricking anyone into seeing what isn't there! So you have to admit you're beaten."

Raymond stiffened. "I admit no such thing. All the tools I would need even for such a test as this I have with me. Believe me, they would be enough."

Hugh laughed aloud, and the sound of it broke into small echoes all down the corridors behind us. It was that sound, I am sure—the living contempt in it rebounding from wall to wall around us—which sent Raymond into the cell.

Hugh wielded the hammer, a short-handled but heavy sledge, which tightened the collar into a circlet around Raymond's neck, hitting with hard even strokes at the iron which was braced against the wall. When he had finished I saw the pale glow of the radium-painted numbers on a watch as Raymond studied it in his pitch darkness.

"It is now eleven," he said calmly. "The wager is that by midnight this door must be opened, and it does not matter what means are used. Those are the conditions, and you gentlemen are the witnesses to them."

Then the door was closed, and the walking began.

Back and forth we walked—the three of us—as if we were being compelled to trace every possible geometric figure on that stony floor, the doctor with his quick, impatient step, and I matching Hugh's long, nervous strides. A foolish, meaningless march, back and forth across our own shadows, each of us marking the time by counting off the passing seconds, and each ashamed to be the first to look at his watch.

For a while there was a counterpoint to this scraping of feet from inside the cell. It was a barely perceptible clinking of chain coming at brief, regular intervals. Then there would be a long silence, followed by a renewal of the sound. When it stopped again I could not restrain myself any longer. I held up my watch toward the dim yellowish light of the bulb overhead and saw with dismay that barely twenty minutes had passed.

After that there was no hesitancy in the others about looking at the time and, if anything, this made it harder to bear than just wondering. I caught the doctor winding his watch with small, brisk turns, and then a few minutes later he would try to wind it again, and suddenly drop his hand with disgust as he realized he had already done it. Hugh walked with his watch held up near his eyes, as if by concentration on it he could drag that crawling minute hand faster around the dial.

Thirty minutes had passed.

Forty.

Forty-five.

I remember that when I looked at my watch and saw there were less than fifteen minutes to go I wondered if I could last out even that short time. The chill had sunk so deep into me that I ached with it. I was shocked when I saw that Hugh's face was dripping with sweat, and that beads of it gathered and ran off while I watched.

It was while I was looking at him in fascination that it happened. The sound broke through the walls of the cell like a wail of agony heard from far away, and shivered over us as if it were spelling out the words.

"Doctor!" it cried. *"The air!"*

It was Raymond's voice, but the thickness of the wall blocking it off turned it into a high, thin sound. What was clearest in it was the note of pure terror, the plea growing out of that terror.

"Air!" it screamed, the word bubbling and dissolving into a long-drawn sound which made no sense at all.

And then it was silent.

We leaped for the door together, but Hugh was there first, his back against it, barring the way. In his upraised hand was the hammer which had clinched Raymond's collar.

"Keep back!" he cried. "Don't come any nearer, I warn you!"

The fury in him, brought home by the menace of the weapon, stopped us in our tracks.

"Hugh," the doctor pleaded, "I know what you're thinking, but you can forget that now. The bet's off, and I'm opening the door on my own responsibility. You have my word for that."

"Do I? But do you remember the terms of the bet, doctor? This door must be opened within an hour—*and it doesn't matter what means are used!* Do you understand now? He's fooling both of you. He's faking a death scene, so that you'll push open the door and win his bet for him. But it's my bet, not yours, and I have the last word on it!"

I saw from the way he talked, despite the shaking tension in his voice, that he was in perfect command of himself, and it made everything seem that much worse.

"How do you know he's faking?" I demanded. "The man said he had a heart condition. He said there was always a time in a spot like this when he had to fight panic and could feel the strain of it. What right do you have to gamble with his life?"

"Damn it, don't you see he never mentioned any heart condition until he smelled a bet in the wind? Don't you see he set his trap that way, just as he locked the door behind him when he came into dinner! But this time nobody will spring it for him—nobody!"

"Listen to me," the doctor said, and his voice cracked like a whip. "Do you concede that there's one slim possibility of that man being dead in there, or dying?"

"Yes, it is possible—anything is possible."

"I'm not trying to split hairs with you! I'm telling you that if that man is in trouble every second counts, and you're stealing that time from him. And if that's the case, by God, I'll sit in the witness chair at your trial and swear you murdered him! Is that what you want?"

Hugh's head sank forward on his chest, but his hand still tightly gripped the hammer. I could hear the breath drawing heavily in his throat, and when he raised his head, his face was gray and haggard. The torment of indecision was written in every pale sweating line of it.

And then I suddenly understood what Raymond had meant that day when he told Hugh about the revelation he might find in the face of a perfect dilemma. It was the revelation of what a man may learn about himself when he is forced to look into his own depths, and Hugh had found it at last.

In that shadowy cellar, while the relentless seconds thundered louder and louder in our ears, we waited to see what he would do.

THE DOG DIED FIRST

Bruno Fischer

Typically of the pulp era, many of the most successful writers were prodigiously prolific and Bruno Fischer (1908-1992) was no exception, producing an endless stream of stories for numerous pulps, though some were not the first tier. While a few sales were to such top magazines as *Black Mask* and *The Shadow,* numerous stories sold to *Dime Mystery, 10-Story Detective,* and *Strange Detective Mysteries.*

In addition to his hundreds of stories, both under his own name and as Russell Gray, he wrote more than two dozen novels, many of which were paperback originals.

Born in Berlin, Germany, Fischer emigrated to the United States at the age of five, his family settling in New York City. He was educated at the Rand School of Social Sciences, which had been established by the Socialist Party in 1906 and closed in 1956 during Joseph McCarthy's anticommunist reign.

Fischer became a sportswriter for the *Long Island Daily Press* before working for the Socialist newspaper *Labor Voice* and then taking over as editor of the *Socialist Call,* the official weekly magazine of the Socialist Party. He went on to run for the New York State Senate on the Socialist Party ticket and maintained his dedication to Jewish causes and socialism until the end of his life, spending his final summers at a socialist cooperative in Putnam County, New York.

"The Dog Died First" was originally published in the Fall 1949 issue of *Mystery Book Magazine.*

The Dog Died First

Bruno Fischer

BLOOD WAS on my mind that night, but it was blood of the French Revolution. I was correcting Modern European History papers while Dot was at a hen party at Marie Cannon's. At midnight I went to bed, knowing that between bridge and chit-chat there was no telling when Dot would be home.

The sound of the car pulling into the driveway woke me. As we have no garage in our bungalow-type stucco house, we leave the car out in the open on the cinder driveway. I heard Dot enter the house through the back door, and then I was listening to water running in the kitchen.

It ran for a long time—too long for her to be getting a drink and she certainly wouldn't be washing herself at the kitchen sink. Drowsily I was wondering what she was up to now, and I wondered a lot more when she turned off the water and left the house again. The radium clock on the dresser said five minutes after one.

I turned on my side and looked through the window. Dot had left the car's headlights on and she was walking into their glare. The pail she carried in her right hand was evidently full of water. The weight of it made her neat hips sway. She opened the back sedan door, switched on the overhead light, dug a dripping scrubbing brush out of the pail and leaned inside the car.

So that explained her antics. No doubt somebody had spilled liquid on the upholstery and she was trying to scrub it off before it dried. I dug my head into the pillow to shut out the glow of the headlights coming in through the window. I was almost asleep when the night lamp went on in the bedroom.

"Are you awake, darling?" Dot asked.

"Um, umph, um," I mumbled, turning my head to let her know I was too sleepy for conversation.

But as nothing ever stopped Dot from talking, my desire for slumber didn't. I'd trained myself to absorb her chatter without listening to it, and that was what I did then until a startling sentence jerked me fully awake.

"I couldn't get all the blood off," she had said.

"Blood?" I breathed, opening my eyes wide. "Did you say blood?"

Dot was taking a nightgown out of a drawer. "He died on the way to the doctor," she said complacently. "I feel like a murderer."

She straightened up with the nightgown in her hand. The soft, dim night light played over her tightly and precisely formed body, and her face was as guileless as a doll's.

"Who died?" I demanded hoarsely.

"The dog, of course," she said, dropping the nightgown over her head.

I sank back on the bed. A dog, of course. Well, what had I really expected?

"I wasn't going to tell you because you're always criticizing my driving," she explained. "Like when I smashed a fender last week. But I really couldn't help what happened tonight. The dog ran right under the wheel. Then when I got home I noticed the blood in the car and I tried to wash it off, but I couldn't quite because it had dried. I decided to tell you because you'll see it tomorrow."

I was drowsy again, but puzzled. "How does blood get inside a car when you run over a dog?"

"He was still breathing, so I took him to the vet, but he was dead when I got there. The dog, I mean. The poor little thing."

She put out the light and got into bed, but that didn't stop her voice. She told me about the dollar and seventeen cents she had lost at bridge and that Ida Walker looked dowdy and Marie Cannon stunning and Edith Bauer—

"How about some sleep?" I complained.

She was quiet—for about a minute, it seemed to me. Then she was shaking me.

"Bernie," she whispered, "there's somebody sneaking about outside with a flashlight."

The radium clock said ten minutes after three, which meant that I'd actually been asleep about two hours. Dot was sitting up, and past the vague outline of her shoulder and through the window I saw a splotch of light move along the side of the car.

"Maybe he's trying to steal the car," she whispered.

"Did you leave the key in the ignition?"

It didn't surprise me when she admitted that she thought she had. Snorting, I got out of bed and went to the window. Whoever held the flashlight seemed to have lost interest in the car and was walking toward the street.

"He's going away," I said hopefully. I was a man who liked to avoid trouble.

"I wonder what he wanted."

"I know what I want," I said. "Sleep."

I had one leg on the bed when the doorbell rang. I froze half on the bed, listening. There are few things more disturbing than a doorbell ringing at three in the morning.

"That must be the thief," Dot whispered.

I roused myself. "Thieves don't ring doorbells."

"Well, it's somebody," Dot pointed out.

It certainly was somebody. The doorbell kept on ringing. I fumbled into slippers and robe, went into the living room, turned on the light, opened the front door.

The man who entered held a flashlight in his hand, so he was the same one I had seen prowling outside. He had more paunch than chest and a lumpy face.

"Mr. Bernard Hall?" he said.

I nodded. "What is it?"

He didn't answer. He stepped past me into the living room, looked it over as if he were thinking of renting it, then fixed me with rather sad eyes.

"My boy Steve is in your History class. Stephan Ricardo."

"Ah, yes," I said, using my teacher-parent manner. But that was absurd. This man hadn't got me out of bed at three in the morning to discuss his son's scholastic problems. Then I remembered what Stephan Ricardo had told me his father did for a living, and I tensed.

"You're a detective," I said.

"That's right." Ricardo massaged his jowls. "Seems there's blood in your car."

"Is that what you were looking at with your flashlight?"

He nodded. "Uh-huh. There was an attempt made to wash it off, but it was soaked into the floor rug."

At that moment Dot came into the living room. She wore her flowered housecoat over the nightgown.

"I'm the one you want," she said. "I suppose I shouldn't have left the body in the bushes."

Ricardo pushed his hat back from his brow and blinked a couple of times. "You admit you did it, Mrs. Hall?"

"Should I have reported it to the police?" She handed him that disarming smile of hers. "The thing is, I didn't want any trouble."

"No," Ricardo said softly, "I guess you didn't want trouble." He kept looking at Dot as if he didn't quite believe she existed. "Why did you do it, Mrs. Hall?"

"It was an accident. He ran in front of the car."

Ricardo shook his head sorrowfully. "That won't get you anywhere, Mrs. Hall. His head was smashed in, but there were no other marks on his body."

"But that's impossible. I held him in my arms and his head looked all right. He seemed to be injured internally. He died before I could get him to the vet."

"The vet?" Ricardo said, blinking.

"Dr. Harrison, the veterinary on Mill Street," she explained patiently. "Where else would you take a dog?"

Ricardo opened his mouth, but he didn't say what he started to. Instead he drew in air. "Suppose, Mrs. Hall, you tell me all about it."

Dot settled herself in the armchair and placidly crossed her fine legs. I stuck a cigarette between my lips and noticed that the match shook in my hand. I didn't for a moment believe that a detective would awaken and question her at three in the morning because a dog had been run over.

"I was driving to a bridge game at Marie Cannon's tonight," she said. "About two blocks from here a little black dog ran in front of the car and I couldn't stop in time. I got out and there was the poor creature in terrible agony. He was a little thing, all black with white paws and a white splotch on his face. I don't know what breed, though he had some Spitz in him, because when I was a little girl I had a Spitz that was the darlingest—"

"What time was this?" Ricardo broke in.

"Close to eight-thirty. Marie Cannon was anxious that we get to her house at eight-thirty, and it was just about that when I left here. I would be late, but I couldn't leave an injured dog lying in the road, so I put him in the car and drove to the vet."

"To Dr. Harrison on Mill Street," Ricardo said rather grimly. "A good seven miles away, though you were late."

"Do you know of a nearer veterinary?"

Ricardo admitted that he didn't.

"So I had no choice," Dot said. "But when I got there, I saw that the poor dog was dead, so there was no point to taking him in to Dr. Harrison. I drove back to East Billford and left the dog in some bushes beside the road."

"Just like that," Ricardo sighed.

Dot flushed guiltily. "I suppose it was a cruel thing to do, but by then it was about ten minutes after nine and the bridge game couldn't start until I got there because I made the fourth and Marie Cannon would be furious with me. And, after all, the dog was dead, wasn't he? And I did look to see if he had a license, but he didn't have even a collar. He was obviously a stray dog, and I didn't know what else to do with him."

After that gush of words there was a silence. I filled it by saying, "I suppose killing a dog should be reported to the police. That's the law, isn't it?"

"Uh-huh." He glanced at me and then returned his sad gaze to Dot. "Did you get blood on your dress when you picked him up?"

"I'm sure I didn't. One of the women at the bridge game would have noticed if I had." She frowned. "He didn't seem to bleed at all, but he must have, because I saw blood in the car when I got home hours later."

"Where did you leave the—ah-body?"

"On Pine Road, in a section where there are no houses. Just this side of that dirt road."

"Wilson Lane," he said.

"Yes, that's it. A short distance past Wilson Lane, coming toward town, there are thick bushes on the right side. That's where I left him."

Ricardo nodded and scratched his cheeks with the backs of his fingers. He was a plump man with too much waist and jowls, but the set of his lumpy face frightened me.

"You better get dressed, Mrs. Hall," he said, "and go there with me."

Her blue eyes widened. "You mean right now?"

"Right now."

"I'm going too," I said.

"Sure," Ricardo said.

We went into the bedroom to put on clothes.

"I don't understand why they make so much trouble about a dog being run over," Dot complained as she slipped her shoes on. "Of course I feel bad about it, but getting people out of bed in the middle of the night! Why doesn't he just give me a ticket and I'll pay the fine?"

I didn't say anything. My stomach was sickishly empty.

We drove in Ricardo's sedan, the three of us in the front seat.

On the way, Dot said, "I suppose Al Wilcox saw me carry the dog into the bushes. He lives down the street and knows me. I saw his white police car pass when I returned to my car."

"That's right, Mrs. Hall," Ricardo said grimly.

It was less than a mile to the spot. Three cars were parked along the side of the road, and by the light of a couple of powerful electric lanterns I saw five or six men gathered on the narrow grassy stretch between the shoulder of the road and the line of thick bushes. One of them was Al Wilcox in his policeman's uniform.

"All these men because a dog was killed!" Dot said. Even she was catching on that something bigger than that must be up.

Ricardo had no comment. He led us across the road and then I saw the long shape under the canvas. The men had become silent and were looking at Dot.

"Mrs. Hall, is this the spot?" Ricardo asked.

She nodded and slipped her hand through my arm. She frowned at the size of the thing under the canvas.

"Give her a look, Cal," Ricardo said.

Wilcox bent over and gripped one end of the canvas and pulled it down. Dot uttered a shrill scream. I felt her sag against my side, clinging to my arm.

"Why that's—that's Emmett Walker!" she gasped. "I played bridge with his wife tonight."

It was Emmett Walker, all right, but no longer the handsome insurance agent Dot and I had known for years. His blond hair was matted with dried blood and some of it had run in ragged streaks over his face.

"Cover him up, Al," Ricardo said wearily. He turned to pot, and there was controlled fury in his voice. "He was murdered, Mrs. Hall."

"But—but where's the dog?" Dot stammered.

"There is no dog, Mrs. Hall."

"But I left him right there in those bushes."

"No, Mrs. Hall," Ricardo said. "You struck Emmett Walker over the head with something and killed him. You dragged him into your car and drove here and dragged him into the bushes. That's how the blood got in your car."

"It's not true!" Dot had recovered from the shock and was now merely indignant.

At that point I should have said something. I should have come to my wife's defense. But even if I hadn't been too choked for words, I couldn't think of any that would do any good.

Al Wilcox spoke up. "I was passing here at a few minutes after nine, Mrs. Hall, when I saw you come out of these bushes and get into your car. At two o'clock I passed this way again, and by my headlights I saw what looked like a man's leg sticking out of the bushes. I investigated and found him."

"Well, I didn't do it," Dot said angrily. "Why would I want to kill Emmett Walker?"

"Suppose you tell us, Mrs. Hall."

Dot turned to me in exasperation. "You try to make him understand, darling."

I gulped air into my lungs. I said, "Of course you didn't do it," but my voice quavered.

Ricardo moved away from us to consult with the other policemen in undertones. When he returned to us, he asked Dot if the dress she had on was the one she had worn at the bridge game. She said that it was. Then he asked me for the keys to my car and handed them to Wilcox.

"Okay, let's go," Ricardo snapped.

I didn't ask him where. I knew where.

This time there were four of us in the sedan. I sat beside Ricardo who drove, and Dot sat in the back seat with another detective. Ricardo didn't waste time. He had questions for Dot as we drove.

"Where did you say that bridge game was?"

"At Marie Cannon's house."

"Is she the wife of George Cannon, the lawyer?"

"Yes."

"Who else was there?"

"There were only four of us. Besides Marie and myself, there were Edith Bauer and Ida Walker." Her voice broke a little. "Poor Ida! Who is going to break the news to her?"

"She knows already," Ricardo said. "She didn't take the news too hard."

"They haven't got along too well lately. There were rumors that Emmett wasn't—well, exactly faithful to her." Dot leaned forward toward the back of Ricardo's neck, and her voice was breathless. "Do you think that Ida killed him?"

"I know who killed him," Ricardo said crisply.

That ended all talk until we reached the County Building, which also contained police headquarters and the county jail. Dot was taken into an office on the second floor, but I got no farther than the door.

"You might as well go home," Ricardo told me. "Your wife is being held."

"What are you going to do to her—give her the third degree?"

His lumpy face smiled a little. "We're going to question her."

"She's entitled to have a lawyer present."

"Sure." He waved a pudgy hand. "You'll find a phone booth down the hall."

I went into the booth and dialed George Cannon's number.

His voice was drowsy, but it got wide awake when I told him what was up.

"I'll be right there," he said.

I waited out in the hall. In ten minutes George Cannon arrived. His hair was mussed and his suit looked like a sack on his frail body, but that wasn't because he'd dressed in a hurry. He always managed to look seedy and disheveled, though he was the most prominent lawyer in East Billford.

Briefly I gave him the details. His thin mouth tightened as he listened.

"Emmett was supposed to call for Ida tonight," he told me. "She waited in my house until one o'clock and then I drove her home. I think she suspected that he was out with another woman. And all that time he was dead."

"Don't stand here talking," I said. "God knows what they're doing to Dot."

"Oh, they won't be rough with a woman. You wait here, Bernie."

He knocked at the door through which Dot had been taken and was admitted.

For a full hour I paced that lonely hall before George came out.

Glumly he shook his head. "They've taken her up to a cell through another door. She hasn't been charged yet. There are still loose ends."

"How does it look?"

"It's too soon to tell," he said, not meeting my eyes. "If the blood in the car is a dog's, their circumstantial case will be shot." He patted my shoulder. "No use hanging around here. Go home and get some sleep."

He dropped me off at my house. Dawn was coming up, and

in the grayness of it I saw that my car was gone. The police had taken it because it was evidence—evidence that might mean life or death.

The house was terribly empty. I went into the bedroom and there was her nightgown flung across the foot of the bed. I remembered how only a few hours ago I had watched her getting into that nightgown, and nobody could have looked less like a woman who had just murdered somebody.

She hadn't. She said so. She was flighty and talkative, but she had never before lied to me.

But she had never before had occasion to lie about murder. . . .

I tossed in bed for an hour and slept fitfully for another hour. Then the doorbell woke me. It was Herman Bauer, a fellow teacher at the high school. His wife Edith was an old friend of Dot's.

Herman, chubby and usually jolly, was now glum and embarrassed. He said that he had stopped off on his way to school to tell me that the police had questioned him and Edith.

"They got us out of bed at six-thirty this morning," Herman said. "They asked Edith about the bridge game last night. When Dot arrived, when she left, if she'd been in the house all that time, and so on. They also asked how well Dot and Emmett had known each other." Uneasily he fumbled with the brim of his hat. "Neither Edith nor I mentioned that Dot used to go out with Emmett."

"That was years ago," I said. "Before Dot and I were engaged."

"Of course." Herman watched his fingers on his hat. "But the police mightn't understand." He turned to the door. "If there's anything I can do for you, let me know."

After Herman Bauer was gone, I stood in the same spot for

a long time. He had it all figured out, the way everybody else figured it and the police certainly did. I couldn't know that they weren't right.

Rousing myself, I went to the phone to call the school that I wouldn't be in that day and maybe for the rest of the week. Before I could start to dial the number, the phone rang.

It was George Cannon, and he said, "Bernie, can you come over to the district attorney's office right away?"

"Did anything new break?"

"Yes, but I'm afraid it's not good. The blood in your car has been analyzed." He paused and then added tonelessly, "It's human blood, and it matches Emmett Walker's blood type."

There went the last hope, I thought as I hung up. Police science had proved Dot's story about the dog a lie, and if that was false, everything else she had said was.

I dressed and left the house. The police had my car, so I had to walk to the County Building.

Detective Ricardo and George Cannon were in the district attorney's office. John Fair, the D. A., was one of those back-slapping politicians who never met a voter without heartily pumping his hand, but when I entered his office he merely nodded gravely and remained in his seat.

"The analysis of the blood in your car leaves no doubt of your wife's guilt," Fair began brutally. "It took her some forty minutes to arrive at the bridge game after she left home—a distance of little over a mile. We know now that her delay was not caused by killing a dog and driving out to Dr. Harrison and back. She told the farfetched story about the dog to explain her delay and also the blood in her car. Obviously she met Emmett Walker and killed him with a blunt instrument, probably as he was sitting in the car with her."

"What time was Walker killed?" I asked, grasping at a straw. "I mean, if he died after she arrived at the bridge game—"

Ricardo shook his heavy head. "The medical examiner can't cut it that fine. Says he thinks Walker died between nine and ten-thirty last night, and he'll give or take half an hour at either end."

"What does my wife say?" I asked weakly.

Fair shrugged irritably. "In spite of virtually conclusive evidence, she sticks to her preposterous story about the dog. A very stubborn young woman and extremely foolish." He rose and came around his desk. "Hall, I'm not out for her neck. We have learned that she and Walker were sweethearts at one time. I'm sorry to have to say this to you, but it appears that she continued to be one of his women up until last night."

"No!" I heard myself shout.

"We haven't proved it yet," Fair admitted, "but that explains her motive for killing him. Let us say that she struck him in jealous rage. In that case, I would not insist on a first-degree murder indictment. I want you to talk to her, Hall. I want you to make her see that it will be to her advantage to make a full confession."

"Prison," I said bitterly. "Is that what you offer her, years and years in prison?"

"It's better than the electric chair," Fair said softly and returned to his desk.

George Cannon hadn't said a word since I entered the office. He was our legal mind. I asked him for his opinion.

"Bernie, I'm against any deal," he declared. "I believe I can get her off free."

He believed! I looked at him standing there, seedy and slight and his pinched face with that perpetually hungry expression.

He was the top lawyer in East Billford, but it was a small city and his reputation didn't extend beyond it. He didn't think her innocent—nobody did—but he was willing to risk her life to build up his reputation in a sensational murder trial.

"I'll talk to her," I told the district attorney.

Ricardo led me upstairs to a small bare room containing only a few chairs, and left me there. A few minutes later a matron brought Dot in.

There were tired lines about her eyes and mouth, but she looked beautiful. She felt wonderful in my arms and her tremulous mouth was unendurably sweet. The electric chair, I thought dully, or years in prison that would be a living death for her.

After a minute she slipped out of my embrace. "I'd like a cigarette, darling," she said.

I lit it for her, and she sat down and crossed her legs and drew smoke into her lungs. "Darling," she said then, "they're saying terrible things about me."

She sounded indignant. Not frightened, not broken up, but merely outraged that she should be accused of having done anything wrong.

"They're even saying that Emmett was my lover," she went on angrily.

"Was he?"

When the words were out of my mouth, I hated myself for saying them. But I had to know.

Her eyebrows arched. "Darling, you don't think that too?"

"Was he, Dot?"

"Certainly not." Again that vast indignation. "Emmett meant little to me, even when I went out a few times with him before I married you."

I bent over her and took her face between my hands and

looked deeply in her blue eyes. They were grave and without deceit.

"Dot," I said, "did you kill him?"

"No."

"How did the blood get in the car?"

"From the dog I ran over."

But police science had proved that a man and not a dog had bled in the car. It didn't make sense that she would tell the truth about everything but that. It was all of one piece. Frantically I wanted to believe her, but deep inside of me I didn't know.

I straightened up. She was my wife and I loved her.

"We'll fight them," I said.

When I returned to the district attorney's office, the same three men were there waiting for me.

"Well, is it a deal?" Fair asked.

"No," I said.

Ricardo sighed. Fair pounded his desk. "Very well, it will be first-degree murder then."

I turned away. George followed me out of the office and put his hand on my shoulder.

"We've got a good chance to lick them," he said. "I don't think, at any rate, that Fair can get a jury to give her the chair. We may get away with temporary insanity if she'll cooperate. I'll tell her exactly what to say on the stand, and if she sticks to it—"

"She's innocent," I said and walked away.

I was running away from his legal logic, but I couldn't run away from my hellish doubts.

Emmett Walker had had an eye for pretty women, but he had married an unattractive one. He hadn't done well as an insurance agent. Financially, being the husband of a woman with a fat bank account had paid off better.

Ida Walker was dumpy, and she had a face to match. When she admitted me into the house, she didn't give the impression of a grieving widow. She was frank about it.

"I'm not a fool," she told me. "I was aware that Emmett was constantly betraying me."

"With Dot?" I asked, looking down at the carpet.

Ida's voice was gentle. "No, Bernie. I never suspected Dot." Then she added, "But a wife is the last to know."

Or a husband, I thought, and the silence that followed was more embarrassing for me than for her. After a minute I asked her what time Emmett had been supposed to call for her last night.

"He wasn't definite," Ida said. "He told me he had work to do at his office and at eight-thirty dropped me off at Marie's in the car. He said he would try to be back before ten to watch a prize fight on the Cannon's television set. At one o'clock I gave up waiting for him and George drove me home."

"Weren't you worried when Emmett didn't show up?"

"Worried?" Ida Walker's lips curled. "Not worried in the way you mean. I assumed that he was with another woman. Then the police got me out of bed and told me he was dead."

I stood up and Ida accompanied me to the door.

"I'm a lot sorrier for Dot than for Emmett," she said. "He deserved what he got. That devil had a way with women. Even I could forgive him a lot. I was willing to accept crumbs from him, but I don't regret that he's gone."

I wondered how much she had forgiven him in the end.

Edith Bauer was Dot's best friend. She was a high-strung, delicately formed woman whose figure would be a delight in porcelain. When I told her that Dot was being charged with first-degree murder, she burst into tears.

Her husband was there. Herman lived close enough to the high school, where he taught science, to walk home for lunch, and I found them seated at the dinette table.

After Edith dried her eyes, she asked me if I would care to have a bite with them. I shook my head. I'd had no desire that morning for anything but coffee. I sat at the table with them and asked Edith if any of the four women at the bridge game last night had left for any length of time.

"You mean left the house?" she said, frowning at the question.

"At least left the room."

"Not for more than a minute or two," Edith replied. "We four were playing bridge all the time, from about a quarter to nine until almost one o'clock when we broke off. Of course we took time off for a snack, but we were all in the same room."

"Who served refreshments?"

"Marie, naturally, but she didn't have to leave the house to do that."

"How could you start playing at a quarter to nine when Dot didn't arrive until after nine?"

"George Cannon made the fourth," she said. "He wasn't anxious to play, and when Dot arrived he gave up his seat to her and went down to the basement to work with his tools. Cabinet making is his hobby, and he showed us the record cabinet he's building out of bleached oak. It was one of the most attractive—"

She broke off. "How can I talk about furniture at a time like this?" she wailed and started to sniffle.

I turned my attention to Herman, whose chubby face was thoughtful as he chewed his food.

"Where were you last night, Herman?" I asked.

"Home alone, catching up on my reading." He scooped up a slice of tomato from his plate. "Why is that important?"

"Because," I said carefully, "Dot wasn't the only woman at the bridge game who used to go out with Emmett Walker."

"Meaning me," Edith said. "I had quite a crush on Emmett when I was a kid." She rose quickly—too quickly, it seemed to me—to go into the kitchen for the coffeepot.

Herman had his fork poised in midair, and he studied me over it. "What are you getting at, Bernie?"

"I'm not sure," I muttered.

And that was the truth. I was groping in the dark, trying to veer guilt away from Dot to somebody else. Anybody else.

I went to see Marie Cannon. Marie was a full-bodied, slow-moving woman who caught and held men's eyes when prettier women were ignored. The housecoat she wore had a tight, high waist and a wide, low neckline that accentuated her lushness. A handkerchief was balled in her fist, and like Edith Bauer she wept at the sight of me, for she too was a close friend of Dot's.

"I can't imagine Dot killing anybody in cold blood," she said. "It must have been an accident, or temporary insanity."

I didn't argue. I had come to ask questions, and my first one was whether Dot had been greatly upset when she had arrived last night.

Marie thought that over. "She seemed somewhat out of breath, but that was all. George played out the hand before he gave up his seat to her, and as she waited she rather calmly told us that she had run over a dog." Marie unclasped her hand to stare at her moist handkerchief. "George is afraid that the fact that she had a story about killing a dog all prepared before she got here will sound bad before a jury."

Somebody came down the stairs. Marie and I turned our heads as George entered the room. He wore a faded bathrobe and flapping slippers.

"I came home for a nap," he explained. "I had only a couple of hours sleep last night when your phone call woke me." He looked at me. "You can use some sleep too, Bernie."

Sleep? Could there be any sleep for me while Dot was shut in by four walls?

"Why would Dot have said she left a dead dog in the spot where she left the body?" I said. "If she'd killed Emmett, she would have known that his body would be found there instead."

George shrugged. "She was aware that Wilcox had seen her come out of the bushes and that when the body was found Wilcox would put two and two together. She was frantic."

"Marie says she didn't seem very frantic when she arrived here a few minutes later."

"No, she didn't," George agreed, "but it's hard to tell with a woman like Dot. She's always breathless and bubbling and excited anyway. And she's—well, Bernie, she's lovely and charming, but her mind jumps about. I mean, that far-fetched story about a dog might have seemed like a valid explanation to her at the time, but she isn't exactly a logical person."

Not at all logical, I thought, and her flightiness used to annoy me. Now it might mean her death or imprisonment. Suddenly I was so tired that I could hardly stand. I leaned against the television cabinet, and I remembered that it was on that screen Emmett Walker had intended to see a prize fight last night. Or so Ida had told me.

I said, "The one who had most reason to kill Emmett Walker was his wife."

Marie sat down abruptly. "Yes," she whispered. "You mean before she got here last night?"

"It's possible," I said. "By the way, where was Emmett's car found?"

"At his house," George replied. "The police believe that he returned home after driving Ida here and then Dot picked him up in her car." He shook his head. "I've considered every angle too, Bernie, but they all lead to Walker's blood in your car and Dot's preposterous story about a dog."

I wasn't being logical either. I looked at Marie, who was opening her handkerchief to blow her nose, and at George, who tightened his lips glumly.

"I'll do my best to save her," George said. "The odds are that she can be got off within the law."

Odds, like gambling odds. Gambling against whether she would die or spend long years in jail or be released with the stigma of blood on her hands.

There was pity in their eyes. Pity for me, as well as for Dot. I could not stand it and I said good-bye and got out of there.

Sometimes, when I was worn out from a day of teaching and wanted quiet to read my paper, Dot's incessant and meaningless chatter would irritate me. Now the absence of her voice made the house terribly empty. I had come back home, but I couldn't endure being there without Dot. I was about to leave when the doorbell rang.

A ten-year-old boy stood there—Larry Robbins, son of the druggist who lived in the next block.

"Mr. Hall," he said, "did you see a little black dog?"

I stared at him.

"He got lost," the boy said. "I let him out for a few minutes last night and he never came back. So I'm asking all the neighbors if they saw him. Did you, Mr. Hall?"

With an effort I kept my voice calm. "What did he look like?"

"A little thing about so big. All black except for a white spot over his nose, and white paws. I got him only last week—my uncle gave him to me—and we didn't get a collar for him yet or a license. Maybe somebody thought he was a stray dog, fed him and took him in."

"What time did you let him out last night?"

"It was after eight o'clock. You didn't see him, did you?"

"Thanks, Larry," I said and patted his head.

He blinked at me. "Thanks for what, Mr. Hall?"

"Never mind," I said, and then added, "No, I didn't see your dog, Larry."

A couple of hours later, the small bulldozer I had hired arrived near the intersection of Pine Road and Wilson Lane. I'd been waiting there for some time. When the bulldozer had trundled off the truck, I told the driver where to start digging. Then I drove to the nearest phone and called Detective Ricardo at police headquarters.

"Can you come right away to where Emmett Walker's body was found last night?" I said.

"You got something, Mr. Hall?"

"I don't know," I said. "But if I have, I want you there as a witness."

I hurried back to where the bulldozer was ploughing up a fifty-feet wide area that started at the bushes along the road. Though he'd dug some three feet deep and twenty feet into the field beyond, he had so far turned up nothing but boulders. I walked beside the bulldozer blade, my feet sinking into the loose, upturned dirt.

The scooped-out area doubled in size before Ricardo showed up. His fat hips waddled as he stumbled over the chewed-up ground. He brooded at the crawling, bucking bulldozer and sighed.

"Faith moves mountains, eh, Mr. Hall?" he commented dryly.

I told him about Larry Robbins' lost dog.

"So why didn't you come to the police and let them do the digging?" he demanded.

"Because there'd be too much red tape before I got them to move, if they moved at all."

Ricardo scratched his jowls reflectively. "This field belongs to Gridley. He wouldn't like what you're doing to it."

"I obtained his permission. I'm paying him and promised to have it leveled off after—"

The driver yelled. He was climbing off the seat. Ricardo and I ran toward him. There, on the ground, half covered by dirt, was a patch of the black fur. It was some fifty feet back in an almost straight line from where Walker's body had been found.

Ricardo stooped, brushed dirt away from the fur, pulled the dead animal out into the clear by one of its legs. I had never before seen that little black dog, but I had heard it described by both Dot and Larry Robbins.

Dot hadn't had a logical mind. She had only told the truth. Suddenly I was feeling fine. I had never felt better in my life.

"Do you believe now that my wife ran over a dog?"

Ricardo straightened up and dusted his hands. "Why should I?"

"W-w-why?" I stammered from sheer incredulousness. "Don't you believe what you see?"

"I see a dead dog, all right, but there are at least two things this dog didn't do. He didn't bleed in your car and he didn't leave Walker's body in the bushes. I think I know how the dog got here."

"He was buried by the murderer."

Ricardo smiled thinly. "That's what you'd like us to think. Early this morning, after you left police headquarters, you decided to try to save your wife by making her cockeyed yarn seem true. You found a little black dog and killed it and buried it here. Then you pretended to find it."

The bulldozer driver was listening open-mouthed. As for me, bitter anger had replaced my elation.

"Are you going to have the dog examined?"

"Sure, Mr. Hall, though it probably won't be possible to tell if a car or a club killed it."

There was nothing to be said. The finding of the dead dog proved everything to me and nothing to the detective. I told the bulldozer driver to shove back the dirt he had scooped out and walked to my car. The car had been returned to me a few hours ago by the police—with the bloody floor rug missing.

Ricardo moved at my side. "I guess I'd do about the same thing for my wife," he said sympathetically, "but I'd be smarter."

I whirled at the edge of the road to face him. "So you're smart! But not smart enough to see that a story can sound so farfetched that it has to be true. My wife isn't quite the fool all of you try to make her out."

Ricardo had no comment for long moments, and his sad black eyes were reflective. He wasn't a bad guy, I thought. Not one of those bullying, blustering cops. He was trying to do what seemed to him the right thing.

"You know," he mused, looking back at the splotch of black

fur on the field, "there's another answer if your wife's story about the dog is true."

"It's about time you saw it."

Suddenly he grinned at me. "You wait here. I have to take the dog's body in. Might be evidence."

He waddled over the chewed-up field. It struck me that I could accomplish more than a policeman could, and by the time he caught up with me I could hand him something. I got into my car and drove off.

Marie Cannon came to the door. Those harsh, stricken lines at the corners of her eyes and mouth had deepened within a few hours.

"George isn't home," she said.

"I'm here to see you," I said.

She led me into the living room. She sat down, keeping her full-fleshed body stiff. I stood over her.

"Marie, you've been weeping all day for Emmett Walker."

She brought the handkerchief to her nose. "Of course I'm sorry he's dead. He was a friend."

"A friend and a lover," I said. "And maybe you're weeping a little for Dot too—or for your own conscience—because you know Dot is innocent. You know that Emmett was alive at around ten o'clock, which means that Dot couldn't have killed him."

I heard a car pull into the driveway at the side of the house. Ricardo, I thought, right at my heels. I hoped that he would have sense enough to let me handle Marie.

"No, no!" Marie was saying.

"We found the dog buried near where Emmett Walker's body was found," I told her. "That proves Dot's story, and it proves that one of the people who was in this house last night killed him. They were the only ones who knew where Dot had left the dead dog."

There was a whisper of feet on the porch. Then silence. That meant that Ricardo was playing along with me. He was letting me break down Marie while he listened through the open window.

Marie was sniffling into her handkerchief.

"This is what must have happened," I went on. "Last night, you went into the kitchen to prepare refreshments. Through the window you saw Emmett Walker arrive to watch the fight on your television. You slipped out through the kitchen door to talk to him."

"I didn't kill him!" she burst out. "Let me alone!"

"You didn't kill him!" I agreed. "None of you four women in the house could have, because none of you was out of the house long enough to drive the body away. But there was a fifth person in the house—your husband."

Now, beside the edge of the curtain on one of the two windows looking out on the porch, I could see a man's hip. Ricardo was taking it all in.

"No!" Marie was wailing. "No, no!"

"Yes," I said. "It's the only possible way it could have happened. George was in the basement making a record cabinet. I've been down there a number of times. There's a ground-level window looking out to the side of the house. George saw you run out to meet Emmett. Maybe you kissed Emmett. Maybe you arranged a meeting with him. Then you returned to the kitchen and took the refreshments out to your guests. Emmett lingered outside so as not to enter the house at the same time you did and give his wife ideas. And George came out of the basement through the garage door, and in his hand he held a hammer, or whatever heavy tool he'd snatched up from his work bench."

Marie wept. In a minute she would be talking for Ricardo to hear.

I glanced toward the window and saw that Ricardo had shifted his position and that considerably more than his hip was now visible.

Only it wasn't Ricardo. The detective had a fat paunch, a padded hip. The man out there was thin, frail. George Cannon, who had seen my car parked in front of his house and had come up on the porch quietly.

All right, let him hear. Maybe he would break down when Marie did. Or he would flee and that would be as good as a confession.

I turned back to Marie. "So George killed Emmett Walker in blind, jealous fury. Then there he was with a murdered man on his hands. He had heard Dot tell that she had run over a dog and where she had left it. He saw how he could divert suspicion wholly from himself by shoving it all on Dot. He dragged the body into Dot's car, and the battered head bleeding on the floor rug fitted in with his scheme. He drove to where Dot had said she'd left the dog and found it and buried it in the fields behind the bushes and left Emmett's body there. He returned and drove Emmett's car to Emmett's house and walked back. The whole business had taken some time, but you women playing cards didn't know he was gone. Maybe he left one of his machine tools running so that you heard it upstairs and assumed he was in the basement."

"The disgrace!" Marie blubbered. "The scandal!"

And then I saw the gun. Outside the window George Cannon held it in his skinny hand against his hip. Rays from the sinking sun glinted on the barrel.

Breath clogged my throat. There was no chance in flight. Only in more words, and in not letting him realize that I knew he was there.

"So that's why you protected him," I said, "though he murdered the man you loved. You knew that George had killed him. Having seen Emmett alive and outside the house at ten, there was no other possibility. Yet you were ready to see Dot die for George's crime."

Her shoulders heaved. "George said he could get her off. And there would have been a frightful scandal if George had gone on trial. Everybody would have known that Emmett had been my—my—" Her voice went completely to pieces.

I looked at Marie as I spoke, but actually my words were directed to the man outside with the gun. "The police know the truth," I said. "When they found the dog's body, the pieces fell into place. With your evidence, there will be no doubt of his guilt. The police are on their way now to—"

Outside, somebody yelled. The man at the window jerked around, and all of George Cannon's slight body became visible. He held the muzzle of his gun against his temple.

The sound of the shot wasn't very loud. Then he crumpled out of sight below the window sill, and I saw Ricardo running up the porch steps.

I dashed out to the porch. Ricardo was looking down at the dead man.

"Shot himself when he saw me," Ricardo said. "Guess he thought I was coming to arrest him."

"Yes," I muttered. "I made him think so."

He raised angry black eyes to me. "Why didn't you wait for me?"

"Does it matter now?" I said, turning away from George Cannon's body.

Inside the house, Marie was sobbing brokenly.

"I guess not," Ricardo said softly. He went into the house.

I walked as far as the porch steps so that I would not be too near the dead man. In a little while, I thought, I would be bringing Dot home.

And I would buy Larry Robbins another dog.

THE AX
Ben Hecht

There are times when an author doesn't require a stretch of time or a ream of pages to let the reader know enough about a character to form an opinion while also knowing, somehow, that a situation isn't going to work out well. Although some stories can make a sharp turn and surprise one and all, including, perhaps, at least one of the characters, I do not believe that is the case in the present story.

The author, the remarkable Ben Hecht (1894-1964) was a child prodigy on the violin, giving a concert in Chicago at the age of ten and, as a young teenager, spent his summer vacations in Wisconsin touring as an acrobat with a small circus. He ran away to Chicago at sixteen, owning and managing an "art theater" before becoming a successful journalist, first as a crime reporter then as a foreign correspondent.

He was an integral part of the Chicago literary renaissance in the 1920s, writing newspaper columns, short stories, novels, and dramas. Co-writing the play *The Front Page* with Charles MacArthur made him famous and wealthy; it has been produced on the stage frequently since it opened in New York in 1928 and has served as the basis for numerous motion pictures under its original title and others, including *His Girl Friday* (1940).

It is fair to say Hecht was the most successful screenwriter in Hollywood history, both critically and in terms of the popularity of his films. Among his nearly one hundred screen credits are *Underworld* (1927), winner of the first Academy Award for Original Screenplay, *The Front Page* (1931), *Scarface* (1932), *Gunga Din* (1939), *Wuthering Heights* (1939), *It's a Wonderful Life* (1939), *Spellbound* (1945), *Notorious* (1946), *Kiss of Death* (1950), and *The Sun Also Rises* (1957). Films on which he worked extensively but did not receive screen credit include *Stagecoach* (1939), *Gone with the Wind* (1939), and *Foreign Correspondent* (1940).

"The Ax" was first published in the November 1930, issue of *Cosmopolitan*.

The Ax

Ben Hecht

Zeller put the ax behind the furnace out of sight, the head of the ax on the cement floor, the long handle leaning against the side of the furnace. Still it wasn't hidden. It showed if you stood in certain places in the basement. Zeller nodded. He would take care she shouldn't stand in those places.

Then it seemed to Zeller suddenly that he was lying, that he was not going to kill Mrs. Lansen. The whole thing was a fake. Coming down in the basement to wait for her, hiding the ax and emptying the barrel in the corner so it would be ready for her—he was making believe. It was a lie. The thought that he was lying to himself became intolerable to Zeller.

He had lain awake all night enjoying the death of Mrs. Lansen. The way she would come walking into the dark basement, angry and proud and sneering as always, calling, "Zeller, Zeller." And he would listen to her. Her complaints. They would be the last complaints she would ever make.

For five years he had never answered her. Just a mumble, his head hanging. This time he would look right at her, straight into her eyes while she hollered at him.

Everybody was afraid of her. How many times he had heard that daughter of hers getting her head banged against the wall and crying, "Mother, Mother, don't!" And how many times he had heard that husband of hers whining while she hollered at him.

The whole neighborhood was afraid of her. The way she held her head and sneered, as if people were dirt under her feet.

But he was lying. He wasn't going to kill her. He was going to hang his head again and mumble. He knew this because his stomach was like ice.

Zeller walked to the ax and picked it up. He could hardly close his fingers on it. It seemed alive, as if it would jump away. Suddenly he swung the ax through the air. There was a metallic crash, a terrible bang of sound that filled the basement. He had cracked the side of the furnace.

He threw the ax to the ground and stood staring at it. He was crying. The tears ran from his eyes down his cheeks.

He remembered how he had come home eight years ago and there was no supper on the kitchen table and his wife was gone. Gone—the rooms empty, all her clothes gone. Gone with some man, loving somebody else; and he had lain in the empty bed hugging her pillow and crying—just like he was crying now.

He picked up the ax and held it against him. It made him feel weak. He wanted to kiss it.

A voice began speaking in his ears. It said, "What do you tell yourself lies for? You ain't gonna kill anybody. You're a liar."

Zeller caught his breath. His body quivered and a soft broken wail came from him.

"Zeller! Zeller! Where are you? Come right here!"

Mrs. Lansen. She was coming down. Her heels banging on the stairs made him wince.

He tried to put the ax back quickly out of sight but the air seemed to have thickened around him so that he had to push against it to move. He was putting the ax behind the furnace but slowly, slowly, as if he were bewitched. What if he didn't get it hidden in time!

"Zeller! Zeller, where are you?"

He was waiting for her.

"Good heavens, why don't you answer me? Standing there like an idiot!"

She was coming across the dark basement. His eyes were on the ground but he could see her: the sneer, the angered face, the proud head that called him dirt.

"You lazy fool, letting the fire go down! On a cold day like this. And the walks unshoveled. What am I paying you for? To stand around and do nothing? Wake up! Don't look so stupid. Look at me! What was that noise down here?"

Zeller shivered and hung his head.

"I heard something smash."

Zeller mumbled.

"Haven't you any common, ordinary sense? Look up at me. I'm talking to you."

Zeller's stomach felt like ice. He lifted his head slowly, fearfully. There she was, an old woman with rouge on her face, and her hair done fancy. Hollering at him.

Why was he so frightened? She would see him trembling. Why couldn't he breathe through his nose instead of keeping his mouth open and panting—so she could see? He hung onto the side of the furnace. It was hot, burning his hand. But if he let go he would fall down. He felt limp.

He wanted to scream something. Go 'way! Go 'way quick, Mrs. Lansen! He wanted to scream this at her, at her rouged old face, at her finger with rings on it shaking under his nose. He was a liar. The ax, the barrel, the banging on the furnace—these were lies. He stood staring at the angry rouged face, shivering. Then he heard a noise, a faint noise behind the furnace. The noise made his heart stop beating. It was the ax. The ax had fallen down. Somebody had knocked over the ax.

No. Not somebody. He had done it himself. He wasn't standing here. He was behind the furnace knocking over the ax and pushing it out so the handle showed. This made him feel queer—that there should be two Zellers in the basement.

He could hear that other one behind the furnace breathing—or it might be the fire in the grate making that noise. He must see what was there. She wanted to know what the noise was. What noise? What noise? That was himself mumbling. But wait a minute—there was somebody behind the furnace.

Zeller leaned over slowly and touched the ax handle. He was afraid it would jump away. But it came into his hand.

Again the air seemed to thicken so he could hardly move. He was moving as fast as he could, yet between each of his movements, between putting his hand on the ax and picking it up; between picking it up and turning around to look at Mrs. Lansen, there were terrible pauses as if he were paralyzed. Something began to whimper in his ears. "Faster . . . faster."

Then everything stopped. Mrs. Lansen stopped. He was looking at her.

A strange feeling was in him, a warm flood that melted the ice in his stomach. There wasn't time for her to run away. She was just as paralyzed as he was.

The air was too thick for her to move in. She was waiting for him, giving him plenty of time, with her eyes raised looking at something in the air and her mouth wide open.

Through this stopping of everything Zeller saw Mrs. Lansen for an instant and this instant seemed longer to him than his whole life. The Mrs. Lansen he saw filled him with so great a happiness that he shouted. A queer Mrs. Lansen with red spots on her withered cheeks like an old clown; a Mrs. Lansen whose face was twisted into a frightened, imploring expression.

In this instant Zeller forgot about the ax. He was going to say something but he couldn't speak fast enough. The ax kept moving, flying. He was killing her.

Zeller closed his eyes. He was flying with the ax, flying in circles up and down as if in a marvelous dream. Then his arms grew tired. The flying was over.

There were noises in the basement. The fire roared. Boards creaked. Lumps of coal slid over each other in the coal bin. Zeller looked around. There was the barrel. He hadn't lied. It had all happened. He felt proud. He pulled Mrs. Lansen along the cement floor toward the barrel and was surprised at the way she looked. Zeller came out of the basement smiling sleepily. He blinked at the sunny winter morning, at the bright, peaceful street. He started walking away and it seemed to him his heart would break with this sense of peace and brightness that was in the world. Then when he had walked several blocks Zeller stopped. A voice was calling behind him.

"Zeller! Zeller! Where are you?" He stood still. "Zeller!"

How could it be that thing in the barrel calling him?

"Zeller! Zeller! Come here at once!"

Yes. Mrs. Lansen! He was a liar. He had only made believe. It hadn't happened. He had fooled himself. The ax, the barrel, hadn't happened. Again his stomach felt like ice.

"Zeller! Zeller! Where are you?"

The voice screamed in his ears. Violent, nagging, like he was dirt under her feet. A sob such as a child gives who has cried too long came from him. Then, as his name repeated itself over and over in his ears, Zeller began to run. He ran wildly, his legs weaving under him.

He was running back to the basement. He would show her if he was a liar. He would show himself who was a liar. He would grab the ax and chase her through the house and keep his eyes open this time.

A crowd of men and women stood around the basement door. At the far end of the dark basement policemen with flash lights were looking into a barrel.

Zeller stood for a moment bewildered. A boy was screaming and pointing at his reddened hands.

MURDER FOR TWO

James A. Kirch

Largely forgotten today, James A. Kirch (1930s-1960s) was a Wall Street trader and turned to writing to earn a living when his company went out of business. He became a regular contributor to various publications including pulp magazines, with more than forty stories to his credit.

The majority of his stories appeared in such second-tier pulps as *Ten Detective Aces*, *Detective Tales*, *10-Story Detective Magazine*, and *Variety Detective Magazine*, but he also sold work to such better-paying publications as *Argosy*, *Dime Detective Magazine*, and *Detective Fiction Weekly*.

Although he tried his hand at creating a series detective series for *Dime Detective* with Ben Harkness, he lasted only two issues in 1947 and 1949; most of his stories are stand-alones, more closely seen as suspense fiction than genuine detective stories.

Despite having his work appear exclusively in pulps, he nonetheless had work selected for several "Best of the Year" anthologies edited by David C, Cooke and the 1958 Mystery Writers of America collection, *A Choice of Murders*, edited by Dorothy Salisbury Davis.

Oddly, as it is a rather narrow field, a large number of Kirch's stories feature everyday characters who do all they can to evade gangsters. It seems to have worked for him as one pulp expert has favorably compared the current story with the best of Cornell Woolrich.

Later in his career, Kirch turned to television and wrote an episode for the popular suspense series *Danger* in 1951, and "The Whistling Room," an episode of *Chevron Theatre*, based on William Hope Hodgson's psychic detective Carnacki; it aired on August 22, 1952.

"Murder for Two" was originally published in the June 1949 issue of Argosy; it was reprinted as "The Eye-Witness Who Wouldn't See" in the Spring 1951 issue of Suspense Magazine.

Murder For Two

James A. Kirch

"WHAT'LL IT be?" I asked.

The big fellow brought his hand up with a wallet, flipped it open and let me look at the badge.

"Okay," I said. "What'll it be?"

He rested his thick hands on the counter and his eyes held mine. "Coffee," he said.

I filled a cup from the glass pot on the stove and ladled milk into it. A little milk spilled out and sputtered on the griddle. I put the cup down in front of him and waited.

He slid a dime across the counter, but I didn't pick it up. That wasn't what I was waiting for. He shook sugar into the coffee and stirred it, then pushed the cup away from him.

"All right, Mac," he said. "Where is she?"

"The name's Joe," I told him. "Joe Raymond." I pointed to the plastic name plate I wore on my shirt.

"I know, Mac," he said. "Joe Raymond, Prop. That's not what I asked you. What I want to know is, where is she?"

They'd been crowding me for days now. Every time I'd think they were going to lay off, one of them would come in and sit down and start the whole thing over again. Always somebody crawling in my hair, asking the question I couldn't answer.

"I told you," I said. "I don't know."

He nodded slowly, as if he believed me. "Oh," he said. "You told us." He thought it over. "Yeah," he said, "you told us. What did you tell Al Vance?"

He threw it at me before I was ready for it. If I'd been set, I wouldn't have laid myself open like I did. I answered without thinking it out. "Al Vance?" I said. "I don't know him. He hasn't even been in."

He let his fingers drum on the counter top. "His boys," he said. "Now don't tell me his friends haven't been around."

I hadn't thought it out right. I knew they were watching the diner. I should have realized they'd have tagged the men who came in from Al Vance. I'd slipped up on that one. I'd have to be more careful.

"Look," I said, "I don't know everybody. Maybe some of those who've been asking questions come from Mr. Vance. I thought they were from you."

"Maybe you couldn't see them clear?" he said. "Maybe your eyes went bad again? Maybe that was it?"

My hands started shaking. I picked up a rag and rubbed the top of the counter, pressing down hard until the twitch went out of them. "My eyes are all right," I said. "I never said there was anything wrong with my eyes."

"No," he said. "But it's funny, Mac. Two men come in here and have coffee. They take a booth in the corner. The waitress sees them all right."

"Molly was serving them," I cut in. "She couldn't help—"

"Yeah," he said. "Molly was serving them. And she sees them clear. She even describes the one that leaves. But not you."

"I told you," I said. "I was cleaning up. I was polishing the stove, shining up under the sink." I pointed to the pipes. "I wasn't thinking of them."

"Not even when you heard the shot?"

"Like I said," I told him, "I was down under the sink. When I heard the shot, I turned around and raised up, but he was gone. All I saw was his back. He had on a gray coat. And a gray hat. I told you everything I could."

"You were a big help," he said. "You cut it down to two million people." He drew his coffee cup toward him and cradled it in his hands. "That girl friend of yours," he said. "Molly. She's quite a girl, Mac."

A lot he cared about Molly. They'd taken her statement about these two men who'd come in and ordered coffee, about how they seemed to be arguing with each other, and how the older one got up and started to the phone and the young one pulled a gun and shot him. She told them everything. I couldn't stop her. The police had come in too fast for me to shake her out of the daze she was in. They questioned me, and I gave them my story, how I'd been polishing the pipes, and then they asked her to go to Headquarters and look at pictures.

I had a minute with her just before she left. I tried to warn her. "Look, Molly," I said, "take it easy. In a case like this you've got to be sure. Don't go overboard. Don't get jammed up, Molly."

Her gray eyes tried to smile at me. "It's all right, Joe," she said. "I won't make a mistake. I saw him clear."

Then the detective said, "Ready, Miss Matthews?" and took her arm and they went up to Headquarters.

And she picked out Dave Vance. Al Vance's kid brother.

If she'd been city-raised, like I was, she'd have known better. People like us couldn't afford to get mixed up with his kind. Al Vance was too big for us. He was even too big for the police. They'd arrested him twice, once on a hot-cars charge and once for murder. Both times, he laughed when he walked off scot-free. The second time, in the murder case, they hadn't even brought Al Vance up in court. The only witness had disappeared. He'd just dropped out of sight. Nobody ever could prove what had happened to him. Nobody ever saw him again. That's what happened to people who got in the way of the Vances. That's what Molly was asking for when she tagged Dave Vance for murder.

They shouldn't have let her do it. A kid like Molly, in a mess like that. But they didn't care. They hadn't even tried to protect her. I told him that now. I let it all spill out of me, leaning over the counter and telling him.

"She'd have been all right," he said. "We had a man on her. But she shook him and dusted. That's where she played it wrong."

That's what he thought, that she'd played it wrong. That's when she started to get smart, when she dropped out of the picture.

"It's too bad," he went on. "She wouldn't have been so important if you'd just seen him, too."

I knew what he wanted. But he couldn't make me do it. He couldn't make me say I'd seen anybody. I told him that.

His eyes tightened a little. "We could, Mac. We could get it out of you, all right. But it's no use. You'd fold. They'd make a monkey out of you on the stand." His coffee was cold, but he drank it down. "This Molly, Mac," he said, as he got up to leave. "You find out where she is, give us a ring. Ask for Sergeant Cotter." He waved his hand toward the coffee stove behind me, where the milk had spilled over. "Better polish it, Mac. Clean it up. Keep it all nice and shiny and clean." He went out without saying goodnight.

The other one didn't come in until late, maybe half an hour before it was time to close. He took a stool near the side door. He had a paper with him and he unfolded it and held it so it shielded his face from the entrance. "Hello, Joe," he said. "What have you got for me?"

"Ham," I said. "Scrambled eggs, roast beef, meat loaf . . ."

"Milk," he said. "But that's not what I meant."

He didn't have to tell me that wasn't what he meant. He'd never been in before, but I knew what he wanted.

He was a thin man, with thin, narrow shoulders and a tight, narrow face. He was the kind you might think would get pushed around. I didn't figure I could push him around. I gave him his milk.

He said, "Joe, don't get me wrong. I want to help her."

"I don't know where she is," I said.

He said, "She's your girl. You two have it bad. We know that. She'd get in touch with you. She should get out of town. That's all we want."

"She maybe is out of town," I said.

He didn't seem to hear me. "That's what she should do. Clear out. We could help her, Joe. We've got ways."

"She's probably already gone," I said. "She probably just beat it."

"A new name," he went on. "And once she gets settled, you could follow her, Joe."

"Look," I said, "you've got it all wrong. You go back and tell Mr. Vance I don't know where she is."

"Uh-huh," he said. He drank his milk. "Joe," he said, "don't be dumb about this. Don't make people sore."

My hands were shaking again. I said, "I don't know where she is."

The door opened and a man came in. He had on a brown coat and a new brown hat. He stood looking at the clock behind the counter. "That clock right?" he asked.

I nodded. The thin man got off his stool, and laid a dime on the counter. "It's certainly a nice place," he said. He went out the side door.

The man who had come in stood there, looking at the clock.

"What'll it be?" I asked him.

He shook his head and then his hand went in under his coat. He brought it out with a watch in it. "Just checking the time," he said, and went out.

I closed at midnight. I locked the doors and dimmed the lights and then spent an hour cleaning the place up. I did everything just the way I always did it.

But when you're keyed up, you imagine things. That's how it was with me. After I had locked the door, I felt eyes watching me from all sides. All the way home to my room I felt the eyes watching and heard footsteps behind me. I had to walk slow and steady, not running or anything, not giving anybody ideas, but all the time I heard the footsteps. Even when I got to my room and closed the door, it seemed as if I could still feel eyes watching me.

I didn't pull down the shade. I sat on the bed for a while, like anybody might who'd just finished a hard shift, and then I undressed and stretched out. I smoked one cigarette before I reached up and pulled out the light.

It was the way I did every night, after I'd closed up and come home. There was nothing to give anyone an idea that I had any special plans. I always did it just like that, had a cigarette and then pulled out the light and went to sleep.

Only this time, I couldn't go to sleep.

I kept thinking how lucky it had been about the cat. When I first saw the jam Molly had got herself into, I'd thought right away what a break that was. Otherwise, it would have been tough. You can't just walk into a hotel, or even a rooming house, when the whole town's looking for you. But this way, because of my cousin's cat, it was all right.

He'd gone away for his week's vacation and stopped in the diner and left me his keys so I could go in and feed Ringo. That's how things go. I was doing him a favor, and then, when it happened, I had what I needed—a place for Molly.

Tomorrow, I'd get the letter. As it was now, Molly couldn't get out of town because the police were watching the stations. So I'd had to figure some way to make them stop watching.

That's when I'd hit on the letter. If they thought she was already out of town, there'd be no sense in their watching for her at the stations. If I got a letter from Chicago, they'd see it. They follow people around; they listen in on phone calls. They'd watch the mail, all right. Before I'd left Molly that night I'd had her write me a letter saying she was okay and would get in touch with me later, and I'd sent it with a quarter to a forwarding place in Chicago. Tomorrow, it would be delivered to me, and then I could call Molly and tell her it was okay to go to the station. And she'd be out of it.

I thought about that for a while, about Molly getting clear of this jam, and then I got out of bed and went to the window and looked out.

There was a car parked halfway down the block, facing my way. I saw a light flicker in the front seat, as if somebody had struck a match under the dashboard for a cigarette. Even then, I couldn't be sure who it was. A policeman wasn't supposed to smoke on duty, but that didn't mean he wouldn't do it. It didn't matter much who it was. He was parked out there hoping I'd lead him to Molly. I went back to bed and waited for morning.

It would have been better if I'd been able to sleep. I wouldn't have been so much on edge. The daytime shift is always a rough one, and I couldn't walk away from it for a phone call, not even after the letter from Chicago came, in Molly's handwriting. It wouldn't have looked right.

It was the usual rush. By evening, I was out on my feet. With a mob like that, I couldn't take the time to tag any of them. I just kept pushing the orders as fast as I could. I wanted them out of there. I wanted the day over so I could phone. I was filling the glass coffee pots when I heard it: "Where's Molly?"

They'd never lay off it. Even when I had a crowd, they'd come in. I didn't answer. I switched the burners to *High* and set the pots on the stove.

"Where's Molly?" He said it again. He was needling me.

"I don't know," I said.

He laughed. "That's a good one."

"Yeah," I said. "That's a good one." I picked up the full pot on the end and turned to the counter.

"Hey!" he said. "What's the . . ." It was Frankie Miller, one of my regulars. He'd been on the road with his truck for a week. He didn't know anything about it.

"Coffee," I said. I poured him a cup.

Frankie said, "Look, Joe. I didn't mean anything. If Molly give you the gate—"

"Vacation," I told him. "Keeps me on the jump." I moved away, to the end of the counter. That had been close. I couldn't let it get me like that. It would always be that way, when somebody asked me. It would be worse for Molly, always on edge, tied up inside. I got a picture of her like that, in some strange place, but I couldn't let myself think about that part. I couldn't let myself think beyond the big thing, to make the phone call and see that she got safe out of town. I'd told her I'd phone after supper. By then, they'd have had time to pull their men out of the stations.

It was nine-thirty before I could make the call. And then I didn't get her. I dialed the number and listened to the buzz. It kept on, unanswered.

It came to me, then, what had probably happened. I was excited and I must have dialed it wrong. I hung up and dialed again. It buzzed twice, and then this fellow came in. He walked up to me at the phone. He said, "Supper?"

I hung up. "Yeah," I said. "Sure. What'll it be?" I went around behind the counter and waited.

"Ham and eggs," he said. He had a quiet, soft voice. He was a trim, small man, with rimless glasses. He carried a fat brief case under his arm. He could have been a lawyer. He sat on the stool and put his case on the counter next to him, watching me.

"You've got a nice place here," he said.

I put a slice of ham in the pan and broke the eggs in with it.

"Good location," he said. "You must run a nice gross."

"How'll you have 'em?" I asked.

He thought it over. "Sunny side up," he decided. He smiled a little.

I got a cup. "Coffee?" I asked him.

"Coffee," he said. "Of course, you've got expenses. You've got taxes and help."

"I make out," I said. I gave him his coffee and turned the heat down under the eggs. "Milk?"

"No," he said. "Insurance, too. Now that runs pretty high. Insurance."

I slid his ham and eggs onto a plate and set it in front of him. "No sale," I said. "I've got plenty."

He laughed. "You've got me wrong," he said. "I'm not selling." He sprinkled salt on his eggs and swallowed a mouthful. "Good eggs," he said. "No. I'm just figuring expenses. You've got to do that—figure what's in it for you."

"I make out," I said.

"Times change," he said. "Expenses go up. Even things like insurance. Right now, you could get a fat price, Joe. I know a party who'd be interested. A smart man knows when to sell out. You look pretty smart, Joe."

"I'm not," I said. "I'm dumb. I'm so dumb I don't even know where she is. You tell Mr. Vance that." I almost screamed it at him. "*I don't know!*"

He cut a piece of ham and chewed on it. "Good ham, too,"

he said. He pointed his fork at me. "You've got it mixed, Joe. We're not talking about Molly any more. It's *you*."

He was nuts. I'd told them all I hadn't seen anything. "Look," I said, "I was busy cleaning up. I didn't see him at all."

"Think back, Joe," he said. "You saw him come in. It wasn't Dave Vance. He was a tall, thin man. Middle-aged. They've got the wrong man, Joe."

"Molly described him," I said. "She picked him out."

"Let's forget about Molly," he said. "We won't worry about her any more."

I didn't get it, at first. I had to let it turn over in my mind a couple of times before it clicked into place.

I swung around the counter to the phone. It was no use. I knew it was no use even before I dialed the number. I let it go on buzzing. Molly wasn't there. They'd found her.

I hung up and walked back to the counter. "What do you want?"

"Like I told you. You saw him come in. It wasn't Dave Vance. It was a tall, thin, middle-aged man. You got a good look." He finished the ham. "It'll pay you, Joe. It'll pay off nice."

"What about Molly?"

He shook his head. "It's too late, Joe. We can't do anything about her. This is just you and me."

I guess I'd known it from the beginning. It was like the time Al Vance had been charged with murder and the witness had dropped out of sight. They'd taken care of him, the way they'd take care of Molly. I'd tried to outsmart them. Me, dumb Joe Raymond, had tried to go up against them, and I'd just made it worse.

"You've got to stop them," I said. "You've got to—"

"Wait a minute, son." He slid off the stool. "I can't do anything."

"You've got to."

"Hold it, man. It's too late. It's . . ."

He must have seen it coming. He said, "Wait a minute . . ." and ducked under my arm toward the door.

He might have made it. He might have gotten away from me, into the street, if the door hadn't opened.

It was the man in brown. The heavy one, with the brown coat and new brown hat. He said, "Something wrong?" He reached out and caught the little man's wrist. "What goes on?"

"They killed her," I said. I took a step forward.

He swung the little man behind him and put a hand on my chest. "Easy," he said. "What's the trouble?"

I knew who he was then. I hadn't thought of it before, but I knew now. He was the man the police had put to watching the diner. That's why he'd come in before, and that's why he'd come in now; both times when Al Vance's men were alone in the place.

"What's the trouble?" he said again.

She wouldn't have been so important, Sergeant Cotter had said, *if you'd just seen him, too.* I knew then what I had to do.

"I want to make a statement," I said.

"Sure," he said. "We'll just run up to Headquarters . . ."

"No," I said. "Now. I want to make a statement *now*."

He closed the door behind him and walked over to the counter. He spread his bulk on a stool and stretched his arm so the little man could sit on the stool next to him.

"Go ahead," he said.

I gave it to him. I gave it fast, but I didn't leave anything out.

I told him now how I'd seen Dave Vance come in, and how I'd recognized him. I told him how, when the shot had come, I'd ducked under the sink.

When I'd finished, he studied me carefully. "You didn't duck down until *after* the shot?" he asked. "That means you saw it all?"

"Yes," I said. "Right from the beginning."

"And you knew Dave Vance?"

"We come from the same neighborhood," I said. "I knew him, all right. That's why I said I didn't see him. I didn't want any trouble."

"That wraps it up," he said. "The sergeant'll like it. Everybody will like it. Except maybe Dave Vance."

The little fellow hadn't said a word.

"Understand," I said, "I'm ready to swear on the stand that it was Dave Vance and that I saw him shoot."

"Fine," the detective said. "Fine. We'll just run up to Headquarters." He looked at the clock on the wall. "I'm due to report. I'll have to phone in, first." He got up, dragging the little man to his feet. "We'll take this one along. The sergeant can decide how to book him."

He walked in front of me, towing the little man after him. He dug a nickel out of his pocket and raised it to the coin slot. He was holding the little man with one hand and the coin with the other when I hit him.

He went down slowly. His head rocked back against the phone and he shook it once, and then he lurched sideways against the little man. He stayed that way a minute, as though the little man were holding him up, and then slid to the floor.

It was the little man's chance to run. That's how I'd figured it; that he'd run out the door as soon as the cop let go of him. He'd phone the Vances and tell them what I'd done. All I'd have to do was wait. This time, they'd come themselves. And this time, Joe Raymond would have a gun.

But the little man didn't run. The little man had the gun. The cop's gun. The one I'd figured on.

"Easy," he said.

I didn't move.

"You played it dumb, Joe," he said.

He didn't have to tell me that. I knew I'd played it dumb. I sat down on one of the counter stools. I didn't say anything. I just sat there.

"You're lucky," the little man said. "You're lucky it's me. I'm a quiet man." He looked down at the top at his feet. "You're in bad, Joe. You're in bad all around." He reached up and jerked the phone wires loose.

"Joe," he said, "if I were you, I'd get out of town. In a hurry, Joe. I wouldn't hang around." He backed to the door and opened it with one hand. "I'm sorry, Joe. Those were very good eggs." He slid out and closed the door.

I stayed on the stool, not moving. I knew the little man was right. I was finished. I couldn't wait for them, without a gun. It wouldn't do any good to just let them come in and shoot me. It wouldn't do Molly any good if I did that.

I could go to the police. They'd take my statement and they'd book me for slugging the cop. They'd keep me in custody, while they tried to find the Vances.

But they wouldn't find them. The Vances weren't like Molly and me, playing it alone. They had connections and money. When they came to the diner and found I was gone, they'd go back into hiding until the whole thing blew over. They could even wait until the police let me go, and then take care of me, the way they'd taken care of Molly.

The little man was right. I had to get out of town.

I locked the end door and went back to the rear of the diner, to get my suit coat. I took off my apron and the white jacket and reached up to the hooks.

And on the hook next to mine, I saw Molly's apron.

It hit me then. For the first time, it really hit me. Molly was dead. She was dead because she'd trusted me. She'd said, "It's all right, Joe. I'm not afraid. You'll take care of me." She'd tried to smile through the terror that gripped her and she said, "You'll take care of me, Joe." Now Molly was dead. And the men who had killed her were free.

I knew I couldn't run away. From the others, maybe. But I couldn't run away from Molly.

I put the apron and the white coat back on. I half carried, half dragged, the cop to the little room at the rear. I didn't want him to spoil the show if he came to too fast, so I locked him in the back room and went back to the counter.

The little man's egg plate and coffee cup were still on the counter, next to his brief case. I put the case on the floor and washed up the dishes and set them back on the shelves and then I wiped off the top of the counter, where a little of his coffee had spilled. I wanted everything to look just right. I turned the gas on in the oven and the open broiler and then I picked up a clever from the meat board and went up front and sat on the stool by the register.

I couldn't just sit there. I opened the cash register and started stacking the money, counting the day's receipts.

The bills stuck to my fingers. I dried my hands on a towel,

but the bills still stuck to them. I gave up and began stacking the quarters, ready for rolls. When I finished, there was one quarter left over.

I fished a cigarette from my pocket and put it between my lips. I got out a book of matches and slid the quarter inside the cover and laid the box down in front of me.

I started counting the halves.

I had three piles in front of me, when I heard them.

I picked up the matches and cupped them in my hand, ready to light my cigarette. I was sitting like that, with a cigarette in my mouth and matches cupped in my hand, when the door opened.

Their coat collars were turned up almost to their lowered hat brims, but I could still see their eyes. The slim one was Dave Vance, the heavy one was Al, his brother. They slid the door closed and stood with their backs to it. They both had their hands in their pockets.

Dave said, "Hello, Joe."

I didn't answer him.

He came a step forward. "Joe," he said, "we heard you were leaving town. We thought you'd be gone by now. We'd better have a talk, Joe. We'll have to straighten you out."

I still didn't answer him.

"It wouldn't look good, Joe," he said. "Your knowing me makes it bad. That would be worse than the girl's picking me out."

I had trouble with my voice. I had trouble keeping my hands from shaking. I said, "I was just leaving town. I was getting ready to go."

"Sure," he said. "That's what we figured. We brought you a car."

Al Vance said, "Stow it, Dave. It won't work. He don't want to come." He brought his right hand out of his pocket. He knew I wasn't coming along. He raised the gun slowly.

I struck the match and the book burst into flame, scorching my hand. I said, "Damn!" and Dave Vance laughed, a high woman's laugh, and I threw the burning box at the unlighted gas oven.

I didn't see it land. I went down, under the counter. I didn't have to see it land. I heard it, and felt it.

The blast rocked the diner. The windows rattled and dishes cracked on the racks, and then I was over the counter. I forgot the cleaver. I forgot everything but getting my hands on Dave Vance's throat.

Al Vance had caught most of the blast. He was huddled on the floor, his arms spread out. Dave was still on his feet. His eyes were blank and his jaw hung loose, but he was still standing. He shook his head once, trying to clear it, before my fingers closed on his throat.

He was done with killing. I had him. I had him down over the counter and I had my hands on his throat and he couldn't move. He was done with killing. I told him that.

"How do you like it?" I said. "How do you like it, Dave?"

I had him where he could never hurt anyone like Molly again. I had him where he belonged.

They were trying to stop me. Hands clawed at my wrists. Voices shouted in my ears. They wouldn't leave me alone. I had him, and they wouldn't leave me alone.

"Leave me alone," I said. "I've got him!"

There were too many of them. They pried my fingers free and forced me back and away from him. They held me, pinning my arms.

"Cut it out," they kept shouting. "Cut it out, Mac."

"Go ahead," I said. "Shoot. Why don't you shoot?"

A hand reached out and slapped my face. A voice kept saying, "Snap out of it, Mac."

The hand kept slapping me, first on one side, then on the other.

"You don't have to do that," I said.

"Take him outside," the voice said.

The cold air hit me. I shook my head and then something happened inside me and I doubled up over the gutter. They let go of me and stood there until I was finished. When I straightened up, one of them said, "Okay?"

"Yeah. I'm okay."

Sergeant Cotter was standing in front of the oven. He'd turned off the gas. The detective from the little back room was there, too. They'd turned him loose and, aside from looking pretty mad, he seemed none the worse for wear. There was a uniformed cop at the end of the diner. The Vances were next to him, handcuffed together.

"You trying to kill him?" Sergeant Cotter looked at me. "You just leave that to us, Mac. That's our job."

Their job. Molly had been their job. And Molly was dead. I told him that, bitterly.

He scowled. "People pay us to protect them, and then they lose their heads. You think I'd let those punks snatch the girl?"

I didn't believe him at first. "You?" I said. "*You* found her?"

His scowl spread. "Who else? Them punks? We got a system, Mac. You think we didn't find out you had a cousin?"

That's what the little man had meant. They couldn't do anything about Molly. He'd meant the police had her.

"She's all right?" I said. "You mean Molly's all right?"

"Sure, she's all right. But you wouldn't have been if we hadn't missed our man's regular report and come down here to see what was wrong. You had one of them, but the other one was just coming to when we got here. Joe Raymond, too scared to testify, but he tangles with two men with guns."

He grinned suddenly. "Get your coat, Joe. We'll go uptown and take down your statement."

The detective in the brown suit, rubbing his jaw where I'd hit him, grinned at me, too, and winked. He wouldn't cause trouble.

"Yeah," I said. "Sure." I went to the rear of the diner and took off my uniform and slid into my coat. I hung the apron and jacket on the hook, and then I just stood there a minute. Molly's apron hadn't been touched by the blast. It was as fresh and clean as when she'd hung it there. I stood there, looking at her apron and my jacket hanging together, and then Sergeant Cotter said, "Shake it up, Joe. We've got to get up to Headquarters pronto. You're keeping a lady waiting."

I shook it up. Fast.

LOVE COMES TO MISS LUCY

Q. Patrick

In a complicated bibliography, Hugh Callingham Wheeler (1912-1987) and Richard Wilson Webb (1901-1966) collaborated with a coterie of writers that mixed and matched on many books published as by Q. Patrick, Patrick Quentin, and Jonathan Stagge. Only when Wheeler and Webb moved to the United States in the 1930s did their books change from a recognizably British style to American in speech and tone.

Wheeler and Webb created the Patrick Quentin byline for their most successful series, beginning with *A Puzzle for Fools* (1936), which introduced Peter Duluth, a theatrical producer who stumbles into detective work by accident, and Iris Pattison, an actress who is irresistibly curious about mysteries and draws her husband into helping her solve them. The highly successful Duluth series of nine novels inspired two motion pictures, *Homicide for Three* (1948), starring Warren Douglas as Peter and Audrey Long as his wife Iris, and *Black Widow* (1954), with Van Hefflin (Peter), Gene Tierney (Iris), Ginger Rogers, George Raft, and Peggy Ann Garner. Webb dropped out of the collaboration in the early 1950s and Wheeler continued using the Quentin name but abandoned the Duluth series to produce stand-alone novels until 1965. He also turned to writing for the theater, winning the Tony Award and the Drama Desk Award for Outstanding Book of a Musical in 1973 and 1974 for *A Little Night Music* and *Candide*, and won both again in 1979 for his book for *Sweeney Todd.*

"Love Comes to Miss Lucy" was originally published in the April 1947 issue of *Ellery Queen's Mystery Magazine*; it was first collected in *The Ordeal of Mrs. Snow* (London, Gollancz, 1961) published in the United States by Random House in 1962.

Love Comes to Miss Lucy

Q. Patrick

THEY SAT around the breakfast table, their black coats hanging sleevelessly from their shoulders in the Mexican tourist fashion. They looked exactly what they were—three middle-aged ladies from the most respectable suburbs of Philadelphia.

"*Mas cafe,*" demanded Miss Ellen Yarnell from a recalcitrant waitress. Miss Ellen had traveled before and knew how to get service in foreign countries.

"And *mas hot—caliente,*" added Mrs. Vera Truegood who was the oldest of the three and found the mornings in Mexico City chilly.

Miss Lucy Bram didn't say anything. She looked at her watch to see if it was time for Mario to arrive.

The maid dumped a tin pot of lukewarm coffee on the table.

"Don't you think, Lucy," put in Ellen, "that it would be a good idea if we got Mario to come earlier in the morning? He could take us out somewhere so we could get a nice hot breakfast."

"Mario does quite enough for us already." Miss Lucy flushed slightly as she spoke of the young Mexican guide. She flushed because her friends had teased her about him, and because she had just been thinking of his strong, rather cruel Mexican legs as she had seen them yesterday when he rowed them through the floating gardens of Xochimilco.

Miss Lucy Bram had probably never thought about a man's legs (and certainly not at breakfast time) in all her fifty-two years of polite, Quakerish spinsterhood. This was another disturbing indication of the change which had taken place in her since her cautious arrival in Mexico a month before. The change, perhaps, had in fact happened earlier, when the death of an ailing father had left her suddenly and bewilderingly rich, both in terms of bonds and a release from bondage. But Miss Lucy had only grown aware of it later, here in Mexico—on the day when she had found Mario in Taxco.

It had been an eventful day for Miss Lucy. Perhaps the most eventful of all these new Mexican days. Her sense of freedom, which still faintly shocked her sedate soul, had awakened with her in her sunny hotel bedroom. It had hovered over her patio breakfast with her two companions (whose expenses she was discreetly paying). It had been quenched neither by Vera's complaints of the chill mountain air nor by Ellen's travel-snobbish remark that Taxco was sweet, of course, but nowhere near as picturesque as the hill towns of Tuscany.

To Miss Lucy, with only Philadelphia and Bar Harbor behind her, Taxco's pink weathered roofs and pink, feathery-steepled churches was the impossible realization of a dream. "A rose-red city half as old as time . . . ."

The raffish delight of "foreignness," of being her own mistress, had reached a climax when she saw The Ring.

She saw it one of the little silversmith shops below the leafy public square. It caught her attention while Vera and Ellen were haggling with the proprietor over a burro pin. It wasn't a valuable ring. To her Quaker eyes, severely trained against the ostentatious, it was almost vulgar. A large, flamboyant white sapphire on a slender band of silver. But there was something tempting in its brash sparkle. She slipped it on her finger and it flashed the sunlight back at her. It made her mother's prim engagement ring, which was worth certainly fifty times as much, fade out of the picture. Miss Lucy felt unaccountably gay, and then self-conscious. With a hurried glance at the stuffy black backs of Vera and Ellen, she tried to take it off her finger.

It would not come off. And while she was still struggling Vera and Ellen joined her, inspecting it with little cries of admiration.

"My, Lucy, it's darling."

"Pretty as an engagement ring."

Miss Lucy flushed. "Don't be foolish. It's much too young for me. I just tried it on. I don't seem to be able . . ."

She pulled at the ring again. The Mexican who owned the shop hovered at her side, purring compliments.

"Go on, Lucy," said Ellen daringly. "Buy it."

"Really, it's annoying. But since I can't seem to get it off, I suppose I'll have to. . ."

Miss Lucy bought the white sapphire ring for a sum which was higher than its value, but which was still negligible to her. While Ellen, who handled all the financial aspects of the trip because she was "so clever" at those things, settled with the proprietor, Miss Lucy said to Vera:

"I'll get it off with soap and water back at the hotel."

But she didn't take it off. Somehow her new disturbing happiness had become centered in it.

In Taxco Miss Lucy's energy seemed boundless. That evening, before dinner, while Vera and Ellen were resting aching feet in their rooms, she decided upon a second trip to the Church of Santa Prisca which dominated the public square. Her first visit had been marred by the guidebook chatter of her companions. She wanted to be alone in that cool, tenebrous interior, to try to get the feeling of its atmosphere, so different from the homespun godliness of her own Quaker meetinghouse at home.

As she stepped through the ornate wooden doors, the fantastic Churrigueresque altar of gold-leaf flowers and cherubs gleamed richly at her. An ancient peasant woman, sheathed in black, was offering a guttering candle to an image of the Virgin. A mongrel dog ran past her into the church, looked around and ran out again. The splendor and the small humanities of the scene had a curious effect upon Miss Lucy. This stood for all that was "popish" and alien and yet it seemed to call her. On an impulse which she less than half understood, she dropped to her knees, in imitation of the peasant woman, and crossed herself, the sapphire ring flashing with some of the exotic quality of the church itself.

Miss Lucy remained kneeling only a short time, but before she rose she was conscious of a presence close to her on the right. She glanced around and saw that a Mexican youth in a spotless white suit had entered the church and was kneeling a few yards away, the thick hair shining on his reverently bent head. As she got up, his gaze met hers. It was only a momentary glance, but she retained a vivid impression of his face. Honey-brown skin and the eyes—particularly the eyes—dark and patient with a gentle, passive beauty. Somehow that brief contact gave her the sensation of seeing a little into the mind of this strange city of strange people. Remembering him, her spontaneous genuflection seemed somehow the right thing to have done. Not, of course, that she would ever speak of it to Vera and Ellen.

She left the church, happy and ready for dinner. The evening light had faded, and as she passed from the crowded Xocalo into the deserted street which led to the hotel, it was almost night. Her footsteps echoed unfamiliarly against the rough cobblestones. The sound seemed to emphasize her loneliness. A single male figure, staggering slightly, was coming up the hill now toward her. Miss Lucy was no coward, but with a tingle of alarm she realized that the oncomer was drunk. She looked around. There was no one else in sight. A weak impulse urged her to return to the Xocalo, but she suppressed it. After all, she was an American, she would not be harmed. She marched steadfastly on.

But the seeds of fear were there, and when she came abreast of the man, he peered at her and swung toward her. He was bearded and shabby and his breath reeked of tequila. He started a stream of Spanish which she couldn't understand. She knew he was begging and, trained to organized charities, Miss Lucy had no sympathy for street beggars. She shook her head firmly and tried to move on. But a dirty hand grabbed her sleeve, and the soft whining words continued. She freed her arm more violently than she intended. Anger glinted in the man's eyes. He raised his arm in an indignant gesture.

Although he was obviously not intending to strike her, Miss Lucy recoiled instinctively and as she did so, caught her high heel in the uneven cobbles and fell rather ungracefully on the ground. She lay there, her ankle twisted underneath her while the man stood threateningly, it seemed, over her.

For a moment, Miss Lucy felt panic—blind overwhelming terror completely unjustified by the almost farcical unpleasantness of the situation.

And then from the shadows, another man appeared. A slight man in a white suit. Miss Lucy could not see his face but she knew that it was the boy from the church. She was conscious of his white-sleeved arm flashing toward the beggar and pushing him away.

She saw the beggar reel backwards and shuffle mutteringly off. Then she was aware of a young face close to her own, and a strong arm was helping her to rise. She could not understand all her rescuer said, but his voice was gentle and concerned.

"*Qué malo*," he said, grinning in the direction of the departing beggar. "*Malo Mexicano*." The teeth gleamed white in the moonlight. "Me Mario, from the church, yes? Me help the señora, no?"

He almost carried Miss Lucy, who had twisted her ankle painfully, back to the hotel and right into her room where she was turned over to the flustered administrations of Vera and Ellen.

As Mario hovered solicitously around, Ellen grabbed at her pocket book with a whispered: "How much, Lucy?"

But here Miss Lucy showed a will of her own. "No. Money would be an insult."

And Mario, who seemed to understand, said "*Gracias, Señora*." And after several sentences, in which Miss Lucy understood only the word "*madre*," he picked up Miss Lucy's left hand—the one with the new sapphire ring—kissed it and then bowed himself smilingly out.

That was how Mario had come into their lives. And having come in, it was apparent that he intended to stay. Next morning he came to the hotel to inquire for Miss Lucy and she saw him squarely for the first time. He was not really handsome. His long-lashed eyes were perhaps a shade too close together. His slight mustache above the full-lipped mouth was perhaps too long. But his figure, though slight, was powerful, and there was something about him that inspired both affection and confidence.

He was, he explained, a student anxious to make a little money on vacation. He wanted to be a guide to the Señoras, and since Miss Lucy could not walk with her twisted ankle, he suggested that he hire a car and act as their chauffeur. The fee he requested was astonishingly small and he stubbornly refused to accept more.

The next day he hired a car at a low price which more than satisfied even the parsimonious Miss Ellen and from then on he drove the ladies around to points of interest with as much care and consideration as if they had been his three "*madres.*"

His daily appearances, always in spotless white, were a constant delight to Miss Lucy—indeed, to all three of them. He was full of plans for their entertainment. One day he drove them around the base of Mount Popocatepetl and for several hours they were able to rhapsodize over what is certainly one of the most beautiful and mysterious mountains in the world. And for a moment when they happened to be alone together, staring at the dazzling whiteness of the mountain's magnificent summit, Miss Lucy felt her hand taken in Mario's firm brown one and softly squeezed.

It was of course, his way of telling her, despite the difficulties of language, that they were sharing a great Mexican experience and he was glad they were sharing it together. Under his touch the large sapphire in the ring pressed into her finger painfully, but another feeling, different from pain, stirred in her.

After the Popocatepetl trip, Miss Lucy decided that it was time to leave Taxco and take up their quarters in Mexico City.

She instructed Ellen to dismiss Mario—to give him an extra hundred pesos and to let him know politely yet firmly that his services were terminated. But Ellen might as well have tried to dispel Popocatepetl or bid it remove itself into the sea. Mario just laughed at her, waved away the hundred pesos, and referred himself directly to Miss Lucy. There were bad Mexicans in Mexico City. He threw out his strong, honey-gold hands. He would take care of them. No, of no importance was the money of Señora Ellen (the other two women were always Señora to him, Miss Lucy alone was Señorita). The important thing was that he should show them everything. Here the strong arms waved to embrace the sun, the sky, the mountains, all of Mexico. And the dark eyes with the too-thick lashes embraced Miss Lucy too.

And Miss Lucy, acting against some deeply rooted instinct, yielded.

Mario went with them to Mexico City.

It was the second week of their stay in Mexico City and they had decided upon a trip to the Pyramids at Teotihuacan. As usual Miss Lucy sat in front with Mario. He was an excellent driver and she loved to watch his profile as he concentrated on the road; loved his occasional murmurs to himself when something pleased or displeased him. She liked it less when he turned to her, flashing his dark eyes caressingly on her face and lowering them to her breast.

His gaze embarrassed her and today something prompted her to say to him laughingly in English:

"Mario, you are what in America we call a flirt. I imagine you are very popular with the girls here in Mexico."

For a moment he did not seem to understand her remark. Then he burst out:

"*Girls—muchachas. Para me, no.*" His hand went into his breast pocket and he brought out a small battered photograph. "*Mi muchacha.* My girl, *mi unica muchacha . . . Una sola . . .*"

Miss Lucy took the photograph. It was of a woman older than herself with gray hair and large sad eyes. There were lines of worry and illness in her face.

"Your mother?" said Miss Lucy gently. "Tell me about her."

Mario rattled on, not in the slow careful Spanish which he generally reserved for the ladies, but in a rapid monologue of which Miss Lucy understood but part. She gathered that Mario's mother was terribly poor, that she had devoted her life in a tiny Guerreros village to raising fatherless children, and was a saint on earth. It was obvious that Mario felt the almost idolatrous love for his mother that is so frequent in young Mexican males.

While he talked excitedly, Miss Lucy reached a decision. Somehow, before her vacation was over, she'd get from Mario his mother's address and she'd write and send her money, enough money to finance Mario at college. A mother surely would accept it even though her son might be too proud to yield to persuasion.

"Is that one of the pyramids?" It was Ellen's disappointed voice that broke the chain of Miss Lucy's thought. "Why, it's nothing compared to the pyramids in Egypt!"

Miss Lucy was thrilled, however, by the pyramids of the Sun and the Moon. And as she gazed at their somber, ancient magnificence, she felt that strange inner elation, which she had felt on the morning when she had genuflected and crossed herself in the church at Taxco.

"I'm not going to climb up those crumbly steps," said Ellen peevishly. "I'm too old and it's too hot."

And Vera, though never too hot, was far too old. She stood at the foot of the pyramid, her coat hanging sleevelessly over her shoulders, the inevitable cigarette held in her clawlike hand. "You go, Lucy—you're young and active."

Lucy went.

With Mario's help she climbed to the very top of the Pyramid of the Sun and she was hardly out of breath when she reached the summit, so great was her sense of mystic exaltation.

They sat alone and close together on the summit, this cultivated woman past fifty with a degree from Bryn Mawr, and this almost ignorant boy from an adobe hut in the hinterland of Guerreros. They looked over the vast design of the square where the ancient village had been with its Temple of Quetzalcoatl of the Plumed Serpents, gazing down at the Road of the Dead which led from the Temple to the Pyramid of the Moon.

Mario started to tell her of the sacrificial rites of the feast of Toxcatl which, in ancient days, took place once a year.

As he talked, Miss Lucy half-closed her eyes and visualized the scene: the assembled public hushed in the huge square beneath them; the priests, each in his appointed place on the steps of the Pyramid; the spotless youth who was, of course, Mario.

And because it was Mario who was being sacrificed in her mind, sacrificed to the futility of life and beauty, she felt a warm human pity for him and instinctively her hand went out—the hand with the cheap sapphire ring that would not come off—and it found his, and was held fast in his warm brown fingers.

Miss Lucy was hardly aware of it when Mario's arm slipped round her, and his dark head dropped against her breast. It was not until she became conscious of a smell like warm brown sugar, which was his skin, and a smell of flowery oil which he used on his hair, that all Philadelphia came rushing back. She jumped up hastily—jumping out of the centuries to this practical moment when two friends would be waiting at the base of the pyramid, hungry for lunch—and there were a great many steps to descend.

On the way home Miss Lucy decided that she and Vera would take the back seat, so Ellen sat in front and argued with the sulky Mario.

When they reached the pension, Miss Lucy said quickly:

"It's a Sunday tomorrow, Mario. You'd better take a holiday."

He began to protest. When Lucy repeated, "No, not tomorrow, Mario," his face fell like a disappointed child's. Then his expression changed, and his dark eyes looked squarely, challengingly into hers.

As she turned into the house, Miss Lucy felt her heart pounding. The intimacy of that glance had brought into the open the thing which she had not dared to contemplate before. She was quite certain of it now.

Somehow—for some reason that she did not understand and in some way that her simple mind had never dreamed of—Mario desired her.

He desired her physically.

That night, before she went to bed, Miss Lucy did something she had never done in her life before. She stood in her plain cotton nightgown for several minutes before the long Venetian mirror in the sumptuous room and took stock of herself as a woman.

She saw nothing new or startling—nothing external to balance the startling changes which were going on inside her. Her face was not beautiful. It never had been, even in youth, and now it was uncompromisingly middle-aged. Her hair was almost white but not white enough. It was soft and plentiful and sat rather prettily on her forehead. Her eyes were clear and pleasing in themselves, but surrounded by the lines and shadows natural to her age. Her breasts were firm beneath the cotton nightgown but her figure was in no way remarkable. In fact, there was nothing externally desirable either about her face or her body. And yet she was desired. She knew it. For some reason a handsome Mexican youth found her desirable. Miss Lucy was sure of that.

There was no nonsense about Miss Lucy and she knew that young men often make up to rich older women in the hopes of eventually obtaining money from them. But Mario, apart from the fact that he'd refused all financial offers, did not even know that Miss Lucy was by far the richest of the three ladies. Only a Philadelphia lawyer or a member of their old Quaker family could possibly know how rich Miss Lucy really was. No, if Mario had wanted money, he would have concentrated on Ellen who held the purse strings and never for a moment let it be known to anyone that it was Miss Lucy's money she was dispensing.

There was nothing about Miss Lucy, drab, black-clad Miss Lucy, to suggest wealth. True, her mother's engagement ring had a rather valuable diamond in it. But only an expert jeweler would recognize that. As for the flashy white sapphire ring, that wasn't worth anyone's time or energy and Miss Lucy would have gladly given it to Mario out of gratitude if only she could have got it off her finger.

No, there were thousands of other women in Mexico City with far more obvious signs of wealth. There were young, beautiful women and any one of them might have been pleased and proud to have Mario as an escort and—yes, Miss Lucy faced it uncompromisingly—as something else.

And yet . . . suddenly Miss Lucy became frightened at the illogicality of it all.

Some virginal instinct stirred in her and warned her of—danger.

And because there was no nonsense about Miss Lucy, she decided that she must do something final about it. Lying there quietly beneath the sheets, she came to her great resolution.

Miss Lucy and Vera were waiting at the bus station. Both of them hugged their coats around them as if cold. Vera was always cold, of course. But today Miss Lucy was cold, too, despite the splendid warmth of the spring sunshine. Her eyes—and her nose—were red.

They were waiting for Ellen who had been left behind to deliver the final *coup de grâce* to Mario. The bus for Patzcuaro was leaving in twenty minutes.

At last Ellen appeared. Her nose was red too.

"You shouldn't have done it, Lucy," she snapped. "It was cruel." She thrust two one-hundred-peso bills into Lucy's hands. "I thought he was going to hit me when I gave him these." She sniffed. "And he burst into tears like a child when he read your letter."

Miss Lucy did not speak. In fact, she spoke very little during the entire length of the tiring bus journey to Patzcuaro.

The three women had been sitting since dinner around their table on the veranda overlooking the serene expanse of Lake Patzcuaro. Ellen restlessly voluble, was discussing possible plans for the next day. Miss Lucy was, apparently, paying no attention. Her eyes studied the evening gray-green waters of the lake with its clustering islands and its obscene bald-headed vultures that squawked and fought greedily over scraps of carrion on the lake shore.

After a short time she rose, saying: "It's getting a bit cold. I think I'll go up to my room. Goodnight."

Miss Lucy's room, with its small veranda, commanded a view of the lake from another angle. Below her, in the growing darkness, the fishermen were pottering with their boats, talking in low, sibilant voices or singing snatches of Michoacan songs.

Miss Lucy sat watching them. She was thinking of Mario, missing him with an intensity that was almost painful. She had thought of him constantly since she left Mexico City and now was appalled at her harshness in dismissing him by proxy through Ellen. She should have spoken to him herself. She would hate to have him think . . . The thoughts went on with a goading persistence. She had done him a wrong, hurt him . . . .

At some indeterminate stage of her reverie she became conscious of a white-clad figure moving among the fishermen below. Miss Lucy's gaze rested on him and then her heart turned over. She strained forward and peered into the darkness. Surely, surely, there was something familiar about those light, graceful movements—that small, compact form.

But it couldn't be Mario! She had left him hundreds of miles away in Mexico City, and Ellen had been particularly instructed not to tell him where they were going.

The figure in white moved away from the lake shore towards her window. He passed through a shaft of light from an open door. There was no doubt about it now.

It was Mario.

She bent over the balcony, her heart fluttering like a foolish bird. He was only about fifteen feet below her.

"Oh, Miss Lucy, I have found you." He spoke in the slow careful Spanish which he reserved for her. "I knew I would find you."

"But, Mario, how . . . ?"

"The bus company told me you had come here. I got a ride and I have been waiting."

She saw his teeth gleaming as he smiled at her. "Miss Lucy, why did you go away without saying *adios*?"

She did not answer.

"But I am back now to take care of you. And tomorrow you and I—we will go on the lake. Before the other two ladies are up. You and I alone together. There will be a moon and then the sunrise."

"Yes . . ."

"At five o'clock in the morning I come. I will have a boat. Before even the birds awake I will be waiting here."

"Yes, yes . . ."

"Goodnight, *carissima*."

Miss Lucy went back into her room. Her hands were trembling as she undid her dress and slipped into bed.

And she was still trembling when—in the middle of the night, it seemed—a low whistle beneath her window told her that Mario had come for her.

She dressed swiftly, patted her soft gray hair into place, threw a coat over her shoulders and hurried downstairs. The hotel was very quiet. No one saw her as she made her way through the deserted lobby and no one saw her as she went down the slope to where Mario was waiting for her with the boat.

He took her hand and pressed it to his lips. Then he drew her gently towards the boat.

She did not resist. It was as though he were Destiny leading her onwards towards the inevitable.

Mario had been right. There was a moon—full and lemon-white, it shed a weird light on the opaque waters of the lake.

Miss Lucy was in the bottom of the boat, lying on her coat. It was cold, but she did not seem to notice it. She was watching Mario as he stood up in the boat, guiding it skillfully past the other craft into the deep waters of the lake. He had rolled his trousers up beyond his knees and his legs looked strong and somehow cruel in the moonlight. He was singing.

Miss Lucy had not realized before what a beautiful voice he had. The song seemed sweet and ineffably sad. Mario's eyes caressed her as his gaze travelled downward from her face and rested on her hands which lay impassive on her lap. The cheap sapphire sparkled in the moonlight.

Miss Lucy was not conscious of time or place as the boat moved slowly toward the secret heart of the lake with its myriad islets. She was not conscious of the dimming stars and the moon paling before the dawn. She felt only a deep, utter tranquility, as though this gentle, almost imperceptible motion must go on forever. She started at the sound of Mario's voice:

"Listen, the birds."

She heard them in the cluster of small islands that were all around her, but she could see only the vultures that hovered silently overhead.

Mario rested from his rowing and produced a parcel. It contained *tortas,* butter, and goat cheese. He also brought out a bottle of red Mexican wine.

He spread butter on a *torta* with his large clasp knife and handed it to Miss Lucy. Suddenly she realized that she was very hungry. She ate wolfishly and drank from the bottle of the sweet Mexican wine. It went to her head and made her feel girlish and happy. She laughed at everything Mario said and he laughed too while his eyes still caressed her.

And so they breakfasted like honeymoon lovers, as a sunrise splashed red gold over the lake, miles away now from anyone, with only the visible vultures and the invisible songsters to witness them.

When the last *torta* was eaten and the bottle drained, Mario took up his paddle again and propelled the boat deeper into the heart of the lake, on and on without speaking.

As soon as she saw the island, Miss Lucy knew it was the one Mario had chosen. It looked more solitary, more aloof than the rest of them, and there was a fringe of high reeds around its edges.

He steered the boat carefully through the reeds which were so tall that they were completely hidden in a little world of their own. When they reached the shore, he took her hand and raised her gently with the one word: "Come."

She followed him like a child. He found a dry spot and spread out her coat for her. Then, as she lay down, he sat with her head in his lap. She could see his face above hers very close; could see those dark eyes set a little too close together; could feel the warm breath, wine-scented, that came from his lips.

She closed her eyes knowing that this was the moment to which everything had been leading—ever since the day in the church of Santa Prisca when she had first met Mario. She could feel his hands caressing her hair, her face, gently, gently. She felt him take her hand, felt him touch the sapphire ring.

The moment he touched the ring, she knew. She could feel it in his fingers, an outflowing, obsessive desire. The whole pattern which had seemed so complex was plain.

His hands moved upward. His fingers, still gentle, reached her throat. She didn't scream. She wasn't even frightened.

As his hands tightened their grasp, the full mouth came down upon hers, and their lips met in their first and only kiss.

Mario threw the bloodstained knife away. He hated the sight of blood and it had disgusted him that he had had to cut off a finger to get the ring.

He hadn't even bothered about the engagement ring that had belonged to Miss Lucy's mother. It was a plain, cheap affair, and for weeks now the great beauty of the sapphire had blinded him to anything else.

He spread the coat carefully over Miss Lucy's body. For a moment he considered putting it in the reeds, but it might float away and be discovered by the fishermen.

Here, on the island, it could be years before anyone came, and by that time—he glanced up at the vultures hovering eternally overhead . . . .

Without looking back Mario went to the boat and rowed towards the deserted mainland shore. There he landed, overturned the boat, and pushed it free so that it would drift into deep water.

An American woman had gone out in a boat on the lake with an inexperienced boatman. They had both been drowned. The officials would never drag so big a lake to find the bodies.

Mario made his way in the direction of the railroad track. He could board a freight car and tomorrow perhaps he would be in Guerreros.

He was sure his mother would like the ring.

CHALLENGE TO THE READER
Hugh Pentecost

Born in Massachusetts, the prolific mystery novelist and short story writer Judson (Pentecost) Philips' (1903-1989) best-known pseudonym is Hugh Pentecost, taken from a great-uncle, a noted criminal lawyer in New York at the turn of the last century. The author's other pseudonym, Philip Owen, was also borrowed from a relative.

During his tireless and highly professional career, Philips wrote more than ninety novels under his own name and as Pentecost and Owen while producing virtually countless short stories for such major fiction magazines as *Colliers, The Saturday Evening Post, Liberty*, and *Cosmopolitan*, with more than a hundred in *Ellery Queen's Mystery Magazine.*

For the pulps, he wrote between forty and fifty thousand words a month for more than a decade. He was the co-author of *General Crack*, John Barrymore's first talkie, and worked on many other motion pictures and television shows, including numerous episodes of *Suspense*, the Father Brown mysteries for radio; and scripts for such TV drama series as *The Web*, *The Ray Milland Show*, *The Hallmark Hall of Fame*, and *Studio One.*

He covered sports for *The New York Times* while still a teenager, was the co-owner and editor of the *Harlem Valley Times*, and founded the Sharon Playhouse, for which he produced plays for twenty-eight years (1950-1977). He was a founder of Mystery Writers of America, became its third president, and was honored with the Grand Master Award in 1973.

"Challenge to the Reader" was originally published in the May 1947 issue of *Ellery Queen's Mystery Magazine.*

Challenge to the Reader

Hugh Pentecost

THE BLOND man lay on his stomach on the lawn near the edge of the lake, a newspaper spread out on the grass in front of him. A large picture of Nancy Bradford and her small daughter, Sybil, stared up at him. Of course the picture showed Nancy Bradford and her child as they had looked *before* the murder, not afterwards.

The blond man's hair and heavy eyebrows were bleached almost white, probably by the bright August sunshine. Those eyebrows were drawn together in a concentrated frown as he read the newspaper story. It was a Sunday supplement with many pictures and a long rehash of the Bradford case written by the paper's leading crime reporter. The article purported to give all the known facts in the particularly brutal and sadistic killing of the lovely actress and her small daughter. They had been beaten to death, almost out of human semblance, with a heavy iron poker. It was the opinion of the medical examiner that the murderous beating had gone on, violently, long after both mother and child were dead. It was called a crime of passion—black, turbulent, sick passion.

The murderer had been described in the usual confusing fashion by the doorman in Nancy Bradford's apartment—described as a tall, short, fair, dark, fat, thin man who wore blue-tinted glasses, a tweed topcoat in July, and a dark-gray snap-brim hat. He had come into the foyer and asked for Nancy. Bradford. The doorman had pointed to the house phone, and the tall, short, fair, dark, fat, thin man had called Nancy Bradford's apartment. The doorman heard him speak. He said: "Hello, darling. It's me." He was evidently invited up because he went directly to the automatic elevator and the doorman watched the indicator needle rise to Nancy's floor.

An hour later a certain Mrs. Carpenter; whose job it was to sit with small Sybil Bradford if Nancy went out for the evening, arrived and went up to the apartment. She reappeared in the foyer presently, screaming hysterically and making no sense whatever. The doorman phoned the police after he was able to distinguish the word "murder" amidst the jumble of Mrs. Carpenter's ravings. The doorman did *not* go upstairs. He justified this on the ground of duty. But there was a result from it. The doorman could swear that the tall, short, fair, dark, fat, thin man with the blue glasses and the tweed topcoat had never left the building. He hadn't come down in the elevator and he hadn't come down the inside fire stairs which also opened into the lobby, and there wasn't any other way out. The papers had made a lot of this, but the police were not overly concerned by this mystery angle. Whatever the testimony, the man was gone—perhaps like Chesterton's postman, perhaps by magic. The puzzle of *how* was not important. The important thing was that he must be found.

There wasn't much to go on. There had been money and jewelry in the apartment. The jewelry had been taken but the money—several hundred dollars—had been left. The police were of two minds about it. The jewelry had been stolen as a blind for the real motive—or it had been a gift from the murderer which he now took back. Outside of this one clue? Well, on the floor of the Bradford apartment were two extinguished lives, two dreadfully mutilated bodies, and—two pine needles.

The blond man raised his eyes from the newspapers and turned his head toward the hotel which was set back about a hundred yards from the lake. Back of the hotel was the dark green mystery of a heavy pine forest. He stared for a long time as if he hoped somehow to penetrate the brooding darkness of the wood to some bright point of clarification. Finally he lowered his eyes to the newspaper once more.

The blond man's concentration was so intense that he was not aware of the approach of the fat man. The fat man came from the direction of the boathouse. He wore faded khaki pants, a corduroy hunting coat with deep, bulging pockets, and a battered gray hat with fishing flies stuck in the band. He was reaming out the bowl of a short, black pipe with the blade of a penknife. The operation completed, he put the stem of the pipe in his mouth and blew hard to clear it. Then he paused, his gray eyes blinking through the lenses of his steel-rimmed spectacles at the newspaper reader. He moved quietly across the grass until he stood directly over the blond man.

"Pretty gruesome business—the Bradford case," he said.

The blond man moved as if someone had jabbed a pin into him. He rolled over onto his side, braced half-upright on his elbow, staring up at the fat man, his eyes dilated, his whole attitude defensive.

"Sorry if I startled you," the fat man said. His smile was slow and friendly.

"I—I didn't hear you coming," the blond man said. He fished for cigarettes in the breast pocket of his blue denim shirt.

"My name is Doyle," the fat man said. "I noticed you in the hotel dining room last night. You just arrived?"

"Yes. I'm Jerry Hartman—radio writer."

Doyle grinned. "You mean—'Love that soap!'?"

"I write dramatic shows. The agencies handle the commercials."

Doyle's mild eyes moved back to the newspaper on the grass. "Maybe you knew Nancy Bradford. I understand she did a lot of radio acting."

"I never happened to meet her," Hartman said.

That seemed to end it. Doyle looked out at the shimmering expanse of the lake. "I was going out to try to catch a few bass," he said. "It's pretty sunny but there are some shady spots along the shore."

"I have a license," Hartman said, "but I don't know one fish from another."

"Same here," Doyle said. "It's just getting out and relaxing that counts. Steep in a little sun. Want to join me?"

Hartman had difficulty lighting the match for his cigarette. He finally managed and dragged the smoke deep into his lungs. "I—I don't know," he said. "I haven't any equipment. I—"

"I've got extra stuff," Doyle said. "We probably won't catch anything anyway. I just thought a little company—But if you feel like being alone—"

"I—I think I'd like it," Hartman said. He scrambled up to his feet and then bent down to pick up the paper. He rolled it up and stuck it under his arm.

"I've rented one of the rowboats," Doyle said. "You ready to start now?"

"Yes. Yes, I'm all ready if you've got some extra tackle."

"Let's go," Doyle said.

The rowboat was chained to the platform inside the boathouse. Doyle's tackle was in the back of the boat along with a small wicker hamper.

"I've got some sandwiches and a thermos of iced tea in there," Doyle said. "If you want some liquor—"

"I don't drink," Hartman said.

"And you in the radio business?" Doyle chuckled.

Hartman seemed to force a smile. "Maybe that's why. I'm on my second ulcer."

"Get in," Doyle said. "I'll row. I know a place where we might have some luck."

Hartman climbed into the back of the boat, balancing himself unsteadily. Doyle unfastened the chain and then climbed in and sat down in the middle seat. He reached out and pushed off with his hand. The boat moved slowly out of the boathouse shade into the bright sun. Once clear, Doyle fitted the oars into the oarlocks and began rowing. He used short but very powerful strokes that shot the boat forward in the water. He was the first one to speak.

"It seems impossible he could have got away without leaving a clearer trail," he said.

"Who could have got away from what?" Hartman asked.

"The Bradford murderer."

"Oh," Hartman said.

"I've toyed with the idea that the man with the blue glasses wasn't the murderer at all."

"Oh?" Hartman tossed his cigarette stub out onto the water. He watched it bob up and down in the boat's wake.

Doyle kept rowing steadily as he talked. "Suppose you were a friend of Nancy Bradford's. You went upstairs and walked into that shambles. *My* impulse would be to get away—not to be involved."

"But that couldn't have been the way it was," Hartman said.

Doyle stopped rowing, leaning forward on the oars. The boat continued to move slowly through the water. "Why not?"

"He spoke to her on the house phone," Hartman said. He tapped the newspaper which lay on the seat beside him. "The doorman heard him say 'Hello, darling. It's me.' He went right up. She must have been alive then, you see,"

"Maybe the man in the glasses was bluffing."

Hartman shook his head. "If he was bluffing then he was involved anyway. No, it must have been that guy all right. Only the description of him just isn't any use. He wouldn't wear those blue glasses again. You can bank on that."

Doyle nodded slowly. "I guess you're right," he said. He began rowing again.

"Those pine needles," Hartman said, after a moment.

"What about 'em?"

"Well, he must have come from some place where he'd walked in pine needles. They stuck to his shoes—or maybe to the bottom of his trousers." Hartman looked back across the lake toward the pine forest behind the hotel. "Here, perhaps."

Doyle laughed. "Pleasant idea! The Bradford murderer may have been around here all the time I've been vacationing."

"It's quite possible," Hartman said. "There's the brooch."

Doyle stopped rowing. His gray eyes were fixed, unblinking,

on Hartman's pale face. It was odd that Hartman's hair should be so bleached by the sun and yet his face was neither sunburned nor brown.

"What brooch?" Doyle asked.

"Why, Nancy Bradford's brooch," Hartman said. "It was found in a path in the woods here. Some local kid picked it up and turned it over to the cops."

"They found it *here*?"

"That's right. A day or two after the murder."

"How do you know that?" Doyle's voice was on a curious dead level.

"Why—I guess I read it somewhere," Hartman said.

"That's funny. I thought I'd read everything about the case and I never saw anything about the brooch."

Hartman moistened his lips. "Well, I must have read it somewhere," he said. "I wouldn't have any other way of knowing."

"No," Doyle said, slowly. "No, I suppose not." He started rowing again, the rhythm a little slower than before. "If they found the brooch here you'd think the place would be swarming with detectives."

Hartman's smile was forced. "Maybe it is," he said. "They wouldn't necessarily come out in the open for fear of scaring off their man."

"Yes," Doyle said, "I suppose they would handle it that way. Since they have no way of identifying the man, they'd just lie low till he made a mistake."

"What kind of mistake?"

"I don't know," Doyle said. "Probably they don't either. They'd just wait and hope." He pulled on the right oar and headed the boat in toward the shore. "Good shady place over there," he said, nodding toward a clump of willows whose branches spread shadow well over the water. When he had his bearings he started pulling on the oars again. He smiled. "You wouldn't kid me, would you, Hartman? About being a radio writer?"

"Well, it's a secret," Hartman said, in a mock-confidential tone, "but I'm really a junior G-man."

They both laughed.

Doyle pulled the boat into the shade of the willows. Then he shipped his oars and climbed to the bow of the boat. He lowered an anchor which was fastened to the boat by a heavy chain. Hartman looked over the side at a colony of water bugs that flitted across the dark blue surface of the lake.

"Push that box of tackle forward and I'll bait a line for you," Doyle said.

There was a can of damp earth from which Doyle extracted worms. He fastened one to each hook on the two lines and handed one line to Hartman. They dropped the lines over the side and the little tan floats bobbed away from the side of the boat. Doyle hooked his line around one of the oarlocks and began filling his pipe.

"How would you go about it, Hartman, if you were a detective?" he asked.

Hartman shrugged. "There isn't much to go on. The doorman's description wouldn't give you any particular physical type to look for."

"Not much."

"About all you'd have to go on from the physical side is that he is extremely strong. It was a man of considerable strength who beat those two into a pulp."

Doyle held a match to the bowl of his pipe. "Not necessarily," he said, after the pipe was going. "I believe it's a medical fact that people who are worked into a homicidal rage often show evidence of strength far beyond their normal capacity. Something to do with the adrenal glands."

"I wouldn't know about that," Hartman said. He looked out across the water. "Say, looks like you have something."

The float on Doyle's line was ducking sharply below the surface. Doyle began to pull in the line. Rock bass don't put up much of a fight. For a moment the silver scales of the fish gleamed in the sunlight and then Doyle hauled it aboard.

"There was a kind of savage cruelty involved in that beating," Doyle said. "I think you could expect to see it crop up in the man in other directions." When Hartman didn't answer he glanced up. The blond man was staring at Doyle, who was holding the bass in one hand and wrenching at the hook in the fish's mouth with the other.

"Stuck good," Doyle said. He gave it another wrench and pulled it free, ripping out the side of the fish's mouth with it. Then he took a short piece of baling wire, jammed it through the fish's gill and out through the mouth. He twisted the wire together so that the fish hung from a loop. He attached the other end of the wire to an oarlock and dropped the fish over the side so that it dragged in the water and would keep fresh there. There had been a kind of ruthless efficiency about it. He looked up and saw the revulsion in Hartman's blue eyes.

"They don't feel anything," he said. "Cold-blooded." He rebaited his hook and dropped the line over the side. "You were saying you'd expect to see some evidence of a cruel streak in the man you'd be looking for—if you were a detective."

"Yes," Hartman said. "Yes—I think you could expect that."

"Not a nice guy to find yourself with alone," Doyle said.

"No . . . not nice at all."

They fished in silence for a long time. The fish weren't biting. Then Hartman glanced down the lake. The sky had taken on a peculiar copper hue. Doyle followed the direction of Hartman's glance and whistled. "Looks like a thunderstorm," he said. "Maybe we better think about getting in. Those things get pretty bad out here on the lake."

"Do you think we can make the hotel before it breaks?"

"We can try," Doyle said. "Here, I'll take in the lines and get things organized. You want to pull up the anchor and start rowing?"

"Okay," Hartman said. He squeezed past Doyle to the bow of the boat. He took hold of the anchor chain with both hands and pulled. Nothing happened. He stopped trying after a moment, breathing hard. "Seems to be caught in something," he said. He took a lower grip on the chain and tried pulling again. He looked back at Doyle. "I'm afraid I can't budge it," he said.

Doyle finished packing away the lines in the wicker hamper and closed the lid. "You come back here and I'll take a whack at it," he said.

The boat rocked slightly as Hartman made his way to the stern seat. Then Doyle worked his way forward and took hold of the anchor chain. As he began pulling at it, the cords stood out in his neck, the corduroy coat seemed to bulge at the shoulders. He didn't yank at the chain. He just applied a steady, powerful pressure. Suddenly he staggered back slightly, the anchor free. In the distance there was the deep, ominous rumble of thunder.

Doyle climbed back into the seat at the oars, grinning. There was a curious tense look about the corners of Hartman's mouth.

"I believe you said the murderer was a strong guy," Doyle said, and laughed. He put out the oars and began rowing back toward the hotel. A jagged streak of lightning split the sky.

Hartman fumbled for a cigarette and lit it. He kept glancing over his shoulder at the approaching storm. Doyle rowed with long, even, powerful strokes. The sun was still bright where they were, but the storm was coming rapidly. At the far end of the lake they could see sheets of rain.

"Of course the murderer would be smarter than that," Doyle said.

"Smarter than what?" Hartman's voice sounded tense, a little frightened.

"To show his strength—since that's what the police would be looking for."

"Oh."

"He might even pretend that he had no strength at all. Now, if I were the murderer I'd have done what you did."

"What I did?"

"Demonstrated that I couldn't do something—like lift an anchor."

"I see." Hartman took a deep drag on his cigarette. "That *would* be the clever thing."

Doyle rowed for a moment in silence. Then he smiled disarmingly. "That anchor wasn't stuck very tight," he said. "I made it look tougher than it was."

"Why?" Hartman asked, sharply.

"Just a gag, Hartman. The idea amuses me."

"What idea?"

"That we're both probably wondering a little bit about each other."

Lightning struck across the sky again and a sudden gust of wind sent water chopping against the side of the boat.

Doyle was still smiling. "Do you ever wear tinted glasses,

Hartman? Most blonds suffer from bright sunshine. Wrong pigmentation."

"Look," Hartman said, "I don't think this gag of yours is very funny."

"Sorry," Doyle said. His smile faded. "I'm afraid we're going to get good and soaked."

Hartman felt a faint spatter of rain against his face. They were still a good five hundred yards from shore. A fork of lightning shot down into the water not far from them and the clap of thunder set the boat vibrating. Doyle kept on with his rowing as if nothing had happened. Hartman's hands were gripping the sides of the boat, his knuckles white.

"Scared?" Doyle asked.

"Not really. But I don't like thunderstorms. Never did."

"Must be a little bit like what happened to the Bradford murderer," Doyle said. "A calm, sunny day—and then—the wrath of God!" He took a deep full stroke with the oars. "Why do you suppose he did it, Hartman? A beautiful woman—charming little girl—"

"Some people can't stand treachery," Hartman said.

The oars remained suddenly poised over the water—water that seemed to have begun to boil slightly. "Treachery?" Doyle said.

"That's the way some men would look at a turndown," Hartman said.

The oars dipped slowly again and Doyle continued his rowing. Lightning and thunder seemed suddenly to engulf them. The rain came—hard—almost painful in the sharpness of its drive. Doyle increased the rhythm of his rowing but he threw his head back, laughing.

"What's the joke?" Hartman shouted at him.

"Your hair!" Doyle shouted back.

"What about my hair?"

Doyle's laughter rang out over the noise of the storm. "I thought it was dyed. So help me, Hartman, I thought it was dyed. I thought the color would run when it got wet."

Hartman lifted his hand to his soaking hair and brought it away again, staring at it as if he, too, expected something odd.

"Everybody always says that . . ." he explained.

And then Doyle nosed the boat into the sanctuary of the boathouse. They sat there, protected from the rain, wiping the water from their faces. Doyle took off his glasses and tried drying them with a damp handkerchief.

"Boy, that really came down!"

Hartman nodded.

"You said you didn't drink, Hartman, but after that soaking maybe you should have something—for medicinal purposes. I've got a bottle of old brandy up in my room."

"Really," Hartman said, "I don't think—"

"Do you good," Doyle said. "You don't want to get chilled."

"Well—"

They walked up across the lawn to the hotel. There was no point in hurrying. They'd never be any wetter than they were now. They crossed the wide porch and went into the big main hall. The water ran off their clothes and made little puddles on the floor. The corner of Hartman's mouth twitched.

"Suppose we each get a quick shower and rubdown before that drink," he said.

Doyle nodded. "Perhaps that's a good idea. But make it snappy. My room's Number Eleven on the second floor."

"See you," Hartman said.

Hartman went to his room. He stripped off his clothes and dropped them on the bathroom floor. He got under the hot shower in the tub and stood there till he was thoroughly warmed. Then he got out and dried himself with a rough bath towel. He walked, naked, into his room and opened the middle bureau drawer. He put on dry socks and underwear, a clean blue flannel shirt. From the closet he got dry trousers and shoes and a worn tweed jacket. Then he stood in front of the mirror and brushed his light blond hair. His mouth twitched again as he looked at his reflection. After he put down his brush and comb he held out his hands in front of him. They were shaking.

Then Hartman pulled open one of the top bureau drawers and moved a pile of handkerchiefs. Under them was a small thirty-two caliber revolver. He slipped it, along with a fresh package of cigarettes and matches, into the right-hand pocket of the tweed coat. Then he looked at his shaking hands once more and swore softly.

Hartman paused outside the door of Room Eleven and then knocked. He heard Doyle call out to him.

"Come on in!"

He opened the door and went in. He could hear water running in the bathtub.

"I got soaking wet here," Doyle called out through the half-open bathroom door. "It felt so good. Be with you in a minute."

"That's okay," Hartman said.

"The brandy's on the bureau. Help yourself."

"Thanks."

Hartman walked over to the bureau. The bottle of brandy and two water glasses stood on the white linen bureau cover. Hartman glanced toward the bathroom. The water was still running in the tub. He reached out—not toward the bottle but toward the top bureau drawer. He pulled the drawer open. He drew in his breath, sharply.

Lying on top of a stack of clean shirts were some photographs—theatrical photographs of Nancy Bradford. They'd been mutilated. Some of them were torn, some of them had been defaced with a heavy black crayon. Hartman picked them up. His hands shook so that the heavy photographic paper rattled in his fingers. Then he heard a faint squeaking noise. He dropped the pictures and swung around. His right hand dove into the pocket of his coat and came out holding the revolver.

"Well, well," Doyle said. He stood in the bathroom doorway, fully dressed. The sound of the water, still running in the tub, came from behind him. And he, too, was holding a gun, quite steadily, pointed at Hartman. "I had a feeling you'd snoop if you had the chance."

Hartman drew a deep breath. He spoke in a loud, very clear voice. "So you're the Bradford murderer," he said.

Doyle's mouth smiled, but the eyes behind the steel-rimmed spectacles were cold. "It won't work, Hartman," he said.

"I knew it," Hartman said, "when I saw you unhook that fish. I knew it when you pulled up that anchor. I knew it when you kept probing and probing to find out who I was. I knew it the way you reacted to my telling you about the brooch."

"It won't work, Hartman," Doyle said.

"How do you explain these pictures of Nancy Bradford in your bureau drawer?"

"They came from Nancy Bradford's apartment." Then Doyle said, still smiling, "The murderer had to destroy even the symbols of Nancy Bradford. You must have hated her like hell, Hartman!"

"It was *you* who hated her," Hartman said. "Even after you'd murdered her you had to go on destroying everything that reminded you of her." His voice was loud, like an attorney addressing a courtroom.

"You ought to know," Doyle said. "You ought to know how the murderer felt. You even told me, Hartman. Some men would think of a turndown as treachery, you said."

"It was you, Doyle. You've been staying around here because you'd lost the brooch. You didn't know whether it had been found or not. No one knew that but the police."

"That's right, Hartman. No one knew but the police. You were fishing when you brought it up. You wanted to know if it *had* been found. You were trying to find out from me because you'd decided that maybe I was a cop looking for you. Well, you were right. I *was* looking for you."

Hartman laughed. "I'll bet you were," he said.

"The pretense that you weren't strong enough to lift the anchor. Your pretended squeamishness when I yanked that hook out of the bass's mouth. I did that on purpose—just to see how you'd behave. You're a good actor, Hartman."

"This isn't getting us anywhere," Hartman said. "You'd better drop that gun."

"You've been in the radio and theater business, Hartman. You knew how easy it would be to fool the doorman at Nancy Bradford's apartment. You made yourself noticeable going in and unnoticeable coming out."

"Drop that gun," Hartman said.

Doyle laughed. "Stop kidding," he said. "It won't work, Hartman." He took a step forward.

Suddenly thunder shook the room—the thunder of two guns fired almost simultaneously. The two men stood there, swaying, pulling the triggers of the two guns. Slowly Hartman slumped to his knees, a bewildered, frightened look on his face. The smoking gun fell out of his hand and he pitched forward on his face.

Doyle leaned against the door jamb. There were bright red stains spreading on the front of his white shirt. He coughed—a wet, choking cough.

There were excited voices in the hall outside and the sound of running feet. The door burst open and the clerk and the hotel porter, in a blue uniform, burst into the room. They stopped just inside the door staring at the man on the floor—and at Doyle.

Doyle coughed. "He was the Bradford murderer," he said. He coughed again. "I'd been looking for him—special assignment."

The porter crossed the room and knelt beside Hartman. Presently he stood up. His face was very pale. "Dead," he said. He looked at Doyle. "You look as though you were pretty badly hurt," he said. "You better lie down on the bed while we get you a doctor." He walked over to Doyle.

"I—I feel a little sick at my stomach," Doyle said, smiling weakly.

The porter reached him. Then suddenly the porter's left hand knocked the gun from Doyle's flabby fingers and his right smashed squarely against Doyle's mouth in a pile-driving punch. Doyle staggered back and fell on the bathroom floor.

"Special assignment!" the porter shouted. "Special assignment for murder—you crazy killer!" He turned to the hotel clerk. From his pocket he took a small leather folder and opened it, disclosing a police badge. "There's your Bradford murderer," he said, pointing at Doyle. "Hartman was a homicide man. We worked as a team." His voice was bitter. "Why wasn't I around when they came in? He might have passed the tip to me. I might have saved him." He looked down at Hartman's body. "Poor guy! He was always scared as hell on a job like this—but he never flinched—never took a backward step."

The clerk's eyes moved from the body of Hartman to the still figure of Doyle.

"Why—why did he k-kill Nancy Bradford?" It was almost a whisper.

"He was her first husband," the homicide man said. "A paranoid killer. She'd been hiding from him—changed her name—remarried. Then he showed up—seemed all right—wanted to see his child. She thought he was cured—everything all right. Then—"

"Maybe—maybe I b-better get a d-doctor for him," the clerk said.

"Let the—let him die," the homicide man said, grimly. "It'll save the state a lot of dough."

TERROR TOWN
Ellery Queen

As Anthony Boucher wrote, "Ellery Queen *is* the American detective story," but the two Brooklyn cousins who collaborated under the pseudonym Ellery Queen, Frederic Dannay (born Daniel Nathan) (1905-1982) and Manfred B(ennington) Lee (born Manford Lepofsky) (1905-1971), also conceived one of the most brilliant marketing decisions of all time by naming their detective Ellery Queen. They reasoned that if readers forgot the name of the author, *or* the name of the character, they might remember the other. It worked, as Ellery Queen is counted among the handful of best-known names in the history of mystery fiction with more than a dozen movies based on their books and several radio and television shows as well as comics.

Lee was a full collaborator on the fiction created as Ellery Queen but Dannay on his own was also one of the most important figures in the mystery world for more than a half-century. He founded *Ellery Queen's Mystery Magazine* in 1941; it remains, more than eighty years later, the most significant periodical in the genre. He also formed one of the first great collections of detective fiction first editions, often leading to reprinted stories in the magazines and anthologies he edited, which are among the best ever produced, most notably *101 Years' Entertainment* (1941), arguably the greatest mystery anthology ever published. He also produced such landmark reference books as *Queen's Quorum* (1951) and *The Detective Short Story* (1942).

"Terror Town" was originally published in the August 1956 issue of *Argosy*.

Terror Town

Ellery Queen

YOUNG SUSAN Marsh, red-haired librarian of the Flora G. Sloan Library, Northfield's cultural pride, steered the old wreck of a Buick around the Stanchion blinker in the center of town and headed up Hill street toward the red-brick Town Hall, coughing as the smoke came through the floorboards. Susan did not mind. She had discovered that the 1940 sedan only smoked going up steep grades, and the road between town and her little cottage in Burry's Hollow three miles out of Northfield, her usual route, was mostly as level as a barn floor.

The vintage Buick had been given to Susan a few weeks before, in October, by Miss Flora Sloan, Northfield's undisputed autocrat and, to hear some tell it, a lineal descendant of Ebenezer Scrooge.

"But Miss Flora," Susan had exclaimed, her ponytail flying, "why me?

"'Cause all that robber Will Pease offered me on her was a measly thirty-five dollars," Miss Flora had said grimly. "I'd rather you had her for nothing."

"Well, I don't know what to say, Miss Flora. She's beautiful."

"Fiddle-de-sticks," the old lady had said. "She needs a ring job, her tires are patchy, one headlight's broken, the paint's scrofulous, and she's stove in on the left side. But the short time I had her she took me where I wanted to go, Susan, and she'll take you, too. It's better than pedaling a bike six miles a day to the library and back, the way you've had to do since your father passed on." And Miss Flora had added a pinch of pepper: "It isn't as if girls wore bloomers like they used to when *I* was twenty-two."

What Miss Flora had failed to mention was that the heater didn't work, either, and with November nipping up and winter only weeks away it was going to be a Hobson's choice between keeping the windows open and freezing or shutting them and dying of asphyxiation. But right now, struggling up Hill Street in a smelly blue haze, Susan had a much more worrisome problem. Tom Cooley was missing.

Tommy was the son of a truck farmer in the Valley, a towhead with red hands, big and slow-moving like John Cooley, and sorrow-eyed as his mother Sarah, who had died of pneumonia the winter before. Tommy had a hunger for reading, rare in Northfield, and Susan dreamed dreams for him.

"There's not an earthly reason why you shouldn't go on to college, Tommy," Susan had told him. "You're one of the few boys in town who really deserves the chance."

Tommy had said, "Even if Pa could afford it, I can't leave him alone."

"But sooner or later you've got to leave anyway. In a year or so you'll be going into the Army."

"I don't know what Pa'll do." And he had quietly switched the subject to books.

There was a sadness about Tommy Cooley, a premature loss

of joy, that made Susan want to mother him, high as he towered above her. She looked forward to his visits and their snatches of talk about Hemingway and Thomas Wolfe. Tommy's chores kept him close to the farm; but on the first Monday of every month, rain, snow, or good New England sunshine, he showed up at Susan's desk to return the armful of books she had recommended and go off eagerly with a fresh supply.

On the first Monday in November there had been no Tommy. When he failed to appear by the end of that week, Susan was sure something was wrong, and on Friday evening she had driven out to the Cooley place. She found the weather-beaten farmhouse locked, a tractor rusting in a furrow, the pumpkins and potatoes unharvested, and no sign of Tommy. Or of his father.

So on Saturday afternoon she had closed the library early, and here she was, bound up Hill Street for Deputy Sheriff Linc Pearce's office on an unhappy mission.

It had to be the county officer, because Northfield's police department was Rollie Fawcett. Old Rollie's policing had been limited for a generation to chalking tires along Main and Hill Streets and writing out overtime parking tickets for the one-dollar fines that paid his salary. There was simply no one in Northfield but Linc Pearce to turn to.

Susan wasn't happy about that, either.

The trouble was, to Linc Pearce she was still the female Peter Pan who used to dig the rock salt out of his bottom when old Mr. Burry caught them in his apples. Lengthening her skirts and having to wear bras hadn't changed Linc's attitude one bit. It wasn't as if he were immune to feminine charms; the way he carried on with that overblown Marie Fullerton just before he went into the Army, for instance, had been proof enough of that. Linc came home quieter, more settled, and he was doing a fine job as Sheriff Howland's deputy in the Northfield district. But he went right back to treating Susan as if they were still swimming raw together in Burry's Creek.

She parked the rattletrap in the space reserved for "Official Cars Only" and marched into Town Hall with her little jaw set for anything.

Linc went to work on her right off. "Well, if it isn't Snubby Sue," he chuckled, uncoiling all six-foot-three of him from behind his paper-piled desk. "Leave your specs home?"

"What specs?" Susan could see the twitch of a squirrel's whisker at two hundred yards.

"Last time I passed you on the street you didn't see me at all."

"I saw you, all right," Susan said coldly, and drew back like a snake. "Linc Pearce, if you start chucking me under the chin again—"

"Why, Susie," Linc said, "I'm just setting you a chair."

"Well," Susan sniffed, off guard. "Is it possible you're developing some manners?"

"Yes, ma'am," Linc said respectfully, and he swung her off the floor with one long arm and dropped her into the chair.

"Some day . . ." Susan choked.

"Now, now," Linc said gently. "What's on your mind?"

"Tom Cooley!"

"The silk purse you're working on?" He grinned. "What's Plowboy done now, swiped a library book?"

"He's disappeared," Susan snapped. And she told Linc about Tommy's failure to show up at the library and her visit to the Cooley farm.

Of course, Linc looked indulgent. "There's no mystery about John. He's been away over a month looking to buy another farm as far from Northfield as he can find. John took Sarah's death last winter hard. But Tommy's s'posed to be looking after the place."

"Well, he's not there."

"Probably took off on a toot."

"Leaving a four-thousand-dollar tractor to rust in a half-plowed lot?" Susan's ponytail whisked about like a red flag in a high wind. "Tommy's got too much farmer in him for that, Linc."

"He's seventeen, isn't he?"

"I tell you, I know Tommy Cooley, and you don't!"

Deputy Sheriff Lincoln Pearce looked at her. Then he reached to the costumer for his hat and sheep-lined jacket. "S'pose I'll never hear the end of it if I don't take a look."

Out in the parking space Linc walked all around Susan's recent acquisition. "I know," he said gravely. "It's John Wilkes Booth's getaway car. Where'd you get her?"

"Miss Flora Sloan presented her to me three weeks ago when she won that Chevrolet coupe at the bazaar drawing."

Linc whistled. Then he jackknifed himself and got in. "Is it safe? The chances I have to take on this job!"

He went on like that all the way into the valley. Susan drove stiffly, silently.

But as they turned into the Cooley yard Linc said in an altogether different kind of voice, "John's home. There's his jeep."

They found John Cooley crouched in a Morris chair in his parlor, enormous shoulders at a beaten-down slope. The family Bible lay on his massive knees, and he was staring into space over it.

"Hi, John," Linc said from the doorway.

The farmer's head came about. The bleached gray eyes were

dazed. "My boy's gone, Lincoln." The voice that rumbled from his chest had trouble in it, deep trouble.

"Just heard, John."

"Ain't been home for weeks, looks like." He peered through the dimness of the parlor. "Where's Tommy at, Sue Marsh?"

"I don't know, Mr. Cooley." Susan tried to keep her voice casual. "I was hoping you did."

The farmer rose, looking around as if for a place to put the Bible. He was almost as tall as Linc and half again as broad, a tree of a man struck by lightning.

"When did you see Tom last, John?"

"October the second, when I went off to look for a new place." John Cooley swallowed. "Found me one down in York State, too. Figured to give Tommy a new start, maybe change our luck. But now I'll have to let it go."

"You hold your horses, John," Linc said cheerfully. "Didn't the boy leave you a note?"

"No." The farmer's breathing became noisy. He set the Bible down on the Morris chair, as if its weight were suddenly too much.

"We'll find him. Sue, you saw Tom last on the first Monday in October?"

Susan nodded. "It was October the third, I think, the day after Mr. Cooley says he left. Tommy came into the library to return some books and take out others. He had the farm truck, I remember."

"Truck still here, John?"

"Aya."

"Anything of Tom's missing?"

"His .22."

Linc looked relieved. "Well, that's it. He's gone off into the hills. He'll show up any minute with a fat buck and forty-two kinds of alibis. I wouldn't worry."

"Well, I would," Susan said. She was furious with Linc. "Tommy'd never have left on an extended trip without bringing my library books back first."

"There's female reasoning for you." Linc grinned. But he went over to Cooley and touched the old man's shoulder. "John, you want me to organize a search?"

The shoulder quivered. But all the farmer said, was, "Aya."

Overnight, Linc had three search parties formed and the state police alerted. On Sunday morning one party, in charge of old Sanford Brown, Northfield's first selectman, headed west with instructions to stop at every farm and gas station. Rollie Fawcett took the second, going east with identical instructions. The third Linc took charge of himself, including in his party Frenchy Lafont, and Lafont's two hound dogs. Frenchy owned the Northfield Bar and Grill across Hill Street from Town Hall. He was the ace tracker of the county.

"You take her easy, John," Lafont said to John Cooley before they set out. "Me, my dogs, we find the boy. Why you want to go along?"

But the farmer went ahead as if he were deaf, packing a rucksack.

Linc's party disappeared into the heavily timbered country to the north, and they were gone two weeks. They came back bearded, hollow-cheeked, and silent. John Cooley and Frenchy Lafont and his two hounds did not return with them. They showed up ten days later, when the first snowfall made further search useless. Even the dogs looked defeated.

Meanwhile, Linc had furnished police of nearby states with handbills struck off by the Northfield *Times* job press, giving a description of Tommy Cooley and reproducing his latest photograph, the one taken from his high-school yearbook. Newspaper, radio and TV stations co-operated. Linc sent an official request to Washington; the enlistment files of the Army, Navy, Marine Corps, and Air Force were combed. Registrars of colleges all over the country were circularized. The FBI was notified.

But no trace of Tommy Cooley—or his hunting rifle—turned up.

Linc and Susan quarreled.

"It's one of those things, I tell you." The cleft between Linc's eyes was biting deep these days. "We haven't been able to fix even the approximate time of his disappearance. It could have been any time between October third and the early part of November. Nobody saw him leave, and apparently no one's seen him since."

"But a grown boy doesn't go up in smoke!" Susan protested. "He's got to be *somewhere,* Linc. He didn't just run away from home. Tommy isn't irresponsible, and if you were half the sheriff s white-haired boy you think you are you'd find out what happened to him."

This was unreasonable, and Susan knew it. For a thrilling moment she thought Linc was going to get mad at her. But, as usual, he let her down. All he said was, "How about you taking my badge, half-pint, and me handing out library books?"

"Do you think you could locate the right one in the stacks?"

Susan stalked out. After the door banged, Linc got up and gently kicked it.

Once, in mid-December, Susan drove out to the Cooley farm. The rumors about John Cooley were disturbing. He was said to be letting the farm go to seed, mumbling to himself, always poring over his Bible.

She found the rumors exaggerated. The house was dirty and the kitchen piled with unwashed dishes, but the farm itself seemed in good order, considering the season, and the farmer talked lucidly enough. Only his appearance shocked Susan. His ruddy skin had grayed and loosened, his hair had white streaks in it, and his coveralls flapped on his frame.

"I've fetched you a blueberry pie I had in my freezer, Mr. Cooley," she said brightly. "I remember Tommy's saying blueberry's your favorite."

"Aya." Cooley looked down at the pie in his lap, but not as if he saw it. "My Tom's a good boy."

Susan tried to think of something to say. Finally, she said, "We've missed you at Grange meetings and church . . . Isn't it lonesome for you here, Mr. Cooley?"

"Have to wait for the boy," John Cooley explained patiently. "The Lord would never take him from me without a sign. I've had no sign, Susan. He'll come home."

Tommy Cooley was found in the spring.

• • • • •

The rains that year were Biblical. They destroyed the early plantings, overflowed ponds and creeks, and sent the Northfield River over its banks to flood thousands of acres of pasture and bottom-land. The main highway, between Northfield and the Valley, was under water for several miles.

When the waters sank they exposed a shallow hole not two miles from the Cooley farm, just off the highway. In the hole lay the remains of John Cooley's son. A county crew repairing the road found him.

Susan heard the tragic news as she was locking the library for the day.

Frenchy Lafont, racing past in his new Ford convertible, slowed down long enough to yell, "They find the Cooley boy's body, Miss Marsh! Ever'body's goin' out!"

How Susan got the aged Buick started in the damp twilight, how she knew where to go, she never remembered. She supposed it was instinct, a blind following of the herd of vehicles stampeding from town onto the Valley road, most of them as undirected as her jalopy. All Susan could think of was the look on John Cooley's gray face when he had said the Lord had given him no sign.

She saw the farmer's face at last, and her heart sank. Cooley was on his knees in the roadside grave, clawing in the muck, his eyes blank and terrible, while all around him people trampled the mud-slimed brush like a nest of aroused ants. Linc Pearce and some state troopers were holding the crowd back, trying to give the bereaved man a decent grieving space; but they need not have wrestled so. The farmer might have been alone in one of his cornfields. His big hands alternately caressed and mauled the grave's mud, as if he would coax and batter it into submission to his frenzy. Once he found a button rotted off his son's leather jacket sleeve, and Linc came over and tried to take it from him, but the big hand became a fist, a mallet, and Linc turned away. The big man put it into the pocket of his coat along with a pebble, a chunk of glass, a clump of grass roots—these were his son, the covenant between them, Mizpah . . .

Afterward, when the heap under the canvas had been taken away by Art Ormsby's hearse, and most of the crowd had crawled off in their cars, Susan was able to come close. They had

John Cooley sitting on a stump near the grave now, while men hunted through the brush. They were merely going through the motions, Susan knew; time, the ebbing waters, and the feet of the crowd would have obliterated any clue.

She waited while Linc conferred with a state trooper lieutenant, and Dr. Buxton, who was the coroner's physician for Northfield. She saw Dr. Buxton glance at John Cooley, shake his gray head, and get into his car to drive back to town. Then she noticed that the lieutenant was carefully holding a rusty, mud-caked rifle.

When the trooper went off with the rifle Susan walked up to Linc and said, "Well?" They had spoken hardly a word to each other all winter.

Linc squinted briefly down at her and said, "Hello, Sue." Then he looked over at the motionless man on the stump, as if the two were painfully connected in his mind.

"That rifle," Susan said. "Tommy's?"

Linc nodded. "Tossed into the hole with the body. They're going to give it the once-over at the state police lab in Gurleytown, but they won't find anything after all this time."

"How long?"

"Hard to say." Linc's firm lips set tight. "Doc Buxton thinks offhand he's been dead five or six months."

Susan's chest rose, and stayed there. "Linc . . . was it murder?"

"The whole back of his head is smashed in. What else there is we won't know till Doc does the autopsy."

Susan swallowed the raw wind. It was impossible to associate that canvas-shrouded lump with Tommy Cooley's big, sad, eager self, to realize that it had been crumbling in the earth here since last October or early November.

"Who'd want to kill him?" Susan said fiercely. "And why, Linc? Why?"

"That's what I have to find out."

She had never seen him so humorless, his mouth so much like a sprung trap. A wave of warmth washed over her. For the moment Susan felt very close to him.

"Linc, let me help," she said breathlessly.

"How?" Linc said.

The wave recoiled. There was no approaching him on an adult level, in the case of Tommy Cooley as in anything else. Susan almost expected Linc to pat her shoulder.

"It's a man's job," Linc was mumbling. "Thanks all the same."

"And are you the man for it, do you think?" Susan heard herself cry.

"Maybe not. But I'll sure give it a try." Linc took her hand, but she snatched it away. "Now, Susie," he said. "You're all upset. Let me do the sweating on this. With the trail five-six months old . . ."

Susan sloshed away, trembling with fury.

In the weeks that followed, Susan kept tabs on Linc's frustration almost with satisfaction. She got most of her inside information from Dr. Buxton, who was a habitué of the library's mystery shelves, old Flora Sloan, and Frenchy Lafont. Miss Flora's all-seeing eye encompassed events practically before they took place, and Frenchy's strategic location opposite Town Hall gave him the best-informed clientele in town.

"Linc Pearce is bellowing around like a heifer in her first season," Miss Flora remarked one day, in the library. "But that boy's all fenced in, Susan. There's some things the Almighty doesn't mean for us to know. I guess the mystery of poor Tommy Cooley's one of 'em."

"I can't believe that, Miss Flora," Susan said. "If Linc is fenced in, it's only because it's a very difficult case."

The old lady cocked an eye at her. "Appears to me, Susan, you take a might personal interest in it."

"Well, of course! Tommy—"

"Tommy, my foot. You can fool the men folks with your straight-out talk and your red-hair tempers, Susan Marsh, but you don't fool an old woman. You've been in love with Lincoln Pearce ever since *I* can remember, and I go back to bustles. Why don't you stop this fiddling and marry him?"

"Marry him!" Susan laughed. "Of all the notions, Miss Flora! Naturally, I'm interested in Linc—we grew up together. This is an important case to him—"

"Garbage," Miss Flora said distinctly, and walked out.

Frenchy Lafont said to Susan in mid-May, when she stopped in his cafe for lunch, "That Linc, he's a fool for dam-sure. You know what, Miss Marsh? Everybody but him know he's licked."

"He's *not* licked, Mr. Lafont!"

The fact was, there was nothing for Linc Pearce or anyone else to grab hold of. The dead boy's skull had been crushed from behind by a blow of considerable force, according to Dr. Buxton. His shoulders and back showed evidences of assault, too; apparently, there had been a savage series of blows. But the weapon was not found.

Linc went back to the shallow grave site time after time to nose around in a great circle, studying the road and the brush foot by foot, long after Tommy Cooley was buried in the old Northfield cemetery beside his mother. But it was time wasted. Nor were the state police technicians more successful. They could detect no clue in the dead boy's clothing or rifle. All they could say was that the rifle had not been fired—"Old Aunty Laura's blind cow could see that!" Susan had snapped—so that presumably the boy had been killed without warning or a chance to defend himself. Tommy's rifle had been returned to his father, along with the meaningless contents of his pockets.

No one remembered seeing Tommy after October third. So even the date of the murder was a mystery.

Motive was the darkest mystery of all. It had not been robbery; Tommy's wallet, containing most of the hundred dollars his father had left with him, had been intact in the grave. Linc went into the boy's life and through his effects, questioned and requestioned his friends, his old high-school teachers, canvassed every farmer and field hand within miles of the Cooley place. But the killing remained unexplained. The boy had had no enemies, it seemed, he had crossed no one, he had been involved with no girl or woman.

"John," Linc had pleaded with Cooley, "can't you think of anything that might tell why Tommy was murdered? Anything?"

But the farmer had shaken his head and turned away, big fingers gripping his Bible. The Book was now never far from his hand. He plodded about his farm aimlessly in the spring, doing no planting, letting the machinery rust. Once a week or so he drove into Northfield to shop in the supermarket. But he spoke to no one.

One night toward the end of May, as Susan was sitting on her porch after supper, rocking in the mild moonlight and listening to the serenade of the peepers in the pond, the headlights of a car swung into her yard and a tall figure got out.

It couldn't be! But it was. Linc Pearce come to Burry's Hollow. The mountain to Mohamet.

"Susie?"

"Well, if it isn't Lanky Linc," Susan heard herself say calmly. Her heart was thumping like an old well pump.

Linc hesitated at the foot of the porch steps, fumbling with his hat. "Took a chance you'd be home. If you're busy—"

"I'll put my dollies away," Susan said. "For you."

"What?" Linc sounded puzzled.

Susan smiled. "Sit down, stranger."

Linc sat down on the bottom step awkwardly, facing the moon. There were lines in his lean face that Susan had never noticed before. "How've you been?" Susan said.

"All right," he said impatiently, and turned around. "See here, Susie, it's asinine going on like this. I mean, you and me. Why, you're acting just like a kid."

Susan felt the flames spread from her hair right down to her toes. "*I'm* acting like a kid!" she cried. "Is that what you came here to say, Linc? If it is—"

He shook his head. "I never seem to say the right thing to you. Why can't we be like we used to be, Susie? I mean, I miss that funny little pan of yours, and that carrot top. But ever since this Cooley business started—"

"It started a long time before that," Susan retorted. "And I'd rather not discuss it, Linc, *or* my funny pan, *or* the color of my hair. What about the Cooley case?"

"Susie—"

"The Cooley case," Susan said. "Or do I go to bed?"

"Hopeless. It'll never be solved."

"Because you haven't been able to solve it?"

"Me or anybody else," Linc said, shrugging. "One of those

crimes that makes no sense because it never had any. Our theory now is that the Cooley boy was attacked on the road by some psychopathic tramp, who buried him in a hurry and lit out for other parts."

"In other words, the most convenient theory possible."

Linc said with elaborate indifference, "It happens all the time."

"And suppose it wasn't a psychopathic tramp?"

"What do you mean?"

"I think it was somebody in Northfield."

"Who?"

"I don't know."

Linc laughed.

"I think you'd better go, Linc Pearce," Susan said distinctly. "I don't like you any more."

"Now, Susie."

The phone rang in the house. It was three rings—Susan's signal, and she stamped inside.

"It's for you, Linc," she said coolly. "The bartender over at Frenchy Lafont's."

"Bib Hadley? Should have known better than to tell Bib I was stopping in here on my way home," Linc growled, unfolding himself from the step. "Some drunk acting up, I s'pose . . . What is it, Bib?"

Discussing me in a bar! Susan thought. She turned away in cold rage.

But then she heard Linc say, I'll get right on out there, Bib," and hang up.

Something in the way he said it made her turn back.

"What's the matter?" Susan said quickly.

"Another murder."

An icy hand seized her heart.

"Who, Linc? Where?"

"Frenchy Lafont." Linc's voice sounded thick. "Some kids out in a hot rod found his body just off the Valley road. Whole back of his head caved in."

"Like Tommy Cooley," Susan whispered.

"I'll say like Tommy Cooley." Linc waived his long arms futilely. "Bib says they found Frenchy lying in the exact spot where we dug up Tommy's body!"

• • • • •

The Valley road was a wild mess of private cars and jeeps and farm trucks.

Susan wormed past. In one car Susan saw Miss Flora Sloan. The withered despot of Northfield was driving her new Chevrolet like a demon, the daisies in her straw hat bobbing crazily.

Linc kept his siren going all the way.

We're scared witless, Susan thought.

Two state police cars had set up roadblocks near the site of the new horror. Linc plowed onto the soft shoulder and skidded around into the cleared space. The road in both directions was a double string of lights. Everywhere Susan looked, people were jumping out of cars and running along the road and the shoulders. In a twinkling the fifty feet of highway between the roadblocks was rimmed with eyes.

Susan almost trod on Linc's heels.

She peeped around his long torso at what lay just off the road on the north side. It sprang at her, brutally detailed, in the police flares. Susan jerked back, hiding her eyes.

She was to remember that photographic flash for the rest of

her life. The mound of sandy earth where the grave had been refilled after the removal of Tommy Cooley's body, pebbled, flint-spangled, scabby with weeds; and across it, as on one of Art Ormsby's biers, the flung remains of what had been Frenchy Lafont.

Susan could not see his wound; she could only imagine what it looked like. They had turned him over, so that his face was tilted sharply back to the stars. It did not look the least bit like Frenchy Lafont's face. Frenchy Lafont's face had been dark and vivid, lively with mischief, with beautiful lips over white teeth and a line of vain black mustache. This face looked like old suet. The mouth was a gaping black cavern; the eyes stared like dusty pieces of glass.

"Just like the Cooley kid," one of the troopers was saying.

His voice raised a deep echo, like a far-off growl of thunder. There was more than fear in the growl; there was anger, and under the anger, hate. The troopers and Linc looked around, startled.

"Sounds like trouble, Pearce," one of the older troopers muttered to Linc. "They're your people. Better do something."

Linc walked off toward one of the police cars. For a moment Susan almost ran after him; she felt as if she had been left standing naked in the flares.

But the eyes were not on her.

Linc vaulted to the hood of the car and flung his arms wide. The rumble choked and died.

"Neighbors, I knew Frenchy Lafont all my life," Linc said in a quiet way. "Most of you did, too. There isn't a man or woman in Northfield wants more to identify the one who did this and see that he gets what's coming to him. But we can't do it this way. We'll find Frenchy's killer if you'll only go home and give us a chance."

"Like you found the killer of my boy?"

It was John Cooley's hoarse bass voice. He was near the west roadblock, standing tall in his jeep, his thick arm with the flail of fist at the end like a wrathful judgment. Linc turned to face him.

"Go home, John," Linc said gently.

"Yeah, John, go home!" a shrill voice yelled from behind the other barrier. "Go home and get yourself murdered like Tommy was!"

"That's not helping, Wes Bartlett," Linc said. "Use your head, man—"

But his voice went down under a tidal wave.

"We want protection!"

"Aya!"

"Who's next on the list?"

"Long as *he's* deputy."

"Resign!"

"New sheriff s what we need!"

"Aya! Resign!"

In the roar of the crowd the clatter of Linc's badge on the hood of the police car was surprisingly loud.

"All right, there's my badge!" Linc shouted. "Now who's the miracle man thinks he can do the job better? I'll recommend him to Sheriff Howland myself. Come on, don't be bashful! Speak up."

He gave them glare for glare. The glares dimmed; the answering silence became uneasy. Something embarrassed invaded the night air.

"Well?" Linc jeered.

Somewhere down the line a car engine started . . .

Ten minutes later the highway was empty and dark.

Linc jumped off the police car, reached for his badge, and went over to the troopers.

"Nice going, Sheriff," Susan murmured.

But he strode past her to the edge of the burial mound, rock-hard and bitter.

"Let's get to it," he said.

• • • • •

At first they thought it had been a murder in the course of a robbery. Frenchy Lafont's wallet was found untouched on the body, but an envelope with the day's café receipts, which he had been known to have on him earlier in the evening, was missing. The robbery theory collapsed overnight. The envelope of money was found in the night depository box of the First National Bank of Northfield on Main Street when the box was unlocked in the morning.

The weapon was not found. It was the Tommy Cooley case all over again.

Everything about the cafe owner's murder was baffling. He was a bachelor who lived with his aged mother on the old Lafont place off the Valley road, a mile out of town. His elder brother, a prosperous merchant of Quebec, had not heard from him in months. The brother, in town to make the funeral arrangements and take charge of the mother, could shed no light on the mystery. Old Mrs. Lafont knew nothing.

On the evening of his murder Lafont had left the cafe shortly before nine, alone, taking the day's receipts with him. He drove off in his new Ford. An hour or so later he was dead some six miles out of town, on the site of the Cooley tragedy. His car was found near the mound. It was towed into the police garage at the Gurley town barracks and gone over by experts. It yielded nothing but Frenchy Lafont's fingerprints. No blood, no indication of a struggle, no clue of any kind. The fuel tank was almost full.

"He dropped the envelope into the slot at the bank," Linc told Susan, "stopped in at Howie Grebe's gas station to fill up, and drove off west on the Valley road. He must have gone straight to his death. Nothing to show that he was waylaid and held up—nothing was taken, and Frenchy didn't touch the pistol he carried in his glove compartment. Bib Hadley says he was his usual wisecracking self when he left the cafe."

"You think he had a date with somebody he knew?" Susan asked. "Well, Hadley says he got a phone call at the cafe," Linc said slowly, "about eight o'clock that night."

"I hadn't heard that! Who phoned him, Linc?"

"Bib doesn't know. Frenchy answered the call himself."

"Did Bib Hadley overhear anything?"

"No."

"Was Frenchy excited? There must have been something, Linc!"

"Bib didn't notice anything unusual. The call might have had nothing to do with the case."

"Maybe it was some woman Frenchy was fooling with. I've heard stories about him and Logan Street."

Susan colored. Logan Street was a part of Northfield no respectable girl ever mentioned to the opposite sex.

"So far all alibis have stood up." Linc passed his hand over his eyes like an old man. "It's no good thinking, theorizing. I have to *know*, Sue, and there's not a fact I can sink my teeth into."

"But there's got to be a reason for a man's getting the back of his head knocked in!" Susan cried. "*Why* was Frenchy murdered? *Why* was his body dumped on the spot where the murderer had buried Tommy? You can hardly say it was another psychopathic tramp, Linc."

Linc looked at her in a persecuted way. He was glassy-eyed with exhaustion. But he merely said, "Maybe not. Only there doesn't seem to be any more sense in Frenchy's death than in Tom Cooley's. Look, Susie, I've got work to do and talk won't help me do it even with you. If you'll excuse me."

"Certainly," Susan said frigidly. "But let me tell you, Linc Pearce, when these murders are solved it'll be talk and theories and *thinking* that solve them!" And she swept out, thoroughly miserable.

Susan tossed night after night, asking herself unanswerable questions. Why had Tommy Cooley been killed? Why had Frenchy Lafont followed him in death? What was the connection between the two? And—the most frightening question of all—who was going to be the next victim?

A week after Lafont's murder Susan was waiting at the cafe entrance when Bib Hadley came to open up.

"You must hanker after a cup of my coffee real bad, Miss Marsh," the fat bartender said, unlocking the door. "Come on in. I'll have the urn going in a jiffy."

"What I want, Bib, is information," Susan said grimly. "I'm sick and tired of moping around, waiting to get my head bashed in."

The bartender tied a clean apron around his ample middle. "Seems like every Tom, Dick, and Mary between Northfield and Boston's been in for the same reason. Even had a newspaperman in yesterday from one of the city wire services. Made a special trip just to pump ol' Bib. So get your list in now, Miss Marsh, while Frenchy's brother makes up his mind what to do with this place. What do you want to know?"

"The connection between Tommy Cooley and Frenchy Lafont," Susan said.

"Wasn't any," Bib Hadley said. "Next?"

"But there must have been, Bib! Did Tommy ever work for Mr. Lafont?"

"Nope."

"Did Tommy ever come in here?"

"Tell you the truth, Miss Marsh," the bartender said, lighting the gas under the urn, "I don't believe Frenchy would have known young Tom Cooley if he'd tripped over him in broad daylight. You know how Frenchy was about teenagers. He'd stand 'em all treat over at Tracy's ice cream parlor, but he wouldn't let 'em come into his own place even for coffee. Gave a good bar a bad name, Frenchy used to say."

"Well, there was a connection between Tommy and Frenchy Lafont," Susan said positively, "and these murders won't ever be solved till it's found."

"And you're going to find it, I s'pose?"

Susan jumped. There he was, in the cafe doorway, jaws working away like Gary Cooper's in an emotional moment.

"I saw you ambush Bib from my office window," Linc said bitterly. "Don't you trust me to ask the right questions, either?"

I don't know why I'm feeling guilty, Susan thought furiously. *This is a free country!*

Linc jammed his big foot on the rim of the tub holding the dusty palm. "You want my badge, too, Sue? Don't you think I've asked Bib every question you have, and a whole lot more? This is a tough case. Do you have to make it tougher for me by getting under foot?"

"Thanks!" Susan said. "People who won't accept help when they're stuck from people trying to unstick them are just—just perambulating *pigheads.*"

"We stopped playing tag in you dad's cow barn long ago, Sue," Linc said. "When are you going to grow up?"

"I've grown up! Oh, how I've grown up, Linc Pearce—and everybody knows it but you!" Susan screamed. "And do we have to stand here screaming in front of people?"

"I'm not people," Bib Hadley said. "I ain't even here."

"Nobody's screaming but you." Linc drew himself up so tall Susan's neck began to hurt. "I thought we knew each other pretty well, Susie. Maybe we don't know each other at all."

"I'm sure of it!" Susan tried to say it with dignity, but it came out so choky-sounding she fled past Linc to her jalopy and drove off down Hill Street with the gas pedal to the floor.

• • • • •

Two nights later the body of Flora Sloan, autocrat of Northfield, was found by a motorcycle trooper just off the Valley highway. The back of her head had been battered in.

As in the case of Frenchy Lafont, the old lady's body had been tossed onto Tommy Cooley's winter grave . . .

Flora Sloan had attended a vestry meeting in Christ Church, at which certain parish and financial problems had been argued. As usual, Miss Flora dominated the debate; as usual, she got her way. She had left the meeting in lively spirits when it broke up just before ten o'clock, climbed into her Chevrolet, waved triumphantly at Sanford Brown, who had been her chief antagonist of the evening, and driven off. Presumably she had been bound for the big Sloan house on the western edge of town. But she never reached it; or rather, she had by-passed it, for the Valley road ran by her property.

When her body was found shortly after midnight by the motorcycle trooper, she had been dead about an hour.

Had Flora Sloan picked someone up, who had forced her to drive to the lonely spot six miles from town and there murdered her? But the old lady had been famous for her dislike of tramps and her suspicion of hitchhikers. She had never been known to give a stranger a lift.

Her purse, money untouched, was found beside her body. A valuable ruby brooch, a Sloan family heirloom, was still pinned to her blue lace dress. The Chevrolet was parked near the grave in almost the identical spot on which Frenchy Lafont's Ford had been abandoned. There were no fingerprints in the car except her own, no clues in the car or anywhere around.

Three nights after Flora Sloan's murder, Sanford Brown, first selectman of Northfield, called a special town meeting. The city fathers, lean old Yankee farmers and businessmen, sat down behind the scarred chestnut table in the Town Hall meeting room under an American flag like a panel of hanging judges; and among them—Susan thought they looked dismally like prisoners—sat County Sheriff Howland and his local deputy, Lincoln Pearce.

It was an oppressive night, and the overflow crowd made the room suffocating. She saw everyone she knew, and some faces she had forgotten.

Old Sanford Brown rapped his gavel hard on the table. A profound silence greeted him.

"Under the authority vested in me," old Brown said rapidly through his nose, "I call this town meetin' to order. As this is special, we will dispense with the usual order of business and get right to it. Sheriff Howland's come down from the county seat at the selectmen's request. Floor's yours, Sheriff."

Sheriff Howland was a large, perspiring man in a smart city suit and black string tie. He got to his feet, drying his bald head with a sodden handkerchief.

"Friends, when I was elected to office in this county I looked for the best man I could find to be my deputy in your district. I asked 'round and about and was told there wasn't finer deputy material in Northfield than young Lincoln Pearce. I want you and him to know I have every confidence in his ability to discharge the duties of his office. Linc, you tell these good folks what you told me today."

The buck having been deftly passed to him, Linc rose. His blue eyes were mourning-edged and he was so pale Susan bled for him.

"I'm no expert on murder, never claimed to be one," Linc began in a matter-of-fact voice, but Susan could see his knuckles whiten on the edge of the table. "However, I've had the help of the best technical men of the state police. And they're as high up a tree as the 'coon of this piece. And that's me."

An old lady chuckled, and several men grinned. *Humility, Linc?* Susan thought in a sort of pain. *Maybe one of these days you'll get around to me . . .*

"Three people have been beaten to death," Linc said. "One was a boy of seventeen, son of a dirt farmer—quiet boy, Congregationalism never in trouble. One was a bar-and-grill owner—French-Canadian descent, Roman Catholic, one of the most popular men in town. The third was the last survivor of the family that founded Northfield—rich woman, tight-fisted, some said, but we all know her many generosities. She just about ran Northfield all her life. She was a pillar of Christ Episcopal Church, on every important committee, with her finger in every community pie."

He thinks he has them, Susan thought, glancing about her at the long bony faces. *Linc, Linc . . .*

"The bodies of these three were found in the same spot. So their deaths have to be connected some way. But how? There doesn't seem to be any answer. At least, we haven't been able to find one so far.

"We know nothing about Tommy Cooley's death because of the months that passed before we found his body. Frenchy Lafont was probably lured to his death by a phone call from somebody he knew and wasn't afraid of. Flora Sloan probably picked her killer up as she left the church meeting, which she wouldn't have done unless it was someone she knew. Tommy Cooley's clothing was too far gone to tell us anything, and the rains this spring wiped out any clues that might have been left in his case. But we found dirt on the knees of Frenchy's trousers and Flora Sloan's skirt, so maybe Tommy was made to kneel on that spot just like Frenchy and Miss Flora afterward, and hit a killing blow from behind."

You can talk and talk, Linc, they won't let you alone any more, Susan thought. *They won't do anything to you—they'll just ignore you from now on . . .*

"That's all we have," Linc said. "No connection among the three victims—not one. No motive. No gain—nothing was taken in any of the three cases as far as we know. Tommy Cooley had nothing to leave anybody, Frenchy Lafont's business and house he left to his eighty-one-year-old mother, and now we're told that Flora Sloan willed her entire estate to charity. No motive—no woman or other man in the case, no jealous husband, wife, or sweetheart. *No motive."*

Linc stopped, looking down. Susan shut her eyes.

"When someone kills for no reason, he's insane. Three people died because a maniac is loose in our town. It's the only answer that makes sense. If anyone here has a better idea, for God's sake, let all of us hear it." Now the noise came back like a rising wind, and Sanford Brown banged it back to silence. But it was still there, waiting.

"I want to say one more thing."

Susan heard Linc's pride take stubborn voice again. *Linc, Linc, don't you know you've had it? Old Sanford, the selectmen, Sheriff Howland—they all know it. Don't you?*

"I'm not going to hand over my badge unless Sheriff Howland asks for it," Linc went on. "Want it, Sheriff?"

The politician squirmed. "No, Linc, course not—unless the good folks of Northfield feel—"

Poor Linc. Here it comes.

"Let Linc Pearce keep his badge!" a burly farmer shouted from the floor. "The boy's doin' his best. But he's just a boy, that's the trouble. What we need's a Committee o' Safety. Men with guns to stand watch near the grave site . . . patrol the roads!"

"Mr. Chairman . . ."

Susan slipped out of the meeting room as motions and resolutions winged toward the table from every corner. She caught up with Linc on the steps of the Town Hall.

"'Lo, Susie," Linc said with a stiffish grin. "Come after me to watch me digest crow?"

"Committee of Safety, men guarding the grave," Susan said bitterly. "What do they expect him to do—walk into their arms?

Linc, *please* let me help. You're not beaten yet. Let's you and I talk it over. There must be something you missed! Maybe if we put our heads together—"

"You know something?" Linc put his big hands about her waist and lifted her to his level like a doll. "All of a sudden I want to kiss you."

"Linc, put me down. Don't treat me as if I were a child. Please, Linc."

"My little old Susie."

"And *don't* call me Susie! I loathe it! I've loathed it all my life! Linc, put me down, I say!"

"Sorry." Linc looked genuinely surprised. He deposited her quietly on the step. "As far as the other thing is concerned, my answer's got to be the same, Sue. They can make up all the committees and posses they want—this is my job and I'll do it by myself or go bust. Can I drive you home?"

"Not *ever?*" And Susan fled to the safety of the old Buick Flora Sloan had given her, where she could burst into tears in decent privacy.

• • • • •

Linc sat in his office long after the last selectman had gone and Rollie Fawcett had darkened the building. He was blackly conscious of the thunderstorm that had sprung up. The rain lashing his windows seemed fitting and proper.

There must be something you missed . . .

Linc was irritated more by the source of the phrase going round in his head than by its persistence. That little fire-eater! She'd singed his tail from the start. Talk about your one-track minds . . .

Suppose she's right?

The thought was like his collar, chafing him raw.

What could he have missed? What? What hadn't he followed up? He'd been over the three cases a hundred times. He couldn't possibly have missed anything. Or had he?

Linc Pearce finally saw it—appropriately enough, during a flash of lightning. The bare office with its whitewashed walls for an instant became bright as day, and in that flash of illumination Linc remembered what he had missed.

It had happened on that first night of the long nightmare. The night Tommy Cooley's body had been found, washed out of its roadside grave by the receding waters of the spring flood. John Cooley had been kneeling in the grave, his hands scrabbling in the mud for some remnant of his son. The pitiful little things he had found and tucked away in the pocket of his checkered red mackinaw . . . *Suppose one of those things, unknown to Cooley, had been a clue?*

Linc grabbed a slicker and ran.

• • • • •

The Cooley farmhouse was dark. Linc turned off his lights and ignition, skin prickling at some danger he could not exactly define.

The rain had turned into a tropical downpour. Lightning tore the sky open in quick bursts, like cannon salvoes, lighting up the shade-drawn windows, the porch with the rickety rocking chairs turned to the wall, the open door of the nearby garage . . .

Cooley's jeep was not in the garage.

Linc reached for a flashlight and jumped out of his car. He

splashed over to the garage and swung his light about. Yes, the farm truck was here, but the jeep was out.

Linc relaxed. He had not noticed John Cooley at the town meeting, but he must have been there. If he was, with a committee of safety forming, he'd surely be one of the men to be staked out in the brush near Tommy's grave.

Linc went up on the porch and tried the door. It was not locked, and he opened it and stepped into the hall.

"John?" He could be wrong. There might be a dozen explanations for the missing jeep. "John?"

No one answered. Linc went upstairs and looked into the bedrooms. They were empty.

He went back to John Cooley's old-fashioned bedroom and played his flash about. Of course, the chifforobe. He opened the doors. It was filled with winter garments.

And there was the red mackinaw.

Linc breathed a prayer and put his hand into the right pocket.

They were still there, all right.

He took them out one by one, carefully, turning them over in his fingers. The button from young Tom's rotted leather jacket. A pebble. A chunk of dirt-crusted glass . . .

The piece of glass!

It was thick, ridged glass with a curve to it, a roughly triangular piece cracked off from something larger. It was . . . it was . . .

My God! Linc thought.

He went over it again and again, refusing to believe. It couldn't be that simple. The answer to the murders that had happened. The warning of the murder that was going to happen. *The murder of Susan Marsh.*

For a moment of sheer horror Linc saw her flying red hair,

the familiar little face, the snub nose he used to tweak, the brook-water eyes, the impudent mouth that had tormented him all his life.

He saw them all, soiled and still.

A world without Sue . . .

Linc never knew how he got out of the house.

• • • • •

Susan had gone to bed swollen-eyed. But she had been unable to sleep. The mugginess, the storm, the thunder crashes, the lightning bolts bouncing off her pond, made the night hideous. She had never felt so alone.

She crept out of bed, got into a wrapper, and pattered about, clicking switches. She put on every light in the house. Then she went into her tiny parlor and sat there, rigidly listening to the storm.

Oh, Linc, Linc . . .

Her first thought when the crash came and the curtains began blowing about and a cold spray hit her bare feet was that the gale had blown the front door loose.

She looked up.

John Cooley stood in her splintered doorway. He had Tommy's hunting rifle cradled in his arm. In the farmer's eyes Susan saw her death.

"They're watching at the grave, "John Cooley said. His voice was all cracked and high, not like his bass at all. "So I can't take you there, Susan Marsh."

"You killed them," Susan said stiffly.

"Get down on your knees, and pray."

He was insane. She saw that now. He had been tottering on

the brink ever since Tommy's disappearance, his only son, the child of his beloved Sarah. And he had toppled over when the body was found. Only no one had seen it—not Linc, not she, not anyone.

Linc, Linc.

"Not Tommy," Susan whispered. "You loved Tommy, Mr. Cooley. You wouldn't—couldn't have killed Tommy."

The farmer's twitching face, with its distended eyes, softened into something vaguely human. Tears filled the eyes. The heavy shoulders began to shake.

Oh, dear God, let me find a way to keep him from killing me as he killed Frenchy Lafont and Miss Flora . . .

"I know you didn't kill Tommy, Mr. Cooley."

With the metal-sheathed butt of Tommy's hunting rifle. That was the weapon that had crushed out their lives . . . *Dear God . . . I mustn't faint, mustn't . . . those dark smears on the butt . . . get him talking . . . maybe the phone . . . No, no, that would be fatal . . . What can I do! Linc . . .*

"Not Tommy. Somebody else killed Tommy, Mr. Cooley. Who was it? Why don't you tell me?"

The farmer sank into the tapestried chair near the door. The rain beat in on him, mixing with his tears.

"You killed him, Susan Marsh," he wept.

"Oh, no!" Susan cried faintly.

"You, or the Frenchy, or the old woman. I knew from the hunk of glass in the boy's grave. A hunk of headlight glass. Headlight from an old auto. He was run over on the road, hit by an auto from the back . . . from the back. You killed him with an auto and you put him in a dirty hole and piled it on him and you ran away. You, or the Frenchy, or the old woman."

Susan wet her lips. "The Buick," she said. "My old Buick."

John Cooley looked up, suddenly cunning. "I found it! Didn't think I would, hey? I looked all over Northfield and I found the auto it come from. I looked for a smashed headlight, and the auto the old woman gave you was the one the hunk of glass fitted. Was it you run Tommy over? Or the old woman, who run the car before you? Or the Frenchy, who owned the Buick before the old woman bought it?"

"Frenchy Lafont sold that car to Flora Sloan—in October?" Susan gasped.

"Didn't think I'd track that down, hey?" John Cooley said with a sly chuckle. "Aya! Lafont sold it to the old woman when he bought his new Ford. And she gave it to you a couple weeks later when she won a Chevrolet in the Grange bazaar. Oh, I tracked it all down. I was careful to do proper justice." The eyes began to stare again; he whimpered. "But which one, which one? I didn't know which one of you killed Tommy in October, 'cause nobody knows what day in October he was run over. So I got to kill you all. That way the Lord's vengeance is mine. The Wrath. With the boy's gun. I phoned that Lafont and I says meet me at the grave, I have to talk to you . . . I walked into the town and I waited for the old woman to come out of the church and I stopped her and made her drive out to the grave. 'Pray, Flora Sloan,' I says. 'Get down on your murdering knees, sinner, and pray for your damned soul,' I says. And then I used the Lord's gun butt on her."

The room was shimmering.

John Cooley was on his feet, the great eyes shining.

"Pray, Susan Marsh," he thundered. "Down on your knees, girl, and pray for your soul."

Now the steel hand was at the back of her neck, forcing her to her knees.

Dear God . . . Linc, you're the one I love, the only one I've ever . . .

The last thing Susan saw as she strained against the paralyzing clutch on her neck was that exultant face, terrible in triumph, and the rusty blood-caked butt of the rifle held high above it.

She fainted just as Linc Pearce plunged into the room and hurled himself at the madman.

Susan opened her eyes. She was in her own bed. Linc's long face was close to hers.

"I thought I heard you say something, Linc, a million years ago," Susan murmured. "Or maybe it was just now. Didn't you say something, oh, so nice?"

"I said I love you, Susie—Susan," Linc muttered. "And something about will you marry me."

Susan closed her eyes again. "That's what I thought you said," she said contentedly.

They never did find out which one had accidentally run over Tommy Cooley, whether Frenchy Lafont or old Miss Flora. They argued about it for years.

THE PERFECT CRIME
Ben Ray Redman

Well known in his day as a true bookman, Ben(jamin) Ray Redman (1896-1961) was one of the unofficial founders of *The Saturday Review of Literature* and became a prolific contributor to it.

During his literary life, he was known as an erudite raconteur, described by Norman Cousins, editor of *Saturday Review*, as "a debonair gentleman . . . elegantly mannered and attired, born for a part in a Noel Coward play."

Redman tirelessly wrote essays, poetry, literary criticism, reviews, introductions to new editions of classics in numerous genres, and fiction, as well as translating works from the French. In the 1920s, he became the editorial and advertising manager of the G.P. Putnam publishing house.

In addition to countless pieces for *Saturday* Review, he often contributed material to *The New York Times*, *Harper's Magazine*, and *The American Mercury*. He created a column titled "Old Wine in New Bottles," devoted to reviews of reissues of great books from the past, for the *New York Herald-Tribune*. Of the more than 200 books to which he contributed, perhaps his most significant volumes were his history, *The Oxford University Press, New York, 1896-1946*, his study, *Edward Arlington Robinson*, and *The Portable Voltaire*, which Redman translated and edited and which is still in print.

His most famous and enduring work is the often-anthologized masterpiece, "The Perfect Murder," which was turned into an episode of *Alfred Hitchcock Presents*. It aired on October 20, 1957, with a screenplay by Stirling Silliphant and starred Vincent Price.

Redman moved to Hollywood for a time and contributed to screenplays for Twentieth Century-Fox. He was married to the actress Frieda Innescourt, who called the police when she found Redman had taken an overdose of sleeping pills, having told her that he was despondent of world affairs.

"The Perfect Crime" was originally published in the August 1928 issue of *Harper's Magazine*.

The Perfect Crime

Ben Ray Redman

THE WORLD'S greatest detective complacently sipped a port some years older than himself and intently gazed across the table at his most intimate acquaintance; for many years the detective had not permitted himself the luxury of friends. Gregory Hare looked back at him, waiting, listening.

"There is no doubt about it," Trevor reiterated, putting down his glass, "the perfect crime is a possibility; it requires only the perfect criminal."

"Naturally," assented Hare with a shrug, "but the perfect criminal . . ."

"You mean he is a mythical fellow, not apt to be met with in the flesh?"

"Exactly," said Hare, nodding his big head.

Trevor sighed, sipped again, and adjusted the eyeglasses on his thin, sharp nose. "No, I admit I haven't encountered him as yet, but I am always hopeful."

"Hoping to be done in the eye, eh?"

"No, hoping to see the perfect methods of detection tested to the limits of their possibilities. You know, a gifted detector of crime is something more than an inspired policeman with a little bloodhound blood in his veins, something more than a precise scientist; he's an art critic as well, and no art critic likes to be condemned to a steady diet of second-rate stuff."

"Quite."

"Second-rate stuff is bad enough, but it's not the worst. Think of the third, fourth, fifth, and heaven-knows-what-rate crimes that come along every day! And even the masterpieces, the 'classics,' are pretty poor daubs when you look at them closely: a bad tone here and a wrong line there; something false, something botched."

"Most murderers are rather foolish," interjected Hare.

"Foolish! Of course they are. You should know, man, you've defended enough of them. The trouble is that murder almost never evokes the best efforts of the best minds. As a rule it is the work of an inferior mind, cunningly striving towards a perfection that is beyond its reach, or of a superior mind so blinded by passion that its faculties are temporarily impaired. Of course, there are your homicidal maniacs, and they are often clever, but they lack imagination and variety; sooner or later their inability to do anything but repeat themselves brings them up with a sharp jerk."

"Repetition is dullness," murmured Hare, "and dullness, as some-body has remarked, is the one unforgivable sin."

"Right," agreed Trevor. "It is, and plenty of murderers have suffered for it. But they have suffered from vanity almost as often. Practically every murderer, unless he has been accidentally impelled to crime, is an egregious egotist. You know that as well as I do. His sense of power is tremendous, and as a rule he can't keep his mouth shut."

Dr. Harrison Trevor's glasses shone brightly, and he plucked continually at the black cord depending from them as he jerked out his sentences with rapidity and precision. He was on his own ground, and he knew what he was talking about. For twenty years criminals had been his specialty and his legitimate prey. He had hunted them through all lands, and he hunted them successfully. Upstairs, in a chiffonier drawer in his bedroom, there was a large red-leather box holding visible symbols of that success: small decorations of gold and silver and bright ribbons bore mute witness to the gratitude that various European governments had felt, on notable occasions, towards the greatest man hunter of his generation. If Trevor was a dogmatist on murder he was entitled to be one.

Hare, on the other hand, was a good and respectful listener, but, being a criminal lawyer of long experience, he was a man with ideas of his own; and he always expressed them when there was no legal advantage to be gained by withholding them. He expressed one now, when he drawled softly, "All murderers are great egotists, are they? How about great detectives?"

Trevor blinked, then smiled coldly, clutching at his black cord. "Most detectives are asses, I grant you, complete asses and vain as peacocks; very few of them are great. I know only three.

One of them is now in Vienna, the second is in Paris, and the third is . . ."

Hare raised his hand in interruption and said, "The third, or rather the first, is in this room."

The greatest detective in the world nodded briskly. "Of course. There's no point in false modesty, is there?"

"None at all. And it might be a little difficult to maintain such an attitude so soon after the Harrington case. The poor chap was put out of his misery week before last, wasn't he?"

Trevor snorted. "Yes, if you want to call him a poor chap; he was a deliberate murderer. But let's get back to that perfect crime of ours."

"Of yours, you mean," Hare corrected him politely. "I haven't subscribed to the possibility of it as yet. And how would you know about a perfect crime if it ever were committed? The criminal would never be discovered."

"If he had any artistic pride, he would leave a full account of it to be published after his death. Besides, you are forgetting the perfect methods of detection."

Hare whistled softly. "There's a pretty theoretical problem for you. What would happen when the perfect detector set out to catch the perfect criminal? Rather like the immovable object and the irresistible force business, and just about as sensible. The fly in the ointment, of course, is that there is no such thing as perfection."

Dr. Trevor sat up rigidly and glared at the speaker. "There is perfection in the detection of crime."

"Well, perhaps there is." Hare laughed amiably, "You should know, Trevor. But I think what you really mean is that there is a perfect method for detecting imperfect crimes."

The doctor's rigidity had vanished, and now he was smiling with as much geniality as he ever displayed. "Perhaps that is what I do mean, perhaps it is. But there is a little experiment that I should like to try, just the same."

"And that is?"

"And that is, or rather would be, the experiment of exercising all my intelligence in the commission of a crime, then, forgetting every detail of it utterly, using my skill and knowledge to solve the riddle of my own creation. Should I catch myself, or should I escape myself? That's the question."

"It would be a nice sporting event," agreed Hare, "but I'm afraid it's one that can't be pulled off. The little trifle of forgetting is the difficulty. But it would be interesting to see the outcome."

"Yes, it would," said the other, speaking rather more dreamily than was his habit, "but we can never see quite as far as we should like to. My Japanese man, Tanaka, has a saying that he resorts to whenever he is asked a difficult question. He simply smiles and answers, *'Fuji san ni nobottara sazo tōku made miemashō.'* It means, I believe, that if one were to ascend Mount Fuji one could see far. The trouble is that, as in the case of so many problems, we can't climb the mountain."

"Wise Tanaka. But tell me, Trevor, what is your conception of a perfect crime?"

"I'm afraid it isn't precisely formulated; but I have a rough outline in my mind, and I'll give it to you as well as I can. First, though, let's go up to the library; we shall be more comfortable there, and it will give Tanaka a chance to clear the table. Bring your cigar, and come along."

Together the two men climbed the narrow staircase, the host leading. Dr. Trevor's house was a compact, brick building in the

East Fifties, not far from Madison Avenue. Its picturesqueness was rather uncharacteristic of its owner, but its neatness was entirely like him. It was not a large house according to the standards of wealthy New York, but it was a perfectly appointed one, and considerably more spacious than it looked from the street, for the doctor had built on an addition that completely covered the plot which had once been the back yard; and this new section, as well as housing the kitchen and servants' quarters below, held a laboratory and workroom two stories high. An industrial or research chemist might have coveted the equipment of that room; and the filing cases that completely lined the encircling gallery would have furnished any newspaper with a complete reference department. A door opened from the library into the laboratory, and the library itself came close to being the ideal chamber of every student. Dr. Harrison Trevor's house was, in short, an ideal bachelor's establishment, and he had never been tempted to transform it into anything else. More than one male visitor had found reason to remark, "Old Trevor does well for himself."

The same idea flitted across Hare's mind as he puffed at his host's excellent cigar and tasted the liqueur that Tanaka had placed on the table beside his chair. He, too, enjoyed the pleasures of bachelorhood, but he had never learned the knack of enjoying them quite so thoroughly. He would make a few improvements in the routine of his life; he could afford them.

"The perfect crime must, of course, be a murder." Trevor's voice broke the silence that had followed their entrance into the library.

Hare shifted his bulk a little and inquired, "Yes? Why?"

"Because it is, according to our accepted standards, the most reprehensible of all crimes and, therefore, according to my interests, the best. Human life is what we prize most and do our best to protect; to take human life with an art that eludes all detection is unquestionably the ideal criminal action. In it there is a degree of beauty possible in no other crime."

"Humph!" grunted Hare, "you make it sound pleasant."

"I am speaking at once as an amateur and as a professor crime. You have heard surgeons talk of 'beautiful cases.' Well, that is my attitude precisely; and in my cases invariably, as in most of theirs, the patient dies."

"I see."

Trevor blinked, tugged at his eyeglass cord, and then continued. "The crime must be murder, and it must be murder of a particular kind, the purest kind. Now what is the 'purest' kind? Let us see. The *crime passionel* can be ruled out at once, for it is almost impossible that it should be perfect. Passion does not make for art; hot blood begets innumerable blunders. What about the murder for gain? Murderers of this kind make murder a means, not an end in itself; they kill not for the sake of eliminating the victim but in order to profit by the victim's death. No, we can't look to murder for profit as the type that might produce our perfect crime."

The sharp-nosed doctor paused and held his cigar for a moment between his thin lips. Hare studied his face curiously; the man's complete lack of emotion in discussing such matters was not wholly pleasant, he reflected.

Trevor put down his cigar. "Now, how about political and religious murders? They can be counted out almost immediately, for the simple reason that the murderer in such cases is always convinced that he is either serving the public or serving God and, therefore, seldom makes any attempt to conceal his guilt. But there is another class to be considered—those who kill for the sheer joy of killing, those who are dominated by the blood lust. Offhand you would think that their killing would be of the purest type. But as I have said before, the maniac invariably repeats himself, and his repetition leads to his discovery. And even more important is the consideration that the artist must possess the faculty of choice, and that the born killer has no choice. His actions are not willed by himself, they are compelled; whereas the perfect crime must be a work of art, not of necessity."

"You seem to have written off all the possibilities pretty well," remarked Hare.

The doctor shook his head quickly. "Not all. There is one type of murder left, and it is the kind we are looking for: the murder of elimination, the murder in which the sole and pure object is to remove the victim from the world, to get rid of a person whose continued existence is not desirable to the murderer."

"But that brings you back to your *crime passionel,* doesn't it? Practically all murders of jealousy, for example, are murders of elimination, aren't they?"

"In a sense, yes, but not in the purest sense. And, as I have said before, passion can never produce the perfect crime. It must be studied, carefully meditated, and performed in absolutely cold blood. Otherwise it is sure to be imperfect."

"You do go at this in a rather fish-blooded way," remarked the good listener as the doctor paused for a moment.

"Of course I do, and that is the only way the perfect crime could be committed. Now I can imagine a pure murder of elimination that would be ideal so far as motives and circumstances were concerned. Suppose you had spent fifteen years establishing a certain reading of a dubious passage in one of Pindar's odes."

"Ha, ha!" interrupted Hare jocosely. "Suppose I had."

"And suppose," continued Dr. Harrison Trevor, not noticing the interruption, "that another scholar had managed to build up an argument which completely invalidated your interpretation. Suppose, further, that he communicated his proofs to you, and that he had as yet mentioned them to no one else. There you would have a perfect motive and a perfect set of circumstances; only the method of the murder would remain to be worked out."

Gregory Hare sat bolt upright. "Good God, man! What do you mean, 'the method of the murder'?"

The doctor blinked. "Why, don't you understand? You would have excellent reasons for eliminating your rival and thereby saving your own interpretation of the text from confutation; and no one, once your victim was dead and the proofs destroyed, could suspect that you had any such motive. You could work with perfect freedom, you could concentrate on two essentials: the method of the murder and, of course, the disposition of the body."

"The disposition of the body?" Hare seemed to echo the speaker's last words involuntarily.

"To be sure; that is a very important item, most important in fact. But I flatter myself," and here the doctor chuckled softly, "that I have done some very valuable research work along that line."

"You have, eh?" murmured Hare. "And what have you found out?"

"I'll tell you later," Trevor assured him, "and I don't think I would tell any other man alive, because it's really too simple and too dangerous. But at the moment I want to impress on you that the disposition of the body is perhaps the most important step of all in the commission of the perfect crime. The absence of a *corpus delicti* is curiously troublesome to the police. Harrington should really have managed to get rid of West's body, although it probably wouldn't have kept him from sitting in the electric chair two weeks ago. He was too careless."

Hare again sat up sharply and exclaimed, "Was he? Speaking of that, it was the Harrington case that I chiefly wanted to talk to you about tonight."

"Oh, was it? Well, we can get around to that in a minute. And, by the way, that came pretty close to being a murder of elimination, if you like; but the money element figured in it, big money, and gold is apt to have a fairly strong smell when it is mixed up with crime. Harrington's motive was easily traced, but his position made it impossible to touch him until we had our case absolutely water-tight."

"Water-tight, eh? That's what I want to hear about. You see I was abroad until last week, and didn't even know Harrington had been arrested until just before I sailed. The North African newspapers aren't so informative. I was particularly interested, you see, because I knew both men fairly well, and West's wife even better."

"Oh, yes, his wife, gorgeous woman. They were separated, and she's been in Europe for the last two and a half years."

"Yes, I know she has—most of the time."

"All the time. She hasn't been in the United States during that period."

"Hasn't she? Well, I last saw her at Monte Carlo, but that's not important at the moment. I want to hear how you tracked down Harrington."

Dr. Harrison Trevor smiled complacently, adjusted his eyeglasses, and then launched forth in his characteristic manner. "It was really simplicity itself. The only flaw was that Harrington finally confessed. That rather annoyed me, for we didn't need a confession; the circumstantial evidence was complete."

"Circumstantial?"

"Of course. You know as well as I do that most convictions for murder are based on circumstantial evidence. One doesn't send out invitations for a killing."

"No, of course not. Sorry."

"Well, as you probably know, Ernest West, Wall Street operator and multimillionaire (as the papers had it), was found shot through the heart one night a little more than a year ago. He had a shack down on Long Island, near Smithtown, that he used as a base for duck shooting and fishing. The only servant he kept there was an old housekeeper, a local inhabitant; he liked to lead the simple life when he could. Never even used to take a chauffeur down with him. The evening he was killed the housekeeper was absent, spending the night with a sick daughter of hers in Jamaica. She testified that West had sent her off, saying that he could pick up a light supper and breakfast for himself. She turned up the next morning, and nearly died of the shock. West was shot in what was a kind of gun room where he kept all his gear and a few books—cosy sort of place and the best room in the house. There was no sign of a struggle. He was sitting slumped in a big armchair. The bullet that killed him was a .25 caliber. Furst, of the Homicide Bureau, called me up as soon as the regulars failed to locate any scent, and I went down there immediately. West was an important man, you know." The doctor tugged self-consciously at his black cord. "I went down there at once, and I discovered various things. First of all, the house was isolated, and there was no one in the neighborhood who could give any useful evidence whatsoever. The body had been discovered by a messenger boy with a telegram at about seven-thirty; medical examination indicated that the murder had been committed about an hour before. Inside the house I found only one item that I thought useful. After going over the dust and so forth which I swept up from the gun-room floor, I had several tiny thread ends that had pretty obviously come from a tweed suit; and those threads could not be matched in West's wardrobe. But they might have been months old, so I didn't concentrate on them at first. Outside the house there was more to go on. The ground was damp, and two sets of footprints were visible: a man's and a woman's . . ."

"A woman's?" Hare was all attention now.

"Yes, the housekeeper's, of course."

"Oh, yes, the housekeeper's."

"Certainly. But it was difficult to identify them, for the reason that the man, apparently through nervousness, had walked up and down the lane leading to the road several times before finally leaving the scene of his crime; and he had trampled over almost every one of the woman's footprints, scarcely leaving one intact."

"That was odd, wasn't it?

"Very, at first glance, but really simple enough when you think it over. The murderer had hurried out of the house after firing the fatal shot; then he hesitated. He was flurried and couldn't make up his mind as to his next step, even though he had an automobile waiting for him at the end of the lane. So he walked up and down for a few minutes, to calm his nerves and collect his ideas. It was a narrow lane, and the obliteration of the other tracks was at once accidental and inevitable."

"He had a car waiting?"

"Yes, a heavy touring car. Its tire marks were plain, as were those of the public hack that West had ordered for his housekeeper that afternoon. And there was one interesting feature about the marks. There was a big, hard blister on one of the shoes, and it left a perfectly defined indentation in the mud every time it came around."

"I see. And both sets of footprints ended at the same spot?"

"Naturally. The hack stopped for the woman just where the murderer later parked his car."

"Hum." Hare had now lighted a new cigar, and he puffed at it reflectively before asking, "And you are quite sure the woman did not get into the car with the man?"

Trevor stared at the speaker blankly and exclaimed, "You must be wool gathering, Hare. The woman was the housekeeper, and she went off in a public hack at least two hours before the crime was committed. In any event, Harrington confirmed the correctness of all my deductions when he finally confessed." Dr. Harrison Trevor was obviously nettled.

"Oh, yes, of course he did; I'd forgotten. Sorry. Let's hear how you nabbed him."

For a moment the detective looked at his companion doubtfully, as though he feared the other might be baiting him; for Hare's questions had not been of the sort that his alert mind usually asked. He seemed to have something up his sleeve. But Trevor thrust his suspicions aside and returned to the pleasant task of describing his triumph.

"With the bullet, the footprints, the tire marks, and the threads, I had considerable to go on. All I had to do was to relate them unmistakably to one man, and I had my murderer. But the trail soon let into quarters where we had to move cautiously. With my material evidence in front of me, I set out to fasten upon some individual who might have had a motive for killing West. So far as anyone could say, he had no enemies; but on the other hand he had few friends. He believed in the maxim that he travels fastest who travels alone. However, he had nipped some men pretty badly in the Street; and it was upon his financial operations that I soon concentrated my attention. There, with the facilities for investigation at my command, I discovered some very interesting facts. During the three weeks prior to West's death the common stock of Elliott Light and Power had risen fifty-seven points; four days after he had been shot it had dropped back no less than sixty-three points. Investigation showed that on the day West was murdered Harrington was short one hundred and thirty-odd thousand shares of that particular stock. He had been selling it short all the way up, and West had been buying all that was offered. Harrington's resources, great as they were, weren't equal to his rival's. He knew that unless he could break Elliott Common wide open he was a ruined man, and he took the one sure way to do it that he could think of. He eliminated West. It was murder for millions."

Trevor paused impressively; Hare did not say a word.

"That's about all there is to the story; the rest of it was routine sleuthing. One of my men found four tires, three in perfect condition, which had been taken from Harrington's touring car and replaced on the day following the murder. They had been put in a loft of the garage on Harrington's country place. Three perfect tires, mind you; and on the fourth there was a large, hard blister. Harrington's shoes fitted the footprints in West's lane, and the thread ends matched the threads in one of Harrington's suits. And, to top it all off, after the man was arrested, we found a .25, pearl-handled revolver in his wall safe. One shot had been fired, and the weapon hadn't been cleaned since. Harrington's chauffeur testified that his master had taken out the big touring car alone on the afternoon of the murder: the man remembered the date because it had been his wife's birthday. It was all very simple, and even such elements of interest as it possessed were lessened by Harrington's confession. The press made much too much of a stir abut my part in the affair." The doctor smiled deprecatingly. "It was really no mystery at all, and if the men involved had not been so rich and so prominent the case would have been virtually ignored. But we nailed him just in time; he was sailing for Europe the following week."

"What kind of a revolver did you say it was?" Hare asked the question so abruptly that Trevor started before answering.

"Why, it was a .25, pearl-handled and nickel-finished. Rather a dainty weapon altogether; Harrington was a bit apologetic about owning such a toy."

"I should think he might have been. Was the handle slightly chipped on the right side?"

Trevor leaned forward suddenly. "Yes, it was. How the devil did you know?"

"Why it got chipped when Alice dropped it on a rock at Davos. The four of us were target shooting back of the hotel."

"Alice!" exclaimed Trevor. "What Alice? And what do you mean by the four of you?"

Hare answered quietly, "Alice West, my dear fellow. You see, it was her gun. And the four of us were West, Alice, Harrington, and myself; we were all staying at the same hotel in Switzerland four years ago."

"Her gun?" The doctor was speaking excitedly now. "You mean she gave it to him?"

"I doubt it, much as she loved him," drawled Hare. "He probably took it away from her, too late."

"You're talking in riddles," snapped the detective. "What do you mean?"

"Simply that that little weapon helped to execute the wrong man," said Hare wearily.

"The wrong man!"

"Well, that's one way of putting it; but in this case I am very much afraid that the right 'man' was a woman."

Trevor's apparent excitement had vanished abruptly, and now he was as calm as a sphinx. "Tell me exactly what you mean," he demanded.

Hare put aside the butt of his cigar. "It all began back in Davos, four years ago. Harrington fell in love with Alice West, and she fell in love with him. West played dog in the manger: he wouldn't let his wife divorce him and he wouldn't divorce her. They separated, of course, but that didn't help Alice and Harrington towards getting married. I was on the inside of the affair from the first, you see; accidentally to begin with, and afterwards because they all made me their confidant in various degrees. West behaved like a swine, because he really didn't love the woman any more. He simply had made up his mind that no other man was going to have her, legally at least. And he stuck to it—until she killed him."

"She killed him?" The great detective spoke softly.

"I'm as sure of it as though I had seen her do it. To begin with, it was her revolver that fired the shot, as you have proved to me. I've seen it a hundred times when we were firing at bottles and what not for fun. There was no reason for Harrington to borrow it; he had a nice little armory of his own, hadn't he?"

"Yes, we did find a couple of heavy service revolvers and an automatic."

"Exactly. He never would have used a toy like that in a thousand years; and besides he would never have committed a murder. He was too level-headed. Alice, on the other hand, is an extremely hysterical type; I've seen her go completely off her head with anger. Beautiful, Lord, yes! But dangerous, and in the last analysis a coward. She's proved that. I never did envy Harrington."

"But she was in Europe, man, when the murder was committed."

"She was not, Trevor. She was in Montreal that very month, to my certain knowledge, and Montreal isn't so far from Long Island. Harry Sands ran into her at the Ritz there; they were reminiscing about it at Monte Carlo the last time I saw her. She was in Europe before and after the murder, but she wasn't there when it happened. Anyway, that's not the whole story."

"Well, what is it?" Trevor's mouth was grim.

Hare's fingers were playing with a silver match box, and he hesitated a minute before answering. Then he spoke quickly and to the point.

"The rest of it is this. As I told you, Alice is hysterical, and during the past few years drink and dope haven't helped her any. Well, one night at Monte, just before I left, she went off the deep end. We had been talking about her husband's death, and I had been speculating as to who could have done it. Harrington hadn't been arrested then. And I'd been asking her, too, if she and Harrington weren't going to get married soon. She dodged that question, obviously embarrassed. Then suddenly she burst out into a wild tirade against the dead man, called him every name under heaven, and finally dived into her evening bag and fished out a letter. It was addressed to her, and the post mark was more than a year old; it was almost broken at the creases from having been read over and over again. She shoved it at me, and insisted that I read it. It was from West, and it was a cruel letter if I've ever read one. It was the letter of a cat to a mouse, of a jailer to his prisoner: West had her where he wanted her, and he intended to keep her there. He didn't miss a trick when it came to rubbing it in. It was so bad that I didn't want to finish it, but she made me. When I gave it back to her her eyes were blazing; and she grabbed my hand and cried, 'What would you do to a man like that?' I hemmed and hawed for a minute, and she answered herself by exclaiming, 'Kill him! Kill him! Wouldn't you?' As calmly as I could I pointed out to her that someone had already done just that; and she burst into a fit of the wickedest laughter I've ever heard. Then she calmed down, powdered her nose, and said quietly, 'It's funny that you can shoot the heads off all the innocent bottles you like and no one says a word, but if you kill a human snake they hang you for it. And I don't want to hang, thank you very much.' "

Hare paused as though he were very tired, and then he added, "That's about all there was to it; it wasn't very nice. I left for Africa the next day, and I scarcely ever saw the papers there. But I hadn't any doubts as to who had bumped off Ernest West."

While the minute hand on the mantel clock jumped three times there was silence in the book-lined room. Then Trevor spoke, and his voice was strained. "So you think I made a mistake?"

Hare looked him straight in the eye. "What do you think?"

The detective took refuge in another question. "Have you any theory as to what really happened?"

"It's hard to say exactly, but I'm sure she did it. Her reference to the bottles showed that she knew what weapon had been used; she must have done in a thousand bottles with it at various times. My guess is that she and Harrington went down to see West together, to see if they couldn't make him change his mind after all, and that they failed. Then she pulled out that little toy of hers. She always carried it around in her bag. I use to tell her it was a bad habit. She shot West before he could move; she was a better shot than Harrington, he could never have found the man's heart. Then they left the house and drove off in Harrington's car; but first of all he went back and thoughtfully trampled out every one of her footprints and, just to make sure he wasn't missing any, he walked over the housekeeper's as well. There were three sets of tracks there, Trevor, not two; I'll bet on that. Then Harrington took the gun away from her—if he hadn't taken it before—and drove her to wherever she wanted to go. She left him; she left him to stand the gaff if he was suspected, and it was like him to do what he did. He loved her if any man ever loved a woman; and she loved him in her own way, but it wasn't the best way in the world. She loved her own white neck considerably more." Hare smiled a wry smile. "She had forgotten that New York State doesn't go in for hanging. Altogether it is not a pretty tale. But Harrington, poor devil, wanted to save the woman even if she wasn't worth it. You see, to him she was."

"It's impossible!" Trevor snapped out the words as if despite himself.

"What is?"

"That I made a mistake."

"We all make mistakes, my dear fellow."

"I don't." The tight mouth was tighter than ever.

"Well, it's a shame, but what's done is done." Hare shrugged his shoulders.

Trevor looked at him with cold eyes. "Obviously you do not understand. My reputation does not permit of mistakes. I simply can't make them. That's all."

Hare mustered a genial smile; he was genuinely sorry that

Trevor was so distressed and he sought to reassure him. "But your reputation isn't going to suffer. The facts won't come out. Alice West will be dead of dope inside of two years, if I'm any judge, and no one else knows."

"You do."

"Yes, I do; but we can forget about that."

Trevor nodded nervously. "Yes, we must. Do you understand, Hare, we *must*."

Hare studied him quizzically. "Don't worry, old chap, your reputation's safe with me; I'll keep my mouth shut."

Trevor nodded again, more nervously and more emphatically. "Yes, yes, I know you will, of course. I know you will."

"And how about a drink?" Hare swung himself out of his chair.

"On the table there. Help yourself. I'm going into the laboratory for a minute."

The doctor disappeared through the low door, and Hare busied himself with the decanters and the bottles in a preoccupied manner. He was sorry that Trevor was so upset; but what colossal egotism! Perhaps he should have held his tongue; nothing had been gained. He would never mention the subject again. It was a stiff drink of brandy that Hare finally poured himself, and he held it up to the light studying it, with his back to the laboratory door. But he never drank it; for he dropped the glass as he felt the lean fingers at his throat and the chloroform pad smothering his mouth and nostrils. He managed to say only the two words, "My God . . ."

About fifteen minutes later, Dr. Harrison Trevor peered cautiously over the banister of his own stairway. There was no one below, and he descended swiftly. In the kitchen Tanaka heard the front door slam, and almost immediately afterwards his master's voice calling him from the first-floor landing. Tanaka responded briskly.

"Mr. Hare has just left," said the doctor, "and he forgot his cigarette case. Run after him; he may still be in sight."

Tanaka sped upon his errand. Yes, there on the corner was a tall man, obviously Hare *san*; but he was getting into a taxi. Tanaka ran, but before he was half way down the block Hare *san* had driven off. Tanaka returned to report failure.

"Too bad," said his master, who met him on the landing. "But it doesn't really matter. Telephone Mr. Hare's apartment and tell his man that Mr. Hare left his case here, and that he is not to worry about it. You can take it to him in the morning."

Tanaka went downstairs to obey orders; and his master was left to wonder at the coincidence of the man who looked like Hare getting into the taxi. The accidental evidence might prove useful, but it was quite unnecessary, quite unnecessary; he had no need of accidental aid. At the door of his library the detective paused and surveyed the scene with a critical eye: everything was in place, comfortably, conventionally, indisputably in place. There were no fragments of the broken tumbler on the floor; only a dark, wet spot on the carpet that was drying rapidly. Brandy and soda would leave no stain. Dr. Harrison Trevor smiled a chilly smile and then walked resolutely toward the laboratory where his task awaited him. Once the door had been locked behind him, his first act was to switch on the electric ventilator fan which carried off all obnoxious odors through a concealed flue. After that he worked on into the morning hours.

The disappearance of Mr. Gregory Hare, eminent criminal lawyer, within a week after his return from abroad, furnished the front pages of the newspapers with rather more than a nine days' wonder. It was Dr. Trevor who was the first to insist upon foul play; and it was Dr. Trevor who worked fervently upon the case, with all the assistance that the police could give him. Naturally he was deeply concerned, for Hare had been an intimate acquaintance, and he had been among the last to see the man alive; but the body was never found, and there was no evidence to go on with. Tanaka repeated what he knew, reiterating the story of the taxi; and a patrolman on fixed post confirmed the Japanese's testimony. The tall gentleman had come from the direction of Dr. Trevor's house, and had driven off just as the servant had come running after him. All of which helped not at all. A certain "Limping" Louie, whom Hare, years before when he was District Attorney, had sent up for a long term, was dragged in by the police net; but he had a perfect alibi. The mystery remained a mystery.

Dr. Trevor and Inspector Furst were discussing the case one afternoon, long after it had been abandoned. Furst still toyed with the idea that it might not have been murder, but the doctor was positive.

"I'm absolutely sure of it, Furst, absolutely sure. Hare was killed."

"Well," said the Inspector, "if you are so sure, I'm inclined to agree. You've never made a mistake."

MAN AFRAID

Ben Ames William

ALTHOUGH BORN in Mississippi, Ben Ames Williams (1889-1953) spent most of his life in New England, achieving his B.A. from Dartmouth in 1910 and going straight to the *Boston American* as a sportswriter. After six years, he had sold some short stories and serials, so quit to become a full-time fiction writer. A steady stream of nearly four hundred short stories followed and were published in numerous magazines but most frequently in *The Saturday Evening Post* and *Collier's*.

The first of his more than thirty novels was *All the Brothers Were Valiant* (1919), on which two films were based, one in 1923, a silent romance starring Lon Chaney, and one presented as adventure in 1953, starring Robert Taylor, Stewart Granger, and Ann Blyth. The novels had a wide range of subjects but they were unfailingly popular, which he ascribed to the fact that, as he said, he "liked to write and the result is stories that people liked to read."

People evidently also liked to see the films that his books inspired, notably *Leave Her to Heaven* (1945), starring Gene Tierney, Cornel Wilde, Jeanne Crain, and Vincent Price, and *The Strange Woman* (1946), starring Hedy Lamarr, George Sanders, and Louis Hayward. Lesser films made from novels and stories by Williams include *After His Own Heart* (1919), *Jubilo, Jr* (1927), *Too Busy to Work* (1932), *Small Town Girl* (1936), *Adventure's End* (1937) and *Johnny Trouble* (1957).

The most ambitious and challenging work that Williams produced was *A House Divided* (1947), for which he researched for twenty years and needed four-and-a-half years to write. A long Civil War novel, it resided on bestseller lists for many months.

"Man Afraid" was originally published in the April 26, 1930 issue of *The Saturday Evening Post.*

Man Afraid

Ben Ames Williams

Simon Gray, by the unanimous opinion of those who knew him best, was an arrant coward; yet this was not altogether surprising. To train a fighting dog, you pit him first against opponents he can surely master; but Simon had fought since babyhood a series of losing battles. Thus in the matter of his profession, he was a drug clerk from choice; but it was his father's choice, not his own. The elder Gary was a snuffy old man with bristling brows; and he had held Simon in a filial terror for so many years that it never occurred to the boy to be anything but what his father wanted. His father wanted an assistant in the pharmacy, so a drug clerk Simon did become.

He was afraid of his father, and he was afraid of many other things. He was afraid of policemen, of automobiles, of indigestion; he was even afraid of caterpillars and of butterflies. Most of all, perhaps, he was afraid of his wife. When he found himself, in some fashion wholly mysterious, committed to marry Alice Field, he thought that marriage would at least remove him from his father's roof, give him some small empire of his own. But he was to find that he had simply bowed the knee before another tyrant. Alice was pretty and soft and helpless to the eye; but she had iron in her, and Simon was wax in her hands.

To be afraid of one we hate is bad enough; but it is infinitely worse to live in daily fear of one beloved. Simon devoted his every waking thought to the effort to avoid doing anything by which Alice might be displeased; yet he was not always successful. If smoking in the house scented her curtains, he could give it up; if she liked to read the morning paper as it came fresh-folded from the presses, he could surrender it to her intact; if she wished to lie late abed in the morning, he could prepare her breakfast and bring it on a tray. He learned to walk softly so that he would not wear holes in his socks. He learned to press his own neckties. He learned to put on overalls before tending the furnace, lest he soil his more formal clothes.

But three times during the first months of their marriage he committed, despite his best precautions, the unpardonable sin. He missed the last train home from town.

The first time he came home by street car, arriving half an hour or more after Alice had expected him, she gave him a chance to explain; but this was difficult, because she began with the assumption that whatever he said was a lie. After his explanations she refused to speak to him for twenty-four hours. The second time he came home late, she wept aloud all night in the bed beside him, sobbing that he had betrayed her for another woman. The third time she went home to her mother for three interminable days; and when she returned, she told him sadly that if he were ever late again, she would kill herself.

"Because I don't want to live, Simon, dear," she wistfully explained, "if I'm once convinced you don't love me any more."

A bolder man would have told her to stop being an idiot; but Simon was not bold. He was afraid of scores of things, though, of course, he was more afraid of some things than of others. He vowed never to be late again; but there was one occasion when in the effort to keep this vow he displayed an extraordinary energy, and a reckless audacity not to be expected of a man afraid.

The drug store was a small establishment, narrow and compact, tucked away in the crevice between a shoe-shine parlor and a fruit counter, just across the street from the South Station. Simon and his father were its only staff; and this meant long hours. Three days in the week Simon came in at eight and stayed till six at night, catching the six-seven train in time to be home for dinner at six-forty-five. On the other days he reported for duty at noon and stayed till eleven at night, arriving home by the train which was due in Newtonville at eleven-forty-two. The routine was absolute, and Simon clung to it tenaciously.

On the occasion about to be related, the elder Gary went home at six and left Simon in sole charge. It was a winter night; a blizzard howled through the street under the Elevated. Snow packed in the window corners, and frosted the windowpanes and banked against the door. The street lamps shone through a nimbus of light reflected from the swirling flakes. But the drug store was warm and comfortable; and Simon had no worry except a fear that his train might be late in getting home. Sometimes on such a night the switches froze.

Business in the little pharmacy was never brisk; and to-night it was even more dull than usual. Simon had time on his hands; and when his father had gone, he sat on a tall stool behind the glass screen which shielded the prescription department, and began to read the evening paper.

He was invisible behind the screen, so that from the street the store appeared to be empty. But Simon could see, through a transparent panel in the glass, anyone who might enter; and about twenty minutes after his father departed, two men came in. They were muffled against the storm, their faces invisible. They came in and closed the door behind them and stood looking out through the snow-crusted glass into the street, as though watching someone there.

Simon noticed that they carried bags: two suitcases and one soft black leather kit of smaller size. He thought this faintly surprising; because if they were about to take a train at the station across the street, they might as well have gone direct to that shelter from the storm.

But he descended from his stool and came around the screen into the front of the store to serve them. The men turned at his appearance, in a faintly startled fashion, and one of them dove quickly into the telephone booth. Simon thought the other had had a like impulse; but the first man closed the door of the booth behind him, leaving his companion outside; and this man, after a moment's hesitation, said:

"Hot chocolate!"

Simon prepared the drink. The man in the booth seemed to be telephoning, for the low murmur of his voice could be heard through the muffling walls. He who had ordered the hot chocolate sipped it slowly, watching the man in the booth, watching the street; and Simon studied him curiously. Till by and by the customer seemed to become conscious of Simon's regard, and to be by it disquieted. He fumbled in his pocket and produced a bank note.

"Here," he said, and laid it on the marble slab.

Simon noticed that the man kept his head bent so that the brim of his hat shadowed his countenance; he was still wondering why the other did this as he picked up the money and turned and pressed the key of the cash register to register the sale. But, as the drawer slid open, Simon looked for the first time at that which he held in his hand, and saw that it was a fifty-dollar bill!

Now the elder Gary had taken most of the day's cash with him. Simon hesitated, then turned to his customer.

"Haven't you anything smaller?" he asked.

"Smallest I've got," the other retorted.

"I can't change it," Simon confessed.

"Well, go get the change," the customer directed, in a quick impatience.

Simon still hesitated; he pointed toward the man in the booth. "How about him?"

"He can't change it either," the other insisted.

And Simon stood shifting from one foot to the other, suddenly a little pale. He was on the horns of a dilemma. There were two rules which the elder Gary held absolute. Never leave a customer alone in the store; and never let the cash register get out of balance. The sale was already registered, or Simon would have forgiven his customer the price of the hot chocolate. He might have done so even now, and made good the deficit out of his own pocket; but Alice required him to keep a punctilious account of his expenditures, and she would miss the nickel. Simon was more afraid of her displeasure than of his father's; and the end was that he went behind the screen and put on his overcoat and hat, and came out again.

"I'll be right back," he promised. The customer made no reply; and Simon went out into the storm.

He hurried, because he was uneasy at having left the store alone. Yet the first shop he tried, and the second, declined to accommodate him. It must have been almost ten minutes before he returned with the change. As he came in sight of the pharmacy, he thought he saw his two customers crossing toward the station through the swirling snow. But he decided this must be a mistake, and he went on to the store.

It was empty. The men were gone.

They must have been compelled to catch a train, Simon decided; and he remembered that there was a six-thirty express west. Trains were a hobby with Simon; he took long journeys in time-tables. Some day, when he could afford it, he meant to follow the routes he traced on paper now; but for the present his travels were purely literary. Yet he knew the time card backward; and he was quite sure in his own mind now where the men had gone.

It did not occur to him to keep the money. He had once short-changed his father, retaining three pennies out of a nickel with which he had been sent to buy papers. This was fifteen years ago; but Simon still remembered very vividly the penalties of theft. So he sprang the lock on the door and ran across the street toward the station. He could catch the two men before the train pulled out, give them their money, and be back in five minutes' time. He ran across the street into the station; and he raced the length of the train shed to the track from which the six-thirty would depart.

He came thus far without having overtaken the men he sought; but he cut through a nearer gate and ran along the length of the train, watching through the windows till in one of the forward cars, near the engine, he discovered them, moving down the aisle.

He climbed the steps, panting with haste, the money clutched in his hand. The train began to move; and he hesitated; but he could always alight at Trinity Place and return. So he went on.

The men were not in sight in the car, and for a moment he was baffled. Then he realized that they must be in the drawing-room; and he tried the door. It was locked; but he knocked; and after a moment the door opened a crack, and a man looked out. Simon said hurriedly:

"You forgot your money!"

Someone inside swore, in a tone of surprise and dismay. The man at the door hesitated, and half closed the door; but Simon was in haste. He must be ready to get off the train at Trinity Place, and they were already rolling through the yards. He pushed the door open and stumbled in, the money in his hand.

"Here it is!" he exclaimed.

The men seemed at a loss. One of them closed the door, and bolted it; but Simon did not notice this. He was not sure for the moment to which one the change was due; and he looked from one to the other searchingly. They were curiously alike, somewhere in their thirties, with alarming *eyes.*

Then the man at the door said: "Pull down the shades!"

The other reached across and did so. Simon tried to protest; and then he choked, and swallowed hard.

For the man behind him jabbed Simon in the ribs with something, and Simon looked down and saw it was a gun. The man said grimly:

"Sit down!"

Simon sat down. He was a jelly of fear.

Simon did not leave the train at Trinity Place. His first frantic appeals had been silenced by the steady menace of that pistol; and he sat trembling while the train stopped and started again. When they were once more under way he listened in horror while his captors devised a working arrangement to meet the situation into which Simon's coming had precipitated them.

They had made Simon sit next the window. Then the younger man put on a black silk scarf like a sling, and rested his right hand in this scarf. The pistol was in this hand, concealed by the black folds. He sat down beside Simon and the pistol pointed across the front of his body at the terrified young man.

When the conductors came to take up the tickets, Simon stared straight ahead, and the young man with his arm in a sling sat beside him, while the other man dealt with the train officials. They had only two tickets, he explained cheerfully; but his friend here—he nodded toward Simon—had decided at the last moment to come along. He paid a cash fare to Chicago with another fifty-dollar bill. The conductors withdrew and the man bolted the door again.

Then he sat down, facing Simon, and he looked at Simon intently. He was not a pleasant man. There was a mustache like a black smudge across his upper lip, and Simon did not like mustaches. This man asked Simon harshly:

"Now, what's the game?"

"I brought back your change," Simon stammered. "That's all." The money was still in his hand, and he extended it toward his questioner.

The other ignored the money. His lip twisted. "Come clean!" he directed. "Come clean!"

"Eh?" Simon protested.

"I said, what's the game?"

"Why, you gave me a fifty-dollar bill," Simon urged. "And I——"

"Not me," Black Mustache corrected scornfully. "I didn't give it to you. It was that simp there!"

The younger man by Simon's side said mildly: "Whose idea was it, ducking in the drug store, anyway? He was sizing me up! I had to get him out of the way."

"I brought back your money," Simon said again.

"Just an honest man, eh?" Black Mustache asked derisively.

"Why, yes," Simon pleaded. "Yes, that's all!"

"I think you're a liar," said the older man vividly. "Who knows you came?"

"Nobody," said Simon.

"Now isn't that too bad!" Black Mustache commented; and he grinned. "Now isn't that too bad!"

And Simon shivered at that grin.

But the younger man, there by Simon's side, shook his head. "No, Ed," he remarked. "I've gone this far with you. We've got the stuff." His eyes rested on the soft leather bag under the other's hand. "But I don't stand for anything else. I don't want to burn."

"I'll burn before I rot in jail," said Black Mustache.

Before the other could reply, the train slowed for Newtonville; and Simon started to his feet. But the mild young man beside him—and he did not in this moment seem so mild—said softly:

"Sit down, buddy. I don't want to hurt you; but I don't mind if I do."

Simon stood shuddering like a frightened horse. He had been till now so full of terror that he could not think. But when the train stopped at this familiar station he had remembered

Alice. She might telephone the drug store during the evening. Certainly she would expect him home on the eleven-forty-two. He had to be there, dared not fail.

But the gun jabbed him in the ribs, and he sat down; stayed silent while the train was at a standstill, waited till it went on once more.

Then he said pleadingly: "I've got to go back. There's no one in the store. And I've got to get home by midnight."

"Why?" asked Black Mustache.

"My wife will worry!" said Simon desperately. He became voluble. "You see, she's always afraid I'll run after other women. I wouldn't. There aren't any other women but her. But she thinks that, so I have to be careful all the——"

"Oh, shut up!" said Black Mustache. He looked toward his ally. "Listen," he urged intently. "We're all right so far. They won't find out a thing about it at the bank till tomorrow morning. We've got that much start. But this sap crabs the show. He's seen us; he can spill the works. I say, curtains for him!"

"I've got to get home," Simon cried. He was thinking in terms of time-tables. "Listen, I'll get off at Worcester and catch the eight-four back."

"Say," Black Mustache assured him malignantly, "you won't catch no train at Worcester, fellow!"

And the younger man amended this. "The best break you can get, buddy, is to wake up in Chicago tomorrow," he told Simon. "Now keep still."

His tone was calm; it was almost friendly. Yet Simon found it had a curiously chilling quality. He sat still; but time-tables came tumbling through his distracted head.

"We've got to let the porter make up the berths," the younger man pointed out. "That's the first thing." He rang, and when the porter presently appeared, this young man held Simon with his eyes, while Black Mustache said briefly:

"Fix us up as soon as you can, porter."

"Yes, sir," the porter agreed. "Upper and couch, sir?"

Black Mustache nodded.

"I'll take care of you right away," the porter promised.

He departed to fetch linen, and Black Mustache asked, with a nod toward Simon:

"What'll we do with him while the porter's in here? Take him in the smoking compartment?"

"Yes," said the mild young man. He looked at Simon. "But you won't talk much, buddy. You won't talk at all. Because my arm's still broke, see."

And he showed Simon the gun, in the black silk sling.

"I just want to get off and go home," said Simon helplessly.

But the porter returned; and he dared speak no more.

They had the smoking compartment to themselves; they returned by and by to find the drawing-room prepared for their occupancy. Black Mustache locked the door; and he said to the mild young man:

"All right, they won't bother us till morning now."

"We'll be in Worcester in ten minutes," Simon pleaded.

Black Mustache ignored him. "I say we finish him, and drop off somewhere and beat it."

The younger man ran his hands over Simon's pockets. "He isn't heeled!" he said then; and to Simon: "Get up there!"

So Simon climbed into the upper berth; and he thought of Alice, and his brow was wet. He began desperately to seek some device by which he could escape. If he submitted to the will of these two deadly men he might come to Chicago alive; to resist was likely to have serious consequences. But even if he survived,

Alice would never believe the fantastic story he must tell; so his thoughts went racing.

There was a penknife in his pocket. A drowning man snatches at straws. Simon opened the tiny blade and hid the knife under his pillow. If the worst happened, it might serve some useful end.

On the couch below him, the men discussed his fate. Black Mustache still favored simple murder; but the mild young man overruled him.

"Here's what we'll do," he said at last positively. "I won't stand for anything else."

"You've got one vote," Black Mustache grimly reminded him.

"And one gun," said the younger man in the gentlest tones. "And I'm that much ahead of you. I say—here's what we'll do."

This was his plan. They would tie Simon securely, with a towel to close his mouth. They themselves would alight at Albany, leaving Simon gagged and bound in the upper berth. And the porter would be instructed that Simon was not to be waked in the morning.

"That way," the younger man pointed out, "they won't find him till they hit Chicago, and we'll have time enough to get across the line, the way we planned. Jim will be at the station in Albany with the car. And that's that!"

"Let's take him with us," Black Mustache urged. "Take him for a ride. We can throw him off a bridge some place."

"I've told you what we'll do," the other reminded him. "Of course, if he makes a break, that's different. But as long as he behaves, that's good enough!"

And with a warning glance at Simon, he opened the door and called the porter in.

"This gentleman and I have had to change our plans," he explained, indicating Black Mustache. "We're getting off at Albany. But Mr. Jones—" he nodded toward Simon, lying very still in the upper berth—"Mr. Jones is going on to Chicago." He spoke to Simon directly. "You want to sleep late in the morning, don't you, Jones? Don't want to be waked, do you?"

"No," said Simon huskily. "Let me sleep. Late as I can."

"Yes, sir," the porter agreed.

When they were again alone, the younger man spoke to Simon.

"Now let's have your hat, and coat, and pants," he directed briefly.

Simon sat up in the berth and took them off as he was bid. "Hang the overcoat up," he begged. "And the coat too. Alice doesn't like it if my clothes are mussed."

"Why, we're pleased to oblige," the young man assented with a smile. He draped the coats over the hanger by the door; and as Simon kicked off his shoes and drew off his trousers, the young man thrust the shoes under the edge of the couch, folded the trousers and put them in the baggage rack. But before he did so, he removed the belt from its loops.

"Now," he directed, "stick your feet out here."

Simon looked at the watch on his wrist. The train was slowing down for Worcester. He shuddered; but there might still be time to get back from Springfield. He must get back; he dared not fail.

He was thinking about trains and time-tables while the young man bound his ankles together with the belt, and strapped them firmly. At the other's direction he rolled on his side and offered his wrists to be secured. His captor climbed half into the berth to affix the towel that would serve as a gag; and Simon bit hard on the rough fabric forced between his teeth.

"There," said the young man, when his arrangements were complete. "You're getting a break! Call yourself lucky, and be a nice boy."

He even pulled up the blankets and tucked Simon snugly in. Then he and Black Mustache sat down on the couch below, and stayed there in lowvoiced conversation while the train stopped at Worcester and went on.

Simon, lying on his side in the upper berth so that he could look down on them where they sat, was in the grip of a horrible despair. His bonds were tight, the towel muffled his mouth and hindered his breathing, and his posture was incredibly awkward and uncomfortable; but he was unconscious of his pains. His thoughts were misery enough. He might not get home for days; his father would discover that the store had gone untended, and Alice—he dared not think what Alice would do. He lay in a dismal grief, curled into a ball like a puppy which is cold in its sleep; and below him the two men talked calmly of black and hideous things.

The trussed captive in the upper berth heard without attending to their words some of the things they said. They were, he gathered, trusted employees of one of the Boston banks who had served loyally for years, waiting the right and proper moment for the coup just consummated. Now the thing was done, their escape accomplished, their prospective flight assured; and there was enough in the soft black bag to make them rich for years.

So much Simon understood, but he did not greatly care. He would have given all the money in the little bag to be safe back in the store.

That which at last turned his thoughts in a more practical direction was a little thing. He lay on his right side, his hands behind him; and he moved his arms now and then to ease the pain of their cramped position. Once when he did this, his hands escaped from under the edge of the blanket and touched the steel plate that formed the side of the berth and at the same time the side of the car. The steel was cool and soothing to the touch; Simon stroked it absently.

And his fingers came in contact with a projection there.

He felt it gingerly, recognized its nature. It was a bell button; to press it would no doubt summon the porter. So long as he could reach the bell he was not wholly lost. And he took quick hope, and began, with a sudden lucidity, to plan and to devise.

He forgot to be afraid, in this new activity. The bell would summon the porter; even with his bound hands, he could press the button. But the porter could do nothing for him now. He must first help himself; and he could do so much more if he were free. He wrenched at his bonds, tentatively; but his thoughts were searching. And suddenly they found something.

His thoughts found the knife under his pillow.

He lay quite still, considering the possibilities, staring blankly. He turned over, so that his captors might not see his face and guess his thoughts; and he thus lay facing the blank wall of the berth, where hung the hammock designed to contain a traveler's clothes. His fingers had found the bell button; his thoughts had found the knife; his eyes found the hammock!

And in a moment Simon's plan was formed.

The first step to its accomplishment was to secure the knife. It was under the pillow, here beneath his head, not three inches from his ear; yet it seemed at first very far away. Moving gingerly lest he alarm the men who sat just below him, he tried to lift his cramped hands far enough to reach the knife; but the effort was a hopeless one. He resorted to indirection. He burrowed with his head under the pillow, found the knife with his chin, dragged it downward toward his chest, pushed it farther down.

This took time; but the men were not alarmed. When Simon was sure of this, he turned over on his other side, his bound hands behind him; and instantly his fingers touch the smooth pearl handle of the pen-knife there.

From that contact a flood of power ran through Simon's whole body; but upon its heels came a surge of fear. For the men stood up, and the mild young man looked at Simon. Simon stared back at him, quaking.

The young man grinned. "Go to sleep, buddy," he directed. "You've got all night. I'll tuck you in when we say bye-bye."

He and Black Mustache proceeded to take off their shoes; they lay down, Black Mustache on the couch, the younger man on the berth below Simon. They would rest a while, till it was time to leave the train at Albany.

When the mild young man turned off the light, leaving the drawing-room in almost total darkness, Simon's eyes shone with delight. He saw triumph waiting for his hand.

Some forty-five minutes later, as the train began to slow down in the outer yards at Springfield, the porter on duty in that particular car heard his bell buzz; he looked at the indicator and saw that the button had been pressed in the upper berth in Drawing-Room A.

There would be time to answer the call before the train stopped, so he went along the curtained aisle between the made-up berths, and pushed the button on the door of the drawing-room. He heard the buzzer sound inside; but for a moment there was no response. The porter rang again.

After a momentary interval, someone called in a cautious voice: "Who's there?"

"You rung for the porter, sir," said the man at the door.

The man inside started to reply; but his words seemed to be cut off. There was a moment's silence, and a movement as though the man might be coming to open the door, and then a tumbling sound. And suddenly a vast confusion, a shot, and a sharp cry.

The porter backed off with some precipitation. He ran headlong to fetch the conductor. There was something going on in Drawing-Room A.

What was going on in Drawing-Room A was this. In that dark interior, illumined only by the dim crack of light beneath the curtain on the window that opened into the corridor, Black Mustache had been lying awake on the couch, while the mild young man slept lightly in the lower berth. Black Mustache was considering the advisability of rising, while his companion slept, to remove all fear of what the captive in the upper berth might later have to say. Only the possibility that the mild young man might wake and resent his action made him hesitate.

While he weighed this murderous project pro and con, someone came to the door of the drawing-room and pressed the button; the buzzer sounded sharply, and Black Mustache sat up in a sudden strict alarm. He sat up and stared at the door, quite forgetting Simon now.

The buzzer rang again, and Black Mustache got lightly to his feet; he touched the elbow of the mild young man, who half rose, fumbling for the weapon by his side. And Black Mustache leaned toward the door.

He called: "Who's there?"

Someone had rung for the porter, it appeared. But Black Mustache said harshly:

"No, we——"

And as he spoke he was already turning toward the upper berth, ready to do destruction there.

But before he could finish what he wished to say, something happened to him. He gasped and was silent, snatching desperately at his throat. Out of the darkness of the upper berth there had dropped around his neck a light, running noose of stout cord, which instantly tightened in a cruel grip and would not easily be loosened. He snatched at it; but it had bitten so deep into his flesh that his fingers found no hold. He tottered and stumbled, and the mild young man in the lower berth ejaculated:

"What's the matter, Ed?"

Black Mustache, by way of reply, fell to his knees on the floor, still fighting at that deadly, choking cord.

The mild young man understood that something was seriously wrong, and he scrambled out of the berth, the gun in his hand. He stood up and looked into the black cavern of the upper berth, where their captive was bestowed. But before he could see anything, he saw a million stars; for something lashed him across the open eyes. The darkness was so complete that his eyes had no warning; the lids had not time to close. The mild young man screamed with pain, and his hands clenched, and the gun exploded, and then another stinging blow in the face made him recoil so that he fell sidewise and down in a heap upon the struggling bulk that was Black Mustache.

Outside the drawing-room, feet were stumbling up the aisle of the car.

Something dropped from the upper berth to the couch, to

the floor. This was young Simon Gary, the man who was afraid. Simon snatched his pants and jumped into them. He fumbled for his shoes, and found them; found also the mild young man's abandoned gun. He thrust his feet into the shoes; and with the gun in his hand he pulled open the door of the drawing-room.

The conductor was there, and a passenger or two, and a gray-faced porter in the background. As Simon opened the door, the train stopped in the Springfield station with a lurch which threw Simon into their arms. He pressed the pistol into the conductor's hands.

"Bank robbers!" he cried. "Hold them! I'll get a cop!"

And he raced along the aisle.

While they were still bewildered, he had disappeared; but there was enough to occupy them here. It was the conductor who turned on the light in the drawing-room, the gun ready in his hand. But the two men in the little apartment were thoroughly subdued. Black Mustache had freed that noose about his neck at last; but he was still gasping for breath. The mild young man was babbling in an awful pain.

Besides these two human beings, there were three things in the drawing-room which the conductor did find interesting. There was a small black bag full of bills of moderate denominations, the whole running to a staggering sum. But there was also a whip like a knout, which had been made by cutting off one end of the clothes hammock in the upper berth, leaving eight or nine inches of dangling cords. And there was a noose made of hammock cord, which had been laboriously braided into a three-ply strand, with a running knot which tightened when the noose was drawn, and held it stubbornly.

Not till the conductor had inspected all these matters did he look about to discover the recklessly daring hero who with no other weapon than a Pullman hammock had overcome two bank robbers and a gun; but by that time Simon was gone!

Simon had departed in haste, because the train to Boston which he hoped to catch must be already in the station. He knew his time-tables. From the car platform he saw the other train on a near-by track, and he jumped from the Pullman vestibule across the fence which divided west- from eastbound tracks, and boarded the other train as it began to move. He dropped into a seat there like a man reprieved.

There was still the chance that his absence from the store might have been discovered; but aside from that one possibility, he had nothing to fear. He had even saved his belt, the belt which had fastened his ankles. When his hands were free, he had unbuckled the belt and buckled it around his waist again; because Alice would blame him if he lost so necessary an article.

Once aboard the train for home, he gave no thought to what was done; his thoughts cast ahead to what there was yet to do. He alighted at Newtonville at eleven thirty-one; and he waited till the eleven-forty-two from town should arrive. By that train Alice would expect him home; when it had come and gone he trudged up the street happily.

He let himself into the house and left his hat and coat and went upstairs. He undressed in the dark; for Alice did not like her sleep disturbed. But when he got into bed, she roused enough to ask:

"What time is it, dear?"

"Two minutes of twelve," he told her gently.

"You came straight home, didn't you?" She sighed approvingly, and touched his arm, and went to sleep again.

And Simon relaxed by her side, unutterably relieved. He had reached home on time; he need no longer be afraid.

DIME A DANCE

Cornell Woolrich

Known as the greatest writer of suspense fiction of the 20th century, the long and prolific career of Cornell (George Hopley) Woolrich (1903-1968) embraced many kinds of fiction. His first novel, *Cover Charge* (1926) was a romance, as was his second, *Children of the Ritz* (1927), which won a $10,000 prize (a staggering sum at that time) jointly offered by *College Humor* magazine and First National Pictures, which produced a film based on the book two years later.

His next four books were also romantic novels and were so well received that critics compared him to F. Scott Fitzgerald. He found magazines eager to buy his varied fiction in the 1920s and '30s, including humor, western, and adventure fiction and, finally, in 1934, his true forte, the noir stories for which he is properly revered today.

Many of his greatest works have been adapted for motion pictures, including *The Bride Wore Black* (1940, filmed by Francois Truffaut in 1967), *Phantom Lady* (1942, under the Irish name, filmed in 1944), "It Had to Be Murder" (1942, filmed by Alfred

Hitchcock as *Rear Window* in 1954), *Black Alibi* (1942, filmed as *The Leopard Man* in 1943), *The Black Angel* (1943, filmed in 1946) and *Night Has a Thousand Eyes* (1945, as by Hopley, filmed in 1948). "Dime a Dance" was adapted as an episode for radio and television several times, most notably for *Fallen Angels* (1995), starring Jennifer Grey and directed by Peter Bogdanovich.

"Dime a Dance" was first published in the February 1938, issue of *Black Mask* magazine; it was first collected in book form in *The Dancing Detective* (Philadelphia, Lippincott, 1946).

Dime a Dance

Cornell Woolrich

PATSY MARINO was clocking us as usual when I barged in through the foyer. He had to look twice at his watch to make sure it was right when he saw who it was. Or pretended he had to, anyway. It was the first time in months I'd breezed in early enough to climb into my evening dress and powder up before we were due on the dance floor.

Marino said, "What's the matter, don't you feel well?"

I snapped, "D'ya have to pass a medical examination to get in here and earn a living?" and gave him a dirty look across the frayed alley-cat I wore on my shoulder.

"The reason I ask is you're on time. Are you sure you're feeling well?" he pleaded sarcastically.

"Keep it up and you won't be," I promised, but soft-pedaled it so he couldn't quite get it. He was my bread and butter after all.

The barn looked like a morgue. It always did before eight—or so I'd heard. They didn't have any of the "pash" lights on yet, those smoky red things around the walls that gave it atmosphere. There wasn't a cat in the box, just five empty gilt chairs and the coffin. They had all the full-length windows overlooking the main drag open to get some ventilation in, too. It didn't seem like the same place at all; you could actually breathe fresh air in it!

My high heels going back to the dressing-room clicked hollowly in the emptiness, and my reflection followed me upside-down across the waxed floor, like a ghost. It gave me a spooky feeling, like tonight was going to be a bad night. And whenever I get a spooky feeling, it turns out to be a bad night all right.

I shoved the dressing-room door in and started: "Hey, Julie, why didn't you wait for me, ya getting too high-hat?" Then I quit again.

She wasn't here either. If she wasn't at either end, where the hell was she?

Only Mom Henderson was there, reading one of tomorrow morning's tabs. "Is it that late?" she wanted to know when she saw me.

"Aw, lay off," I said. "It's bad enough I gotta go to work on a empty stomach." I slung my cat-pelt on a hook. Then I sat down and took off my pumps and dumped some foot powder in them, and put them back on again.

"I knocked on Julie's door on my way over," I said, "and didn't get any answer. We always have a cup of Java together before we come to work. I don't know how I'm going to last the full fifteen rounds—"

An unworthy suspicion crossed my mind momentarily: Did Julie purposely dodge me to get out of sharing a cup of coffee with me like I always took with her other nights? They allowed her to make it in her rooming-house because it had a fire-escape; they wouldn't allow me to make it in mine. I put it aside as unfair. Julie wasn't that kind; you could have had the shirt off her back—only she didn't wear a shirt, just a brassière.

"Matter?" Mom sneered. "Didn't you have a nickel on you to buy your own?"

Sure I did. Habit's a funny thing, though. Got used to taking it with a side-kick and—I didn't bother going into it with the old slob.

"I got a feeling something's going to happen tonight," I said, hunching my shoulders.

"Sure," said Mom. "Maybe you'll get fired."

I thumbed my nose at her and turned the other way around on my chair. She went back to her paper. "There haven't been any good murders lately," she lamented. "Damn it, I like a good, juicy murder wanst in a while!"

"You're building yourself up to one right in here." I scowled into the mirror at her.

She didn't take offense; she wasn't supposed to, anyway. "Was you here when that thing happened to that southern girl, Sally, I think, was her name?"

"No!" I snapped. "Think I'm as old as you? Think I been dancing here all my life?"

"She never showed up to work one night, and they found her—that was only, let's see now . . ." She figured it out on her fingers. "Three years ago."

"Cut it out!" I snarled. "I feel low enough as it is!"

Mom was warming up now. "Well, for that matter, how about the Fredericks kid? That was only a little while before you come here, wasn't it?"

"I know," I cut her short. "I remember hearing all about it. Do me a favor and let it lie."

She parked one finger up alongside her mouth. "You know,"

she breathed confidentially, "I've always had a funny feeling one and the same guy done away with both of them."

"If he did, I know who I wish was third on his list!" I was glowering at her, when thank God the rest of the chain gang showed up and cut the death-watch short. The blonde came in, and then the Raymond tramp, and the Italian frail, and all the rest of them—all but Julie.

I said, "She was never as late as this before!" and they didn't even know who or what I was talking about. Or care. Great bunch.

A slush-pump started to tune up outside, so I knew the cats had come in too.

Mom Henderson got up, sighed, "Me for the white tiles and rippling waters," and waddled out to her beat.

I opened the door a crack and peeped out, watching for Julie. The pash lights were on now and there were customers already buying tickets over the bird cage. All the other taxidancers were lining up—but not Julie.

Somebody behind me yelled, "Close that door! Think we're giving a free show in here?"

"You couldn't interest anyone in that second-hand hide of yours even with a set of dishes thrown in!" I squelched absent-mindedly, without even turning to find out who it was. But I closed it anyway.

Marino came along and banged on it and hollered, "Outside, you in there! What do I pay you for anyway?" and somebody yelled back: "I often wonder!"

The cats exploded into a razz-matazz just then with enough oompah to be heard six blocks away, so it would pull them in off the pave. Once they were in it was up to us. We all came out single file, to a fate worse than death, me last. They were putting the ropes up, and the mirrored tops started to go around in the ceiling and scatter flashes of light all over everything, like silver rain.

Marino said, "Where you goin', Ginger?" and when he used your front name like that it meant he wasn't kidding.

I said, "I'm going to phone Julie a minute, find out what happened to her."

"You get out there and goona-goo!" he said roughly. "She knows what time the session begins! How long's she been working here, anyway?"

"But she'll lose her job, you'll fire her," I wailed.

He hinged his watch. "She is fired already," he said flatly.

I knew how she needed that job, and when I want to do a thing I do it. A jive-artist was heading my way, one of those barnacles you can't shake off once they fasten on you. I knew he was a jive, because he'd bought enough tickets to last him all week; a really wise guy only buys them from stretch to stretch. The place might burn down for all he knows.

I grabbed his ticket and tore it quick, and Marino turned and walked away. So then I pleaded, "Gimme a break, will you? Lemme make a phone call first. It won't take a second."

The jive said, "I came in here to danst."

"It's only to a girl friend," I assured him. "And I'll smile pretty at you the whole time." (*Clink! Volunteer* 8-1111.) "And I'll make it up to you later, I promise I will." I grabbed him quick by the sleeve. "Don't go way, stand here!"

Julie's landlady answered. I said, "Did Julie Bennett come back yet?"

"I don't know," she said. "I ain't seen her since yesterday."

"Find out for me, will ya?" I begged. "She's late and she'll lose her job over here."

Marino spotted me, came back and thundered: "I thought I told you—"

I waved the half ticket in his puss. "I'm working," I said. "I'm on this gentleman's time," and I goona-gooed the jive with teeth and eyes, one hand on his arm.

He softened like ice cream in a furnace. He said, "It's all right, Mac," and felt big and chivalrous or something. About seven cents worth of his dime was gone by now.

Marino went away again, and the landlady came down from the second floor and said, "She don't answer her door, so I guess she's out."

I hung up and I said, "Something's happened to my girl friend. She ain't there and she ain't here. She wouldn'ta quit cold without telling me."

The goona-goo was beginning to wear off the jive by this time. He fidgeted, said, "Are you gonna danst or are you gonna stand there looking blue?"

I stuck my elbows out. "Wrap yourself around this!" I barked impatiently. Just as he reached, the cats quit and the stretch was on.

He gave me a dirty look. "Ten cents shot to hell!" and he walked off to find somebody else.

I never worry about a thing after it's happened, not when I'm on the winning end anyway. I'd put my call through, even if I hadn't found out anything. I got back under the ropes, and kept my fingers crossed to ward off garlic-eaters.

By the time the next stretch began, I knew Julie wasn't coming any more that night. Marino wouldn't have let her stay even if she had, and I couldn't have helped her get around him any more, by then, myself. I kept worrying, wondering what had happened to her, and that creepy feeling about tonight being a bad night came over me stronger than ever, and I couldn't shake it off no matter how I goona-gooed.

The cold orangeade they kept buying me during the stretches didn't brace me up any either. I wasn't allowed to turn it down, because Marino got a cut out of the concession profits.

The night was like most of the others, except I missed Julie. I'd been more friendly with her than the rest of the girls, because she was on the square. I had the usual run of freaks.

"With the feet, with the feet," I said wearily, "lay off the belt-buckle crowding."

"What am I supposed to do, build a retaining wall between us?"

"You're supposed to stay outside the three-mile limit," I flared, "and not try to go mountain climbing in the middle of the floor. Do I look like an Alp?" And I glanced around to see if I could catch Marino's eye.

The guy quit pawing. Most of them are yellow like that. But on the other hand, if a girl complains too often, the manager begins to figure her for a trouble-maker. "Wolf!" you know, so it don't pay.

It was about twelve when they showed up, and I'd been on the floor three and a half hours straight, with only one more to go. There are worse ways of earning a living. You name them. I knew it was about twelve because Duke, the front man, had just wound up "The Lady Is a Tramp," and I knew the sequence of his numbers and could tell the time of night by them, like a sailor can by bells. Wacky, eh? Half-past—"Limehouse Blues."

I gandered at them when I saw them come in the foyer, because customers seldom come in that late. Not enough time left to make it worth the general admission fee. There were two of them; one was a fat, bloated little guy, the kind we call a "bellywhopper," the other was a pip. He wasn't tall, dark and handsome because he was medium-height, light-haired and clean-cut looking without being pretty about it, but if I'd had any dreams left he coulda moved right into them. Well, I didn't, so I headed for the dressing-room to count up my ticket stubs while the stretch was on; see how I was making out. Two cents out of every dime when you turn them in.

They were standing there sizing the barn up, and they'd called Marino over to them. Then the three of them turned around and looked at me just as I made the door, and Marino thumbed me. I headed over to find out what was up. Duke's next was a rhumba, and I said to myself: "If I draw the kewpie, I'm going to have kittens all over the floor."

Marino said, "Get your things, Ginger." I thought one of them was going to take me out; they're allowed to do that, you know, only they've got to make it up with the management for taking you out of circulation. It's not as bad as it sounds, you can still stay on the up and up, sit with them in some laundry and listen to their troubles. It's all up to you yourself.

I got the backyard sable and got back just in time to hear Marino say something about: "Will I have to go bail for her?"

Fat said, "Naw, naw, we just want her to build up the background a little for us."

Then I tumbled, got jittery, squawked: "What is this, a pinch? What've I done? Where you taking me?"

Marino soothed: "They just want you to go with them, Ginger. You be a good girl and do like they ast." Then he said something to them I couldn't figure. "Try to keep the place here out of it, will you, fellas? I been in the red for six months, as it is."

I cowered along between them like a lamb being led to the

slaughter, looking from one to the other. "Where you taking me?" I wailed, going down the stairs.

Maiden's Prayer answered, in the cab. "To Julie Bennett's, Ginger." They'd gotten my name from Marino, I guess.

"What's she done?" I half sobbed.

"May as well tell her now, Nick," Fat suggested. "Otherwise she'll take it big when we get there."

Nick said, quietly as he could, "Your friend Julie met up with some tough luck, babe." He took his finger and he passed it slowly across his neck.

I took it big right there in the cab, Fat to the contrary. "Ah, no!" I whispered, holding my head. "She was on the floor with me only last night! Just this time last night we were in the dressing-room together having a smoke, having some laughs! No! She was my only friend." And I started to bawl like a two-year-old kid, straight down my make-up and onto the cab floor.

Finally this Nick, after acting embarrassed as hell, took a young tent out of his pocket, said: "Have yourself a time on this, babe."

I was still working on it when I went up the rooming-house stairs sandwiched between them. I recoiled just outside the door. "Is she—is she still in there?"

"Naw, you won't have to look at her," Nick reassured me.

I didn't, because she wasn't in there any more, but it was worse than if she had been. Oh God, that sheet, with one tremendous streak down it as if a chicken had been—! I swiveled, played puss-in-the-corner with the first thing I came up against, which happened to be this Nick guy's chest. He sort of stood still like he liked the idea. Then he growled, "Turn that damn thing over out of sight, will you?"

The questioning, when I was calm enough to take it, wasn't

a grill, don't get that idea. It was just, as they'd said, to fill out her background. "When was the last time you saw her alive? Did she go around much, y'know what we mean? She have any particular steady?"

"I left her outside the house door downstairs at one-thirty this morning, last night, or whatever you call it," I told them. "We walked home together from Joyland right after the session wound up. She didn't go around at all. She never dated the boys afterwards and neither did I."

The outside half of Nick's left eyebrow hitched up at this, like when a terrier cocks its ear at something. "Notice anyone follow the two of you?"

"In our racket they always do; it usually takes about five blocks to wear them them out, though, and this is ten blocks from Joyland."

"You walk after you been on your pins all night?" Fat asked, aghast.

"We should take a cab, on our earnings! About last night, I can't swear no one followed us, because I didn't look around. That's a come-on, if you do that."

Nick said, "I must remember that," absent-mindedly.

I got up my courage, faltered: "Did it—did it happen right in here?"

"Here's how it went: She went out again after she left you the first time—"

"I knew her better than that!" I yipped. "Don't start that. Balloon Lungs, or I'll let you have this across the snout!" I swung my cat-piece at him.

He grabbed up a little box, shook it in my face. "For this," he said. "Aspirin! Don't try to tell us different, when we've already checked with the all-night drugstore over on Sixth!" He took a couple of heaves, cooled off, sat down again. "She went out, but instead of locking the house-door behind her, she was too lazy or careless; shoved a wad of paper under it to hold it on a crack till she got back. In that five minutes or less, somebody who was watching from across the street slipped in and lay in wait for her in the upper hallway out here. He was too smart to go for her on the open street, where she might have had a chance to yell."

"How'd he know she was coming back?"

"The unfastened door woulda told him that; also the drug clerk tells us she showed up there fully dressed, but with her bare feet stuck in a pair of carpet-slippers to cool 'em. The killer musta spotted that too."

"Why didn't she yell out here in the house, with people sleeping all around her in the different rooms?" I wondered out loud.

"He grabbed her too quick for that, grabbed her by the throat just as she was opening her room-door, dragged her in, closed the door, finished strangling her on the other side of it. He remembered later to come out and pick up the aspirins which had dropped and rolled all over out there. All but one, which he overlooked and we found. She wouldn't 've stopped to take one outside her door. That's how we know that part of it."

I kept seeing that sheet, which was hidden now, before me all over again. I couldn't help it, I didn't want to know, but still I had to know. "But if he strangled her, where did all that blood—" I gestured sickly. "—come from?"

Fat didn't answer, I noticed. He shut up all at once, as if he didn't want to tell me the rest of it, and looked kind of sick himself. His eyes gave him away. I almost could have been a detective myself, the way I pieced the rest of it together just by following his eyes around the room. He didn't know I was reading them, or he wouldn't have let them stray like that.

First they rested on the little portable phonograph she had there on a table. By using bamboo needles she could play it late at night, soft, and no one would hear it. The lid was up and there was a record on the turntable, but the needle was worn down half-way, all shredded, as though it had been played over and over.

Then his eyes went to a flat piece of paper, on which were spread out eight or ten shiny new dimes; I figured they'd been put aside like that, on paper, for evidence. Some of them had little brown flecks on them, bright as they were. Then lastly his eyes went down to the rug; it was all pleated up in places, especially along the edges, as though something heavy, inert, had been dragged back and forth over it.

My hands flew up my head and I nearly went wacky with horror. I gasped it out because I hoped he'd say no, but he didn't, so it was yes. "You mean he danced with her *after* she was gone? Gave her dead body a dime each time, stabbed her over and over while he did?"

There was no knife, or whatever it had been, left around, so either they'd already sent it down for prints or *he'd* taken it out with him again.

The thought of what must have gone on here in this room, of the death dance that must have taken place . . . All I knew was that I wanted to get out of here into the open, couldn't stand it any more. Yet before I lurched out, with Nick holding me by the elbow, I couldn't resist glancing at the label of the record on the portable. "Poor Butterfly."

Stumbling out the door I managed to say, "She didn't put

that on there. She hated that piece, called it a drip. I remember once I was up here with her and started to play it, and she snatched it off, said she couldn't stand it, wanted to bust it then and there but I kept her from doing it. She was off love and men, and it's a sort of mushy piece, that was why. She didn't buy it, they were all thrown in with the machine when she picked it up second-hand."

"Then we know his favorite song, if that means anything. If she couldn't stand it, it would be at the bottom of the stack of records, not near the top. He went to the trouble of skimming through them to find something he liked."

"With her there in his arms, already!" That thought was about the finishing touch, on top of all the other horror. We were on the stairs going down, and the ground floor seemed to come rushing up to meet me. I could feel Nick's arm hook around me just in time, like an anchor, and then I did a clothespin act over it. And that was the first time I didn't mind being pawed.

When I could see straight again, he was holding me propped up on a stool in front of a lunch counter a couple of doors down, holding a cup of coffee to my lips.

"How's Ginger?" he said gently.

"Fine," I dribbled mournfully all over my lap. "How's Nick?"

And on that note the night of Julie Bennett's murder came to an end.

Joyland dancehall was lonely next night. I came in late, and chewing cloves, and for once Marino didn't crack his whip over me. Maybe even he had a heart. "Ginger," was all he said as I went hurrying by, "don't talk about it while you're on the hoof, get me? If anyone asks you, you don't know nothing about it. It's gonna kill business."

Duke, the front man, stopped me on my way to the dressing-room. "I hear they took you over there last night," he started.

"Nobody took nobody nowhere, schmaltz," I snapped. He wore feathers on his neck, that's why I called him that; it's the word for long-haired musicians in our lingo.

I missed her worse in the dressing-room than I was going to later on out in the barn; there'd be a crowd out there around me, and noise and music, at least. In here it was like her ghost was powdering its nose alongside me at the mirror the whole time. The peg for hanging up her things still had her name penciled under it.

Mom Henderson was having herself a glorious time; you couldn't hear yourself think, she was jabbering away so. She had two tabloids with her tonight, instead of just one, and she knew every word in all of them by heart. She kept leaning over the gals' shoulders, puffing down their necks: "And there was a dime balanced on each of her eyelids when they found her, and another one across her lips, and he stuck one in each of her palms and folded her fingers over it, mind ye! D'ye ever hear of anything like it? Boy, he sure must've been down on you taxis—"

I yanked the door open, planted my foot where it would do the most good, and shot her out into the barn. She hadn't moved that fast from one place to another in twenty years. The other girls just looked at me, and then at one another, as much as to say: "Touchy, isn't she?"

"Get outside and break it down; what do I pay you for anyway?" Marino yelled at the door. A gob-stick tootled plaintively, out we trooped like prisoners in a lock-step, and another damn night had started in.

I came back in again during the tenth stretch ("Dinah" and

"Have You Any Castles, Baby?") to take off my kicks a minute and have a smoke. Julie's ghost came around me again. I could still hear her voice in my ears, from night-before-last! "Hold that match, Gin. I'm trying to duck a cement-mixer out there. Dances like a slap-happy pug. Three little steps to the right, as if he were priming for a standing broad-jump. I felt like screaming: For Pete's sake, if you're gonna jump, jump!"

And me: "What're you holding your hand for, been dancing upside-down?"

"It's the way he holds it. Bends it back on itself and folds it under. Like this, look. My wrist's nearly broken. And look what his ring did to me!" She had shown me a strawberry-size bruise.

Sitting there alone, now, in the half-light, I said to myself: "I bet *he* was the one! I bet *that's* who it was! Oh, if I'd only gotten a look at him, if I'd only had her point him out to me! If he enjoyed hurting her that much while she was still alive, he'd have enjoyed dancing with her after she was dead." My cigarette tasted rotten, I threw it down and got out of there in a hurry, back into the crowd.

A ticket was shoved at me and I ripped it without looking up. Gliding backward, all the way around on the other side of the barn, a voice finally said a little over my ear: "How's Ginger?"

I looked up and saw who it was, said, "What're you doing here?"

"Detailed here," Nick said.

I shivered to the music. "Do you expect him to show up *again*, after what he's done already?"

"He's a dance-hall killer," Nick said. "He killed Sally Arnold and the Fredericks girl, both from this same mill, and he killed a girl in Chicago in between. The prints on Julie Bennett's phonograph records match those in two of the other cases, and in the third case—where there were no prints—the girl was holding a dime clutched in her hand. He'll show up again sooner or later. There's one of us cops detailed to every one of these mills in the metropolitan area tonight, and we're going to keep it up until he does."

"How do you know what he looks like?" I asked.

He didn't answer for a whole bar. "We don't," he admitted finally. "That's the hell of it. Talk about being invisible in a crowd! We only know he isn't through yet, he'll keep doing it until we get him!"

I said, "He was here that night, he was right up here on this floor with her that night, before it happened; I'm sure of it!" And I sort of moved in closer. Me, who was always griping about being held too tight. I told him about the impression the guy's ring had left on her hand, and the peculiar way he'd held it, and the way he'd danced.

"You've got something there," he said, and he left me flat on the floor and went over to phone it in.

Nick picked me up again next dance.

He said, shuffling off, "That was him all right who danced with her. They found a freshly made impression still on her hand, a little off-side from the first, which was almost entirely obliterated by then. Meaning the second one had been made after death, and therefore stayed uneffaced, just like a pin-hole won't close up in the skin after death. They made an impression of it with moulage, my lieutenant just tells me. Then they filled that up with wax, photographed it through a magnifying lens, and now we know what kind of a ring he's wearing. A seal ring shaped like a shield, with two little jewel splinters, one in the upper right-hand corner, the other in the lower left."

"Any initials on it?" I gaped, awe-stricken.

"Nope, but something just as good. He can't get it off, unless he has a jeweler or locksmith file it off, and he'll be afraid to do that now. The fact that it would press so deeply into her hand proves that he can't get it off, the flesh of his finger has grown around it; otherwise it would have had a little give to it, the pressure would have shifted the head of it around a little."

He stepped all over my foot, summed up: "So we know how he dances, know what his favorite song is, 'Poor Butterfly,' know what kind of a ring he's wearing. And we know he'll be back sooner or later."

That was all well and good, but I had my own health to look out for; the way my foot was throbbing! I hinted gently as I could, "You can't do very much watching out for him, can you, if you keep dancing around like this?"

"Maybe you think I can't. And if I just stand there with my back to the wall, it's a dead give-away. He'd smell me a mile away and duck out again. Keep it quiet what I'm doing here, don't pass it around. Your boss knows, of course, but it's to his interest to cooperate. A screwball like that can put an awful dent in his receipts."

"You're talking to the original sphinx," I assured him. "I don't pal with the rest of these twists anyway. Julie was the only one I was ever chummy with."

When the session closed and I came downstairs to the street, Nick was hanging around down there with the other lizards. He came over to me and took my arm and steered me off like he owned me.

"What's this?" I said.

He said, "This is just part of the act, make it look like the McCoy."

"Are you sure?" I said to myself, and I winked to myself without him seeing me.

All the other nights from then on were just a carbon copy of that one, and they started piling up by sevens. Seven, fourteen, twenty-one. Pretty soon it was a month since Julie Bennett had died. And not a clue as to who the killer was, where he was, what he looked like. Not a soul had noticed him that night at Joyland, too heavy a crowd. Just having his prints on file was no good by itself.

She was gone from the papers long ago, and she was gone from the dressing-room chatter, too, after a while, as forgotten as though she'd never lived. Only me, I remembered her, because she'd been my pal. And Nick Ballestier, he did because that was his job. I suppose Mom Henderson did too, because she had a morbid mind and loved to linger on gory murders. But outside of us three, nobody cared.

They did it the wrong way around. Nick's superiors at Homicide, I mean. I didn't try to tell him that, because he would have laughed at me. He would have said, "Sure! A dance-mill pony knows more about running the police department than the commissioner does himself! Why don't you go down there and show 'em how to do it?"

But what I mean is, the dance mills didn't need all that watching in the beginning, the first few weeks after it happened, like they gave them. Maniac or not, anyone would have known he wouldn't show up *that* soon after. They needn't have bothered detailing anyone at all to watch the first few weeks. He was lying low then. It was only after a month or so that they should have begun watching real closely for him. Instead they did it just the reverse. For a whole month Nick was there nightly. Then after that he just looked in occasionally, every second night or so, without staying through the whole session.

Then finally I tumbled that he'd been taken off the case entirely and was just coming for—er, the atmosphere. I put it up to him unexpectedly one night. "Are you still supposed to come around here like this?"

He got all red, admitted: "Naw, we were all taken off this duty long ago. I—er, guess I can't quit because I'm in the habit now or something."

"Oh, yeah?" I said to myself knowingly. I wouldn't have minded that so much, only his dancing didn't get any better, and the wear and tear on me was something awful. It was like trying to steer a steam-roller around the place.

"Nick," I finally pleaded one night, when he pinned me down flat with one of his size twelves and then tried to push me out from under with the rest of him, "be a detective all you want, only please don't ask me to dance any more, I can't take it."

He looked innocently surprised. "Am I that bad?"

I tried to cover up with a smile at him. He'd been damn nice to me even if he couldn't dance.

When he didn't show up at all next night, I thought maybe I'd gone a little too far, offended him maybe. But the big hulk hadn't looked like the kind that was sensitive about his dancing, or anything else for that matter. I brought myself up short with a swift, imaginary kick in the pants at this point. "What the heck's the matter with *you*?" I said to myself. "You going soft? Didn't I tell you never to do that!" And I reached for the nearest ticket, and tore it, and I goona-gooed with a: "Grab yourself an armful, mister, it's your dime."

I got through that night somehow but I had that same spooky feeling the next night like I'd had *that* night—like tonight was going to be a bad night. Whenever I get that spooky feeling, it turns out to be a bad night all right. I tried to tell myself it was because Nick wasn't around. I'd got used to him, that was all, and now he'd quit coming, and the hell with it. But the feeling wouldn't go away. Like something was going to happen, before the night was over. Something bad.

Mom Henderson was sitting in there reading tomorrow morning's tab. "There hasn't been any good juicy murders lately," she mourned over the top of it. "Damn it, I like a good murder y'can get your teeth into wanst in a while!"

"Ah, dry up, you ghoul!" I snapped. I took off my shoes and dumped powder into them, put them on again. Marino came and knocked on the door. "Outside, freaks! What do I pay you for anyway?"

Someone jeered, "I often wonder!" and Duke, the front man, started to gliss over the coffin, and we all came out single file, me last, to a fate worse than death.

I didn't look up at the first buyer, just stared blindly at a triangle of shirt-front level with my eyes. It kept on like that for a while; always that same triangle of shirt-front. Mostly white, but sometimes blue, and once it was lavender, and I wondered if I ought to lead. The pattern of the tie across it kept changing too, but that was all.

"Butchers and barbers and rats from the harbors
Are the sweethearts my good luck has brought me."

"Why so downcast, Beautiful?"

"If you were standing where I am, looking where you are, you'd be downcast too."

That took care of him. And then the stretch.

Duke went into a waltz, and something jarred for a minute.

My timetable. This should have been a gut bucket (low-down swing music) and it wasn't. He'd switched numbers on me, that's what it was. Maybe a request. For waltzes they killed the pash lights and turned on a blue circuit instead, made the place cool and dim with those flecks of silver from the mirror-top raining down.

I'd had this white shirt-triangle with the diamond pattern before; I remembered the knitted tie, with one tier unravelled on the end. I didn't want to see the face, too much trouble to look up. I hummed the piece mentally, to give my blank mind something to do. Then words seemed to drop into it, fit themselves to it, of their own accord, without my trying, so they must have belonged to it. "*Poor butterfly by the blossoms waiting.*"

My hand ached, he was holding it so darned funny. I squirmed it, tried to ease it, and he held on all the tighter. He had it bent down and back on itself . . . .

"*The moments pass into hours—*"

Gee, if there's one thing I hate it's a guy with a ring that holds your mitt in a strait-jacket! And he didn't know the first thing about waltzing. Three funny little hops to the right, over and over and over. It was getting my nerves on edge. "If you're gonna jump, jump!" Julie's voice came back to me from long ago. She'd run into the same kind of a—

"*I just must die, poor butterfly!*"

Suddenly I was starting to get a little scared and a whole lot excited. I kept saying to myself: "Don't look up at him, you'll give yourself away." I kept my eyes on the knitted tie that had one tier unraveled. The lights went white and the stretch came on. We separated, he turned his back on me and I turned mine on him. We walked away from each other without a word. They don't thank you, they're paying for it.

I counted five and then I looked back over my shoulder, to try to see what he was like. He looked back at me at the same time, and we met each other's looks. I managed to slap on a smile, as though I'd only looked back because he'd made a hit with me, and that I hoped he'd come around again.

There was nothing wrong with his face, not just to look at anyway. It was no worse than any of the others around. He was about forty, maybe forty-five, hair still dark. Eyes speculative, nothing else, as they met mine. But he didn't answer my fake smile, maybe he could see through it. We both turned away again and went about our business.

I looked down at my hand, to see what made it hurt so. Careful not to raise it, careful not to bend my head, in case he was still watching. Just dropped my eyes to it. There was a red bruise the size of a small strawberry on it, from where his ring had pressed into it the whole time. I knew enough not to go near the box. I caught Duke's eye from where I was and hitched my head at him, and we got together sort of casually over along the wall.

"What'd you play 'Poor Butterfly' for that last time?" I asked.

"Request number," he said.

I said, "Don't point, and don't look around, but whose request was it?"

He didn't have to. "The guy that was with you the last two times. Why?" I didn't answer, so then he said, "I get it." He didn't at all. "All right, chiseler," he said, and handed me two dollars and a half, splitting a fiver the guy had slipped him to play it. Duke thought I was after a kickback.

I took it. It was no good to tell him. What could he do? Nick Ballestier was the one to tell. I broke one of the singles at the orangeade concession—for nickels. Then I started to work my way over toward the phone, slow and aimless. I was within a yard of it, no more than that, when the cats started up again!

And suddenly *he* was right next to me, he must have been behind me the whole time.

"Were you going any place?" he asked.

I thought I saw his eyes flick to the phone, but I wasn't positive. One thing sure, there wasn't speculation in them any more, there was—decision.

"No place," I said meekly. "I'm at your disposal." I thought, "If I can only hold him here long enough, maybe Nick'll show up."

Then just as we got to the ropes, he said, "Let's skip this. Let's go out to a laundry and sit a while."

I said, smooth on the surface, panic-stricken underneath: "But I've already torn your ticket, don't you want to finish this one out at least?" And tried to goona-goo him for all I was worth, but it wouldn't take. He turned around and flagged Marino, to get his O.K.

His back was to me, and across his shoulder I kept shaking my head, more and more violently, to Marino—no, no, I don't want to go with him. Marino just ignored me. It meant more money in his pocket this way.

When I saw that the deal was going through, I turned like a streak, made the phone, got my buffalo in. It was no good trying to tell Marino, he wouldn't believe me, he'd think I was just making it up to get out of going out with the guy. Or if I raised the alarm on my own, he'd simply duck down the stairs before anyone could stop him and vanish again. Nick was the only one to tell, Nick was the only one who'd know how to nail him here.

I said, "Police headquarters, quick! Quick!" and turned and looked over across the barn. But Marino was already alone out there. I couldn't see where the guy had gone, they were milling around so looking over their prospects for the next one.

A voice came on and I said: "Is Nick Ballestier there? Hurry up, get him for me."

Meanwhile Duke had started to break it down again; real corny. It must have carried over the open wire. I happened to raise my eyes, and there was a shadow on the wall in front of me, coming across my shoulders from behind me. I didn't move, held steady, listening.

I said, "All right, Peggy, I just wanted to know when you're gonna pay me back that five bucks you owe me," and I killed it.

Would he get it when they told him? They'd say: "A girl's voice asked for you, Nick, from somewhere where there was music going on, and we couldn't make any sense out of what she said, and she hung up without waiting." A pretty slim thread to hold all your chances on.

I stood there afraid to turn. His voice said stonily, "Get your things, let's go. Suppose you don't bother any more tonight about your five dollars." There was a hidden meaning, a warning, in it.

There was no window in the dressing-room, no other way out but the way I'd come in, and he was right there outside the door. I poked around all I could, mourning: "Why don't Nick come?" and, boy, I was scared. A crowd all around me and no one to help me. He wouldn't stay; the only way to hang onto him for Nick was to go with him and pray for luck. I kept casing him through the crack of the door every minute or so. I didn't think he saw me, but he must have. Suddenly his heel scuffed at it brutally, and made me jump about an inch off the floor.

"Quit playing peek-a-boo, I'm waiting out here!" he called in sourly.

I grabbed up Mom Henderson's tab and scrawled across it in lipstick: "Nick: He's taking me with him, and I don't know where to. Look for my ticket stubs. Ginger."

Then I scooped up all the half tickets I'd accumulated all night long and shoved them loose into the pocket of my coat. Then I came sidling out to him. I thought I heard the phone on the wall starting to ring, but the music was so loud I couldn't be sure. We went downstairs and out on the street.

A block away I said, "There's a joint. We all go there a lot from our place," and pointed to Chan's. He said "Shut up!" I dropped one of the dance checks on the sidewalk. Then I began making a regular trail of them.

The neon lights started to get fewer and fewer, and pretty soon we were in a network of dark lonely side streets. My pocket was nearly empty now of tickets. My luck was he didn't take a cab. He didn't want anyone to remember the two of us together, I guess.

I pleaded, "Don't make me walk any more, I'm awfully tired."

He said, "We're nearly there, it's right ahead." The sign on the next corner up fooled me; there was a chop-suey joint, there, only a second-class laundry, but I thought that was where we were going.

But in between us and it there was a long dismal block, with tumbledown houses and vacant lots on it. And I'd run out of dance checks. All my take gone, just to keep alive. He must have worked out the whole set-up carefully ahead of time, known I'd fall for that sign in the distance that we *weren't* going to.

Sure, I could have screamed out at any given step of the way, collected a crowd around us. But you don't understand. Much as I wanted to get away from him, there was one thing I wanted even more: to hold him for Nick. I didn't just want him to slip away into the night, and then do it all over again at some future date. And that's what would happen if I raised a row. They wouldn't believe me in a pinch, they'd think it was some kind of a shakedown on my part. He'd talk himself out of it or scram before a cop came.

You have to live at night like I did to know the real callousness of passers-by on the street, how seldom they'll horn in, lift a finger to help you. Even a harness-cop wouldn't be much good, would only weigh my story against his, end up by sending us both about our business.

Maybe the thought came to me because I spotted a cop ahead just then, loitering toward us. I could hardly make him out in the gloom, but the slow steady walk told me. I didn't really think I was going to do it until we came abreast of him.

The three of us met in front of a boarded-up condemned house. Then, as though I saw my last chance slipping away—because Nick couldn't bridge the gap between me and the last of the dance checks any more; it was too wide—I stopped dead.

I began in a low tense voice: "Officer, this man here—"

Julie's murderer had involuntarily gone on a step without me. That put him to the rear of the cop. The whole thing was so sudden, it must have been one of those knives that shot out of their own hilts. The cop's eyes rolled, I could see them white in the darkness, and he coughed right in my face, warm, and he started to come down on top of me, slow and lazy. I sidestepped and he fell with a soft thud and rocked a couple of times with his own fall and then lay still.

But the knife was already out of him long ago, and its point was touching my side. And where the cop had been a second ago, *he* was now. We were alone together again.

He said in a cold, unexcited voice, "Go ahead, scream, and I'll give it to you right across him."

I didn't, I just pulled in all my breath.

He said, "Go ahead, down there," and steered me with his knife down a pair of steps into the dark areaway of the boarded-up house it had happened in front of. "Stand there, and if you make a sound—you know what I told you." Then he did something to the cop with his feet, and the cop came rolling down into the areaway after me.

I shrank back and my back was against the boarded-up basement door. It moved a little behind me. I thought, "This must be where he's taking me. If it is, then it's open." I couldn't get out past him, but maybe I could get *in* away from him.

I turned and clawed at the door, and the whole framed barrier swung out a little, enough to squeeze in through. He must have been hiding out in here, coming and going through here, all these weeks. No wonder they hadn't found him.

The real basement door behind it had been taken down out of the way. He'd seen what I was up to, and he was already wriggling through the gap after me. I was stumbling down a pitch-black hallway by then.

I found stairs going up by falling down on top of them full length. I sobbed, squirmed up the first few on hands and knees, straightened up as I went.

He stopped to light a match. I didn't have any, but his helped me too, showed me the outline of things. I was on the first-floor hall now, flitting down it. I didn't want to go up too high, he'd only seal me in some dead-end up there, but I couldn't stand still down here.

A broken-down chair grazed the side of my leg as I went by, and I turned, swung it up bodily, went back a step and pitched it down over the stair-well on top of him. I don't know if it hurt him at all but his match went out.

He said a funny thing then. "You always had a temper, Muriel."

I didn't stand there listening. I'd seen an opening in the wall farther ahead, before the match went out. Just a blackness. I dived through it and all the way across with swimming motions, until I hit a jutting mantel slab over some kind of fireplace. I crouched down and tucked myself in under it. It was one of those huge old-fashioned ones. I groped over my head and felt an opening there, lined with rough brickwork and furry with cobwebs, but it wasn't wide enough to climb up through. I squeezed into a corner of the fireplace and prayed he wouldn't spot me.

He'd lit another match, and it came into the room after me, but I could only see his legs from the fireplace opening, it cut him off at the waist. I wondered if he could see me; he didn't come near where I was.

The light got a little stronger, and he'd lit a candle stump. But still his legs didn't come over to me, didn't bend down, or show his face peering in at me. His legs just kept moving to and fro around the room. It was awfully hard, after all that running, to keep my breath down.

Finally he said out loud: "Chilly in here," and I could hear him rattling newspapers, getting them together. It didn't sink in for a minute what was going to happen next. I thought, "Has he forgotten me? Is he that crazy? Am I going to get away with it?" But there'd been a malicious snicker in his remark; he was crazy like a fox.

Suddenly his legs came over straight to me, without bending down to look he was stuffing the papers in beside me. I couldn't see out any more past them. I heard the scrape of a match against the floor boards. Then there was the momentary silence of combustion. I was sick, I wanted to die quick, but I didn't want to die that way. There was the hum of rising flame, and a brightness just before me, the papers all turned gold. I thought, "Oh, Nick! Nick! Here I go!"

I came plunging out, scattering sparks and burning newspapers.

He said, smiling, pleased with himself, casual, "Hello, Muriel. I thought you didn't have any more use for me? What are you doing in my house?" He still had the knife—with the cop's blood on it.

I said, "I'm not Muriel, I'm Ginger Allen from the Joyland. Oh, mister, please let me get out of here, please let me go!" I was so scared and so sick I went slowly to my knees. "Please!" I cried up at him.

He said, still in that casual way, "Oh, so you're not Muriel? You didn't marry me the night before I embarked for France, thinking I'd be killed, that you'd never see me again, that you'd get my soldier's pension?" And then getting a little more vicious, "But I fooled you, I was shell-shocked but I didn't die. I came back even if it was on a stretcher. And what did I find? You hadn't even waited to find out! You'd married another guy and you were both living on my pay. You tried to make it up to me, though, didn't you, Muriel? Sure; you visited me in the hospital, bringing me jelly. The man in the next cot died from eating it. Muriel, I've looked for you high and low ever since, and now I've found you."

He moved backwards, knife still in hand, and stood aside, and there was an old battered relic of a phonograph standing there on an empty packing-case. It had a great big horn to it, to give it volume. He must have picked it up off some ash-heap, repaired it himself. He released the catch and cranked it up a couple of times and laid the needle into the groove.

"We're going to dance, Muriel, like we did that night when I was in my khaki uniform and you were so pretty to look at. But it's going to have a different ending this time."

He came back toward me. I was still huddled there, shivering. "No!" I moaned. "Not me! You killed her, you killed her over and over again. Only last month, don't you remember?"

He said with pitiful simplicity, like the tortured thing he was: "Each time I think I have, she rises up again." He dragged me to my feet and caught me to him, and the arm with the knife went around me, and the knife pressed into my side.

The horrid thing over there was blaring into the emptiness, loud enough to be heard out on the street: "Poor Butterfly." It was horrible, it was ghastly.

And in the candle-lit pallor, with great shadows of us looming on the wall, like two crazed things we started to go round and round. I couldn't hold my head up on my neck; it hung way back over my shoulders like an overripe apple. My hair got loose and went streaming out as he pulled me and turned me and dragged me around . . . .

"I just must die, poor butterfly!"

Still holding me to him, he reached in his pocket and brought out a palmful of shiny dimes, and flung them in my face.

Then a shot went off outside in front of the house. It sounded like right in the area-way where the knifed cop was. Then five more in quick succession. The blare of the music must have brought the stabbed cop to. He must've got help.

He turned his head toward the boarded-up windows to listen. I tore myself out of his embrace, stumbled backwards, and the knife point seemed to leave a long circular scratch around my side, but he didn't jam it in in time, let it trail off me.

I got out into the hall before he could grab me again, and the rest of it was just kind of a flight-nightmare. I don't remember going down the stairs to the basement; I think I must have fallen down them without hurting myself—just like a drunk does.

Down there a headlight came at me from the tunnel-like passage. It must have been just a pocket-torch, but it got bigger and bigger, then went hurtling on by. Behind it a long succession of serge-clothed figures brushed by me.

I kept trying to stop each one, saying: "Where's Nick? Are you Nick?"

Then a shot sounded upstairs. I heard a terrible death cry: "Muriel!" and that was all.

When I next heard anything it was Nick's voice. His arm was around me and he was kissing the cobwebs and tears off my face.

"How's Ginger?" he asked.

"Fine," I said, "and how's Nick?"

DISCUSSION QUESTIONS

- Reading this anthology, did you learn anything about the Golden Age mystery short story that you didn't already know? If so, what?
- Which story's mystery did you find the most perplexing?
- Did any of the solutions stretch credibility?
- Were you able to solve any of the mysteries before the main character? If so, which ones?
- How did the cultural history of the era play into these stories? Did anything help date them for you?
- Did any stories surprise you in terms of subject, character, or setting? If so, which ones?
- Did any stories remind you of work from authors today? If so, which ones?
- What characteristics do you think made these authors so popular in their day? Do you think readers today still want the same things from their reading material?

DISCOVER MORE
GOLDEN AGE ANTHOLOGIES
AVAILABLE NOW FROM

AMERICAN MYSTERY CLASSICS

OTTO PENZLER PRESENTS
AMERICAN MYSTERY CLASSICS

All titles are available in hardcover and in trade paperback.

Order from your favorite bookstore or from
The Mysterious Bookshop, 58 Warren Street, New York, N.Y. 10007
(www.mysteriousbookshop.com).

Charlotte Armstrong, ***The Chocolate Cobweb.*** When Amanda Garth was born, a mix-up caused the hospital to briefly hand her over to the prestigious Garrison family instead of to her birth parents. The error was quickly fixed, Amanda was never told, and the secret was forgotten for twenty-three years ... until her aunt revealed it in casual conversation. But what if the initial switch never actually occurred? **Introduction by A. J. Finn.**

Charlotte Armstrong, ***The Unsuspected.*** First published in 1946, this suspenseful novel opens with a young woman who has ostensibly hanged herself, leaving a suicide note. Her friend doesn't believe it and begins an investigation that puts her own life in jeopardy. It was filmed in 1947 by Warner Brothers, starring Claude Rains and Joan Caulfield. **Introduction by Otto Penzler.**

Anthony Boucher, ***The Case of the Baker Street Irregulars.*** When a studio announces a new hard-boiled Sherlock Holmes film, the Baker Street Irregulars begin a campaign to discredit it. Attempting to mollify them, the producers invite members to the set, where threats are received, each referring to one of the original Holmes tales, followed by murder. Fortunately, the amateur sleuths use Holmesian lessons to solve the crime. **Introduction by Otto Penzler.**

Anthony Boucher, ***Rocket to the Morgue.*** Hilary Foulkes has made so many enemies that it is difficult to speculate who was responsible for stabbing him nearly to death in a room with only one door through which no one was seen entering or leaving. This classic locked room mystery is populated by such thinly disguised science fiction legends as Robert Heinlein, L. Ron Hubbard, and John W. Campbell. **Introduction by F. Paul Wilson.**

Fredric Brown, ***The Fabulous Clipjoint.*** Brown's outstanding mystery won an Edgar as the best first novel of the year (1947). When Wallace Hunter is found dead in an alley after a long night of drinking, the police don't really care. But his teenage son Ed and his uncle Am, the carnival worker, are convinced that some things don't add up and the crime isn't what it seems to be. **Introduction by Lawrence Block.**

John Dickson Carr, ***The Crooked Hinge.*** Selected by a group of mystery experts as one of the 15 best impossible crime novels ever written, this is one of Gideon Fell's greatest challenges. Estranged from his family for 25 years, Sir John Farnleigh returns to England from America to claim his inheritance but another person turns up claiming that he can prove he is the real Sir John. Inevitably, one of them is murdered. **Introduction by Charles Todd.**

John Dickson Carr, ***The Eight of Swords.*** When Gideon Fell arrives at a crime scene, it appears to be straightforward enough. A man has been shot to death in an unlocked room and the likely perpetrator was a recent visitor. But Fell discovers inconsistencies and his investigations are complicated by an apparent poltergeist, some American gangsters, and two meddling amateur sleuths. **Introduction by Otto Penzler.**

John Dickson Carr, ***The Mad Hatter Mystery.*** A prankster has been stealing top hats all around London. Gideon Fell suspects that the same person may be responsible for the theft of a manuscript of a long-lost story by Edgar Allan Poe. The hats reappear in unexpected but conspicuous places but, when one is found on the head of a corpse by the Tower of London, it is evident that the thefts are more than pranks. **Introduction by Otto Penzler.**

John Dickson Carr, ***The Plague Court Murders.*** When murder occurs in a locked hut on Plague Court, an estate haunted by the ghost of a hangman's assistant who died a victim of the black death, Sir Henry Merrivale seeks a logical solution to a ghostly crime. A spiritual medium employed to rid the house of his spirit is found stabbed to death in a locked stone hut on the grounds, surrounded by an untouched circle of mud. **Introduction by Michael Dirda.**

John Dickson Carr, ***The Red Widow Murders.*** In a "haunted" mansion, the room known as the Red Widow's Chamber proves lethal to all who spend the night. Eight people investigate and the one who draws the ace of spades must sleep in it. The room is locked from the inside and watched all night by the others. When the door is unlocked, the victim has been poisoned. Enter Sir Henry Merrivale to solve the crime. **Introduction by Tom Mead.**

Frances Crane, ***The Turquoise Shop.*** In an arty little New Mexico town, Mona Brandon has arrived from the East and becomes the subject of gossip about her money, her influence, and the corpse in the nearby desert who may be her husband. Pat Holly, who runs the local gift shop, is as interested as anyone in the goings on—but even more in Pat Abbott, the detective investigating the possible murder. **Introduction by Anne Hillerman.**

Todd Downing, ***Vultures in the Sky.*** There is no end to the series of terrifying events that befall a luxury train bound for Mexico. First, a man dies when the train passes through a dark tunnel, then it comes to an abrupt stop in the middle of the desert. More deaths occur when night falls and the passengers panic when they realize they are trapped with a murderer on the loose. **Introduction by James Sallis.**

Mignon G. Eberhart, ***Murder by an Aristocrat.*** Nurse Keate is called to help a man who has been "accidentally" shot in the shoulder. When he is murdered while convalescing, it is clear that there was no accident. Although a killer is loose in the mansion, the family seems more concerned that news of the murder will leave their circle. *The New Yorker* wrote than "Eberhart can weave an almost flawless mystery." **Introduction by Nancy Pickard.**

Erle Stanley Gardner, ***The Case of the Baited Hook.*** Perry Mason gets a phone call in the middle of the night and his potential client says it's urgent, that he has two one-thousand-dollar bills that he will give him as a retainer, with an additional ten-thousand whenever he is called on to represent him. When Mason takes the case, it is not for the caller but for a beautiful woman whose identity is hidden behind a mask. **Introduction by Otto Penzler.**

Erle Stanley Gardner, ***The Case of the Borrowed Brunette.*** A mysterious man named Mr. Hines has advertised a job for a woman who has to fulfill very specific physical requirements. Eva Martell, pretty but struggling in her career as a model, takes the job but her aunt smells a rat and hires Perry Mason to investigate. Her fears are realized when Hines turns up in the apartment with a bullet hole in his head. **Introduction by Otto Penzler.**

Erle Stanley Gardner, ***The Case of the Careless Kitten.*** Helen Kendal receives a mysterious phone call from her vanished uncle Franklin, long presumed dead, who urges her to contact Perry Mason. Soon, she finds herself the main suspect in the murder of an unfamiliar man. Her kitten has just survived a poisoning attempt—as has her aunt Matilda. What is the connection between Franklin's return and the murder attempts? **Introduction by Otto Penzler.**

Erle Stanley Gardner, ***The Case of the Rolling Bones.*** One of Gardner's most successful Perry Mason novels opens with a clear case of blackmail, though the person being blackmailed claims he isn't. It is not long before the police are searching for someone wanted for killing the same man in two different states—thirty-three years apart. The confounding puzzle of what happened to the dead man's toes is a challenge. **Introduction by Otto Penzler.**

Erle Stanley Gardner, ***The Case of the Shoplifter's Shoe.*** Most cases for Perry Mason involve murder but here he is hired because a young woman fears her aunt is a kleptomaniac. Sarah may not have been precisely the best guardian for a collection of valuable diamonds and, sure enough, they go missing. When the jeweler is found shot dead, Sarah is spotted leaving the murder scene with a bundle of gems stuffed in her purse. **Introduction by Otto Penzler.**

Erle Stanley Gardner, ***The Bigger They Come.*** Gardner's first novel using the pseudonym A.A. Fair starts off a series featuring the large and loud Bertha Cool and her employee, the small and meek Donald Lam. Given the job of delivering divorce papers to an evident crook,

Lam can't find him—but neither can the police. The *Los Angeles Times* called this book: "Breathlessly dramatic … an original." **Introduction by Otto Penzler.**

Frances Noyes Hart, *The Bellamy Trial.* Inspired by the real-life Hall-Mills case, the most sensational trial of its day, this is the story of Stephen Bellamy and Susan Ives, accused of murdering Bellamy's wife Madeleine. Eight days of dynamic testimony, some true, some not, make headlines for an enthralled public. Rex Stout called this historic courtroom thriller one of the ten best mysteries of all time. **Introduction by Hank Phillippi Ryan.**

H.F. Heard, *A Taste for Honey.* The elderly Mr. Mycroft quietly keeps bees in Sussex, where he is approached by the reclusive and somewhat misanthropic Mr. Silchester, whose honey supplier was found dead, stung to death by her bees. Mycroft, who shares many traits with Sherlock Holmes, sets out to find the vicious killer. Rex Stout described it as "sinister … a tale well and truly told." **Introduction by Otto Penzler.**

Dolores Hitchens, *The Alarm of the Black Cat.* Detective fiction aficionado Rachel Murdock has a peculiar meeting with a little girl and a dead toad, sparking her curiosity about a love triangle that has sparked anger. When the girl's great grandmother is found dead, Rachel and her cat Samantha work with a friend in the Los Angeles Police Department to get to the bottom of things. **Introduction by David Handler.**

Dolores Hitchens, *The Cat Saw Murder.* Miss Rachel Murdock, the highly intelligent 70-year-old amateur sleuth, is not entirely heartbroken when her slovenly, unattractive, bridge-cheating niece is murdered. Miss Rachel is happy to help the socially maladroit and somewhat bumbling Detective Lieutenant Stephen Mayhew, retaining her composure when a second brutal murder occurs. **Introduction by Joyce Carol Oates.**

Dorothy B. Hughes, *Dread Journey.* A big-shot Hollywood producer has worked on his magnum opus for years, hiring and firing one beautiful starlet after another. But Kitten Agnew's contract won't allow her to be fired, so she fears she might be terminated more permanently. Together with the producer on a train journey from Hollywood to Chicago, Kitten becomes more terrified with each passing mile. **Introduction by Sarah Weinman.**

Dorothy B. Hughes, *Ride the Pink Horse.* When Sailor met Willis Douglass, he was just a poor kid who Douglass groomed to work as a confidential secretary. As the senator became increasingly corrupt, he knew he could count on Sailor to clean up his messes. No longer a senator, Douglass flees Chicago for Santa Fe, leaving behind a murder rap and Sailor as the prime suspect. Seeking vengeance, Sailor follows. **Introduction by Sara Paretsky.**

Dorothy B. Hughes, *The So Blue Marble.* Set in the glamorous world of New York high society, this novel became a suspense classic as twins from Europe try to steal a rare and beautiful gem owned by an aristocrat whose sister is an even more menacing presence. *The New Yorker* called it "Extraordinary … [Hughes'] brilliant descriptive powers make and unmake reality." **Introduction by Otto Penzler.**

W. Bolingbroke Johnson, *The Widening Stain.* After a cocktail party, the attractive Lucie Coindreau, a "black-eyed, black-haired Frenchwoman" visits the rare books wing of the library and apparently takes a head-first fall from an upper gallery. Dismissed as a horrible accident, it seems dubious when Professor Hyett is strangled while reading a priceless 12th-century manuscript, which has gone missing. **Introduction by Nicholas A. Basbanes**

Baynard Kendrick, *Blind Man's Bluff.* Blinded in World War II, Duncan Maclain forms a successful private detective agency, aided by his two dogs. Here, he is called on to solve the case of a blind man who plummets from the top of an eight-story building, apparently with no one present except his dead-drunk son. **Introduction by Otto Penzler.**

Baynard Kendrick, *The Odor of Violets.* Duncan Maclain, a blind former intelligence officer, is asked to investigate the murder of an actor in his Greenwich Village apartment. This would cause a stir at any time but, when the actor possesses secret government plans that then go missing, it's enough to interest the local police as well as the American government and Maclain, who suspects a German spy plot. **Introduction by Otto Penzler.**

C. Daly King, *Obelists at Sea.* On a cruise ship traveling from New York to Paris, the lights of the smoking room briefly go out, a gunshot crashes through the night, and a man is dead. Two detectives are on board but so are four psychiatrists who believe their professional knowledge can solve the case by understanding the psyche of the killer—each with a different theory. **Introduction by Martin Edwards.**

Jonathan Latimer, ***Headed for a Hearse.*** Featuring Bill Crane, the booze-soaked Chicago private detective, this humorous hard-boiled novel was filmed as *The Westland Case* in 1937 starring Preston Foster. Robert Westland has been framed for the grisly murder of his wife in a room with doors and windows locked from the inside. As the day of his execution nears, he relies on Crane to find the real murderer. **Introduction by Max Allan Collins**

Lange Lewis, ***The Birthday Murder.*** Victoria is a successful novelist and screenwriter and her husband is a movie director so their marriage seems almost too good to be true. Then, on her birthday, her happy new life comes crashing down when her husband is murdered using a method of poisoning that was described in one of her books. She quickly becomes the leading suspect. **Introduction by Randal S. Brandt.**

Frances and Richard Lockridge, ***Death on the Aisle.*** In one of the most beloved books to feature Mr. and Mrs. North, the body of a wealthy backer of a play is found dead in a seat of the 45th Street Theater. Pam is thrilled to engage in her favorite pastime—playing amateur sleuth—much to the annoyance of Jerry, her publisher husband. The Norths inspired a stage play, a film, and long-running radio and TV series. **Introduction by Otto Penzler.**

John P. Marquand, ***Your Turn, Mr. Moto.*** The first novel about Mr. Moto, originally titled *No Hero*, is the story of a World War I hero pilot who finds himself jobless during the Depression. In Tokyo for a big opportunity that falls apart, he meets a Japanese agent and his Russian colleague and the pilot suddenly finds himself caught in a web of intrigue. Peter Lorre played Mr. Moto in a series of popular films. **Introduction by Lawrence Block.**

Stuart Palmer, ***The Penguin Pool Murder.*** The first adventure of schoolteacher and dedicated amateur sleuth Hildegarde Withers occurs at the New York Aquarium when she and her young students notice a corpse in one of the tanks. It was published in 1931 and filmed the next year, starring Edna May Oliver as the American Miss Marple—though much funnier than her English counterpart. **Introduction by Otto Penzler.**

Stuart Palmer, ***The Puzzle of the Happy Hooligan.*** New York City schoolteacher Hildegarde Withers cannot resist "assisting" homicide detective Oliver Piper. In this novel, she is on vacation in Hollywood and on the set of a movie about Lizzie Borden when the screenwriter is found dead. Six comic films about Withers appeared in the 1930s, most successfully starring Edna May Oliver. **Introduction by Otto Penzler.**

Otto Penzler, ed., ***Golden Age Bibliomysteries.*** Stories of murder, theft, and suspense occur with alarming regularity in the unlikely world of books and bibliophiles, including bookshops, libraries, and private rare book collections, written by such giants of the mystery genre as Ellery Queen, Cornell Woolrich, Lawrence G. Blochman, Vincent Starrett, and Anthony Boucher. **Introduction by Otto Penzler.**

Otto Penzler, ed., ***Golden Age Detective Stories.*** The history of American mystery fiction has its pantheon of authors who have influenced and entertained readers for nearly a century, reaching its peak during the Golden Age, and this collection pays homage to the work of the most acclaimed: Cornell Woolrich, Erle Stanley Gardner, Craig Rice, Ellery Queen, Dorothy B. Hughes, Mary Roberts Rinehart, and more. **Introduction by Otto Penzler.**

Otto Penzler, ed., ***Golden Age Locked Room Mysteries.*** The so-called impossible crime category reached its zenith during the 1920s, 1930s, and 1940s, and this volume includes the greatest of the great authors who mastered the form: John Dickson Carr, Ellery Queen, C. Daly King, Clayton Rawson, and Erle Stanley Gardner. Like great magicians, these literary conjurors will baffle and delight readers. **Introduction by Otto Penzler.**

Ellery Queen, ***The Adventures of Ellery Queen.*** These stories are the earliest short works to feature Queen as a detective and are among the best of the author's fair-play mysteries. So many of the elements that comprise the gestalt of Queen may be found in these tales: alternate solutions, the dying clue, a bizarre crime, and the author's ability to find fresh variations of works by other authors. **Introduction by Otto Penzler.**

Ellery Queen, ***The American Gun Mystery.*** A rodeo comes to New York City at the Colosseum. The headliner is Buck Horne, the once popular film cowboy who opens the show leading a charge of forty whooping cowboys until they pull out their guns and fire into the air. Buck falls to the ground, shot dead. The police instantly lock the doors to search everyone but the offending weapon has completely vanished. **Introduction by Otto Penzler.**

Ellery Queen, ***The Chinese Orange Mystery.*** The offices of publisher Donald Kirk have seen strange events but nothing like this. A strange man is found dead with two long spears alongside his back. And, though no one was seen entering or leaving the room, everything has been turned backwards or upside down: pictures face the wall, the victim's clothes are worn backwards, the rug upside down. Why in the world? **Introduction by Otto Penzler.**

Ellery Queen, ***The Dutch Shoe Mystery.*** Millionaire philanthropist Abagail Doorn falls into a coma and she is rushed to the hospital she funds for an emergency operation by one of the leading surgeons on the East Coast. When she is wheeled into the operating theater, the sheet covering her body is pulled back to reveal her garroted corpse—the first of a series of murders **Introduction by Otto Penzler.**

Ellery Queen, ***The Egyptian Cross Mystery.*** A small-town schoolteacher is found dead, headed, and tied to a T-shaped cross on December 25th, inspiring such sensational headlines as "Crucifixion on Christmas Day." Amateur sleuth Ellery Queen is so intrigued he travels to Virginia but fails to solve the crime. Then a similar murder takes place on New York's Long Island—and then another. **Introduction by Otto Penzler.**

Ellery Queen, ***The Siamese Twin Mystery.*** When Ellery and his father encounter a raging forest fire on a mountain, their only hope is to drive up to an isolated hillside manor owned by a secretive surgeon and his strange guests. While playing solitaire in the middle of the night, the doctor is shot. The only clue is a torn playing card. Suspects include a society beauty, a valet, and conjoined twins. **Introduction by Otto Penzler.**

Ellery Queen, ***The Spanish Cape Mystery.*** Amateur detective Ellery Queen arrives in the resort town of Spanish Cape soon after a young woman and her uncle are abducted by a gun-toting, one-eyed giant. The next day, the woman's somewhat dicey boyfriend is found murdered—totally naked under a black fedora and opera cloak. **Introduction by Otto Penzler.**

Patrick Quentin, ***A Puzzle for Fools.*** Broadway producer Peter Duluth takes to the bottle when his wife dies but enters a sanitarium to dry out. Malevolent events plague the hospital, including when Peter hears his own voice intone, "There will be murder." And there is. He investigates, aided by a young woman who is also a patient. This is the first of nine mysteries featuring Peter and Iris Duluth. **Introduction by Otto Penzler.**

Clayton Rawson, ***Death from a Top Hat.*** When the New York City Police Department is baffled by an apparently impossible crime, they call on The Great Merlini, a retired stage magician who now runs a Times Square magic shop. In his first case, two occultists have been murdered in a room locked from the inside, their bodies positioned to form a pentagram. **Introduction by Otto Penzler.**

Craig Rice, ***Eight Faces at Three.*** Gin-soaked John J. Malone, defender of the guilty, is notorious for getting his culpable clients off. It's the innocent ones who are problems. Like Holly Inglehart, accused of piercing the black heart of her well-heeled aunt Alexandria with a lovely Florentine paper cutter. No one who knew the old battle-ax liked her, but Holly's prints were found on the murder weapon. **Introduction by Lisa Lutz.**

Craig Rice, ***Home Sweet Homicide.*** Known as the Dorothy Parker of mystery fiction for her memorable wit, Craig Rice was the first detective writer to appear on the cover of *Time* magazine. This comic mystery features two kids who are trying to find a husband for their widowed mother while she's engaged in sleuthing. Filmed with the same title in 1946 with Peggy Ann Garner and Randolph Scott. **Introduction by Otto Penzler.**

Mary Roberts Rinehart, *The Album*. Crescent Place is a quiet enclave of wealthy people in which nothing ever happens—until a bedridden old woman is attacked by an intruder with an ax. *The New York Times* stated: "All Mary Roberts Rinehart mystery stories are good, but this one is better." **Introduction by Otto Penzler.**

Mary Roberts Rinehart, *The Haunted Lady*. The arsenic in her sugar bowl was wealthy widow Eliza Fairbanks' first clue that somebody wanted her dead. Nightly visits of bats, birds, and rats, obviously aimed at scaring the dowager to death, was the second. Eliza calls the police, who send nurse Hilda Adams, the amateur sleuth they refer to as "Miss Pinkerton," to work undercover to discover the culprit. **Introduction by Otto Penzler.**

Mary Roberts Rinehart, *Miss Pinkerton*. Hilda Adams is a nurse, not a detective, but she is observant and smart and so it is common for Inspector Patton to call on her for help. Her success results in his calling her "Miss Pinkerton." *The New Republic* wrote: "From thousands of hearts and homes the cry will go up: Thank God for Mary Roberts Rinehart." **Introduction by Carolyn Hart.**

Mary Roberts Rinehart, *The Red Lamp*. Professor William Porter refuses to believe that the seaside manor he's just inherited is haunted but he has to convince his wife to move in. However, he soon sees evidence of the occult phenomena of which the townspeople speak. Whether it is a spirit or a human being, Porter accepts that there is a connection to the rash of murders that have terrorized the countryside. **Introduction by Otto Penzler.**

Mary Roberts Rinehart, *The Wall*. For two decades, Mary Roberts Rinehart was the second-best-selling author in America (only Sinclair Lewis outsold her) and was beloved for her tales of suspense. In a magnificent mansion, the ex-wife of one of the owners turns up making demands and is found dead the next day. And there are more dark secrets lying behind the walls of the estate. **Introduction by Otto Penzler.**

Joel Townsley Rogers, *The Red Right Hand*. This extraordinary whodunnit that is as puzzling as it is terrifying was identified by crime fiction scholar Jack Adrian as "one of the dozen or so finest mystery novels of the 20th century." A deranged killer sends a doctor on a quest for the truth—deep into the recesses of his own mind—when he and his bride-to-be elope but pick up a terrifying sharp-toothed hitch-hiker. **Introduction by Joe R. Lansdale.**

Roger Scarlett, *Cat's Paw*. The family of the wealthy old bachelor Martin Greenough cares far more about his money than they do about him. For his birthday, he invites all his potential heirs to his mansion to tell them what they hope to hear. Before he can disburse funds, however, he is murdered, and the Boston Police Department's big problem is that there are too many suspects. **Introduction by Curtis Evans**

Vincent Starrett, *Dead Man Inside*. 1930s Chicago is a tough town but some crimes are more bizarre than others. Customers arrive at a haberdasher to find a corpse in the window and a sign on the door: *Dead Man Inside! I am Dead. The store will not open today*. This is just one of a series of odd murders that terrorizes the city. Reluctant detective Walter Ghost leaps into action to learn what is behind the plague. **Introduction by Otto Penzler.**

Vincent Starrett, *The Great Hotel Murder*. Theater critic and amateur sleuth Riley Blackwood investigates a murder in a Chicago hotel where the dead man had changed rooms with a stranger who had registered under a fake name. *The New York Times* described it as "an ingenious plot with enough complications to keep the reader guessing." **Introduction by Lyndsay Faye.**

Vincent Starrett, *Murder on 'B' Deck*. Walter Ghost, a psychologist, scientist, explorer, and former intelligence officer, is on a cruise ship and his friend novelist Dunsten Mollock, a Nigel Bruce-like Watson whose role is to offer occasional comic relief, accommodates when he fails to leave the ship before it takes off. Although they make mistakes along the way, the amateur sleuths solve the shipboard murders. **Introduction by Ray Betzner.**

Phoebe Atwood Taylor, *The Cape Cod Mystery*. Vacationers have flocked to Cape Cod to avoid the heat wave that hit the Northeast and find their holiday unpleasant when the area is flooded with police trying to find the murderer of a muckraking journalist who took a cottage for the season. Finding a solution falls to Asey Mayo, "the Cape Cod Sherlock," known for his worldly wisdom, folksy humor, and common sense. **Introduction by Otto Penzler.**

S. S. Van Dine, ***The Benson Murder Case.*** The first of 12 novels to feature Philo Vance, the most popular and influential detective character of the early part of the 20th century. When wealthy stockbroker Alvin Benson is found shot to death in a locked room in his mansion, the police are baffled until the erudite flaneur and art collector arrives on the scene. Paramount filmed it in 1930 with William Powell as Vance. **Introduction by Ragnar Jónasson.**

Cornell Woolrich, ***The Bride Wore Black.*** The first suspense novel by one of the greatest of all noir authors opens with a bride and her new husband walking out of the church. A car speeds by, shots ring out, and he falls dead at her feet. Determined to avenge his death, she tracks down everyone in the car, concluding with a shocking surprise. It was filmed by Francois Truffaut in 1968, starring Jeanne Moreau. **Introduction by Eddie Muller.**

Cornell Woolrich, ***Deadline at Dawn.*** Quinn is overcome with guilt about having robbed a stranger's home. He meets Bricky, a dime-a-dance girl, and they fall for each other. When they return to the crime scene, they discover a dead body. Knowing Quinn will be accused of the crime, they race to find the true killer before he's arrested. A 1946 film starring Susan Hayward was loosely based on the plot. **Introduction by David Gordon.**

Cornell Woolrich, ***Waltz into Darkness.*** A New Orleans businessman successfully courts a woman through the mail but he is shocked to find when she arrives that she is not the plain brunette whose picture he'd received but a radiant blond beauty. She soon absconds with his fortune. Wracked with disappointment and loneliness, he vows to track her down. When he finds her, the real nightmare begins. **Introduction by Wallace Stroby.**